Other books by Robert Mendelsohn
published by Prion

*Footsteps on a Drum*
*Clash of Honour*
*The Red Pagoda*

# THE
# HIBISCUS
# TRAIL

*Robert Mendelsohn*

**PRION**

Published in the United Kingdom by
PRION, an imprint of Multimedia Books Ltd
32–34 Gordon House Road, London NW5 1LP

First printing June 1993
Second printing July 1993
Third printing August 1993
Fourth printing August 1993

A catalogue record for this book is available from the
British Library

ISBN 1–85375–111–1 (hardback)
ISBN 1–85375–110–3 (paperback)

Printed in the United Kingdom by
HarperCollins Manufacturing, Glasgow

# To Paul, Rebecca and Natasha

*who have survived their father's eccentricities
and may forgive his mistakes.*

# BOOK ONE

## CHAPTER ONE

———■———

The funeral is at three o'clock this afternoon. They are having it across the border from here, in San Remo, Italy. I have no idea why. Nobody's expecting me, but I'm going all the same. The limousine will be downstairs soon.

I bet they will all be there. Family, friends and, more than anything, there will be the inevitable passers-by. Plenty of them. Down here people love funerals. You don't have to know anyone to go see him buried. It's just something to do, like watching weddings or going to the movies.

I haven't seen either of these two in years. I knew them, sure; I knew them well. I met Charles in Thailand after the war and Sam in Jamaica later. I knew Charles better than anyone. Our paths had crossed over the years and sometimes we were partners.

Sometimes we were enemies. Once we were almost close. But Charles Paget-Brown and Sam Baker were more than friends. They only spent a few short years together, yet their lives were so interwoven, so interdependent, that if one didn't exist you'd have to invent him for the other. What will happen now that one has crossed over to the other side is anyone's guess.

They were the most unlikely couple, Sam and Charles. One was what they call a pukka Englishman and the other was a Levantine. One was educated, the other a peasant. They were both adventurers. They don't make people like that any more.

This afternoon they are putting one of them into the ground. I saw it happen. I saw the man die. And I am going to be there when they put him away.

I have been spending real time in the South of France ever since I retired. Of course, no one ever gets out in my business. But I had managed to build a great big cobweb of trust and mistrust around myself. No one can touch me. I advise both sides of the family and, because they hate each other's guts, they figure reliability and truth shine out of my backside. They both make sure I stay alive and well. They've got to, or I open my mouth real big and everybody ends up in deep shit.

It's fun sitting here on the terrace watching the world go by. Seeing the expensive cars and the beautiful people as they stroll along, impressing each other. Movie stars and singers and big-shot businessmen strut about in their designer rags, trying hard to look casual. Women of all shapes and ages parade in tow, dressed to outdo the world, like they've walked straight out of glossy magazines. It's Cartier and Levi jeans and everybody's got a tan. The restaurants are always full. The jewellers are busy as hell. I don't know where all the money comes from.

I always stay in this place. In or out of season it's always full. It's a classy joint but it's cosy and familiar. I like the old-fashioned architecture, the atmospheric gilt decor, and the courtesy they treat you with.

They know my name here, and there are always flowers or fruits in the room from the management. They get me anything I want. Reservations for eats and planes, cars – everything. I don't tip much but I do talk to everybody. Something I could not do when I was in active service. No one knows how I used to earn a living. They think I'm just a nice guy who got lucky.

'Welcome home, Mr Perotti,' the porter says every time I arrive.

Not bad for an orphan-boy from the Bronx.

I have a sea-view room at no extra cost. The outside spring temperature is just right. Not too cold and not too hot. There's a carpet of flowers sprawling all along the palm trees. I've been here only once in summer but had to get out quick. There were too many people and the heat nearly killed me. It wasn't that long ago. Five years maybe. That was the time Paco the Filipino turned up in this town. He came after me and I had to dodge him or damage him so I took off.

Maybe the guy was just passing through, but I could take no chances. He knew Charles Paget-Brown well and was once thick with him. Come to think of it, he was the one who pushed Charles over to the wrong side of the law. I figure I owed the limey the favour of having the Filipino wasted, but I could get him any time. Charles had enough on his plate that year. On the whole, it seemed Charles was prone to ups and downs later in his life. These swings were sometimes violent, but mostly he managed to end up top of the heap again.

As soon as you met Charles Paget-Brown you realized you couldn't call him plain Charlie. I always did, only to annoy him, but of course he didn't care. He had that superior air about him some English people have. He reminded me of the guy who played Ashley Wilkes in *Gone with the Wind*. He spoke beautifully, and his deep voice was friendly and loaded with confidence. He was just like what you'd imagine an English lord to be, and when he was up he sure lived like one.

Charlie never put on airs and graces, even though he was entitled. As I figure it, he was born to be boss of this estate his family owned, but had chosen to go out and make it on his own. He was an only son, and went to some exclusive private school the English call public. Don't ask me why. He was no great scholar, but he was a competent sportsman and much liked by his friends. He had an uncanny interest in radios and early electrics. He had constructed his own crystal set and used to listen to stations all over the world. The foreign voices captured his imagination and he dreamed of romance and exotic mountains and tropical oceans. This fascination with faraway places, and his addiction to books by a character called Joseph Conrad, formulated his plans. He became obsessed with converting his dreams into reality, and made up his mind to go see the world for himself. I understand his old man was dead against it. He was what the English call landed gentry and had never done a job of work in his life. He couldn't see why young Charles insisted on continuing his studies when his school years were over. He objected, too, to his son's ideas of roaming the world when all he needed was right there in England.

He took a course in wireless engineering and, at the age of twenty-one, some company in that business offered him a job in Ceylon. They were installing radio stations all over what was then called the British Empire, and Charles Paget-Brown went out there on a three-year contract. His father hated the idea, but his two elder sisters loved it. They didn't like their brother much, and having him out of the way meant they'd have the run of the family joint themselves. The origins of that relationship had their roots in the past. Something to do with his mother's death. I never found out what it was because Charlie didn't talk about it. Anyway, he didn't get on with his sisters and I figure they were plain greedy. But Charlie was naive in some ways. He didn't even know his sisters hated him. He thought everybody was the good guys.

He did good in Ceylon. He liked it so much he didn't go back to England all that time. Instead, he used his vacations to travel about. Went to Singapore and Hong Kong and Bangkok and Manila. He was lucky to do that then. In those days of slow sea travel, a man got a chance to know where he was going. You didn't fly in and out of town inside a day. Usually you stayed for weeks and saw all of it. You got to know the people and the local food and customs. Travel then was like an education. Charlie saw places and learned about them. The Orientals taught him how to recognize a deal and he learned to pick out what was available in some places and missing in others.

He was always polite and could charm the pants off anyone. He made lots of friends all over. They loved him. Charlie liked the women there, and I know there was always some local lady in his circle.

At the end of three years the company promoted him and he was sent to Hong Kong. That was where they had their local headquarters. He was the youngest manager they have had there in years. He continued to travel around and make connections.

Three big things happened in that city. That was where Charles Paget-Brown first began to get involved in smuggling. That's one. The second was Rose, the woman he was going to marry. He met her there. The third thing was my seeing him for the first time. Yeah. It was right after the war. In 1947 or something, in Hong Kong.

I saw him walking into the Peninsula Hotel. He was tall, had blond reddish hair, and was as handsome as a prince. He wore a white linen suit that sat on him like he was born in it. There was not one drop of sweat on his forehead, and that haunting smile of his stuck in the middle of his face. I saw him then because I looked at him. Everybody did. I remember his eyes. They were wild. There was something of the rogue in the light that burst out of them as soon as he looked at you. Nothing shifty, just wild. As if he was looking for some adventure everywhere and always, even in front of the Peninsula Hotel, that most peaceful of settings. Anyway, the hotel porters greeted him like a long-lost God and the uniformed Brits patted his shoulders as if he was some returning hero. Of course, that was, in a way, exactly what he was, but I did not know it then. We were miles apart. No one introduced us. In Charlie's world I was only a beginner. I had only just started working for the family again having been out of uniform for a short time. I was trying to get them interested in the Orient and still had to prove there was money to be made there. In those days I was nowhere near the top, but I was doing good.

Rose? From what I had heard of her I thought I wasn't

going to like her. People said she was a snob, and though she was a practical woman she was not aware of her limitations. The trouble with snobs is they never listen to anybody and never learn a damn thing. She thought she knew it all. People said she was a little too aggressive to be feminine, but to each his own. She must have had something that had turned him on. She was fair, with looks you could tell would turn horsy later on in her life. She too had dreams. She dreamed of becoming a part of what the British called society. You know, Wimbledon and Ascot and that.

I took all I heard with a pinch of salt because I knew people were jealous of her. When we first met she kind of looked down on me, and hard as I tried, I couldn't bring myself to get on with her. I don't know anyone who did. She came to Hong Kong as a nurse, and I was told he finally married her because he put her in the family way. It was the decent thing to do, but that was Charlie all over.

His sisters wanted nothing to do with her. They'd heard she was a butcher's daughter from some place called Streatham in London. When he wrote to tell them about her they didn't even bother to answer. When he married they did not congratulate him. The British can be funny that way. But not him. He was a very approachable guy. Talked to everybody. Did business with everybody. Trusted everybody.

He was very strictly legit until the day he ran into a Filipino guy on the Hong Kong–Kowloon ferry. His name was Paco, which is short for Francisco. Everybody has Spanish names in the Philippines on account of the place having been Spanish for yonks. He was in import-export and specialized in bringing goods in and out of places without telling the authorities. It was no big deal at that time and no one called it smuggling. Nothing was organized, and if you paid someone a few bucks he'd let you bring in anything you liked to bring in. In those days there was no mileage in drugs. You didn't need to smuggle those because the stuff grew right in the villages and people used it and bartered with it for years. The money was in whisky and car parts and cigarettes and so forth. This Paco was on the right spot for that because he owned an old ship on which he had his merchandise transported from place to place. She was an 800-tonner, built in Rotterdam, and at one time she had ferried building materials between the Indonesian islands.

It was all very romantic, and Charles Paget-Brown listened to Paco's stories of how he had built his business from nothing. It was as though the books he'd read and the voices he'd heard on his first radio had come alive.

The Filipino had made himself a small fortune. He had come to Hong Kong to shop for a bunch of Chinese sailing junks. Those fat-assed vessels with their large, funny-ribbed sails could slip in and out of ports without attracting much attention. Nowadays you don't see them much, but at that time there were plenty of them around. Fishing was a hobby they both shared, and by the time Paco and Charles got to the other side of the bay the partnership was formed. Charlie would supervise the purchase of the junks and any refitting jobs they needed. Once ready, he would pick up the merchandise Paco was after, load the junks, and make sure they got out of the territorial waters to meet Paco's ship. There, when no one was looking, the boxes would be transferred and shipped to Manila where Paco would take over. For that he was offered fifty per cent of the profits.

The main problem with this Paco was he did not score big in the loyalty department, and would sell his own mother COD to the highest bidder. But during the first years of that partnership he did not cheat. Charlie made money and he kept it in a small Portuguese bank in Macao. He never thought much about money. It was the excitement that turned him on. Perhaps he didn't even like money. Maybe it was because he was born rich. Anyway, a couple of years into this association he was making plenty of dough, but his lifestyle didn't change. He went into his office every day and broke the law after working-hours, and no one knew. He was getting used to living a double life, and I reckon he began to like it that way.

# CHAPTER TWO

■

In 1936 Charlie walked into his boss's face and told him he was leaving. It happened to be on the day his old contract had expired, and no amount of money or promotion was going to change his mind. It was all very quiet and civil and businesslike. He said he was willing to stick around for a few months until they found a replacement, but he wasn't going to stay after that.

That was also the year he married Rose. There's no question in my mind she saw the potential in the young man. Of course, he came from what she considered to be the right background. She dreamt of a grand return to England, in which she would join the glitterati there. She took to reading *Country Life* and *Tatler* and with the money Charles was making they lived great. She dressed like a queen and drove around in a Rolls and was generally very visible. She began dropping stories about her own family. Like how they were important back in England and how they went to the Ascot races and holidays in the South of France and stuff. She got invites to all the parties and people soon forgot who she was when she first arrived. The socializing made them popular. When she lost her first baby everybody came to see her at the hospital and brought flowers. All the while they were clearly getting rich quick. Could be the local police were beginning to suspect him, but no one took any serious action to stop him. He was still a gentleman and a member of all the clubs, and with Japan killing all these people in China they had other worries.

But Charlie wasn't fooled by any of it. Always one to be a step ahead of his pursuers, he decided it was time to up and go. He gave everybody a big song and dance about how he had discovered a new source of fish in some undisturbed stretch of water. How he was going to settle down there and let his fishing fleet loose and catch enough fish to feed the whole world. He and Rose threw the biggest party of the year. There were fireworks and food and booze and all kinds of different music and the carnival lasted three days. People were still talking about it months after they were gone. They talked about the party, but mostly they talked about how Charlie had surprised everybody by hitting the road. He was great at springing surprises on people and he was getting better at it all the time. Later on it became so bad you never knew what he would do next.

They did move to a small Siamese island off the Malay Peninsula, but none of his friends knew where it was. Charlie knew every inch of water from Penang to Manila, and I bet he had it all worked out long before they shoved off. It was certainly no desert island seeing as it was crowded with natives who all, one way or another, ended up working for him.

That was before the war and I did not know him then, but from all accounts Rose did great, considering the island was as primitive as it was. All of a sudden the designer gowns and the parties and the gossip and the bridge games didn't matter. She set up home there and they grew their own food and beef cattle. There was no doctor on the island, and Rose started a small dressing-station in an outhouse. People came to her for bandages and injections and she delivered babies. She was a strict woman and the natives had a lot of respect for her. They were, mostly, fearful of her too. But she did throw herself into her work while Charles was at sea for weeks on end. By the time the war was over there were cattle farms and rice-packaging and a cannery on the island, and all put up by her.

The way I see it, this was when she came into her own. I heard her talk about it, years later, at the British Club in Bangkok. She said her time on that island was the happiest time of her life. I didn't believe a word of it then. Maybe I didn't listen good. I reckon I'd have liked her better sooner if I had. Of course, Charlie's life was much more exciting and adventurous. People generally prefer to hear about wartime macho exploits than to learn about how corn-bread is baked. Maybe that was why Rose never became as popular or famous as her husband once the war was over.

Charlie turned out to be a top-class organizer. On the back of the five junks he owned when they arrived there, he had built a fleet of some twenty sea-going vessels, and his business thrived. The only fishing they did was for feeding themselves and the islanders, because the real money was in trading. He was smuggling agricultural machinery, fishing nets, seeds and liquor, cigarettes, and a whole bunch of other saleables including medicines. All his boats were equipped with the latest word in wireless communication. He had the stuff fitted on himself and no one got a job on board unless they knew how to use the radio. It gave him total control over who was where and for what. His junks operated like a small navy. On land and on sea, Charlie was now the undisputed boss of the island. The people who lived there were as faithful to him as if he was some kind of old-time king.

His daughter Roberta was born on the island in 1939. Rose said later that her marriage to Charles ended with that event. It seems he was besotted by the little girl. She was a bouncy, happy child whose free spirit and obvious sense of humour appealed to him. He spent hours walking the fields with her on his back. He took her out to sea. He told her stories and sang nursery songs to her at bedtime. He spoilt her rotten.

Then, in 1942, he was approached by some South African who turned up on the island. The man was an officer in the Royal Navy. He had, he said, an important job for Mr Paget-Brown. With his inter-communicating fleet he could be of great use to the Allies. Would he play ball?

That's how the wartime alliance between Charlie and his homeland started. He sailed all over the place taking pictures of Japanese warships, and I was told he had three vessels blown out of the water. Where and how big I don't know. Painted all over, his head and face clean-shaven, he took to dressing up as a native. With papers the British supplied him with, Charles managed to get into enemy ports all over the South China Sea. It was in the Siamese ports that he really scored great. He brought photographs of the latest Japanese boat and weapon designs. He watched troop movements and oil shipments and God knows what else. All useful stuff for the Allies.

There were other operations. All, to quote the Brits who told me about it, very hush-hush. One time Charlie collected an entire platoon of Australians and ferried them into occupied Singapore. How he got in there and how he got out no one said. But he did get them in and they kidnapped someone or collected some hidden gold bullion or blew something up. I don't remember what it was but it was big-time. The best part was how he managed to get most of them out again. He once stole a boatload of guns and ammunition and had it delivered to Burmese guerillas in a mountain village which produced the best rubies in the business. I reckon that was when his interest in precious stones began.

It was a reckless, exciting time, and the adventures Charlie lived with became a way of life he got drunk on. It sharpened his senses, and by his own admission he was making a fortune. You would have thought his doing this hero thing would have interfered with his business, but it didn't. On the contrary. He got more and more daring, took more chances. And as things got hotter his mind became more fertile. New ideas flashed through him like crazy; new projects and deals were born every minute.

He didn't much believe in paper money in those days. He hoarded his dough in heaps of gold and gemstones, just like those book characters did. Siam was a terrific joint for spies because it was badly run and you could snoop around all day if you were careful. It was a rich country with tons of rice and fish and fruits and other stuff the Japanese needed, and they came and went like they owned it.

Charlie took to Siam like a fish to water. In no time at all he learned to speak Thai like a native. He brought goods in and shipped goods out and anyone involved was making his cut. Charlie turned many simple country folk and fishermen into out-and-out businessmen. He was known as a fair trader, and had made such close friends there they would have gone to war for him. And lots of them did.

He fell in love there, too. With the country, its people, and mostly with a woman called Nappaporn. She was the greatest-looking girl in Pataya, daughter and sister of a couple of traders Charlie did business with before the war. I bet these guys kept Nappaporn locked up every time Charlie came in, but that didn't help. He met her one night when he sailed into the port to photograph a new Japanese destroyer which lay in the bay. Her father and brother were out of town. From that time on Charlie came into Pataya so many times the girl had to have been special. Of course, he had his spying to do and that. He was selling fishing nets and canned milk and seeds and medicines, and he bought rubies and gold and rice and dry fish, but that was just an excuse. Charlie was not interested in money. He wasn't even interested in the power he had. Sure he loved adventure, but there was plenty of that everywhere at that time. No one would have put their neck on the line so many times unless they got it bad in the loving department. I figure the girl Nappaporn got under his skin, and that's why he kept on going back there.

One time they nearly got him. Three Japanese, a private and two officers, came into Nappaporn's house and found him there. First he told them he was a German priest or something, but that didn't work. They even knew his name. They were about to take him away when he pulled a Schmeisser submachine-gun out of somewhere and shot them to pieces. He took off on Nappaporn's bicycle and rode to the port and boarded his junk and sailed away. There was no one watching the boat. The guy who told me that story insisted it was a miracle.

There was no miracle. The Japs did not watch the boat because they were sure they were going to get him. And they were sure of it because they knew where he was and with whom. They didn't expect any opposition. They didn't want him dead. They would have sent a whole goddamn Imperial Army to Nappaporn's house if they did. He was a big deal, and they figured he was a giant, so why did they send only three men? Because they wanted to take him alive quietly. Then go and surprise the whole Japanese Empire with what they'd caught. I bet no one else even knew about it. Only these three Japs. That's how these things are done. You tell too many people and you blow it. That's why there was nobody watching his boat.

I figured out he was shopped because of who I heard the story from. I didn't hear it from Charlie. He never talked much about that time. He wasn't a guy to tell you how great he was. No, I heard it from Paco the Filipino, and he wouldn't have known all the details unless he was involved on the inside. How did he know there was a private and two officers? How did he know Charlie pretended to be a German priest? He even knew it was a Schmeisser, not a tommy-gun. Charlie wouldn't have told him about it because Charlie never discussed his Royal Navy business with anyone. No, no. The guy first with the news is always guilty. Paco shopped him but the Japs screwed up. Nappaporn's friends got rid of the bodies and by morning she was out of the house. Later she went into hiding.

I don't know how and where they met after that but they must have because he made the girl Nappaporn pregnant. She gave birth to a little girl who was named Nalini, and moved to Bangkok. Her brother was killed by the Japanese for spying, and her father was lost at sea just after. There was nothing left for her in Pataya. I reckon Charlie didn't see her again until after the war because you couldn't get into Bangkok that easy. Maybe he did. I don't know. Some people would have you believe Charlie sailed up the river straight into downtown Bangkok right under the nose of the Japanese. There were so many stories about him and what happened. You can't believe everything. But the island business was true. I went there myself once in the mid-fifties. Paco the Filipino took me and I saw it all with my own eyes. During the war his house had been there and his family lived there and he had his headquarters there. That was where he came back to after each trip.

Rose told me life on the island was a dream. Roberta grew up in a world of duck-ponds and palms. She could roam the rolling hills and pick flowers and feed the chickens. Rose said many things, but I didn't listen much because I didn't like her at that time. I was wrong. Maybe I should have listened to her, but I was too busy trying to learn about Charlie. He was the one I was really after, businesswise.

At the end of the war the British government decorated Charlie for his services. Rose said he should have been knighted. I bet she would have loved to have been Lady Paget-Brown, but I reckon it was a non-starter. The Brits knew damn well what Charlie was doing, and a knighthood would have been one deal too much. They arranged a big show at the house of the Governor of Hong Kong. I heard he didn't even turn up for the ceremony. I heard Rose went instead.

Anyway, the war was over and it was time to leave the island. Rose wanted to move back to Hong Kong, and you don't have to be a genius to guess why. There would be better schools there and more fun, and after years in the wilderness you could forgive her for remembering the parties and the high life and that, but Charlie would have none of it. It was Bangkok or bust.

He told her the authorities would prefer him to stay away from the Colony on account of his business being a little on the shady side. If he returned to Hong Kong they would eventually be forced to arrest him. I think it was bullshit but she bought it.

It was very British, I remember her saying when we discussed that. The way guys at the top look after each other and that. They call it the old-boy network in England, she said. The old school tie. I wouldn't understand that, she said. I could have told her that was not exclusive. We do just the same where I come from, but we call it different. I didn't want to spoil it for her and went right on listening.

She never doubted Charlie's word and never complained. At least not to me, and she had plenty of opportunity. I used to talk to her a lot while we waited around for Charlie to turn up. Usually we would sit in the British Club in Bangkok sipping tea and she would talk. At the beginning of our acquaintance I was ordered to get on with him. So I was polite and I'd sit and wait and she was always there and I'd listen to her and think to myself what a boring broad she was. She did have a lot of dignity though. She had more, but I was shooting for him and didn't reckon her at all.

Perhaps, she said, they should have stayed on the island. They were happy there. Still, she said, and shrugged her shoulders, it was time for her daughter Roberta to go to school, and as Charlie wanted to go to Bangkok that was where they were going.

The whole community came to the quay to see them off. Men, women, children and the elderly. The old wooden pontoon creaked under the people's weight. There were, Rose told me with pride, kisses and tears and promises of everlasting friendship. Bunches of flowers and rafts with lit candles were thrown into the water and followed the boat on which the family sailed off.

Sometimes I imagine the scene, with Charlie standing on the deck watching the island disappear into the evening sun, but I'm no poet. I figure he was just the type to do that, but maybe he didn't. He was in one hell of a hurry to get out.

# CHAPTER THREE

◼

Nappaporn was the real reason for his move to Bangkok after the war. He was crazy about her. It wasn't just the sex thing, and certainly not because she gave him another daughter.

There was something about her he adored. You could spot it in his behaviour; I mean the way he walked about and talked every time he was getting ready to go visit her. There was a happy light in his eyes; the wild man in them would calm down. He was relaxed and agreeable and open to anything. I remember people walking up to his office. I remember them asking the secretary if he was in one of those comfortable moods. It was always the best time to negotiate with him, but no one knew why. No one except me. And I only found that out when I needed to watch her real close. Close enough to get at him.

The way he went on should have made Rose suspect something, but she never found out about Nappaporn. Not until years and years later, and by then it was too late. His friends knew nothing about it either. Crazy, huh? I mean, we're not just talking about some broad a guy keeps on the side. It was a woman and a daughter, a house, a garden, a maid, the whole deal. A real-life family for Chrissakes. How he managed to keep them under the ground in a small place like Bangkok, where foreigners knew everything about each other, is amazing.

In those days there weren't many foreigners in Bangkok. There were no hippies or addicts or shoppers, no do-gooders, no youngsters trying to find themselves or plane-loads of sex tours. No sun-worshippers, no multinationals, no nothing. There were Army guys and a few businessmen and diplomats and a couple of church guys and journalists and that's it. They were an exclusive bunch.

He got more and more involved in the shipment of drugs. Medical drugs. People over there love medicines. It's still a great business to be in. There's plenty of dough in it even today. There are drug stores on every street corner of every Oriental city. They sell everything from Chinese herbal stuff to Tylanol. But in those years drugs were in very short supply; but not for Charlie. Charlie had them coming out of his ears. I figured he had someone in the Army or the Navy medical corps supplying him. I was only able to find out who that was much later, and only by force.

By a natural progression he drifted into other, rarer drugs. That was how he became a target for us. Us was the people I worked for, and we were after what he had. Nothing was planned. Nothing was personal. It was just a question of supply and demand.

Life's funny. None of this would have ever happened if it wasn't for the war. I would have stayed in New York had I not been drafted. The military machine built for the war shipped me out to the Orient and there I came up against the likes of Charlie. The Brits needed someone to sail around the South China Seas to take pictures for them there. Charlie owed meeting his great love and living in Bangkok to the British Royal Navy.

Little Nalini Brown, Charlie's illegitimate child, owes her being born to them. And because of the surprise she was going to spring on all of us later, I reckon the whole world owes something to the British Navy.

I owe meeting Charlie face to face to that same guy, Paco the Filipino. I was still in the Army when I first met him. He was interested in buying stuff from the Commissary, and I'd arranged a few introductions for him and made a bit of dough on the side. After the war I got back to Manila to look for some business angles. Paco knew everybody, and he was the best guy to have on your side. The family didn't care who I picked as long as I came up with the goods. Soon we started working seriously.

We began buying and selling stuff together, and I was moving around the place like crazy. I began to know the Orient better than I knew Manhattan. I liked it so much I thought I'd never go home. I travelled all over. China, Japan, Indonesia, Macao, the Philippines. You name a place up there and I can tell you I've been there. I knew every hotel and every eating-place and every taxi-driver. I had plenty of dough and American cigarettes and Hershey bars and nylons and lipstick, and they liked what I had. The stuff got you plenty then. Remember, there was little luxury around after the war. And the money we earned bought us stuff New York was looking for.

It so happens that Paco was visiting with me when one of the big bosses flew in. I wasn't too sure what he came over for. Maybe it was to check me out because I was living in Hong Kong and spending a fortune. Maybe he just wanted to see the sights. He called me, and as Paco was in town I set up a meeting with him to show New York I wasn't just sitting on my ass.

There's nothing significant to remember about that meeting except this: it was the reason for my meeting Charlie face to face at last.

The Filipino was kind of used to working with me alone. Maybe he thought I was in business for myself. He got quite a surprise when he met the big shot. He didn't understand the respect I showed him. My guy was dressed in a dark suit and did no small-talk at all. Nothing but business. He sounded out of place there. He didn't understand you have to take it easy when you deal in the Orient. You talk about the weather and family and women and that, but my guy talked tough. He said Paco's merchandise was becoming too expensive and stuff.

'You're taking us for a ride, Paco,' he said again and again.

'What you mean?' Paco asked again and again. That was a kind of password of his when he wanted time to think.

'You're too fucking expensive,' my man said. 'That's what I mean.'

Paco understood that, and that was when he got a little arrogant.

Of course he would never have dared to shoot his mouth off the way he did had he known who he was talking to. I kicked him under the table, but he went on. I figure he was a little drunk or something, because Paco wasn't a rude kind of guy.

'You full of shit,' Paco said. 'You not alone customer in the world.'

'What's that you say?'

'He's drunk,' I said. 'He doesn't understand . . .' But Paco was flying high. He got up and he slammed his fist on the table.

'Me no drunk. Me understand everything. Your friend is shit, Mister Vincent. You tell him he shit. Me no need him. You no need him. Why he come here?'

I wanted to say something like he was talking to my boss, but they were now shouting at each other and I didn't get a word in. The place was busy so no one paid any attention to us. My guy nearly burst a blood vessel. He was good and mad. I've seen him kill for less.

'Vince Perotti works for me, Paco,' he said.

'What you mean?'

'I mean I'm Perotti's boss. From America. You talk to me.'

'Me no need you. Me do plenty business with people. Better people. No rude like you. You go back America shoot Indians.'

He said many things, and I was beginning to worry there would be blood. Especially when he said we could go fuck ourselves if we weren't happy, but by that time my guy was full of booze himself and he went all quiet.

'Why don't we listen to Paco,' I asked, and I prayed. 'Maybe we learn something.'

That was when the Filipino mentioned Charles Paget-Brown for the first time. Of course, I had heard of him and had seen him, but I had no way of meeting him personally. And I said so.

'This is a big fish,' I told my guy. 'A British celebrity. I've been trying to meet him for a long time.'

The guy was always interested in new angles so he listened. Paco said he could sell all he wanted to the Englishman. Mister Charlie, he called him, and he talked about him like he was his brother. He talked a lot.

'Mister Charlie important,' he said, 'and always pay in time. He no just customer, he supplier, too. You know morphine? You know penicillin? Nobody have nothing but Mister Charlie he have plenty.'

'Would you believe it,' my guy said quietly. God was tuned in after all.

'Why don't we check this Mister Charlie out?' I asked. 'Maybe we could work with the limey ourselves? Can we use morphine?'

I knew the answer but I needed to give him his say.

'Are you kidding me?' he asked quietly, and gave us the first smile of the evening.

All of a sudden the war was over. My guy offered Paco a light and Paco offered my guy a Manila cigar and one thing led to another. My guy tapped Paco's shoulder and turned to me.

'We can sell that stuff in Europe all day. They kill for it over there.'

'Great,' I said with relief.

'My friend Paco'll introduce you,' my guy whispered, and he winked.

Paco thought that meant he wanted a woman, and for once he was right.


You couldn't get close to Charlie just like that. It wasn't easy, because he moved in circles that were Oh Yoo Tee to me. Paco had gone back to Manila after my guy left, and I was waiting for him to get me an introduction. He took his time and kept me waiting and gave me different excuses every time. Meanwhile I watched Charlie from afar, like a hawk, every time he came to Hong Kong. I followed him to Bangkok. I followed him to Macao. I went everywhere. After a few months I began to get through to some guys who knew him personally. Some police informers and that. These guys weren't necessarily close to him. Some didn't even like him, but they all talked about him like he was special. They talked and I was learning fast and soon there was little I didn't know about him. The more I learned of him, his way of life and work and the courage of his character, the more I admired him. His friends from the war were not interested in talking to me at all. And they were the ones who counted. There was only Paco, and he was just sitting around taking his time about the introduction. I couldn't get near any straight policemen. Not when they thought I was interested in Charlie. They wanted to keep him all to themselves.

He got away with murder because he was a war hero and the police shut their eyes. He was able to come and visit in Hong Kong now that the Japanese were gone and everybody was always happy to see him. There was something about the way he talked to people that made them feel like things were going to be better. And things were not easy there after the war. They had a rough time under the Japanese. No wonder his optimistic way and easy manner pleased people. They were not going to turn him in even though they knew damn well what he was up to. Maybe they even protected him. Most of them had fought against the Japanese during the war and considered it an honour to look the other way. They were rough on Paco, though. And on me. Maybe because I was American. They say I look like Edward G. Robinson. You've got to remember they saw plenty of movies and plenty of tough guys like James Cagney and Bogart and maybe they thought I belonged behind bars. And Charlie, well he was Charles Paget-Brown, a decorated gentleman and one of them. He could have lived in Hong Kong if he wanted to because they would have taken him in with open arms.

During the war, with the Japanese crawling all over the place, Charlie was top of their hit list. They knew about him and they knew what he was doing, but they never caught him. That made him a hero. But he didn't think he was a hero, because he was having the time of his life. Only once did he get close to being done. And that was because of Paco the Filipino.

One of my contacts in the Hong Kong police told me he once asked Charlie why he was still doing business with the Filipino. With all he had done that time in Pataya and his bad reputation and that. Charlie said it wasn't Paco's fault. He said the man was tortured and wouldn't have done it otherwise, but then Charlie never believed anyone could be plain bad. He said Paco had sent word to warn him, but I'm sure he was lying. He defended his friends even when they weren't his friends any more.

I mention Paco even though I didn't like him. I didn't trust him. I mention him because he was the guy who did finally introduce me to Charlie and I owe him.

I had a chance to take care of Paco the Filipino years later in France, but I didn't.

By that time we were so big no one messed with us. I prefer the old days. No computers, no planning and conferences. In those days you did an honest day's work and you saw immediate results. A guy was good to you, you made him rich. He fucked with you, you killed him.

The Orient, too, has lost its charms now. You fly there and back in hours. They have more skyscrapers than Manhattan. It doesn't even smell different any more. You used to know you were there, with soy and fish and piss and frying shrimpy rice and pork coming at you from every sidewalk. Nowadays people dress just like they do anywhere. McDonalds and Toyotas have replaced the rice bowls and the rickshaws. By the paper lanterns they have Christian Dior signs and, boy, are they rich.

For three years after 1942, Charlie lived the lives of ten men. Rose told me once he did that more for the adventure than love of country. She used any opportunity she had to put him down. Whatever she says, his exploits are still talked about today by those who knew him and had worked with him. Mister Charlie, they called him in the Orient. Waiters, company directors and whores alike. In the Caribbean and South America they would have written songs about him. They would have called their first-born kids Mister Charlie after him. Rose couldn't stand the name, but he didn't care. When Roberta, aged two, called him that one day, Rose smacked her across the face, but Charlie loved it. Roberta called her father that ever since.

As soon as they got to Bangkok, they rented a big house near where the American Embassy stands today. He had maids and two gardeners and a boat in the canal they call a klong, which ran at the end of his garden. Bangkok was then still a city of canals, like Venice. You could get from place to place quickly on a boat. With all the traffic there nowadays and the bad air I bet people regret they filled so many of those old canals in.

He set up business downtown, a few minutes' walk from the Oriental Hotel. It was a large office, above a jewellery store. His main business was still import and export, and because he had made friends with the Burmese ruby-dealers during the war, he was in the gem business too. Morphine and penicillin, though, were where the real dough was, and my people were interested in getting in on that. They were sure he was playing around with narcotics. The wise guys in New York figured they knew more than I did.

It's funny, how the world figures things. We, with our so-called swarthy, oily dark hair and Mediterranean faces are all villains. Charlie, who spoke like a gentleman and went to cocktail parties, was doing mostly the same as us but he was invited to the best houses. Yes, all the diplomats and attachés and that were proud to have him in the house. His picture often appeared in the social pages of the Bangkok English-language papers.

People must have guessed he had a local woman stashed away somewhere. Everybody did it and everybody lied about it at home, but not among the men in the club or the office. Charlie kept very quiet about his all the time, but he didn't fool me. Hindsight is a Mister Smartass. I mean, anyone could have seen the signs. They were so loud and clear it was pathetic. But only loud and clear to me, because I knew. And I knew because I had the guy followed night and day from the moment his operation became interesting to us. You can't just pounce on a guy and tell him, Hey, we want in. Not a guy like Charlie, and not out there in Bangkok where it was going to happen. You had to know all about him. Collect enough dirt about him and maybe use it later for pressure. I don't care what people say, there's dirt in everyone. Everyone's got something to hide.

Nappaporn and Nalini lived on the other side of the river, in a small house built on stilts. There was another house there which they used for visitors. The kind of guys who crossed borders illegally and couldn't be put up in hotels where you needed a passport, or people he didn't want around the office. Charlie had turned over two of his fishing junks to Nappaporn. Like all Oriental women, his mistress knew about money, and she ran her small fishing business with great success. He used to go and see her two or three times a week.

Very few people knew about Nappaporn, but no one knew about her daughter Nalini. He never talked about her at all. He didn't even hide a picture of her somewhere in his drawers at the office, like other such fathers had. Nappaporn was a business partner of his, and on occasion people met her in the fish market or rented her boats from her, and they respected her, even though they knew she was his woman. Not so the little girl. There was no sign of her anywhere.

On Charlie's desk there was a silver-framed photograph of his English daughter, Roberta. Everyone knew her and he bragged about her and she could get anything she wanted out of him.

Roberta was sent first to an English-speaking school in town. It was a kind of American school, and all the teachers were from the States. All the kids there were foreign. It was, and I believe still is, a very good school, and Charlie fought hard to keep her there. As long as she went to that school she lived with them in Bangkok and that was how he wanted it. He brought her into the office and took her shopping and introduced her to all his smart friends. But that didn't last. Listening to man-talk in Charlie's place of business, she was becoming vulgar. At school, her King's English was going too American, and Rose hated that. She couldn't wait to get Roberta out of there and send her somewhere where they would make a proper English lady out of her.

They argued and they fought and in the end Charlie lost out. Roberta was sent to Hong Kong to some hoity-toity school. Charlie, on the quiet, got his own back. A month after Roberta left the American school, he sent Nalini there instead. The kids there didn't know how to say Nalini, and that's how her name became Nellie. Little Nellie Brown. Yeah, that one. The one.

I am not a great lover of children. Maybe things turned out the way they did because I felt guilty about Charlie. No. That's not it. I don't feel guilty now and I certainly didn't feel guilty then. All that happened many years ago in Bangkok and it was not personal. What I did to Charlie was strictly legit because it was business.

# CHAPTER FOUR

■

Then there is the other one, Charlie's friend Sam. Everything about him was real foreign. He spoke foreign and he looked foreign. Where he came from and where he got to had nothing to do with me. I had no business dealings with him. Everything I know about Sam came from Charlie because he told me about it. More than once. He loved him and he loved talking about him.

When Charlie talked about Sam Baker his expression was always the same. His eyes looked straight at you and his smile would vanish. He'd go all pensive and serious and wait for you to shut up as if he was about to read from the Bible. He'd mention the name carefully, slowly, with dignity, just like a priest would mention Jesus.

I can't talk the way Charlie could. I don't just mean his accent. When we first met I didn't even understand half of what he was saying. Yes, I knew the words, sure I did. It was the way Charlie put words together that was different. I had spent plenty of time with him and I listened to him and in the end I learned to understand what he said.

People sometimes say I sound like a limey. My guys in New York often say that and maybe I do. They are pulling my leg, but there could be some truth in it. I have spent so much time with the English in the Orient and later in Jamaica. Right after the war it was the English who did all the trading everywhere. Banking, shipping, customs, policing and even smuggling. You name it. I admired Charlie and I listened to him almost every day at one time. Him and Rose too. Sometimes, when that happens, a man imitates people without noticing it. I might have imitated him. I might still be doing it today, but I could never really talk like him. Certainly not when he talked about Sam Baker. I'm going to try. Give it a shot, as Charlie would say. I'll do it my way. It might not come out so good, and I'm only doing it because I want to remember them both. I didn't know Sam that well. I had little to do with him. I can only talk about Sam the way Charlie told it.

You want to know about Sam Baker? That's how Charlie always started. I can't say he's a friend. I can't say he's a brother, he would continue. I can't even say he was the closest any man ever got to me. He was much more than that. He took me in when I thought I had reached the end of the road. When my credibility and money were gone to the dogs, he took me on. He was born with the sort of loyalty one reads about but rarely meets. You look at him today, you see his homes and his business and his friends and his money, and you think he walked into privilege. You see the way people respect him and welcome him and you are envious. You think of him as a man of few words. A quiet sort of chap, but then you don't know the passion Sam Baker has. Passion not for things, not for places, only for people and, above all, friends.

To begin with, Sam Baker was not born Sam Baker. He was born in a small village outside the town of Ramalla in Palestine. The name he had been given was Samir. The family's name was Al Bakr. It is an Arab name.

He was brought up by a young, unmarried aunt and his grandfather. His parents, he was told at an early age, were both victims of the cholera that had plagued the area in the year after his birth. All the softness, compassion and understanding his aunt gave him were needed to inoculate Samir against the unyielding, strict and sometimes abusive treatment his grandfather had dealt him. Until he was seven years old, his grandfather hardly spoke to him at all, except when telling him off for something. These were the starving years, when jobs were scarce and those who could left Palestine for other pastures in Egypt and the Lebanon. Samir's grandfather, in addition to working his own little dusty plot of land, was the village baker.

The rocky, often barren Judean hills have seen peoples come and go. Some were conquerors, others swarmed through with armies that were meant to do battle further afield. Some of these strangers stayed a while, others stayed longer, but all left something behind. The Greeks built temples, the Romans left aqueducts and amphitheatres, and the Crusaders built ports and castles. They stayed in Palestine for a long time. They left blond, blue-eyed children who continued to appear amongst swarthy local families hundreds of years later. The Turks who had ruled Palestine with an iron fist left the locals with a deep mistrust of authority and fear of the law. At the time of Sam's youth, the British were there, and were called Ingleezie by one and all.

In those hard years everyone Samir and his family knew dreamed of going to America. That was a country where God reigned. He filled the streets with gold. America was far, so far it could have been close to the moon. Anybody who had actually arrived there was considered to be lucky.

The golden boys, they called them in the village. They had gone and were now living far away and were rich, but none of them ever forgot the old country or the family they had left behind. There were letters, some money orders, and, most important, a photograph of themselves and their new life. It was always displayed in a prominent part of the house where everybody could see it and admire it and talk of the absent son with great affection and esteem. To be the owner of such a picture put one at the social top of the town. It usually depicted the emigrant, dressed 'frangie', a real dandy, in a suit and tie, shoes and a hat. You saw him smiling as he was leaning on his gleaming 'trombeel'. There were hardly any trombeels to be seen in Ramalla in those days. And those that did exist belonged to the rich or the Ingleezie police who drove their trombeels up and down the streets to keep law and order. Everybody else walked or rode their donkeys.

Charlie loved this part. He'd show off what he'd learned from Sam. He'd stop and explain to me that a trombeel was a car in Arabic. He'd look at me like I was a nobody. He'd wait for me to applaud him and tell him what a smart guy he was, but I never did. There was always silence at that point, and then he'd shrug his shoulders and go on with the story.

While I languished in a fee-paying school in England, Charlie would say, living off the fat of my privileged father and his social position, Samir Al Bakr sweated it out in the village bakery. He had been good at learning and was meant to become a teacher. But his grandfather insisted the boy learned a proper trade, and Samir was sent to the bakery to help.

He was a strong, sturdy boy, if a bit on the short side. If you take the silvery hair away and ignore the lines across his face you'd see him as he used to be. His virile, good eyes caressed the world with the same burning, curious grey light we all grew to love. Inside he hadn't changed at all. He was a hard-working boy, and his aunt had promised he could go back to school full-time once another member of the family had reached fourteen and could take his place.

Samir did not get much sleep. The baker worked nights in those days, and during the day Samir Al Bakr continued to go to school and work the land. He also waited on customers at Abu Hanna's coffee house, where the elderly and the rich converged. It was there that he first heard people talk of America. Everybody talked about America, but at Abu Hanna's coffee house you could hear about it from those who were actually there.

Not many came back to the village from America. And those few who did only returned when they were old. For a while they would be the centre of attention in the village, dressed frangie and oozing eau de cologne. They would sit for hours in Abu Hanna's, basking in the glory of America, the shoeshine boys and waiters hovering over them like bees. They usually said they had come back to die there. They brought sackfuls of money with them to see them through, and they passed the time of day sipping coffee, sucking at their water-pipes, and telling the story of America to anyone who had the time and inclination to listen. Samir Al Bakr listened.

America, where the top of the buildings clashed with the clouds. The wheat fields in America stretched from horizon to horizon, and there was always food to eat. In America everyone had his own trombeel to drive in. America. Where all the women had golden hair and long white legs and thin painted eyebrows. America, where if you wanted to work you never starved. This was what they heard, and with that famous Oriental imagination, it formed an irresistible magnet to which listeners were drawn.

Of course, the local rich did not need to go to America, but there were very few of those about. The boy Samir did not want to go either. The second baking shift started at two o'clock in the morning, and Samir's aunt woke him up for that. It was a small bakery, and while the oven was aflame the heat was unbearable. The master baker himself, who owned the place, was fond of the boy. Fond enough to discuss a possible matrimonial arrangement between Samir and his only daughter. She was a pretty, green-eyed girl and, at thirteen, as local tradition had decreed, she did not visit the village school any longer. Her life, like that of every daughter in the village, was planned for her. In due course she would be married, cook and clean, work the field with her husband, and bear children. Samir's future in the village was assured.

But somewhere in between, something happened to him. The urge he had always been free of, the urge to emigrate, to find gold in America, had suddenly hit him too. He started talking about it to his aunt and to his friends. He talked to some of the golden boys themselves, while waiting on them at Abu Hanna's. He asked for guidance on life and success in the new world. They were happy to give it to him.

When Samir was twenty, his only cousin Latif was brought into the bakery. One morning, long before the village woke, Samir took his shoes and slung them over his shoulders. He stood over the sleeping figure of the woman who had brought him up. He looked at her for a long while and he kissed her broad, tired forehead. He was memorizing her shape, the sound of her breath, and the voice that was now lost in sleep. He would carry the image of her with him. He would carry it in his mind all the way to America, and it would stay imprinted on his mind until he saw her again. He had no doubt of that, for when he became rich he would send for her. He would have her come out to him to witness the success that would surely be his. He could feel his ambition burning through his very soul. He knew he would miss her, but to find his fortune he must go away from her first.

There was, of course, a reason for his departure. He could have stayed in the village or gone back to school or got a job of work somewhere in the village, or even in the town of Ramalla. Samir was a well-known boy. The poor knew him from the bakery and the rich knew him from his days as a waiter at Abu Hanna's cafe. He was always patient with them. He listened to them and he waited patiently when they counted the coins to pay him. He had a smile and a good word for all. Samir would have made a success anywhere, but he could not stay in his village.

No one, Charlie said, no one saw him that last night, as he prepared to leave. I can only imagine the passionate emotions that filled him on his lonely walk through the dark, deserted streets. He was to be a driven man after that, and nothing could have stopped him. He was driven by ambition born of shame.

All that came about because Sam's aunt was not his aunt at all. She was his grandfather's daughter. She was his mother. She was raped by a Turkish soldier in the olive grove one early morning when the village slept. Until that day the soldier came to the village almost every day. He used to wait for her and follow her and had tried to talk to her, but she never stopped.

Charlie said that because he liked fairy tales. He was romantic and made out the Turkish soldier was in love. But the soldier never even got close to talking to her. He had watched her and had desired her, and one day he lay in wait for her behind a thick, ancient olive tree. He pounced on her as she passed, bending down to collect dry branches that had fallen onto the ground. He covered her mouth and took her by force. She did not scream or cry out and never said a thing to anyone.

No one saw the Turkish soldier on his own in the village after that. He used to turn up with two or three other soldiers. They even sat at Abu Hanna's cafe stretching their legs and sipping coffee as if nothing had happened.

Sam never forgot the anguish he had suffered when he first learned the true circumstances of his birth. It happened late one night, when his grandfather came back from the bakery. The old man was tired and irritable, and something in the meal his daughter had served displeased him. He pushed the plate off the table. It fell on the stone floor and broke.

'You whore,' Samir heard his grandfather scream. 'You shameless daughter of Satan.'

Samir came running from behind the rug that separated his sleeping-quarters from where the old man and his daughter sat. His fists were clenched.

'Go back to hell, you little bastard,' the old man yelled.

'You talk like that to my aunt and I will kill you,' the boy shouted.

Whether he overcame his inbred respect for the elderly that night and hit his grandfather will remain a mystery. Sam never spoke of what followed. For a long time after that his life in the house must have been miserable. He tried to work even harder at school, and in the afternoon he followed the old man and his mother to the field. He did everything that was demanded of him and more. But nothing changed. The old man accepted his sweat and his servility but did not open to him.

Then, some years after that revelation, the Turkish soldier's body was found. He lay, dead but open-eyed, in the very same olive grove. Under the same ancient tree where Samir was tearfully conceived. This came to pass within days of General Allenby's victorious entry into Jerusalem. The finding of the body created a commotion in the village, but it remained strictly within the realm of whispers. There were rumours, of course. People said the soldier could have died of starvation or exposure. With battles raging between the Turks and advancing British forces, there were, in those uncertain days, scores of Turkish soldiers roaming the countryside. They were begging and stealing food on their way north. He could have been one of them. Sam always hinted it was his grandfather who had killed the man to restore the family honour.

He had good reason to believe his grandfather did it. The old man seemed different in the year that followed. His hard attitude toward Samir had changed. The constant snide remarks and the scolding were gone. The old man started taking notice of his grandson. He started talking to him. Telling him stories of family members who had gone to America and what had happened to them there. He spoke of his own youth and tried to help the boy with his homework. The discovery of the body had given Samir's grandfather a new, gentler soul. But this new relationship was not meant to last very long. One night, a few months after the soldier was found, the main oven in the bakery exploded. It was during Samir's grandfather's shift, and the old man died in the fire.

There's something fishy here. I reckon the two guys died a little too close to each other. I figured Sam had killed the Turkish soldier himself and blew his grandfather up in his bakery later. He was entitled on both counts, I thought, and I said so to Charlie. He never understood the heat and the passions that rule the Mediterranean. He never understood what blood feuds meant. Sure, he knew people over there carried grudges for generations. He could talk about it and he had read about it, but he didn't really accept it in his heart. Charlie never understood revenge. His life would have been different if he had. When I told him what I thought, he just looked at me with eyes that turned to ice and said I was crazy. He said Sam was a mere child and would never do such a thing. He said Sam didn't have it in him.

I don't care what Charlie thinks. Not every killer is over eighteen. I know that from personal experience. I was just a kid when I shot my first man. I am sure the Arab did it all. But at the time I needed Charlie's help and needed to get along with him, so I didn't argue and said nothing more about it. I just sat there and let Charlie run with his story.

Perhaps he had made up his mind to leave the village because he was the only living evidence of his mother's shame. Perhaps he thought her life would be simpler when he was not there to remind her. People were generally kind and no one said anything, but there was no doubt they all knew. His grandfather's harsh treatment of him could have stemmed from that. In any case, Sam did not waste any time once the opportunity to leave presented itself.

That last dawn, before leaving the house, he stood there and looked at his mother. He made a silent vow that he would continue to support her from America, touched her face one last time, and was gone.

# CHAPTER FIVE
■

He had never spent a night away from his village before. Anything that lay beyond the surrounding countryside was new. He started out walking west and passed other villages on the way. He crossed the hills and the valleys and for the first few days he lived on the bread he had carried on his back. He found water to drink at the bottom of every drying brook that happened on his way. There are a lot of fruit trees strewn about the Judean hills. There are dates and figs and oranges and lemons and there are peaches and carobs. Samir Al Bakr knew the trees and when the fruits were ripe and ready to be eaten. When the bread ran out he was prepared. Every night he started a small fire. He took a handful of flour and salt from his bag and he mixed it with water and baked his own bread.

It took him three months to reach the ancient port of Jaffa, for he walked all the way. He had passed many new villages settled by newly arrived European Yahood, who had started to flock to Palestine in those years. Their Old Testament prophets had told them they must return there. They considered the Holy Land their country too.

He worked for the Yahood in their orange groves and their vegetable fields and he slept under the summer sky. He had saved all his money. Three pounds and seventeen silver shillings, almost all freshly minted with the King's head in the centre.

He was a friendly youth whose polite, dignified manner and open smile were attractive. Once inside the port, he soon made friends with a man who selected labourers for the ships. It was the citrus-shipping season, and within a week of his arrival he boarded an orange-carrying ship bound for England.

Samir saw little of the sea. He often said he had spent most of his time sorting fruits in the hold. On rare evenings he would climb up to walk on deck in search of some fresh air. He was liked by all hands, and even the Captain took to him and wrote a letter of recommendation for him. Samir kept that letter all his life and I saw it myself, hanging on a wall in his house, gilt-framed. It was the only certificate he owned, and he was proud of it. A yellowing, handwritten document with a ship's stamp. The writing was old-fashioned and meticulous. And at the time it came in useful. The Captain's letter got him a job on a vessel crossing the Atlantic.

When Samir Al Bakr came aboard the ship to America he was extremely well off. Some ten paper pounds and two small bagfuls of silver shillings. The ship was loaded with English Austin trombeels, which surprised him. Back in his village they only talked about those American Ford and Chevrolet trombeels. Everyone at Abu Hanna's cafe said they were the best trombeels in the world, but he did not ask any questions. They took almost three weeks to cross the ocean, and when they finally arrived in America he was paid off and discharged.

The port was hot. Hotter than he'd ever imagined America to be. The place was full of black people they called Abeed in his village. But strangest of all was the flag that fluttered above the big white customs house. It was the Ingleezie Union Jack. Samir well remembered the pink colour of British possessions all over the world. India was pink, most of Africa was pink, and many places in Asia were pink too. That map was in every classroom in Palestine. But in America there had been a revolution. The Ingleezie flag had left America many years ago. It had no business there now.

There must have been some mistake, he thought, as he walked down the gangway. It did not occur to him to go aboard again and ask somebody. The Ingleezie had been correct with him and had paid him handsomely as soon as they had docked. Yes, they had kept themselves to themselves, but they had been good to him to take him thus far. He looked about for some of the other hands, but they had all gone. No matter, he thought, as he walked down and felt the hot air hit his face. He smiled at the new world. He was not afraid. He was a strong young man and in his pocket he had the princely sum of twenty-seven pounds and many, many silver shillings. Perhaps another five pounds' worth of shillings. Or ten. He did not count his silver because he was now richer than he had ever been.

Where does a young Levantine boy go when he finds himself in an unknown place? They had taught him the answer to that at Abu Hanna's cafe. Go to the market-place, they had told him. It is a place that needs no schooling or language. It does not favour old-timers over immigrants. It only knows people who sell things and people who buy things. Our people always started there on their way to find their fortune, they had told him. They were drawn there as soon as they set foot in America. When you get there, go to the market. You are bound to find someone there who knows the world you have come from. Someone from the old country. Everybody knows the sons of Ishmael are the best market traders in the world.

It was a large market. It spread over an area bigger than the village olive grove. There were many palm trees there, but they were taller than the ones he had known and bore no dates. He had never seen such an abundance of fruits and vegetables in his life. They were heaped in great quantities and were colourful, almost as colourful as the dresses that covered the women who sold them.

They sold everything. Old furniture and baskets and buckets and pots and straw mats and cotton for dresses and bread. They sold eggs and red meat that hung from metal wires along lines of freshly caught fish. It was hotter than the hottest summer in his village and the merchandise was different, but it was still a market. People pointed and touched their wares and they chanted and screamed and sang in praise of what was on offer. They were speaking in English, but the English they spoke sounded like a song. There were gesticulating and shouting but no one was angry. Everybody appeared to be smiling. There was humour in the air. People were tapping on makeshift drums and they chatted with each other and laughed. The old men at Abu Hanna's were right. America was a happy place.

There were not a lot of white faces to be seen.

Sam bought himself a banana and an orange for half a penny and continued to walk about amongst the shouting and the dust. He was in no hurry because he could spend this first day watching and learning. He found a wooden barrel in the shade and he sat down on it and he ate. He watched people and listened to them argue and nodded when they shook hands as if he was one of them.

Then he heard a voice that was sweet to his ears with its unmistakable guttural sound. It was so familiar it could have been his own.

'Jerusalem lemon water,' the voice proclaimed. 'Holy Jerusalem lemon water. Cold and fresh and sweet.'

He looked up and saw a small blue wooden wagon. There were glass containers filled with crushed ice and a heap of lemons and limes strewn around. A small, dapper man, middle-aged and dressed in a white suit, chanted the words as he pushed the wagon forward.

They soon got talking.

'My name is Samir.'

'My name is Phillip.'

'From Jerusalem?'

'No, Hebron.'

'Why do you say Jerusalem lemon water?'

'Because they all know about Jerusalem. No one's heard of Hebron.'

'Of course they have,' said Samir. 'Everyone in America is educated.'

The older man laughed.

'Another one,' he said.

'How do you mean another one?'

'You are not the first. It's almost become a joke here.'

'I don't see anything funny.'

'You are not the first man to land here thinking he's arrived in America. The very same thing happened to me years ago.'

'We are not in America?'

'No. We are not in America. Not exactly in America. This is the British Colony of Jamaica. The name of this town is Kingston.'

The young man did not smile. He was not angry. He did not ask himself why he had been put ashore in a place he knew nothing about. He accepted it as if it had been God's will, the way he would accept everything.

'There are many like you here on this island, Samir,' Phillip said as he squeezed another lemon into the glass jug. 'When they landed here they thought they were in America too.'

'And what happened to them?'

'Mostly, they landed on their feet like our people always do. We are all much more successful when we live away from home. Anyway, the old country has hardly ever been ours, has it?'

'What do our people do here?'

'Buy and sell, that's what they do. They trade. Dry goods. They own most of the shops in King's Street . . .'

'King's Street?'

'I forgot. You've just walked off the ship. You haven't seen this town at all. Look, it's not a bad place. The locals are happy and friendly and a little lazy. They like to dance and sing and have a drink of rum. The Ingleezie don't do much except ruling this island and running their sugar estates, so we get a chance to make a living. Some of our people made a fortune here.'

'Anyone gone back?'

'You must be crazy. What for? Go back to the old country? I'd rather forget about it. The old country was suffering – Turks and beatings and hunger. If I never saw it again I wouldn't care. This is my country now.'

'What about your family?'

'All dead. You?'

'My aunt lives there . . . my mother . . . one cousin.'

'If you want to make it in this island you'd best forget all about the old country . . . Samir . . . you better think of an easier name, too. No one can say Al Bakr here. Give yourself an English name.'

'Did you?'

'Sure. My name was Walid . . . Phillip is simpler. What work did you do in the old country?'

'I worked in the bakery . . . And . . .'

'That's good. You can call yourself Baker. Samir . . . no. You call yourself Sam. Sam Baker. That's it. You have a name now. You have a place to live?'

'No.'

'You come and stay in our place. It's a big house. Belongs to a widow. She rents rooms.'

'Will there be place for me?'

'The widow will give you one. She will do what I say. She is my woman.'

'Your wife?'

'No. Just my woman. You will have a room.'

'I have very little money.'

'You can work.'

'What work can I do?'

'You can help me. Go buy the fruit. Push this wagon around. Squeeze some lemons, you know . . .'

'Yes.'

'You get a tenth of the takings. On good days it can almost be one pound.'

'When can I start?'

'You have started, Sam. You have started. I can smell it's going to be a good day.'

That night Sam sat on the terrace of the rooming-house and wrote a letter. He addressed it to Abu Hanna's coffee house. His mother could not read or write but someone there would read it to her.

'I have arrived in a place near America. It is an island called Jamaica. I have found work and a place to live and I think I will stay here for a year or so. Until I make enough to go to America and bring you there. During the day it is very, very hot here. Like in the village in summer. The people are nice and happy. I have met a man from Palestine and I work with him. I will work hard.'

He enclosed a one-pound note with his letter and sealed the envelope. Phillip had promised him he would arrange to post it the next morning.

Here Charlie always paused. He'd look around as if we were sitting somewhere in the desert listening to old Arab fables by the fire. He'd make out as if that first sleepless night Sam had spent in Kingston, Jamaica was the turning-point in his life. In a way it was. Not six months after his landing he and Phillip had five lemon-water wagons which were operated by young street urchins Sam had befriended. He had constructed these himself out of old perambulators he had bought in the market. They also had one selling hot coffees. Phillip offered Sam a fifty-fifty partnership and the young man accepted.

He was indeed a hard worker. Within one year they had a total of nine vending trollies and hired more youngsters to operate them. He could now afford a larger room, all for himself, and he used the back-garden shed as a warehouse.

The trollies sold patties and sandwiches and soon Sam became the sole purveyor of fast food to shopkeepers and office workers in the centre of Kingston. Two years after he arrived he had more than fifty people on his payroll. Phillip was put in charge of distributing materials to the vendors while Sam looked after the cash. Later that year, Sam bought his friend Phillip out and gave him a handsome profit and a permanent working position as his right-hand man.

At twenty-three, Sam was able to acquire his first car. By then he didn't call it a trombeel any more. It was an old Packard, but with the polish his boys gave it every day it looked brand new. At that time he was the proud owner of five restaurants, two coffee houses, and a thriving street catering business that covered the town from the harbour to Half Way Tree.

When Sam Baker was twenty-four, he leased the entire house from Phillip's woman, the widow, and converted it into a working man's boarding-house. A year after that he bought another building closer to the port. This time he added two bathrooms on each floor, and the customers were given their own sheets. The large terrace in front was converted into a restaurant. The place did well, and it signalled Samir's entry into the hotel business. Every month, during all that time, Samir wrote to his mother at Abu Hanna's cafe and he told her about his life. His letters always included a five-pound note.

He found out that the baker's daughter had married another. On hearing that, Samir sent Phillip to the old country to buy the bakery from her father and give it to his only cousin Latif, who had replaced him there. That was the year he started importing foodstuffs from America and Greece.

Around about that time he changed his name by deed poll to Sam Baker. It seemed nothing could stop his meteoric rise. He began buying and building more and more hotels all over the island. All that filled every hour of every day in his life. Somehow, he was too busy to fulfil his childhood ambition of going to see America. In a way, the need for that was losing ground because America, in the shape of sun-starved tourists from the cold East Coast, was coming to him.

I think Charlie said it was during the summer of 1931 that Sam Baker got to see America at last. It was an important visit for him. It was the first time he met Jake Mafood, his agent in New York. Jake was a pleasant man of Lebanese origin. Until that time they had conducted their business through the post. Sam was importing frozen meat and cereals, hotel furnishings and electrical goods from the United States, and all his orders were processed by Jake. More importantly, Mafood's daughter, a fiery, petite beauty by the name of Jean, was seconded to show him the sights. You must remember that Sam, at over thirty years of age, was an extremely attractive man. Within the Arab community in Kingston he was considered a most eligible bachelor. His name was sometimes linked to one or another unmarried daughter. The fact was, however, that Sam Baker had dedicated himself purely to work, as though there was no room in his life for a woman.

But all that changed when he met Jean Mafood. She was nearly twenty-one years old and just out of university. She was a cultured girl who liked the theatre and the arts, and she took great pleasure in introducing Sam to Broadway and the galleries along Madison Avenue. He seemed an eager student and, given her strong mind and persuasive personality, almost putty in her hands. She enjoyed having this mature, strong man tamed at her feet. He followed her everywhere and appeared to listen to everything she said. He did not talk much about himself, but she had heard of his past from her father. The earthy strength that emanated from his eyes and his body excited her. Perhaps his accent reminded her of her grandfather.

The long and the short of it was that Sam Baker had got himself a wife. The lavish wedding took place on her twenty-first birthday. They took a train to Florida where they started their honeymoon through the Caribbean. The trip took many days and many nights. The young couple hardly ever left their cabin, but when they did the bride looked as if she had found the true meaning of happiness in the beaming man by her side. Charlie said it was animal magnetism that had drawn her to Sam.

Romantic stuff, but that's Charlie all over. He always lost his head around love. Not his own. He never talked about his feelings in that department, but other people's love excited him. As though love was something that happened only to the chosen few. I figure it was something he got from all those books he always read.

That was one big difference between them. Sam never read a thing. Not even the newspaper. He did not know what was going on in the world. All his concentration was pinned on his business –the hotels, the food imports, and the island of Jamaica. He knew nothing about the rest of the world, or what was going on. In this way you could say he was completely ignorant. He knew his village and the country route to the coast of Palestine. He heard the village gossip from his mother's letters, written for her by Abu Hanna. He knew the inside of the ships which had taken him all the way to the Caribbean and that was all. That ignorance was to cost him very dearly later on.

When he was in New York he must have seen other things or perhaps he pretended. He allowed Jean to think she was leading him all the way. But as soon as they were back in Kingston he stopped acting the pupil. The window Jean had so proudly thought she had opened for him was firmly shut. Sam had distanced himself from the written word. Any written word.

Of course, there were letters to and from suppliers and agents and travel people, but his people did that. All he wanted to know was how much money was coming in and how much was being spent on expansion. Much as Jean tried to get him to further his education, back in Jamaica the culture trip was over. I mean, he let her do what she liked, but she could never again push him to see a show or an exhibition. He went on to increase his wealth while she became a pillar of local society. She helped young painters and had a piano brought into the house to await the hands of the baby she was carrying.

While they were waiting for the birth, Phillip was dispatched to Palestine again to bring Sam's mother to Jamaica. It was to be a first-class passage, no less. Jean threw a big party for her mother-in-law. Everyone who was anyone was there. But the music and the entertainment and the fireworks all went way above the guest of honour's head. The old lady was given a small apartment in the large house and a servant to cater for all her needs. Her son came to see her every evening and made sure she was invited to every social function in the house. If she was surprised to see how successful her son had become, there was no one she could tell. She never learned to speak English.

With his mother's arrival, Sam's connection and interest in his village near Ramalla appeared to have ended. The only family left there were his great-uncle and his son Latif the baker, but his mother had told him he had sold the bakery and was rich enough to do nothing. He no longer wrote to Abu Hanna, nor noticed the events that were to shape Palestine's future. He ceased talking of his village. To those who knew him then, it seemed he had forgotten the old country. Jean settled down to the local social life, and there were tea parties and excursions and the odd afternoon of poetry-reading. Sam took no part in that at all.

I don't want to go into all of that now. They had a good marriage, but when their son was born they started to argue about him. The child was a sturdy, strong boy who had inherited Jean's independent mind and Sam's tenacity and resolution. In his looks, it was as though Jean had nothing to do with him. He was an exact replica of his father, straight from the Middle East. Except that he was going to be taller.

The main difference between them was in their manner. While Sam was quiet and pensive and said little, his son Richard was certainly of a more extroverted nature. He talked a lot and screamed a lot and, boy, he was funny. You could see that laughter shine right out of his mischievous eyes from a very early age.

Come to think if it, there was another difference between Sam and Charlie. Sam did not have a sense of humour. He did not understand jokes and frowned at pranks. No one ever dared tease him. Charlie said something about it once. He said Sam's total sincerity was so great, one could not expect him to make fun.

Richard Baker was clearly the son and heir Sam had been waiting for. The boy was taken over by his father as soon as he could walk. Sam took his son with him everywhere. He knew everyone at the office by name before he was four years old. He knew every hotel and every restaurant. He watched his father and his friends play backgammon and dominoes, swam in the pool, and brawled with the gardener's boys in the yard. Sam wanted to send the boy to a public school in England, while Jean preferred America.

'England is too stuffy, Sam. Too conservative. This is the new world.'

'Jamaica is part of the British Empire. He needs an English education to succeed.'

'He'll become a snob there. On this island all you need to be is approachable.'

'On this island you need to be a trader,' Sam said.

'And you think they'll teach him that in an English school?'

'No one needs to teach him that. His blood is a trader's blood.'

'America is an equal, open society, Sam. He'll learn how to get on with people.'

'The streets have taught him that. People love him. He's like one of them.'

'So what will an English school do for him?'
'It will teach him how to be boss.'

There was, by now, quite an empire for Richard Baker to inherit. The company produced canned goods and soft drinks, and the profits bought more hotels and import agencies. It kept Sam too busy to notice anything that happened outside his island paradise. There were no yesterdays, only tomorrows. A great part of his tomorrow was Richard's place in it, and when the idea of making an Englishman of his son hit him there was no room for anything else.

Sam is a kindly and considerate man, but his word, both in his office and in his house, was the law. When Jean fought tooth and nail for her son's education he just sat there and heard every last word. He did not scream. He did not listen. He sat there quietly while she ranted and raved. The one-sided battle lasted almost a year. At the end of it he said the boy was going to England to learn how to talk and behave like a gentleman and that was that.

It was, therefore, with a heavy heart that Jean and young Richard Baker, aged seven, were put on a ship belonging to the Elders and Fyffe line for their trip across the Atlantic.

# CHAPTER SIX

When Sam Baker's son Richard became a man he turned mean on Charlie, and at one time he caused him real damage. I would have known what to have done, but Charlie's revenge button was missing from his system. He always made excuses for people, even those who screwed him the way Richard Baker did. He wasn't mad at them. He'd talk about them, tell you what great guys they were, even though you knew for sure they were shits.

That was another thing Charlie and Sam Baker had in

common. As far as these two were concerned, there were no bad guys in the world. Period. That was OK for a man like Sam, who ran straight businesses all his life. But Charlie, who was nearly always cooking crooked deals, couldn't afford such generosity. Let's face it, to be a villain you got to end up in bed with other villains. When they refuse to toe the line you get rid of them. Sure, Charlie wasn't a crook all the time and maybe, the way things turned out, he wasn't cut out to be one at all. I mean, if Charlie had his way, some bastards would be alive and well today. I didn't get my way all the time, though. Had I done, Sam Baker's son Richard would not be where he's at. He wouldn't have been going to all these international meetings. You wouldn't have read about him in the papers. He'd be supporting a headstone, I can tell you.

But by that time it was too late. My interest in Charlie was over, and that saved Richard Baker's neck.

I am jumping again. Where we're at is when Sam's boy was still a boy. Richard Baker arrived in England at the age of seven a free-spirited Jamaican of Arab blood. He had a few problems at the beginning because no one was quite sure what he was. He was from Jamaica but he was white. He was white but he did not look like a European. His sense of humour was a little on the vulgar side. He had this fast temper, and though Sam had warned him to forget about brawling, no one had prepared him for the intolerance some Europeans have.

As he got into bed on his first night his roommate started taunting him.

According to Charlie it went something like this:

'You aren't English, are you, Baker? Where did you spring from?'

'West Indies,' Richard said politely.

'Aren't they all black down there?'

'Not all.' He was trying hard.

'How come you've got an English name?'

'My father's name was Al Bakr. He was born in the Middle East.'

'You're a wog, then.'

'I suppose so,' Richard said. 'What's a wog?'

'You want the polite definition?'

'Sure.'

'A Western Oriental Gentleman,' the boy said.

'Thank you.'

'You know what a wog really is?'

'You tell me.'

'A wog lives in a tent in the desert and eats camel shit.'


He had only known clear skies and the heat of the tropics. He must have hated the cold, wet English weather. During his first term, sturdy as he was, Richard had gone all blue every morning at wake-up time. But he kept his spirits up and his mouth shut for as long as he could. The other boys went on teasing him. They took his silence for weakness. His patience was running out, and as time went on he would have been in real trouble, but then his nerves gave out. After beating up his roommate for calling him names, they left him in peace.

He went through the private school system with its soggy cucumber sandwiches. He excelled at games and managed to pass his exams. His ability to get on with people was at last allowed to flower. He became popular, and was invited to spend weekends and holidays in people's country houses. He could talk the pants off anyone. He learned table manners and how to dance and dress and he nearly lost his accent.

He would have gone back to Jamaica a real English gent had it not been for something that happened in 1947. In the spring of that year Sam decided to go visit the old country, and he took Richard with him. The austere discipline of his schooldays in wartime England had prepared him for that trip. The adventure itself put meat on his balls and made him the man he became.

★   ★   ★

It was certainly the wrong time for Sam to go visiting his home town. Nobody with his head screwed on right would have gone to Palestine then. He was a big-shot hotel owner, thirty years out of his village and a pillar of the local business community. He was loved and respected by all. He was made chairman of social committees. He was invited to join all the clubs. But he had no interest in politics and without ever reading the newspapers his ignorance of world events persisted.

Charlie said it all started when Sam promised Jean a trip around the world. She was entitled. After all, the war years were safe but boring. No one went anywhere, and Jean kept herself busy building their new house on Stony Hill where the rich lived. Sure, you could look down on the whole of Kingston from there, and through the palms and flowers the Caribbean Sea stretched blue and calm and seemed near enough for you to touch it. But the woman was used to culture. She wanted all kinds of furniture and lamps and jars and carpets for the house, and none of that was available there. She did go to New York a few times and could have found replicas there, but she wanted the real McCoy. Someone had told her the Orient was a treasure-chest of stuff, and the Orient is where she wanted to go. Sam preferred to go pick Richard up in England and take a tour of Europe, but she stuck to her guns. She said she had been to Europe after her graduation. It was the Orient or bust. Europe, she said, was in ruins. She had, she said, always wanted to go to China, and now that the war was over there was no reason not to.

She bought brochures and maps and travel books, and one night when they looked at the routes Sam agreed he would go on condition they stopped in Palestine on the way. She said it was crazy. Didn't he ever listen to what people were talking about? Didn't he know it was dangerous there? Jews were fighting Arabs and both fought the Brits and the whole country was going to blow up any minute. But Sam was stubborn, and when Jean said she wasn't going near the place he told her he would take his son anyway. With her or without her. It was, he said, important for Richard to know where his father had come from.

Sam wasn't the kind of guy you'd argue with. He would give you the shirt off his back and never turned you down when you needed a loan or a job or something. He would listen to any sob story and was a sucker for other people's troubles, and his generosity was immediate. He was approachable and stuff, but not when he'd made his mind up about something. He'd look at you with his big grey eyes and say in all sincerity that the subject was closed, and anyone who knew him reckoned it was time to quit talking. That was the second argument he had with Jean, the first being the business about making Richard an English gentleman when he was a boy. Like that time, he did not shout. He listened to her until she ran out of words and he smiled and told her quietly she could have her trip. He said he would be more than happy for her to buy up the whole Orient and ship it back to Jamaica. But he was taking his son to the old country first and that was that. She could go on ahead, sail to Egypt and Hong Kong and wait for them there.

Christ, here it comes again. The story Charlie loved best of all. Sam's return to his village, a rich and powerful golden boy who would go sit at Abu Hanna's cafe and tell everybody about America like all the other boys who came back. Except it wasn't America Sam was going to tell about, or any other place for that matter. He wasn't going to be like any of those other golden boys.

Years later I got to read all those books Charlie read myself. I had time then, and they made me understand him and Sam and their lives better than I did when I knew them in person. Books can do this for you if you know which to pick.

I have heard this one plenty of times. I figure Charlie liked it because it was exciting and stuff, but mostly because it happened close to the time these two finally met.

Charlie would take a deep breath and take a sip of any drink he could lay his hands on and point his eyes at mine and talk. I reckon he was living through some of his boyhood adventure books again. But Sam was no English sailor, Palestine was no African river, and this was no Joseph Conrad script, yet Charlie sure made it sound like it was.

The last European port of call for the Baker family was Athens. A visit to the cradle of democracy was part of Jean's deal, and she sure made use of their stay. While Sam and Richard were taking their daily swim in the Aegean Sea, she took every available tour of the town. There weren't many of those because the country was having problems, but she sure found things to do. In spite of the local political turmoil she climbed the rocks to the Acropolis, saw three Greek tragedies performed in its amphitheatre. She saw many churches and listened to every lecture on Ancient Greece.

That last evening they drove down to the port to dine by the waterfront: small tables parked on ancient, giant stones; gay Greek music, bazookas and the sound of breaking plates pulsating into the warm night. Across their table, fishermen rearranged their nets for the coming night's work, their boats nodding with the tide. Older men played lively dice games while couples huddled in dark corners, hiding from their chaperones.

The food they ate that night was close to home. Their table was laden with all Sam's favourite Middle Eastern delicacies. He dipped his pita bread into the little dishes, savouring each in turn with great relish.

'Beirut is just across the water, son,' he said, licking his fingers. 'Where your mother's grandfather was born.'

'Fancy a trip, Mother?'

'No way,' Jean said. 'Your father's pilgrimage is plenty.'

'You're going to love my old village, Richard,' Sam said.

'Of course I will.'

'I wish your mother was coming with us.'

'She'd much prefer to see the pyramids, Dad.'

'Shall we have a game of backgammon?'

'I'm a little out of practice.'

'I'll let you win.'

'Don't take too long you two. The ship leaves at midnight.'

In their cabin there was a bouquet of flowers and a small Arabic phrase-book from Sam's olive-oil supplier. She sat on the bed and looked at it. She laughed.

'What is it, Jean?'

'It's useless. It's Greek Arabic.'

'He meant well.'

'Of course he did. Where's Richard?'

'Talking to one of the officers.'

'He gets on with people, doesn't he?'

'Yes.'

Sam turned to look out of the copper porthole. In his white suit, with his thick greying hair and olive skin, he was particularly attractive that night. His virility seemed to fill the cabin, and with his silent energy he looked like a tiger about to pace his cage. His broad, muscular back excited her. He turned round to face her, his eyes exuding tender fire. She smiled.

'What's funny?'

'I was thinking of the number three.'

'Three?'

'Three delicious nights with you in this cabin. All to myself. Like our honeymoon, remember?'

'Yes.'

'Come over here, Sam.'

'Aren't you tired?'

'It will have to last me.'

'Last you?'

'Yes. Last me until you get to Hong Kong.'

'I see.'

Suddenly she was naked and the light went out and he felt her arms pull him down to her and her lips searched his and her hands probed and travelled all over him as if she was discovering him all over again. She seemed in a tearing hurry to take him and wrap him inside of her and keep him there, and soon she was coming apart in sharp, sweet explosions.

'I love you so much. So much.'

'I love you too.'

'Why do you have to go back there? There's nothing in the village for you, Sam.'

'There is.'

'What? Who?'

'One night I'll tell you.'

'Make it a dark night like this.'

She was tired, she thought. No, much more than that, she was beautifully exhausted. She smiled as she converted her feelings into words for him. But only in her mind; she'd save it all to share with him later, when the reverie was over.

Later he lay on the cool wooden floor and she rubbed his chest. Her fingers were cold, and he listened to the thump of the propellers sending shivers through the vessel. He held Jean's hand and he thought of what had gone, of the passion and the release, and then he felt her hand go limp and he knew she had fallen asleep. There were no more mysteries in his mind. He knew why he had come back even if she did not understand. He came to seek a release. Put an end to the torture that had brought him to life and cut him off from his past forever. But for that he would have to see his beginnings one more time. To grow up and away a man must sever his childhood cord. He would visit his grandfather's grave near the old olive grove and ask permission to stay away forever.

# CHAPTER SEVEN

■

'I don't get this.'

'You don't?'

'No, I don't. It's all bull. Ask permission to stay away?

If Sam wanted to get away, why go there at all? And why take the kid?'

'There were two reasons for that. The first was simple. With Richard being away at school all these years, Sam wanted to get to know him. The trip would have been an ideal opportunity for that.'

'And what was his other excuse?'

'You're a cold-blooded fool, Perotti. You wouldn't understand.'

'Yeah? Try me.'

'He needed a witness, Perotti. There was no one left there to see him do it. He needed someone to represent both worlds, you understand? Someone who had the blood of the old country in his veins. Richard had that. And he needed someone from the new world, too. And Richard was that because in Sam's eyes he was now an Englishman from British Jamaica in the new world. Only someone from both his worlds could help him cut himself off. The old country, the village, all were to be erased before Jamaica could become Sam's country.'

'If Sam wanted a new country why was he risking his life visiting the old one?'

'He went back there to say goodbye. He was born of a rape, Perotti. There was passion in his hate for that olive grove. He had ignored his village after his mother came out because the whole village became that olive grove for him. He had buried it somewhere, and now he was going to dig it up one more time and then spit it out. He had to see it again and feel it again before he could attempt to forget it, not just forget but forgive, too. It's just like leaving someone for good. You can't part in a vacuum. You've got to see them in person, talk to them, touch them, make peace with them before you leave. Shake hands, understand?'

'Is that what you got in mind for me, Charlie?'

'Oh no, Perotti. We'll never part. We're together for the duration.'

'Stuck like a married couple? Till death do us part and

that shit?'

'Yes, that shit.'

'I like the bit about the dark night. That was nice.'

'That was a prophecy.'

It sure was. I thought of that dark night business every time Charlie told the story, and he did that plenty of times. Charlie was some shrink and he understood people, but he didn't practise what he'd preached. He didn't talk or feel or touch anyone when he got ready to run somewhere. He just left his past standing there and was gone. I won't give him a hard time for that because it was mostly my fault. But I will say this: he was going to run out on Sam himself when the time came, and on that occasion it was all his own doing. I had nothing to do with it.

Anyway, that night on the ship Sam got dressed again and walked up the steps to the deck. It was a calm, moonless night and the stars filled the sky above the Mediterranean, but there was no sparkle in them. Sam was too emotional that night, and Charlie said his head was full of thoughts.

There was no one left in his village just outside Ramalla. No one except his great-uncle and his only cousin Latif who had sold the bakery and was spending most of his waking hours playing backgammon at Abu Hanna's cafe.

He thought of the port of Haifa three days away. Of how his wife would go on to Alexandria and see the sights of Egypt and then go on to the Orient without him and wait for him there. Of how he would leave the ship there and go off to chase his childhood away. I reckon he got no sleep at all.

They were going to take a taxi all the way. Richard had asked to go to Nazareth first, but they were told the roads were not safe. Arabs and Jews were shooting at anything that moved. The British Army was doing all it could to keep law and order, but they were having problems. Soon, the driver said, they would leave Palestine, and only Allah knew what sort of carnage would ensue. He would have loved the fare, the driver had lamented, but it was much safer to go by train. There was one leaving for Jerusalem via Lydda in an hour, and the station was a short drive away.

The bustling streets of lower Haifa reminded Sam of Kingston. The difference was in the nervousness that emanated from the people and the presence of military vehicles everywhere. The station itself was reminiscent of wartime England in that it swarmed with soldiers. But these, in their short-sleeved summer uniforms, walked about with suspicion in their eyes, their weapons at the ready.

Sam did not talk much. The sights and sounds of the old country were alien to him. His crystal ball had deserted him. Perhaps it was all a mistake, he thought to himself, but it was all too late now. It seemed to him he could not escape his destiny, and as they got into their compartment he sat down and leaned back and left his fate in the hands of the gods.

'I reckon Mother is well on the way to Alexandria by now.'

'Yes.'

'We might as well make the best of it.'

'Yes.'

'What's the matter, Father?'

'I think I am tired.'

'Sleep a little, then.'

'My town is at the end of the track.'

'How far?'

'Very far.'

'Take a nap. I'll wake you.'

The countryside was like that of Greece all over again. At first they rolled along the coastline, and then the train started a gentle climb. There were rocky hills and cypress trees and olive groves and vineyards and sheep. Fortified police stations stood out amongst picturesque villages that were dotted on the hills. Some boasted churches, others minarets. There was nothing menacing about the varied country-side that came at them from the window. Orderly, stone-walled fields of green and golden wheat rolled down to border the railway line. There were people riding on donkeys and an hour into the trip Richard saw his first camel.

'What are all these soldiers doing on this train?'

'Maybe they are going on leave.'

'They are armed to the teeth, Father. They are expecting trouble.'

'Better just sit here and rest.'

'Who the hell would want to die for this place?'

'No one will die, Richard.'

A paratrooper passed by and winked. The train raced through the plains and valleys and the motion sent Richard to sleep. Much later it began to climb and eked its way up the mountains, and Sam recognized the ancient Judean hills of his childhood. They were surely coming closer to Jerusalem, he thought, and he stretched and sat upright to watch. The hills had changed. There were more settlements than he remembered. It was all a strange place now. There were white houses and electricity pylons and tin-roofed factories. There were lines of trees and vineyards and thick orchards, and there were tractors in the fields. He had been away for many years and a new life had come into the land. Where did all these people get their water from, he asked himself, but no answer came. And then the train ended the long, long climb and slowed down for its crawl into the city, and he was pleased to see his son fast asleep by his side. He stroked the boy's head and a foreboding feeling of doom came upon him and refused to leave.

'It was no feeling of doom, Charlie. He was depressed, that's all . . . Anyone in his shoes would have been.'

'What makes you say that?'

'I reckon he knew what was coming to him.'

'Rubbish. He knew nothing of the future. It was his past that was coming at him. The past he could never forget. The way his mother was violated. The hard years he had left behind him in Palestine. His grandfather's treatment of him. The family shame . . .'

'Don't hit me with big words, Charlie. He was stupid, that's what he was. We've all had to eat shit in our time, but I wouldn't go back for another dose, would you?'

'He had no choice in the matter. I've told you before, Sam needed to go back to cancel all that out. It was going to be a new life from then on.'

'Some life it was going to be . . .'

'Where were you when they created human beings?'

'You're making me cry.'

'You never listen, Perotti.'

'You talk like my mother.'

'She must have known you well.'

'Yeah. That and some.'

'You respect nothing, do you, Perotti.'

'I respect plenty, but not my mother.'

'Why is that?'

'You know why.'

Charlie always sulked when I mentioned my mother. He'd go all quiet and then he'd change the subject. He must have had some big hang-ups in that department. But I didn't press the point because I liked him and he was about to tell me again what happened to Sam and how it happened and so forth. Charlie took all that very personally, as if the pain that waited for Sam around the corner was his own. Sometimes I think Charlie needed to suffer. Maybe he wanted to be punished for being a crook.

There was nervous bustle at the station. Hard-faced people clutched their luggage and raced about, like mice avoiding a trap. Those Sam had managed to talk to appeared abrupt and unfriendly. Out in the street there was confusion. Only the third cab they had flagged down agreed to take them to Ramalla. All the others had declined. The afternoon sun spread a bright desert light over the stone-walled houses they passed on their way through the ancient town.

Filthy city, your Jerusalem, Richard mumbled to himself as the driver and his father chatted. There were churches everywhere. Catholic and Anglican and Greek Orthodox. There were brown-gowned, sandalled Benedictine priests and there were nuns. There was magic in the colour of the sky, but there was nothing holy about the narrow streets. The shops were all locked behind iron shutters. Red-tiled roofs reached down to high stone walls whose closed windows seemed menacingly dark. The people, too, appeared to have come from another planet. Tall, pale, pious Jews clad in long black coats hurried about, their eyes pointing forward, staring at nothing.

Graceful, slow-moving, buxom Arab women, their faces buried behind white shawls, followed their men along the road. There were children, but no one played and no one smiled. There were sandbagged fortifications sprawling out of every corner.

'Looks like they're expecting a blitz,' Richard said.

'Your son doesn't speak Arabic?'

'No. He's an Ingleezie.'

'He shouldn't be here, sir. The Ingleezie are packing their bags. Palestine is not a good place for them any more.'

'Thanks for taking us. We've had trouble finding a taxi.'

'I'm not surprised. The roads are not safe any more. Are you staying long?'

'No. You could wait for us if you like.'

'Of course.'

'I appreciate your kindness.'

'War or no war, I have three children to feed.'

'My son thinks there will be a war.'

'There are rumours of Arab armies massing on the borders. As soon as the Ingleezie go back to England there will be a massacre. The shabab will liberate Palestine.'

'Liberate Palestine? Didn't you say the Ingleezie are leaving?'

'Yes.'

'Liberate Palestine from whom, then?'

'I don't understand politics, sir. The shabab are young and they are hot-blooded. They want to throw the Yahood back to the Sea . . .'

'Why? Didn't you live in peace with them all these years?'

'You have been away a long time, sir.'

'Yes.'

'Things have changed here.'

'The world's just ended one big war. Can't you settle things in peace here?'

'Don't ask me, sir. I am only a driver.'

Up there, out of town, the hills seemed unchanged to his eye. Scenes of his childhood village mingled with the houses and the small farms carved through the countryside. A bored expression settled across Richard's face.

'Soon,' Sam said. 'We'll soon be there.'

'How long are we staying?'

'Not long.'

'Where will we spend the night?'

'I expect we'll go back to Jerusalem.'

'I'd love a hot bath.'

'Later.'

'Aren't you happy you've left this place?'

'I haven't left yet.'

'This isn't Jamaica, is it?'

Just then the driver hit the brakes and the car stopped abruptly. Outside, by a large ruin on the side of the road, sat two armed men. A third stood in the middle of the asphalt, aiming a submachine-gun at them.

'I am sorry,' the driver said as the man came closer. He pushed his head through the windows and looked at them.

'These people are tourists,' the driver said. 'I swear I know them personally.'

'Passports,' the man barked.

'What is the meaning of this?'

'Tourists, you say?' the man at the window shouted. 'Yahood more likely. Passport,' he growled as he stuck the gun barrel into Sam's shoulder. In his eyes hate blended with suspicion. Sam looked straight at him. Richard froze.

'Is this some sort of a joke?'

'Show him your passport, sir,' the driver pleaded.

'Let me see some identification,' Sam said defiantly.

'Do as he says, sir,' the driver said. 'Please.'

'By whose authority are you standing out there?'

'By the authority of the new Palestine.'

'I was born in Old Palestine. Here, look for yourself.'

The man grabbed the passport and looked inside.

'Baker? Sam Baker? That's an Ingleezie name.'

'My name is Samir Al Bakr.'

'It says Sam Baker.'

'Sam Baker means Samir Al Bakr in English, you understand? It's a translation.'

The driver shrugged his shoulders and the young man pointed at Richard.

'Who is this?'

'My son.'

'Tell him to get out of the car. He looks like a Yahood to me.'

'You touch my son and I'll break your head.'

'You speak Arabic well.'

'Of course I do. I was born here.'

'Why did you come back?'

'To visit my village.'

That seemed to satisfy the intruder and he gave Sam his passport. He pulled his gun and his head out of the window and waved them on.

'I am sorry, sir,' the driver said.

'Not your fault.'

'Let's turn back,' Richard said.

'We'll soon be there. We'll have a coffee and then we'll go back.'

'Have we come all this way for a bloody cup of coffee?'

'What is your son saying, sir?'

'He's hot. He wants to have a bath.'

'The sun will be down soon, sir. He'll cool off then.'

'Yes. I suppose he will.'

There were no more road blocks after that. With tyre-shrieking speed the driver negotiated the curving road, and Sam's mind raced with the car. Jean had been right all along. He was chasing a dream that never was. He was risking his boy's life, he thought, as the car entered the main street. The evening was coming down on the village.

'Here we are, Richard. This is where I started from.'

'I see.'

# CHAPTER EIGHT

Sam tapped the driver's shoulder as soon as they got to the old family house. It now belonged to his only cousin Latif, and as he got out of the car and surveyed the deserted, dusty street it seemed to him the place had been locked in a time capsule. Nothing had changed. The smell of cooked meat and donkey dung came into his nostrils, and he was not sure whether it was really out there or only in his memory. Richard's expression betrayed a measure of disgust.

'Don't forget you have a share in this place,' Sam said as they got to the door.

'What share?'

'A part of you was born here, Richard. Never forget that.'

'If you say so.'

Sam told the driver to stay where he was and knocked on the door. Soon there were voices, and then he heard someone call his name. It was his great-uncle, Latif's father.

'Samir,' the old man sobbed. 'By God, you are a man now. You are the image of your poor grandfather. He would have thrilled to see you looking so frangie and clean. It seems you have only left here yesterday, a hungry, hopeful boy. America has been good to you. Did you find happiness there?'

Twenty-seven years of sweat and life and success had evaporated with the old man's voice. Inside there was his only cousin Latif and his wife and children and their children, and they were all called Al Bakr. His blood was the same as theirs but his name was now another. He was Sam Baker, a rich foreigner who looked like his poor old grandfather, and as they sat and talked it occurred to him how little they knew of him. Yet the warmth of the reception brought a lump to his lower throat, and he cried. The family were visibly moved at the sight of his tears.

'Thank you for all the money and your kindness, Samir,' the old man said. Latif himself, corpulent and middle-aged, sat in his corner and said little. The respect for the old still ruled supreme. Richard sat in the corner and sulked.

In the neat, sparsely furnished family room there were old photographs of forgotten men in Turkish uniforms. Over the fireplace there was a sword. One by one the old man introduced the members of his son Latif's family. From the wall, an old picture of his grandfather in his youth looked on.

'Do you remember my cousin Giddo?'

He did not, but he nodded.

'He is in America too. A place called Haiti. Giddo has many shops and a French trombeel. He has become very fat in America and cannot get out of his bed any more. He writes to us every month. He says he would come back here but he cannot leave his bed. He has a wife and many children and many, many grandchildren, but no one talks to him. He writes about Abu Hanna's cafe and how much he . . .'

'Enough, Father,' Latif's hesitant voice came from his corner. 'Let Samir say something too. Let us hear his story.'

'How dare you talk like that to me, boy,' the old man roared. 'I am your father. I am Samir's great-uncle. Samir is

63

the guest of honour and he will talk when he wants to talk. He doesn't need your protection.'

'You know all about me. I have written.'

'Your cousin Latif wants to thank you for all the money you have sent. He has become lazy with the easy life you have sent him, but thank God we manage. My cousin Giddo never sent any money at all. All this new furniture we have bought with the money you have given us. And we bought Degani's plot of land near the cemetery. Do you remember the Degani family?'

The old man did not wait for an answer. 'They have all gone to America. They used to be the biggest family in town. So many children. When I was a boy old man Degani, who was half-blind, used to talk to every child in the street. Around noon time he'd come out of the house and if you were a child he'd stop you, look into your face and ask, "Are you a Degani?" If you said yes he'd tell you to go home quick because mother was serving food. They have all gone now, and my cousin Giddo never sends any money. He says he will bring it all with him when he comes back. But I know my cousin Giddo. He will never come back here.'

'He's too fat and cannot leave his bed,' Sam's cousin Latif said with a wink.

They wanted to show their returning relative off. They had waited many years for this moment. It was part of the ritual. He had remembered it well from his own childhood. When the conversation slowed down he knew it was time to go to Abu Hanna's, to sip coffee and arak and talk men's talk. The women would all stay behind to prepare the evening meal.

'You have a trombeel?'

'Yes. A taxi. He's waiting outside the door.'

'Then you and I will take it to Abu Hanna. Latif and your son can walk.'

'Can we go to the olive grove first?'

'Olive grove? What olive grove?'

'You remember. My grandfather's olive grove.'

'Your grandfather never owned an olive grove. He was a baker.'

'Yes he did. I was there many times. They found the Turkish soldier there . . .'

'That was Degani's olive grove, not your grandfather's . . . Oh yes, maybe he leased it. I don't remember. But it was not his. No. Never his.'

'Can we go there?'

'There is no olive grove there any more. The Deganis have pulled the trees out before they left for America. Then they sold it. There is a vineyard there now. Or apricots, I don't know. I haven't been out that way in years. Let's go to Abu Hanna's, Samir. The people know you are coming. So does Abu Hanna himself. They are waiting for you. You are a golden boy now.'

The taxi reached Abu Hanna's cafe and stopped outside. The same little tables, the same little woven chairs. The place was full as it had always been. Every man in the village seemed to be there. All eyes were on the car, and then Sam climbed out and walked towards the terrace. The evening had arrived in the village.

'Wait here,' Sam said, and he motioned his son to follow. They were all sitting there, all his childhood friends. They looked older and their faces were haggard but they were there. The second cable he had sent from Athens must have arrived after all. An old man came running off the terrace and threw himself on Sam's shoulder.

'Samir,' he sobbed, 'Samir . . . By God, you are a man, Samir. You look like your poor old grandfather. How thrilled he would have been to see you looking so frangie and clean. By God, you're dressed like an Ingleezie. It was only yesterday that you left here.'

'So it seems, Abu Hanna. So it seems.'

'He remembers me,' Abu Hanna cried. 'He remembers poor old Abu Hanna.'

'Of course I do. You were good to me.'

The old man turned to Richard.

'And that is who?'

'That is my son.'

'Looks like you, Samir. Just like you did when you left here. America was good to you, I hear. Will you sit now?'

'Where is your own son, Abu Hanna?'

'He is in Beirut. Three shops, one garage and an American trombeel. Your poor old grandfather would have been so proud of you.'

They all sat down and they talked and laughed and asked questions. There was no need for Sam to talk at all. His good colour, his frangie, elegant suit and the taxi that waited up the street with Richard fast asleep in the back said it all. His cousin Latif's father was telling the story of his success for him. How he owned streets and streets full of hotels in America. How he had fleets of trombeels in America. Chevrolet and Ford and Hudson, all shiny and new. It was late in the night, and it seemed the whole village was there. Someone new appeared to arrive every now and again. Sometimes Sam remembered who they were and sometimes he did not. There were words of happiness and congratulations and thanks and memories were brought back to life. The word of his return had spread into every house, and every male in the village came to see him and talk to him and touch his hand.

Then at last there came silence. Sam saw a truck approach the corner. Something told him it was time to take his leave. He would be able to go without offending anyone. There had been tears, stories were told and retold, and plenty of coffee and arak had been consumed. He had fulfilled his part of the bargain now. He had seen them all and touched them all. He got up to say something just as the truck passed by. He looked at the people and as he opened his mouth he saw a blinding light and he heard the explosion. He heard glass being shattered and he heard screams. People were running out into the street. As he fell onto the floor he opened his eyes. He felt the pain at the back of his head. He saw nothing and heard nothing, and then he heard his son Richard's voice above him. He felt the boy's body close to his.

'I want to see the olive grove,' Sam said, and then he was out.

# CHAPTER NINE

Of course, Sam never saw that olive grove where his mother was raped. Where the man who'd fathered him died. He wasn't going to see a damn thing ever again. Charlie would tell the story of what happened and get real sentimental about it. He'd talk and cry and laugh and cry again. How Sam lost his sight on account of his optical nerve being busted in the explosion. How he got into a hospital in Jerusalem and how he got out of there in the middle of the night. How he walked through the narrow, dangerous streets of that dangerous city with his head bandaged and his son Richard leading him like a baby.

Charlie loved this part of the story best of all because this was when Richard Baker became a man in his eyes. The limey was proud of his Arab friend's son as if he were his own. Of course, the poor bastard didn't know what that little shit was going to do to him later. I myself never liked Richard. But people in Jamaica must have done because they kept voting him into office so often you'd have thought he was the only candidate in the country. His own opinion of himself was high enough so you could sit on it and touch the sun. I won't bother to go into details again. Charlie had done it often enough, and I reckon the whole of Jamaica if not the whole world knows it all because Richard used it forever in his election campaigns. You can look it up in the *Gleaner* if you haven't heard it.

In short, Richard got his father out of the battle-zone that was Palestine at the end of 1947. Through Jewish and

Arab and British lines, he pulled him out of Jerusalem. From somewhere they got a couple of donkeys to ride and a third to carry food and water. With a map Richard procured they started their track through the desert, dressed like Bedouin tribesmen, a blind father and his deaf and dumb son. Richard, never uttering more than a few groans whenever they met someone, pulled Sam through the rocky hills and the barren fields and the valleys and the dry rivers all the way to Amman, Jordan. They were stopped more than a few times and Richard's heroics saved the day.

I don't doubt Charlie's sincerity in all this. This was some trip. I mean, a blind man travelling through a country at war with a boy who had never seen a desert in his life is tough enough. I am sure the boy was great, but each time Charlie told the story Richard's heroics became more and more daring. In the end it became so you'd think they faced a different hostile army every day.

Maybe I begrudge the guy his finest hour because I never liked him. But the reason I won't go into detail is because I'm sick and tired of it. In any case, I'm not about to give Richard Baker any more publicity. Take it from me, he doesn't need it. And Charlie should have known better. After all, Richard Baker screwed him real good when the time came.

But all that was going to happen much, much later. At the end of 1947, after one hell of a saga that would make ten adventure movies look like a Christmas story, they got to Amman, Jordan. They chartered a small plane there and flew to Alexandria, Egypt, and from there they sailed to Hong Kong.

Their arrival in that city is important because it was where Sam finally met Charles Paget-Brown. Strangely enough, Charlie, excited as he became when he talked about their first meeting, never got sentimental. I like the story because it told me something about the way Charlie really saw Sam. His courage, his strength of character, and his acceptance of destiny. They were going to meet and then they parted and didn't come together for a long time. Even then, they didn't stay together. But after that Sam played the lead in Charlie's life in the nostalgia department. I like this bit even though much of it was only in Charlie's mind, but that doesn't matter. It was the way he wanted to see it, and I'm going to tell it the way Charlie did. I'll try not to miss one word.

# CHAPTER TEN

■

They did not cable Jean from the ship the way everybody else did. She did not come to the port to welcome them. In those days you were never sure when the ship was going to dock, and Sam wanted to face his wife by himself. They took a cab to the Peninsula Hotel where she was staying, and ran into Charlie and his daughter Roberta at the reception desk. Charlie was helping Sam to locate Jean's room number while the youngsters struck up a conversation. The reception chief noticed Charlie's concern.

'Are you a friend of Mr Paget-Brown, Mr Baker? He's an old and valued guest of this hotel.'

'We've only just met.'

'Sorry. It's just that I saw you two talking. Anyway, we were expecting you, Mr Baker. Shall we call Mrs Baker for you?'

'No, thank you. I'll go straight up.'

Right behind them, Richard and Roberta were still talking.

'I apologize for my son,' Sam said. 'There wasn't anyone younger than fifty on the ship.'

'Don't worry about it. It's a new experience for my daughter, too. There are no boys in her school.'

They laughed.

'My colleague will show you to your room as soon as

he's free, Mr Baker,' the receptionist said. 'It won't take a minute.'

'Why don't I take Mr Baker up,' Charles said. 'I believe we're on the same floor.'

'It's very kind of you,' Sam said.

'I was going up to my room anyway. What about the boy?'

'I'd rather he stayed down here. I have to see my wife by myself. Need some time. It's a difficult situation, Mr Paget-Brown. I am sorry to drag you into it, but I don't know anyone else here and my son is too young to understand . . .'

'Why don't you and I have a cup of tea in the lobby while your son goes up to see his mother? We'll arrange something later, when he comes down.'

'That won't work. As soon as my wife sees him she'll know . . .'

'I see . . . No, frankly, I don't see. What do you mean?'

'My wife does not know I am blind. It is something I have to break to her myself.'

'Oh . . . You'll need some time for that.'

'A few hours.'

'That's no problem, Mr Baker. I can have my man take the children out on the town.'

'Could you really do that?'

'With pleasure . . . If your son doesn't mind.'

'He'll do what I ask him to do.'

'That's more than I can say for Roberta.'

'I am asking too much of you. He can go to his room . . .'

'At ten in the morning, at his age, in Hong Kong? Why don't you let me suggest it to them. My man is right outside.'

'Thank you.'

The two men took the lift up.

'How are you going to do it, Mr Baker?'

'I don't know. I pray she is still asleep.'

'Something will occur to you when you get there.'

'Yes.'

'It always does.'

'Yes.'

'Well, this is it.'

'Yes.'

'I'll take you to the door.'

'I shall never forget you, Mr Paget-Brown.'

'I won't give you a chance to. I'll expect you to have dinner with me sometime.'

'That will be my pleasure.'

'Just leave a note with the porter.'

'When will it be convenient?'

'Any time.'

'Did you say any time? Aren't you a busy man?'

'I said any time. Here we are, Mr Baker. Go for it.'

'Thank you.'


Sam listened to Charlie's steps as they turned the corner at the end of the corridor, then he knocked on the door, bracing himself for the answer. A nervous 'Yes, who is it?' came rolling at him from the inside. He knocked again. The door opened. Sam turned his back to it.

'Sam,' she screamed.

She came close to him and they embraced.

'Not out here,' he said.

She pulled him in and he locked the door behind him.

He stood there, facing the window, and he felt the light hitting his face.

'Draw the curtains, Jean,' he said. 'Please.'

He heard her run and he heard the curtains swish. He heard her come back.

'Shall I hang the "Do not disturb" sign?'

'Yes.' She went away again and he heard her open and shut the door, then she came into his arms.

'What about Richard? Where is he?'

'He's made a new friend. An English girl. She goes to school here. She's giving him a tour of the town. Turn the light off, Jean.'

'Not before I hold you some more.'

The feel of his body and the familiar smell of his skin blew her mind. The time that had passed since that last night in the Greek ship, the worry, the waiting, and all she had seen and done and all she had wanted to tell him, gave way to an impossible yearning for his touch. All thoughts of her son or anyone else evaporated as she felt her knees giving in. She pulled herself away from him with great difficulty. She walked towards the bed and he heard a light switch.

'It's been a long time. Such a long time. Gee, it's dark in here . . .'

'Yes,' he said. 'Where is the bed?'

'Just walk straight on, big lover. It's right here and I'm right on it.'

She was in a frenzy. He approached the sound of her tearing her nightgown off. He reached the bed and he felt her arm and into his nostrils came the sharp smell of her.

He lay down on his back.

'Let me undress you,' she said. 'This is the Orient.'

'Thank you.'

'You have lost a lot of weight. Where is that sexy paunch, Sam?' She didn't wait for an answer. She wanted him. She wanted him so bad it hurt. There were silent screams inside of her, and she was in a tearing hurry to silence them. She sucked at his shoulders and his chest and lower and lower, and then she came to it and could no longer wait. She found herself on top of him and with him and her body surrounded him and she could not stop moving and then she felt on the edge and her body gyrated and smashed all of him and she felt him all through her and more and more and then she thought she would die and she wailed and fell, spent, on him.

'Selfish of me,' she said. She thought he was quieter than before. He had hardly moved. Perhaps she hadn't given him a chance. She had done it all, for both of them, she thought, and her body and soul laughed.

'I am so out of breath, Sam; getting old before my time. It's been so long. So long.' She took his hand and she kissed it, and through the dim light she saw his eyes gaze at her and yet they looked into space. His face was sad.

'What is it, Sam?'

'You wanted me to tell you something once, remember?'

'I wanted you to tell me many things. Which one was that?'

'About life. About why I had to go back to my village, remember, on the boat?'

'Sure I remember. You were going to tell me on some dark night, yes?'

'Yes. It is dark, but it is morning.'

'I don't care. You tell me.'

'Yes,' he said, and he told her. He told her all of it as he held her close. He told her about it as if it had happened to someone else. There was no self-pity in his voice, nor remorse.

'It's all from God,' he said, and he smiled. 'When I was born, the first thing I saw was my village near Ramalla. It was the last place I saw, too. That is how I said goodbye to the old country, Jean. It's God's will. I am a free man now.'

How the hell Charlie found out about what went on in that bedroom I will never know. Sam was not a great talker, but then perhaps he was when he was alone with Charlie. They saw each other every night after that, and Charlie stayed on in Hong Kong a lot longer just to be with him. He even had Rose come out from Bangkok to be with Roberta so that he'd have more time with his new friend. He might have invented the intimate bits or imagined them. After all, Charlie was a romantic and had read all those books of adventure and so forth, and even if all of it was only in Charlie's imagination it doesn't really matter.

What did Charlie see in Sam? I think it was his naivety. His acceptance of his fate. His childish admiration of Charlie's wartime exploits and way of business. All that was true even if Charlie had to invent Sam's reaction to things to make me understand his character. Charlie told him about the way his junks smuggled stuff from one country to another. He told him how his Burmese gem dealers brought rubies across the border without ever declaring them. He told him of payments made to local chiefs of police and government officials. And Sam, a man who had never broken any law, a man who paid his taxes in full, Sam accepted it all. Never once did it ever occur to him that Charlie could rot in jail for years for ten per cent of what he did every day. Above all, Charlie loved the way Sam accepted his need for excitement and adventure without a hint of warning or envy. Sam did not think of Charlie's adventures as crimes. Not the sales of penicillin or morphine or any other toxic stuff. He saw Charlie's obsession with danger as the norm, not as the addiction it was. Perhaps he thought that was the way things were done in this part of the world. I mean, for all his success and ability, Sam was extremely naive.

'What did you talk about?' I asked Charlie once.

'Nothing much. He told me about his life and I told him about mine. We didn't hide a thing from each other. At first I felt a little sorry for him, the way he lost his sight and all that. But later I realized it didn't bother him at all. It was as if he had been expecting it.'

'Sam was a sucker for punishment?'

'Never. Sam did not think of his blindness as a handicap at all. You see, the man did not have an ounce of self-pity in him. It was his destiny. It was meant to happen. And when it did he got on with his life regardless.'

'What if he'd lost his sight in his youth?'

'He didn't.'

Sam was Charlie's favourite man in the whole world. To Charlie, Sam was the greatest human being, the greatest bene-factor, and the greatest conversation piece. Sometimes I got so fed up with his stories about Sam I'd switch off, but Charlie never tired of talking about him. On the whole, Charlie was quite a talker for an Englishman, but only when he told you about Sam. It wasn't that way at all the other way round. Sam might have been born in the Middle East where people like a good story, but he was not a great one with words.

# CHAPTER ELEVEN

Only once did Sam speak to me of Charlie. It was when he was in deep shit with us. Not Sam. Charlie. He was in real trouble, I can tell you, and it was all his own fault. Had it not been for me he could have been killed. I had to invent a whole new script to keep him safe.

I don't rightly remember how that conversation with Sam came about. He acted like a defence attorney without a brief. Sam must have felt the limey was in danger.

It was the only time I had seen him alone to speak to. He took the trouble to invite me for dinner in his house up in Stony Hill. He was a real big shot then, and being the only dinner guest up there was some great honour. Jean was in the house too, but she left us to ourselves. Richard was out doing his big-time politics or screwing someone's wife. We were alone in the room. Sam waited until I had settled down. He made sure I had a drink in my hand and we sat in the big living-room, by the wide picture window that overlooked Kingston. It spread there below us like a sea of lights, with the harbour on the right and Palisados Airport on the left. There were planes taking off and landing, ships crawling out to sea and others coming in. Closer to the house I saw the moon reflected inside the pool. It fitted into a big star-shaped mosaic they had on the bottom. It was like watching a silent movie screened right there, on the thick glass window. Of course, Sam did not bother to look at the view. He couldn't see a thing. He was too busy trying to defend his pal Charlie. That's all he talked about that night.

*   *   *

'I only met Charles Paget-Brown in 1948 in Hong Kong, but he has become my brother. Different as he was to myself and the people I had grown up and worked with, there was something irresistible in him. He was then at the height of his success and I regretted that, because I would have liked him to come back to Jamaica with me then, much sooner than he did.

'There was, from the way he shook your hand to the soft way he spoke, an Englishness you could not mistake. I have always wanted my son Richard to be like that. There is a lot to be admired about the English. Their tolerance especially. His manners were impeccable, and his belief all people are good was appealing. He was helpful at a time when the greatest mishap in my life had hit me. I required compassion. He was obviously very well known at the Peninsula Hotel where we all stayed, but he never made a thing of it. Charles is a man of strange habits and unconventional ways. He is a generous man. Not just with his money, but with his time and his ear and his affection. He knows how to give, and that giving never stopped. Not even when he could not afford it. Above all, he was a marvellous listener. And never once did he make you feel inferior. You know I have become blind, and not being born blind it took a lot of adjustment. You suffer, and you suffer most from the way people treat you when they find out. They try being gentle with you and they speak slowly as if you are hard of hearing, and I know it is because they feel sorry for you. But Charles never made me feel like I was only half a man. I wish people knew how unnecessary all that was. It was God's will. And no man can interfere there.'

'You are a very brave man, Mr Baker,' I said.

'I hardly think so.'

'Yes you are. The way you accepted what had happened to you like it was written in the stars. The way you went on with the business of life like nothing happened. I don't know what I would have done. I would have shot myself. You are lucky you have such faith.'

'Who ever told you I just accepted it?'

'Didn't you just say it was God's will?'

'I only learned that later.'

'That's not what I heard.'

'Do you think I am God? I am a human being. A man can accept other people's misfortunes. He can accept their nature; it's difficult, but he can. But a man doesn't accept he's been crippled for life. A human being pities himself. I didn't accept my blindness at all.'

'Charlie said you took it that way right from the word go.'

'Did he really tell you that?'

'You bet he did.'

'He told you I just took it as if it was my destiny?'

'I promise you he did. I swear it.'

'It didn't happen like that at all. I was devastated. I was finished. I wanted to die. I thought the end of the world had come to me. There was no one I could open up to. I had my young son there with me, and with the bravery he had shown, the selfless way in which he dragged me all the way from Jerusalem to Hong Kong, how could I tell him what I felt inside? I had to keep a brave face, but inside of me I promise you I was often suicidal. I followed Richard through the desert like a machine. I had no time to think because we were moving. I listened to my son and I walked. Later I sat with him through endless, countless dinner parties on board the ship that took us to the Orient, and only one night, on the one occasion he left me in the cabin by myself, did I get the chance to ask God why he did that to me. I didn't dare cry in case my son came back and saw me. How could I let him down? I had forced him to come with me on a mad, selfish pilgrimage to a village he knew nothing about. A part of my life that had nothing to do with him but with me alone. Me a hero? Had I been a hero I would have gone there by myself. I put my son's life in danger for what? For wanting to cut myself off from my roots? He would have been better off thinking I took him with me because I was afraid to face my past by myself . . . But he did not. He came along, and even though I knew he wasn't keen on it he never complained. How could I have told him how I felt? Not feeling sorry for myself? Of course I did. I am not a hero. I am not an angel. I am a man, and after what had happened to me I felt less than a man. I had no one I could blame for it but myself, no one I could talk to. Not really talk to.'

'But Charlie said you faced it all like a tiger . . . He said you went up to your wife and told her you had lost your sight as if you were discussing the weather . . .'

'I might have spoken to her about it in a detached way . . . I might have been, what do they say these days, cool about it . . . But I was pretending, Mr Perotti. This is not how I really felt. She was waiting for me, fretting about Richard and me and what happened to us. Everyone knew what was going on in Palestine, and especially Jean. She did try to warn me but I didn't listen because I was stubborn. And when I . . . When I lost my sight . . . I had to make out it didn't matter but, Mr Perotti, it did. It did a lot. It mattered more than anything, and as soon as I felt the pain come up and threaten to burst out of my face I had to go somewhere. Away from my wife. Away from my son . . . But where could I go? I couldn't see a thing . . . I was in a strange city . . . I knew no one . . . And that was where Charles Paget-Brown became my brother . . . He became that because he was there and he saw me the way I really was inside . . .'

'I don't understand.'

'Charlie, as you call him, was sent by God. That first day after I had told my wife what had happened I stayed in our bed. I could feel a breaking-point was coming. I pretended to doze off, and she went out to wait for Richard in the lobby. I staggered out of bed and pushed my way through half the furniture to look for the telephone. I don't know how long it took, but I know I made a big mess of the room before I found it. You see, Mr Perotti, it was a new room and a new situation, and for the first time I was really alone. I thought I was going mad . . . I wanted to be dead . . . And then the operator's voice came on and I asked her to connect me with Mr Paget-Brown's room. I was lucky. I was lucky because he was there. I heard his voice. "Come over here quickly," I said. I didn't need to explain. I knew where the door was and I got to it and opened it and waited for him. Panic was approaching, Mr Perotti, and just before it took me he arrived.

'"Get me out of here, Mr Paget-Brown," I said. I didn't need to say anything to him. He knew exactly what was happening to me. I was stark naked. He helped me dress up. He called the maid and had her make the room up. He took me into his room and ordered me a stiff drink. He made me call my wife down at the lobby and tell her where I was. Tell her I was having an important business meeting and did not wish to be disturbed. Tell her to take a tour of the town. Go shopping. I told her all of that; like a parrot I repeated what he said. When all that was done we sat down and I burst into tears. Yes, I cried. I cried like any wreck of a man without a future would. I was inconsiderate. I was selfish. I was crying my dead eyes out and cursing God and myself and my village and the whole world. I cried with the bitterness of defeat, of despair . . . It was the first time I let myself go, and it was in the company of a man I did not know at all. I loaded a stranger with truckloads of self-pity.'

'And what did Charlie do?'

'What did he do? He pulled me out of the chair and he hugged me . . . Yes, would you believe it, that well-spoken, well-born English gentleman hugged me and held me close and stroked my head and let me go on until there were no more tears in me. Then he sat me down and I said I was sorry. And do you know what he said? He said think nothing of it. Shell-shock, he said. Happens to everyone. He said he saw it in the war every day. He said he saw bigger men than me cry a lot longer for much less. He said I could stay with him there until I felt I could face my family dry-eyed.'

'And did you stay with him?'

'Yes I did. I heard him send cables to his wife and his office to say he was delayed in Hong Kong and did not know when he would be back. He arranged for my wife and my son to spend time with his daughter and he introduced them to everybody he knew . . . And he knew everybody, Mr Perotti. I slept nights with my wife, but for one week I spent every daylight hour, every waking moment, every meal with him. It was the most intense week of my life. He listened and he let me talk all the bitterness and all my self-pity out of my system. He didn't say much. He was close to me, and he understood how I felt as if he had known me all my born days.

'He really cured me when he started to bring strange people up to the room. This is Sam Baker, Charles would say. This is my friend Sam Baker from Jamaica who is in trouble because he's just become blind. Don't ask him about it yet, Charles would say, don't ask him because he doesn't know about blindness. He hasn't been blind long enough yet and he is suffering. He made me feel naked in front of all these people, and that taught me to face myself the way I was going to be from then on. He never allowed me to pretend nothing had happened because they could see it, and that made me see it too.

'At the end of that week I was myself again. I began to understand what had happened and why it had happened, and had it not been for Charles Paget-Brown I would not be sitting here with you today, Mr Perotti. I would have thrown myself out of the window. I must tell you one thing. On the second or third day, when I said I wanted to kill myself, Charles took me to the window and he opened it and said he would help me jump if that was what I wanted. He said there were only two conditions. First, he wanted me to talk of my family and my work and my life before he'd help me put an end to it all. He said he wanted to know all of me first. Second, he said I must bring my wife and son up to his room and tell them I wanted to die. They have the right to know you the way you are, understand the way you feel. After that he would help me, he said. He would even push me out of the window himself. And that was the turning-point. It was the turning-point because I saw how ridiculous we looked . . . I looked, and I laughed and he laughed. We laughed so much it hurt, and that other pain started to go away from me.

'Nobody, Mr Perotti, before that week or after, had

been so selfless, so giving, so kind to me like Charles was. That was how we became brothers. He is a valiant man, and I am proud to have him as a brother.

'I had a lot of time on my hands at the hotel and we spent hours and hours together. He never tried to hide the sort of work he was doing, and I could not help feeling that he had a lot of growing up to do. He couldn't help it. People who fight for their country get hurt, Mr Perotti. They are wounded and they need painkillers and then the taking of painkillers becomes an addiction. People see and admire the medals on a hero's chest, not the blood that earned them. The adventurous nature of his business was a relic from his exploits during the war. He recounted those to me, but he never bragged. It was all very matter-of-fact. All the hair-raising dangers he had encountered amounted to nothing. You would have thought he was telling you someone else's story.

'Hong Kong was a strange place at that time. Charles said old empires were being reconstructed and new ones erected. The thin line that bordered the rights and the wrongs was mostly ignored. With the war years and the shortages there were many ways to earn a living. You could never be sure what was legal and what was not. Until that time I had little interest in the world. I knew very little about history or politics or anything. It was Charles Paget-Brown who introduced me to all that. At a time when I badly needed something to save me. He was shipping agricultural machinery and fishing nets and canned foods and other dry goods. He was also importing medicines to the Orient, and he owned a fleet of fishing boats that worked out of a Siamese port called Pataya.

'Charles had an international business while all I knew was Jamaica and tourists. I had never been to Bangkok, but I know Charles Brown was living there at the time and he loved it. He came to Hong Kong often, to see his daughter Roberta who was at school there. It was our children who had, in actual fact, brought our families together. But I have told you that already. I am getting old. You tend to repeat yourself when you get old. I only wish Charles had joined me earlier than he did . . . That way things would have turned out different.'

I could hardly breathe. I listened to what the man had said. I thought of my part in forcing Charlie to go to Jamaica. Maybe I wasn't that bad. Maybe I had done God's job for him, if there is a God, by bringing these two men together against Charlie's will.

'Mr Baker,' I said, 'Charlie never told me that. And I promise you he told me everything about you. He feels as close to you as you do to him . . . But I never knew all this. His story was very different. Did he forget?'

'Never. He knows the truth. Every word of it.'

'So why didn't he tell me?'

'Because he is a modest man. He never meant to be a hero. I think it embarrassed him.'

I sat back. I was dying for a drink but I was so weak I couldn't lift the glass.

'Mr Perotti,' Sam said. His guttural, accented way of talking had gentility in it. He got out of his chair and walked towards me. He knew where I sat and he touched my hand. 'I am not sure what it is you or your company think Charles has done. If it's a question of money, I will guarantee it. Any amount.'

'It's not money. It's a question of honour.'

'In that case I am not worried. Charles is the most honourable man I have ever met. You will find you are wrong to doubt him. I am willing to go anywhere to speak on his behalf. Another thing, Mr Perotti. You must promise me something . . .'

'What's that?'

'Charles must never know of this conversation.'

That was the only time I was alone with Sam. I listened

to his words. I saw his slow movements and the grey light of honesty in his dead but expressive eyes. He talked like a man who had nothing to hide. The years of hard work seemed like they never were. There he was, rich as they come, yet with the simplicity of a Dominican priest. He said he never had any education and he told me how he had started from nothing. He talked about his business and his hotels and the people who worked for him. There was no pride of possession in him, no showing off. He talked of his career as if anyone could have done it. He talked of his deep admiration for America and Americans. Of how he had dreamed of going there all through his childhood. How America was something to look up to. How he had read about the American war and its Constitution. He said a true American would certainly see Charles for what he was. He talked of his problems with his son Richard and how the youngster was interested in women and politics and nothing else. How he had wanted Richard to take the business over, and how lucky he was to have Charles as a friend and partner. It would be Charles who would own the business once he was gone. Charles will keep it in trust for the next generation, Sam whispered, and he made me swear I wouldn't breathe a word of it. He said that was all arranged in his will.

If he could trust Charles with his business, the work of his life, so should I. I must, he said, me and my people too, trust Charles the same way he did. After all, no one knew Charles better than he did. He said he was willing to do anything for me. Anything for my people. Here or in the States.

Of course, there was nothing at all Sam could do for us. We were, the family and me and Charles, in a totally different business. As far from Sam as Australia. Sam thought he knew Charles, and in a way of course he did. Maybe he knew his character better than any man alive, but he knew nothing else about him. He did not know exactly what Charles was doing when he was out of the office. What he got himself into after dark. And I wasn't going to wise him up. As far as my people were concerned, I figure Sam knew nothing about us. He called the family your people. He didn't know what the family meant. You'd mention the word to him and he'd think you meant your cousin or an old aunt. He probably never heard of the organization or how it operated. He didn't even know it existed. He had no idea how deeply involved Charlie was. He was backing him blind. He loved Charlie and I respected him for that.

There was a lot more to him. He was hiding something, but I could not make it out. Sam was, in spite of his condition, a formidable guy. Even then, close to old age.

# CHAPTER TWELVE

I don't know where the line lies between the likes of me and the likes of Sam. How come people turn out the way they do. In the movies they tell you of that hard childhood criminals had and show you these dark, swarthy guys who rob banks. Believe me, I have seen crooks who looked like angels and angel-faced shits who'd kill their mothers. There's this fascination people have with gangsters. Bestsellers and blockbusting movies show them. Sing songs for them. People faint at the dentist's but love watching other people's guts spilled out on the screen.

I will always remember the time Charlie and me talked about it. About how people get their start in this. It was also a one-to-one meeting, in Bangkok, Thailand, years before he moved to Jamaica. In Charlie's club. In the garden over drinks. Just the two of us. Years before I ever saw Sam. It was not my first meeting with Charlie. We had met and we had talked and he knew all about the family. Until that time he did not think we were a threat to his business. That conversation took place right after New York told me to quit stalling and move in on him.

And when the chips are down you've got to be honest.

'How did you get to be a villain?' he asked. 'You know how I did.'

'You really interested?'

'Of course I am.'

'I was thirteen, maybe fourteen. My mother used to take me to visit a guy called Don Antonio. Always on a Sunday and always in his office. I knew she and he had something going. Anyway, he was some important guy. Head of a large family that controlled our part of town. He was a big man, always dressed in a suit and tie, and he always gave me a couple of dimes for ice-cream before sending me for a walk. One Sunday we got into his office. He was on the telephone. By the side of the table, near where I was always made to sit, there was this enormous automatic. I was playing with it under my jacket. My mother did not see. I think she went out of the room for a minute. Don Antonio smiled at me. He had great big eyes and bushy brows and I was always a little scared of him. But not that Sunday. I don't know why. Anyway, suddenly the door bursts open and a guy walks in. I have never seen him before. He pulls a .45 out of his holster. Slowly. He points it at Don Antonio as if he's got all the time in the world. He doesn't give me a thought. I was small for my age but always stocky. Well, fat. I cannot say what hit me. I didn't think much. I didn't say a thing. Anyway, I pointed Don Antonio's big revolver at the man and pulled the trigger. I didn't know if it was loaded or what but I heard a shot and the gun jerked out of my hand and fell on the floor. So did the intruder.

'Don Antonio finished his conversation quietly. He said something and he smiled and then he put the phone down. He got up. I was terrified. But he smiled and came over and took me in his arms and hugged me. My mother came from nowhere and stood by the door, pale as a wall.

'Vincente saved my life,' Don Antonio said. 'He saved my fucking life.'

My mother would have beaten me for using bad words, but when Don Antonio said it she smiled like he'd said something funny.

Don Antonio gave me a couple of dollars and told me to go to a movie. It was a double bill, and by the time I got back to the office the body was gone.

I didn't go back to school after that. I went to work for Don Antonio. That was how I became a villain, Charlie. Now, will you play ball with us?'

That was our conversation. Christ, must be twenty years ago. We saw plenty of each other in between. Not me and Sam. Me and Charlie. I will never know why I opened up so big to him. I could have invented something. I could have told him about how I shot someone and that's it. I didn't need to tell him of Don Antonio and my mother and that. Humiliating stuff. Hurts like hell even now. Still, time is running. One has now gone.

I have had no time to think about it. To decide whether I'm happy or sad or what. Death comes to everybody and never waits. Downstairs they all know where I'm going and what for. The funeral won't wait. That's one thing they are punctual about. They are late for appointments and late in paying. But they are never late praying to God or seeing someone off on their way to Him.

The porter just called to say the limo is on its way. And I'm going to go see the guy off. I won't go in there. Just do it from a decent distance. I'm not going for anyone, except these two. One is dead, and I don't want the other to know I was there. I don't care what anybody else thinks. They won't even recognize me. It was all a long time ago and they will have other things on their minds.

# BOOK TWO

## CHAPTER THIRTEEN

The American was dressed to kill. He looked a little out of place in his three-piece suit, and in spite of the ceiling fan working at full speed he was sweating. He was a short, broad-shouldered, powerful man, his thick black hair combed backwards, Edward G. Robinson-style. His smile revealed two lines of perfect white teeth. The smile never left his face, and he was always soft-spoken. Even when what he had to say had threatening undertones.

Why did he bother to let the man in, Charles asked himself. Why did he talk to him at all? Why did he let him blabber on about his first murder, his mother, his first boss? He should have stayed clear of the bugger. Why did he get involved?

The answer came back into his mind in a flash. Because he had no option, that's why. He had been introduced to him by Paco the Filipino. It was a question of honour. You didn't ignore introductions from an old partner and colleague like Paco. Not in the Orient, where introductions are a sign of friendship and trust. Paco was the man who had introduced him into the shipping business long ago. And, except for that little problem during the war, Paco could always be trusted. The American was talking and Charles heard his voice but did not listen to the words. Was he, himself, that superficial? Did the way people look matter that much to him? Was there something about the man's appearance that had put him off? Until today he had always been cordial enough.

He was a little less so today. No doctor can operate on a man's body without spilling blood. Vincent Perotti was after his business. He might be the nicest chap in the world, but his employers were not. Charles had heard about them. Everybody had. They were dangerous.

Why did he have to confront the man today. He was running late as it was. He had a plane to catch in the evening, and before that he was going to see Nappaporn.

Charles looked at the other man's face. No words came from him. Perhaps Perotti had stopped talking a long time ago and he had failed to notice the silence. Perhaps he was just watching his expression.

Out here in the Orient that was impolite.

The American would know he had not been listening.

'You don't frighten me, Perotti.'

'I wasn't trying to.'

'Yes you were. Why else would you brag about bumping that chap off when you . . .'

'You asked. I only answered your question. You wanted to know how I started in this business. Maybe I told you too much. Maybe you can't stomach the truth. Maybe you've had it too easy for too long.'

'You are right. Listen. I'm going to Hong Kong tonight. We'll talk when I return.'

'What's in Hong Kong?'

'If it were your business, I'd remind you I have a daughter at school there.'

'You ain't being very friendly.'

'You aren't either. You come into my office and you dare tell me you want me out? You must be mad, Perotti. Do you know how long it took me to build this thing up?'

'Sure I do. And we don't want you out. You haven't been listening. You'll still be in charge. You'll be running it for us, that's the only difference. You'll have as much money as you need. You won't need the banks. You'll sell a million times more than you do now. We're big bucks, Charlie.'

'I know that, Perotti. Everyone knows that. Surely your people are adventurous enough to start their own thing. Hire people here and do what I do. There's room for everybody.

It's wide open. What do you need me for?'

'You know the people and the places and all the ropes. You will save us time. We cannot afford to sit around too long while the market waits. No one wants you out. We want you in. You can hire and fire. Nothing needs to change. No one needs to know. The less people know the better. You'll be rich.'

'I am doing fine as it is.'

'Yeah, but you'll have so much money you won't know what to do with it. You'll be able to retire in two years.'

'I don't want to retire.'

'Why not? You could live in the sun and have servants and travel and . . .'

'I do that now. I'd be bored.'

'You keep slipping away from the main issue. Are we gettin' together or what?'

'I told you, we'll talk when I get back.'

'We're running out of time.'

'I am not.'

'Yes you are. Delays are problems and problems can hurt.'

'Don't threaten me, Perotti.'

'I never do. If we were mad you'd know it.'

'There . . . that's a threat.'

'No it ain't.'

'Well, we'll have to talk when I come back. I have things to do.'

'Yeah. See your local sweetheart, huh? Go local before you fly off to your classy friends with your classy wife?'

'You're a nasty piece of work, Perotti . . . I don't know what you're talking about.'

'Oh yes you do. The pretty Thai girl across the river there. The one with your little girl. You call me nasty? Maybe I am, but I don't pretend to be clean, like you do . . .'

'How dare you . . .'

'Cut the crap, Charlie. We make it our business to know everything about anyone we're interested in. And I mean everything. We gotta know.'

'I simply have to leave now. Do you need a lift anywhere?'

'I can walk it. I'm just around the corner at the Oriental. When can I call you?'

'I'll contact you when I get back. We'd better meet somewhere else next time.'

'I don't mind, Charlie.'

'Will you see yourself out? I need to make a few calls.'

'You keep talking down to me, Charlie. As if I was scum.'

'You said it, Perotti. Not I.'

'We both know there's little difference between us. Sure, you're a gentleman and that, and I may not look as good as you, but inside, Charlie . . . Inside, we're the same.'

'I think not. Now, if you'll excuse me . . .'

'Don't forget to take your papers, Charlie.'

'That's the big difference between us, Perotti. We trust each other. We do our business by word of mouth here. You know bloody well there are no papers in our business. Unless of course you have changed . . . I suppose these days you require a letter of credit before you'd agree to shoot someone's head off.'

The American exploded into laughter.

'You're funny, Charlie, did anyone ever tell you that? You sure are funny.'

'Would you mind enjoying my latest joke somewhere else?'

'Sure,' the American said, and got up. In the silence the fan seemed to roar like an engine. They looked at each other.

Please God make him disappear, Charles thought. This is not happening.

'Nice place you got here, Charlie,' the American said with a smile, and was gone.

He'd talk to Paco. See if he could get the American off his back. Would Paco have known what this was about?

Surely not. He would have warned him.

It was twelve o'clock. One o'clock in Manila. He'd have to use the radio. It was infinitely more reliable than the telephone.

The wireless room was on the roof. Perhaps he should go home and use the one there, but Rose might get worried. God knows who she was having for lunch. No. Better do it from here. He got up and walked to the door.

There was a crackle and the usual whistles but the Filipino's voice came through the airwaves clearly.

'You sound tired, Paco.'

'I was sleep.'

'Sorry to disturb you, but I've got a problem.'

'Shipment late?'

'No. Nothing like that. It's your friend Vincent Perotti. The American.'

'What you mean?'

'Oh Christ, Paco, don't start that now. You know Perotti.'

'What he do?'

'It's not what he's done. He's done nothing yet. It's what he wants to do.'

There was silence. There were whistles and a screech. The soft, melodious sound of Glenn Miller's 'Moonlight Serenade' infiltrated into his ears from somewhere.

'Are you there, Paco?'

'Sure Mister Charlie. I am here.'

'You went off the air . . .'

'No. I am here.'

'What do you know about Vincent Perotti? What do you know about his people?'

'What you mean?'

'Go fuck yourself, Paco. You know what Perotti is capable of . . .'

'Anyone can hear us, Mister Charlie.'

'I don't care.'

'Radio is bad communication today. It no legal here. We

talk together me face you face.'

'You haven't answered me.'

'We meet.'

'I'll be in Hong Kong tonight.'

'How is Roberta?'

'I don't know. That's why I'm going there.'

'How long you stay?'

'A week. Ten days maybe.'

'I come see you Hong Kong in three days.'

'Fine, Paco. Thank you. What do I do about Perotti?'

'We talk Hong Kong, you face me face alone,' the Filipino said. He wasn't going to say any more. Charlie said goodbye and switched the set off. His ears hurt.

Back at his desk Charles fished his passport and tickets out of his drawer. He opened his safe. He took a wad of American dollars out and stuffed them into his jacket pocket. A smile landed on his face as he thought of Nappaporn. They would have most of the afternoon for themselves. He would collect Rose on the way to the airport. She had been ready and packed for days. She was only too glad to go somewhere. She didn't like Bangkok.

Perhaps, he thought as he got into the car, she had good reasons. Perhaps he hadn't been the sort of husband he had promised to be when he gave her his vows all those years ago.

The smooth wooden floor caressed his bare feet. From the kitchen, the scent of the food she had cooked floated through the room and reached him, and he smiled in anticipation. There was always food for him in the house. Rice and curried chicken and stir-fried vegetables. Even when he was away. He was always expected. As if he always lived there. As if, whenever he left the house, he would soon be back. He felt much at ease in Nappaporn's house. This was the real Thailand. The wooden walls and the sound of the river and the boats sheltered him from the hustle and bustle he had come from and was going back to. Perhaps he liked it because it was smaller. The outside realities could not invade him there because there was no telephone.

'Sawadee,' she said softly. This word of welcome represented another world to him. There was no room for Vincent Perotti in there.

'Nalini is out,' Nappaporn said of her little daughter. She always mentioned her as soon as Charles walked in. As if in passing, yet hoping he would say something. 'The maid took her for a walk. She is happy in the American school, Mister Charlie. Do you know she is refusing to speak Thai?'

'I am going to Hong Kong tonight.'

'They call her Nellie now. Everybody. Even she call herself Nellie now.'

'The food smells divine, Nappaporn.'

'You have to go soon?'

'We have time. The plane doesn't leave before evening.'

'You look tired. You sleep before you eat?'

'No.'

She loved cooking for him. She loved to look at his expression when she served, the gratified smile that came at her as soon as he had finished. She loved the foreign way he pronounced her name, even though his Thai was nearly perfect. He was the most handsome man she had ever seen. The only man she had ever known. He had, she knew, another life on the other side of the river. He worked and talked to many people and lived in a big, solid colonial house with his other family. Nappaporn had seen the house from the outside many times, and twice she saw his other woman and his other child. He knew all the important people in the town, and that made her proud of him because he was her man. Even if sometimes he was not there he was her man. People talked of him and she had cut his picture out of the newspaper and hidden it in the metal box that contained her special things. Little presents he often gave her – jewels and gold trinkets and his old wartime watch. The box was like a second temple to her, and sometimes, when she was lonely, she would look inside and touch the items and gaze at his picture and remember. In truth he did not come every day, but when he did, and when he ate the food she had cooked, he was hers alone. She so wished Nalini could have him, too. Even for a little.

Why did Mister Charlie estrange himself from her daughter, she often asked herself. There was so much of him in the little girl, no one could have mistaken it. She had his pale almond eyes and his high cheekbones and his nose, and only her skin was Nappaporn's. The child's skin was paler than her own; it was smooth and soft and without blemish. Nalini was, after Mister Charlie, the most beautiful person in the world. A living symbol of their love and their union. A proof for all to see that she was not some woman alone. It was true he never brought any of his Farang friends to this house. His wartime comrades from Burma and of course other locals did too, but they only came when Mister Charlie was not there. They came to discuss business. Some stayed in the little guest-house she had on her grounds. They used her boats sometimes, and sometimes they brought new customers for her fish. They never stayed long, and when she was alone they did not come inside, as if her house were out of bounds to them. At most they would accept a cup of tea on the terrace outside, and then they would leave in a hurry. She did not mind too much because she wanted him, when he did come to the house, all to herself. In any case, Mister Charlie was her lord and her master and her everything, and he knew what he was doing and why. Probably, Nappaporn told herself, this house was his refuge, the monastery into which he could escape from whatever it was that had caused him worry. And she did notice worry in him lately. He was still a young man, but not as young as he had been during the war, when he knew no worry and no fear in spite of the dangers.

But why did he ignore his daughter? She was half Farang now, and she considered herself even more than half. She was now called Nellie and that was a Farang name, and still it made no difference to him. Secretly, Nappaporn thought he would have liked to have had a boy child. She was not sure of that because he never talked to her about children. If it had been a boy perhaps he would have talked about him. A boy can grow to be a priest or a warrior or a husband and many other things. Men prefer boys. She had tried but she had failed him. She had gone to the temple every day, and often she went to the temple where a woman could pray for fertility and conception. Near the form of the Buddha, in that place where women lit candles and put rings of flowers around the smooth phallic shape and knelt and prayed for a man child. She had three men in her life to look after. There was her father and then her brother before he was killed, and now there was Mister Charlie. No woman can ask for more than three men in her life. Yet still she had prayed for a boy child, but the Buddha did not hear her. Or maybe she did not understand the ways of the Buddha. Maybe she was not meant to have another child.

Or, best of all, maybe Mister Charlie wanted her for himself alone. If that was what he wanted she would be the happiest woman in the world. If he told her that, she would gladly stop going to the temple of fertility. But he never said anything, so Nappaporn continued to visit that temple and place flower rings around the stone organs.

Now her Mister Charlie sat on his chair, by his table, in the corner of the living-room in which no one else ever sat. He was eating the food she had cooked with great relish. He was wrapped in the silk kimono she had made for him. From the back, with his narrow waist and slim body, he could have passed for a tall Thai. Only his hair, with its golden-reddish wheat colour, betrayed the Farang blood that ran all through his veins.

As soon as he had entered her house she had taken his shirt and underwear off and washed them and hung them outside. They would be dry and ironed by the time he left. She did it herself, always. She never let the maid touch anything of Mister Charlie's. It was a holy ritual, like cooking for him every day.

She loved watching him. Just he and she in the house. She loved listening to him, for he spoke her language, and the sound of his voice and the soft light in his eyes pleased her no end.

He would soon finish and he would get up and go to the other room. She would follow. He would take his kimono off and his beautiful white skin would fill the large bed. He might open his arms for her, and if he did she would come to him. She would not hesitate. Her Mister Charlie knew how to give pleasure to a woman. He was gentle yet strong, he was sweet and full of ardent passion all at the same time. A woman is born to give pleasure to a man and serve him and suffer his temper in silence.

That was what Nappaporn had learned. When her mother had been alive, a long time ago, that was how she had lived. Many of the women she knew followed that. Some were unhappy because their men did not appreciate what was given to them. But they did not dare to start a new life on their own, or go back to their villages and take their children and live alone. But they did dream about it and talk about it to her because she was a strong, independent woman of business.

Some broke the barrier of shame and good manners and spoke of what occurred between them and their men when they were alone at night. They all talked together. The maids talked while washing clothes in the rushing waters of the klong; her friends talked while they traded in the fish market and the little shops. They laughed and they talked of men and their love.

She never talked of that to a living soul. She thought of it. And when she thought of Mister Charlie in that way she smiled and her insides beamed. Because her Mister Charlie was different. When Mister Charlie was with her, it was her pleasure he cared about more than his own. She often wanted to tell about him. Tell of his tenderness and his care. The beautiful caresses of his that brought such sharp sweetness and release. Tell of the happiness he had brought her. How he catered for her every need. But she could not talk of him because it would bring bad luck. And Nappaporn had been a lucky girl ever since she had met Mister Charlie in Pataya, during the war, when the Japanese roamed in Siam as if it were their own.

There was another side to her as there was to their relationship. She had grown to become his equal in many things, and he relied on her and would listen to her. He was involved in business affairs about which no one knew but her. She was a good dealer, and he often asked for her advice and did as she said. He had learned many ways of trade from her and often, when her opinions prevailed, she was stronger than him. But that did not make him resent her because he loved all of her. Today he summoned her love alone, and the other part of her would wait until he had need of it.

He got up and he rubbed his stomach. He smiled at her and Nappaporn felt the blood race to her face. His eyes told her she was the only love in his life. He did not sweat, but she wiped his brow, then went back and sat on the floor-mat and watched him. He got up and he walked over to her and stretched his hand and gently pulled at her arm.

'You come with me, my witch,' he said. She did not hear what he said, but there was no mistaking what he meant.

When they got to the bed he sat down. It was their bed, and she only slept there when he was in the house. The room was closed when he was gone. But there were flowers there and a table with drinks and even the shining American gramophone he had brought from Manila. Sometimes he asked her for music. But not today. There was something different about him today. Usually he would go on and on about her food and how beautiful she was and how lovely the flowers were, but today he hardly spoke.

He lay back and his handsome face looked at hers. It seemed troubled. She did not ask him what the matter was.

Mister Charlie would tell her when he was ready. He always told her everything, good and bad. But he never talked of bad unless it was over.

The shape and form and brash voice of the American came back to him. A slow, slimy shiver crawled up his spine. He would have to do something about the man. He had met him many times before, but until today their meetings had always been social. It was Paco who had introduced them, and for old time's sake Charlie had obliged. He had introduced him to Rose and to others at the Club. They had drinks and meals and long conversations. Now Perotti had finally come out with his true intention. He wasn't interested in friends or contacts. He was, as he himself had put it, muscling in. The way Charles and his friends worked, it would be impossible. What they had could not be called a business enterprise. Not in the Western sense. They were a group of independent people with a common interest. Some were merchants and others owned boats. Some knew the mountain paths that crossed borders and others were miners. Some lived in the cities and had friends in high places. Each group complemented the other. There were no departments or exclusivity contracts or agreements. It was all based on trust. Each part retained its independence. But how could he ever explain it to him? Perotti would never understand. To the American, Charles was the boss. All he needed to do was say yes. Once he agreed to let them in they could roll.

But that wasn't so at all. In his way of life no one was boss. Many others were involved. By his own admission the American knew nothing of the place. He had met Paco the Filipino and Paco would sell his own mother for money. Paco must have told him they were partners, but that was over long ago, before the war. He was one of many suppliers now. Charles was still buying from him, but he had long been taken out of the inner circle. There were others there now. There were Burmese ruby-dealers and Chinese merchants and Thai seamen. They were all old and proven friends. They had worked closely together all through the war. Many times they relied on each other's trust and actions for their very lives. Together they shared a life of hide and seek and adventure when the Japanese were there.

If he allowed Perotti in there would be new faces. Ugly faces belonging to people motivated by greed alone. Loyalty was hard to come by in these parts. Perotti would not know what loyalty was. He would never understand how these friendships came about. And they would never understand the likes of him, much less work with him.

How were they going to take to such a change. He must never give in. If he did it would be worse than betrayal. Perotti's people would only use them and then throw them to the dogs. He knew how they would operate.

He himself could always go away. Cut loose and run to England or Hong Kong or accept Sam's constant offers to join him in Jamaica. Give it all up. But these people were from here. They had to stay here. There was no other place for them to go. And they had often told him they loved and needed him, and as long as they did he had to stay. He lay there and he fretted.

And then he saw her come into the room. She came close and sat by his side, and as his body shook she hugged him close. He felt her warmth hover all about him. He was not alone. He had many friends. Here and across the mountains in Burma he had friends too. They loved him well, like Nappaporn did. He would find a way. He would have to. He would stay as long as they wanted him to stay. As long as they needed him.

He couldn't let them all down. They had all been through far too much together.

As he saw her and felt the eternal peace of her close by, a fresh gust of optimism entered him and he smiled.

'What have I done to deserve you?' he asked as her face came closer to his.

She looked at him. The aggravation she had noticed before seemed to have gone. She laid her head on his shoulder, and he felt her skin close to his. The flowery scent of her skin brushed his face. He felt her hand touch him and he was aroused, and then Vincent Perotti evaporated into nothing.

# CHAPTER FOURTEEN

Lady Musgrove's School for girls stood on its own grounds on the way to Repulse Bay. Its carefully tended gardens and lawns made a visitor forget he was on the edge of the China Sea. There were roses and honeysuckle, red bricks and Georgian windows. The language heard on the grounds was impeccable and made the English-style uniforms seem very much in place.

There were long, bare corridors and cricket pitches, croquet lawns, tennis courts and indoor swimming-pools. There were sewing classes and music rooms and there was French tuition. There was hymn-singing on Sundays, Brownies and Girl Guides. The school was a miniature slice of pre-war England at its best. Parents were not encouraged to visit Lady Musgrove's too often.

'I wish I had my life again,' Rose said in the car.

'Why is that?' Roberta asked.

'I'd have my father send me to a school like yours.'

'You must be joking.'

'I'm dead serious.'

That she was, Charles thought. He knew an argument was about to erupt. He'd have to defuse it before it caught fire.

'Why don't you two go shopping?' he asked.

'Is that all we'll be doing for half-term?'

'No. Just this afternoon. Maybe tomorrow.'

'What are we doing?'

He didn't answer.

'Shopping is boring,' Roberta said.

'You appreciate nothing,' her mother retorted.

'I thought we were going to Manila . . .'

'Change of plans.'

'You promised.'

'You are right, I did. But things have changed. We'll have to do something else.'

There was no need to go to Manila. Paco the Filipino was coming into town later in the afternoon. He would have to invent something else for them to do. But not now.

'Nothing pleases you, does it, Roberta,' Rose said. 'How many of your friends' parents come to Hong Kong as often as we do?'

'Plenty, Mother,' the girl said, and turned her head away.

'You're a spoilt brat,' Rose snapped. 'Nothing is good enough for you any more. You don't know how lucky you are to be here. You keep forgetting where we were before. You forgot the island . . . A good education is everything.'

'Oh don't bore me with that, Mother.'

'How dare you talk to me like that?'

'Who do you think you are? Lady Musgrove?'

That's precisely who she thinks she is, Charles whispered to himself. The sentence pierced his ear like a scream, and he looked at their faces to make sure no one had heard. He wasn't being fair. Why did he keep putting Rose down, if only in his own mind? What had she ever done to him?

Useless, thinking like that now. There were other problems. How he hated the school, the uniform. Was he getting at Rose through his daughter? No, he was not. Roberta had changed. There was a new stiffness in her he had not known before. It was this bloody school. She was being trained for a way of life he had hated enough to escape from. They were going to stifle her there. She would become like his sisters. No she wouldn't. She was beautiful and intelligent and could hold her own anywhere. And she was warm and loving always. But where were those wild hugs now? Why had they given way to cold, miserable 'how do you do's. He was crazy. Children grow up. She had other needs now. She wasn't becoming aloof; she was becoming a young lady. Yes. Rubbish. She was only eleven years old. He'd have to have a word with her sometime. No he wouldn't. She was advanced for her age. She was a grown-up. Maybe that was what had upset him. Yes. That was it.

No. Not that. The man Perotti was back. What of it? Perotti was only a man. He was a threat, sure, but not to him. He was too well known around here. Too well established. Yes, he was a threat because he knew about Nappaporn. No matter. The Burmese and some of the Thais knew too. She wasn't someone to mess with. And she had powerful friends of her own. No. No threat. Yes it was. Those who knew were his friends and had shared other secrets with him. Secrets that must never see light. Perotti was not a friend.

He must stop this. He must not allow this confusion to interfere with his life.

He looked about him and wondered whether anyone noticed the storms that were raging through him. His wife and daughter were still arguing about something.

Maybe the Arab was right. Maybe he should go to Jamaica. To hell with the pressures. Life would be so much simpler there.

For over six years, sometimes once a month, Sam had written to him asking him to join him out there. He painted the island in bright colours. He offered Charles a chance. You choose any position you like in my organization. You create the position yourself. Be my right-hand man. Maybe he should just drop everything and go. Take the easy way out and live in the Caribbean paradise island and forget the rest. It would be a quieter life. And it would suit Rose down to the ground. Sam had told him of the social life there – the race-courses, the music and the fashions, the parties.

Never. He knew nothing about hotels. So what? He'd soon learn; a business is a business. He could get his teeth into working with the man there. And the climate was just the same. People were the same everywhere. But it would not be the same. Nappaporn would not be there. Rubbish, this was 1953. The world didn't spread as wide or as far as it did before the war. There were ships and there were planes. He could have her come out to Kingston in no time at all. Put her up somewhere. See her every day. Yes, yes, he could do that, but what of her life here? Her family? Her business? She would never leave without her daughter.

And what about that complicated forest of friends and trust that was his trade? What would his friends and suppliers and shippers do without him here?

They'd live. Like they had all lived before he came out. They would all do very well, thank you. He was not indispensable to anyone.

If anything he might be that to Sam Baker. He had looked at Sam's last letter only briefly. It was totally different to anything his friend had written before. It was handwritten on a tatty sheet of grey paper. Very unlike the orderly, typed foolscap page Sam had used all these years. Some other hand had written the letter, and its contents came as a complete surprise. Could be they shocked him, but he was far too preoccupied with Perotti and Paco to react. He'd read it again, carefully, as soon he got a moment to himself.

The man really needed him now. It was all too clear from what little he'd managed to decipher and retain. Sam needed him badly. Maybe he needed him more than anyone out here ever did? For the first time since they had parted Sam Baker was in serious trouble with himself. That could be the best reason to go.

Could he be sure of anything? He was living a lie. One day it was bound to come out and he'd have to go.

No, everybody is living a lie, he thought, and he looked at his wife and his daughter and as he listened to their bickering and their plans he told himself to calm down. But the disturbing itch in the shape and sound of the stocky American refused to leave.

# CHAPTER FIFTEEN

—■—

'How's tricks?' Paco asked.

'You even talk like Perotti, Paco,' Charles said. The Filipino sat across the table from him. He must have been tired, but his face looked fresh.

'Family OK?'

'Yes. They are fine. Tell me, Paco, what's up with Perotti?'

'What you mean?'

'You know damn well what I mean.'

'No,' Paco said. He lit another cigar.

'You've got one burning right there in the ashtray, Paco. It's not even half gone. Are you nervous?'

'Why you say that?'

'You tell me.'

'What you mean?'

'Let's stop beating around the bush, shall we? You introduced me to the man. You told me he was important to you. You said he was a good customer. You asked me to look after him . . .'

'Sure.'

'Well, that's exactly what I've been doing. He's not the easiest man to sit around with. I was nice to him. Introduced him to everybody in Bangkok . . .'

'He come your house?'

'Not yet. But I've taken him out. He comes to the Club very often . . . He turns up in my office any time . . .'

'Why he no come your house?'

'Didn't get a chance yet . . . But I promise you, I have been very nice to him . . . And more than that, Paco.

'He's become quite friendly with Rose. They talk all the time.'

'That's good.'

'That's not good, Paco.'

'What you mean?'

'If you say that one more time I'll hit you.'

'What . . . Why you talk me bad, Mister Charlie . . . We old friends. We friends before war . . . In war. You remember . . .'

'I do, Paco, I do. I'd like to forget some of it.'

'What you mean?'

'Look, Paco. You are tired. You've had a long trip . . . You should have gone to sleep a little before we met. It's my fault. I'm sorry. Why don't we see each other at dinner?'

'Dinner is family time, Mister Charlie. Your wife and daughter. Better we talk now.'

'Fine with me.'

'You start, Mister Charlie.'

'Did you know Perotti was going to try and get into my business?'

'No.'

'Are you sure?'

'Sure.'

'I don't like what you're saying. I don't like the way you say it. You'd better tell me the truth. Does Perotti have something on you?'

'What you mean?'

'Do you owe him money? Does he know some secret about you? Is he threatening you with something? Blackmailing you?'

'What you mean?'

'I'd better go now, Paco. I'd better leave you. You go back to Manila. I am wasting my time here. I thought we were old friends . . . Obviously I'm wrong.'

'I'm sorry, Mister Charlie,' Paco said. His eyes were moist. His voice cracked. 'You no wrong. Perotti want meet you bad. He never say why.'

'What did they promise you for this introduction?'

'No promise nothing.'

'You're lying.'

'No lie. They no promise nothing, Mister Charlie. They say if I no introduce you they kill my father first then my wife then me.'

'I see. I guessed that much. You should have told me that . . .'

'If I tell you you worry. I no like you worry.'

'I wish you had told me.'

'If I tell you, you fight Mister Vincent and you get big trouble. I no want you trouble.'

'I know. I know, Paco. I appreciate that.'

'Why you no work with them, Mister Charlie? They big. They rich.'

'They are dangerous, Paco. And you know it.'

'They never kill my wife. He only say, no?'

'He doesn't just say. He'll kill. You'd better believe he'll kill.'

'They pay good. Sometime they pay before shipment.'

'They don't want to trade with me, Paco. They want to become partners with me.'

'What you mean?'

'You'd better go now, Paco.'

'I see you dinner time?'

'I think you won't, Paco. You'd better go back to Manila.'

'You sell penicillin to me still? You buy?'

'I'll have to think about that, Paco. We'd better talk about things next time we meet. I'll see how I manage with Perotti first.'

'I can help.'

'No you can't, Paco. I wish you could, but you can't. It's far too late now.'

'I can. I can arrange in Manila, Mister Charlie.'

'Arrange what?'

'Can arrange Perotti never leave Manila.'

'You're full of shit, Paco. Perotti is only one man. There are others where he comes from. You will be dead before he's buried, Paco.'

'I know everybody in Manila. I am big man there.'

'You surprise me, you know. I would have expected you

to come clean with me. You insult my intelligence, Paco.'

'I kill him if you like.'

'Don't be naive. You can't do that. It will do no good, anyway.'

'Can do, Mister Charlie. Can kill then take father and wife to jungle. Hide. Hide many years until you safe. Same same wartime. Never mind I live in jungle if you safe.'

'You're a good chap, Paco, and I appreciate what you are saying, but you don't know what you're talking about. Just forget it.'

'We friends?'

'Of course we are friends. I know you mean what you say, but it's hopeless. You don't realize what we're up against.'

'I swear I never know. I know he big people. I never introduce him if I know what you say is truth.'

'I believe you.'

'No worry too much, Mister Charlie. People come to Orient, many people, many years. They come and they go. Orient people always stay. Mister Vincent, he no stay.'

'Maybe you're right. We'll see.'

'You still buy from me? Still sell?'

'Of course I shall, Paco.'

'We eat tonight? You and family and me?'

'Of course. See you at seven, Paco.'

Back up in his room Charles sat on his bed and looked at the bay. Hong Kong beckoned across the water. Three junks glided, all sails up, out into the open sea. They were dwarfed by the giant grey shape of a Royal Navy aircraft-carrier at anchor. The ferry was busily transporting people back and forth. He was always amazed by this miracle of efficiency and how quickly it had been restored. It was five o'clock. Roberta and Rose were going to be a couple of hours at least. He pulled Sam Baker's letter out of his pocket.

*Dear Friend,*

*It seems there is nothing anyone can do for me. I am going to stay blind, but there are people in the world who are blind and not as fortunate as I am. So why is it I cannot find contentment?*

*It will all come as a surprise to you, or maybe it will not. You are the only man who has seen me in a situation similar yet different to this. This is why I am writing to you and telling you everything that has happened to me. You may have noticed I have not written for three months, and what happened is the reason. I have only just recovered, and I owe you an explanation. Your older brother Sam, your reliable friend from across the sea, has been going through a change. Maybe it will never come back. I pray it doesn't. But the person who is writing it for me shares my life and shared my last few weeks of hell with me and she deserves to know.*

*It came all of a sudden. I don't know how and when. One morning two months ago it hit me. It was time to get up. My servant came into the bedroom to bring my coffee in. I was about to get out of bed, go to my bathroom and shave. I shave myself now with an electric shaver Jean bought me for Christmas. Then it happened. I was not tired but I could not get up. There was no pain. I walk a lot and swim and I am as fit as ever, but that morning I could not move. I did not want to sleep. I did not want to get up. I did not want to eat or drink. I did not want to talk to anyone or see anyone. All I wanted to do was cry.*

*Luckily Jean was in New York. I sent my man out of the room and when I heard the door shut I started crying. I don't know why. I covered myself up and I stayed in my bed all day. I would have written to you but I could not bring myself to face my secretary. Could not face anyone. I had no one to confide this to, and afterwards I did not need anyone. After that I forgot about everybody. I even forgot about you, dear Charles. I had lost the need for human contact because I began to fear it.*

*Richard called in the evening. He is at university in California and he rarely calls. I wanted to speak to him, but I did not. I could not. I didn't talk to anyone. Not even to say I wouldn't speak to my son. The staff were bewildered. They must have told Richard something because he flew into Kingston the next day. He came to my room and he sat on my bed, but I pulled the sheet over my head* and refused to speak to him. Not refused. Just couldn't talk to him, and then he left because he had to get back for his exams. No one has ever seen me like that except you. And that was five years ago and I thought it was all over. It seems not.

I don't know how long I was like that. Maybe days, maybe weeks. I didn't know how to deal with myself, and then Jean came back. I cannot say when that was. Maybe within days of Richard's departure, maybe within hours.

For many days and nights she sat by the side of my bed in the day and slept next to me in the night. I am not telling you a lie when I say I did not care one way or another. I did not react to anything she did or said. I did not hate her. I did not love her. I was indifferent to her and everything else in this world. The world around me became a slow-moving selection of pictures. People, food, furniture, the things I used to see and love around me when I could see. The difference was I only saw them in my mind and did not care.

I have been thinking of you today because the American doctor who comes to see me has just left. He says I have been suffering from a reactive depression. I am not sure what it means, but he says it is very curable. He says it is a bursting of a problem I have had inside myself ever since I lost my sight. When I asked why it came all of a sudden, he said it was triggered by something.

As I have written to you, my mother died peacefully in her sleep six months ago. She never forgave herself for what had happened to me because she never stopped me from going back to my village. She used to hold my hand every time I came up to her room at the end of each day. Hold my hand and say, 'My son, I have failed to protect you. After all you have done for me, I have failed.' Old people sometimes get an idea into their mind and never let it go. She kept saying that until the year before she died. By then she could not talk any more. She had become a vegetable, but she was the last link between myself and the old country. Maybe her death was the trigger. The doctor is not sure.

He will have to work on me for a while to find out what has brought this about. I can't tell you who brought him to my house and when. I remembered that yesterday, but not today. He says you lose a little of your memory when you're depressed. He says I need to take medication. He says it is not serious, and he says I shall recover. He cannot guarantee this won't come back, and so I thought of you. My poor, dear brother Charles. I always fall on you when things are hard. You saved my life, and now I write to you and I am asking you to help me again. It is I who owes you a debt yet I seem to ask for more. You should never have offered to take me up to Jean's room that time.

Richard will be long in returning. His education is important, and he won't be able to come and help me here for two or three years. Maybe he will never come and help me at all. Jean says he wants to join one of the parties here for when Jamaica becomes independent. But he is young still, and I hope he will change his mind.

I know you are busy and I know you have commitments, but I am a little down, and when I am like this I am like a child. And like a child I am a little selfish.

Could you come here? I don't mean for a visit. Just come here and work with me?

I have trusted friends and people who have been with me for years, but I am afraid, Charles. I am afraid this will come back and when it does I can only face you. You could sell your business and if no one wants it you can sell it to me.

Or maybe you can come for a little while. Yes, OK, come for a visit and stay in my house and go to my office and see if you like it.

As you can see, I am much better now. I have been going to my office almost every day, and I believe no one knows why I have been away. Jean has worked wonders keeping my condition secret. I know I am blessed with trusted friends and people who have worked with me for many years, but none of them knows what I was like when this sickness hit me. If you come they need never know.

Please believe me, my brother, I would rather not write to you in this vein. You know I have asked you to come and join me before. To come as a matter of a business proposition. To make money. Good for me and good for you. This time I am writing to *ask you to come and save my life once more. In a few days I shall be my old self again, and then I will probably laugh at myself and write and tell you to stay right where you are and only come when you are ready to come. This is a beautiful island, Charles. You will live well here. You will like it here. And I will have you with me. There is a big future on this island.*

*Forgive me for this. It is hard for me to write because I cannot write to you myself, and must share all this with another person. You may recognize her writing. It is Jean, my wife. The words are all mine but they were spoken. She has promised me not to add any comment to this and she sends you her love. Maybe you could think of my proposition sometime.*

*As I do feel better there is no urgency now, but there may be in the future and I know you need time. I feel sure you understand me and that you will forgive this outburst.*

*I am sorry this came on you without warning, but it did on me too.*

*There is something else. It has lurked inside of me for many years, and it keeps threatening to burst out of me. I hope it waits, because if I allow it to come to light without warning it will destroy me. I shall have to talk to you about it one day, Charles. When I am ready.*

*Your brother, Sam Baker*

# CHAPTER SIXTEEN

◾

He was about to do his collar-button up when the scent of her perfume came into the bathroom. He saw her materialize behind him in the large mirror.

'What d'you think of the dress?' she asked.

'Ravishing.'

'You're not even looking at me . . .'

'Of course I am.'

'Your face is strained.'

'I'm struggling with this bloody tie. I hate dressing up.'

'If you prefer shorts you can buy Paco a shrimp in the street somewhere.'

'I wouldn't mind.'

'Come on, Charles, you love this place. We are bound to see someone we know.'

'I'm not in the mood for reminiscing tonight.'

'Stop it. You know it's important for Roberta. She needs to be seen in the right places.'

'What she needs is a hiding. She's a naughty little lady.'

'You should have said something about it this morning,' she chided him.

'The way it was between you two she was in no mood to listen.'

'Oh yes, she would have listened . . . You always take her side.'

'I am a very naughty boy too.'

'Make fun if you like . . . but undermining my authority is bad . . . Not just for me. It's bad for her, too.'

'I am sure you're right, but I haven't the patience for a lecture right now.'

'Don't put me down, Charles.'

'I've got problems.'

'That does not give you the right to make out I am nothing.'

'You're right, of course. I am sorry, dear. Honestly I am.'

'All right.'

'Thank you.'

'You had a letter from Sam?'

'Yes.'

'What's he got to say for himself?'

'Nothing much. The boy's still in the States, Jean sends love. You know, the usual.'

'Is he still on about you coming out to Jamaica?'

'Well, yes. I suppose he is.'

'Cooled off a bit about it has he?'

'Not really.'

'We can talk later. 'We should be going down now. It's seven o'clock.'

'It's only Paco, for Chrissakes.'

'That's no excuse for bad manners. Is he giving you a hard time?'

'Absolutely not. On the contrary, Paco is a friend.'

'That's not what you said when we left Bangkok.'

'I was wrong. I misjudged him. He'd go through fire for me.'

'There's something shifty about him, Charles. Women have intuition.'

'That they have, but you can sleep easy about Paco.'

'I never trusted him, you know. He's a smuggler and a cheat.'

'Come now, Rose. I don't make my living working for the Church of England.'

'When I met you you were different.'

'Do you mean I was honest?'

'I don't mean that. I don't want to talk about that.'

'It's too late for regrets, Rose. My business pays for everything. Even for making a lady out of Roberta.'

'We are talking about Paco. And I am telling you he's not your friend.'

'Oh yes he is.'

'What about that time in Pataya?'

'It was a storm in a teacup.'

'I wasn't there. All I know is what I've heard.'

'Don't listen to gossip.'

'I only want what's best for you.'

'I know that.'

'You better make sure about him.'

'I am sure. More than ever after today.'

'Vince doesn't trust him either.'

'So it's Vince now, is it?'

'Vincent Perotti is your friend.'

'You talked to Perotti about Paco?'

'Yes.'

'You shouldn't do that.'

'You shouldn't leave him with me all the time. We spend hours together waiting for you to turn up. I have to say something. I can't just sit there staring into thin air.'

'Well . . . yes, anyway, Paco is not the problem.'

'What is it then?' she asked.

'Don't worry about it now.'

'You never tell me anything these days.'

'You said we were in a hurry.'

'I wouldn't be if we talked more.'

'We'll talk. It's a bad patch, that's all.'

'You could share it, you know, Charles. I used to be able to help you.'

'It's nothing. It's just business. It will pass.'

'If you say so.'

'I say so.'

'Do you really like the dress?'

'I told you, it is ravishing. You look marvellous.'

'You look quite dashing yourself, Charles. Shall we stay in? Get room service?'

'We have a dinner party to go to.'

'Roberta and Paco can entertain each other. I'd love to have you for myself tonight. It wouldn't take me a minute to . . .'

'Come on, Rose, let's go down, shall we?'

'What is happening to us?'

'We're going for dinner with Roberta and Paco. That is what is happening.'

All through the meal he was quiet. Rose and Paco talked of this and that and Roberta sulked. Too many things were going wrong. His beautiful daughter was becoming someone he wasn't going to like. His wife was unhappy. Perotti loomed over him like an iceberg. Maybe it was time to call it all a day and go. He had enough money to take him to the end of the course, but where? England? From what he had read in the papers it was a grey place these days. And what would he do there? Even his English friends said he'd been away from there too long. He could go home to the estate. No he couldn't. He had signed it all away to his sisters last year. Quite right too. He was rich enough and he never saw himself as a gentleman farmer. There he was again. He was not going anywhere. Life was too exciting. Even the dangers were stimulating because he had always managed to over-come. Retirement was not for him. Read the papers and walk some dog? There would be no problems to solve, nothing to fight for, nothing to rack his brains about, nothing to protect. Go work in Jamaica? He'd have to think hard about it in view of Sam's letter. The man was not himself, and he was in no position to help him right now.

What was happening to him? Why was he thinking in terms of defeat? He should stay here and fight for a way of life he loved. The fight would be his cure. The sweet smell of a solution would soon be his and he'd forget.

He looked at Paco's face. Where in England would he ever find the likes of him? He was having an animated con-versation with Rose. His eyes shone with excitement. You could see he believed in whatever it was he was talking about. How could she doubt him?

She must have been drinking. She was answering Paco back. You didn't do that to a man in these parts. Never in the company of others. And she was becoming aggressive.

'You're a rogue, Paco. You're all rogues.'

'What you mean?'

'You are breaking the law . . . You . . .'

'How you say that? Why you say we bad people? Tell her, Mister Charlie. Tell her about our work.'

'She knows,' Charles said, and he winked, pointing his face at Roberta.

'Some other time, perhaps?' his daughter mimicked. 'Not in front of the children? I know all about your work, but you can tell her . . .'

'Don't you dare call me her,' Rose said. 'I am your

mother.'

'Apologize at once, Roberta,' Charles snapped.

'I am sorry,' the girl said, and her eyes smiled.

'Off to bed with you,' he commanded.

She did not expect this, and for a moment there was surprise in her face. Then she got up. She looked at her mother and then at Paco. She said goodnight to them, and granting her father a quick, icy glance she was gone.

'Thank you, Charles,' Rose said. 'Better late than never.'

'Do you really think we are criminals?'

'I did not say that.'

'Not in so many words.'

'Don't tell me you're a saint. You break the law, don't you?'

'Let me tell you something, dear. Maybe I do break the law. Even the law breaks the law. What was right and permissible yesterday is a crime today . . .'

'That's far-fetched.'

'Far-fetched? Come down to earth, Rose. Was it against the law to deliver fishing nets to those people in Pataya? Sure, we had to do that while Nippon looked the other way, but the fishermen there thought I was Jesus, and so did the Royal Navy.'

'Sure they did. You were bringing pictures back.'

'And that was against the law too. Japanese law. Someone's law, dammit. Punishable by death, if you remember . . .'

'That was war, Charles . . .'

'What's the difference? Life is a war. A war for survival. A war that goes on forever. How would we have survived, how would our customers have survived, without us breaking the law. Sure I brought pictures back. That was buying and selling, Rose. I was buying rubies, the Navy was buying pictures and selling a possible end to this war by sinking a few more ships.'

'You are wrong, Charles. There's a difference between fighting a war and making profits out of it.'

'No there isn't, dear. You think there are no profits in war?'

'Of course there aren't.'

'Really? Well, you're wrong, Rose. The profit of war is victory. Territory. The throwing out of someone's government. Loot. Business contracts. In any case, I never noticed you objecting to all that beautiful money I was making. You wanted to send Roberta to this expensive school. Do you think it is blood money that pays the fees? Will blood money pay for your glorious return to England? Have you ever stopped spending the money I made, according to you, robbing those banks of virtue? I haven't noticed any objection on your part . . .'

'I did not say I object. I wouldn't. I can't. But you must at least admit you are far from legit, as your friend Perotti would say.'

'Evidently, he's your friend . . .'

'Whatever . . .'

'Yes. Whatever. You've had too much to drink, Rose.'

'You want to send me up to bed too?'

'Nothing of the sort. But asking me to admit I'm The Highwayman is rubbish.'

'There are legitimate ways of making a living.'

'Sure. Police inspectors are legitimate too, and they take bribes so that their wives can spend money on buying legitimate bracelets from legitimate jewellers.'

'You're cynical.'

'Life's cynical, my dear. Innocent bystanders get killed by legitimate bombs dropped by legitimate governments in Korea as we speak. Grow up, Rose.'

'It's hopeless talking to you.'

'I don't think you mind what we do at all. It's the fun we are having doing it that irks you.'

'I'm going to bed.'

'That's legitimate too,' Charles said as he got up.

'You don't have to be polite with me,' she said, and was gone. She did not bid the Filipino goodnight.

'Best talk tough to women,' Paco said with a smirk of admiration.

# CHAPTER SEVENTEEN

We both hated Paco the Filipino, Rose and I. The reasons were different, but it was one thing we had in common. There was another, but Charlie never found out about us, and I have been trying to forget it, but I can never deny it happened.

Rose and I didn't become lovers in the usual way. You know, guy meets girl, they talk, they have dinner and dance, and they get the heats and so forth. We kind of drifted into it through circumstance. I am an old man now, and I have learned never to make predictions or rely on promises. The word never doesn't exist. The word always doesn't exist either. If you'd told me what happened was going to happen on the day I first met her I'd have said you were crazy.

Christ, this sure is the wrong day to think about it. I have not seen her since Jamaica, but I bet she'll be there because she always loved formal occasions. Nothing is more formal than a funeral. They will all be dressed in black and there will be flowers and the priest will run the show and talk of God and man as if he knew the guy in the box personally. Every time we met she tried to get this thing going again, because she was unhappy with Charlie even before they went their own separate ways. I was always worried she'd say something, and if she sees me today she might spill the beans. I figure it's stupid to be caught for something you haven't done for twenty years. OK, he didn't know about it then and he certainly wouldn't care now, but what's the sense hurting someone for nothing. I don't want anyone to suspect she used to be my girl, so I won't even let them know I am there. I'll be sitting inside the limousine and will say my goodbyes from the window.

You'd think no woman married to someone like Charlie would ever dream of getting laid on the side. And why choose someone like me? I never looked like a movie star and was always overweight, and Charlie was the envy of every man. I mean, the guy was rich and handsome and exciting and a hero and a villain, so what more does a dame want? When I was starting out in New York I thought of women all the time. Yes, I know everybody does. I didn't understand women though. Maybe I didn't hear what they were saying because I was young and in a hurry to get into their pants.

I did listen to Rose. You couldn't help that. She was a strong woman, and she had firm opinions and had gone through more dangerous experiences than any man. It's funny, as long as she was that way I wasn't interested in her at all. The older I get the less I can figure things out. Not just women, but men too, me included. People do crazy things. I wasn't in love with her, I didn't even think she was a great looker, so why did I? I mean, OK, she was always open with me. She liked me as a friend. She liked to have me around because I was the only guy who listened to her. Charlie certainly didn't. Not when I knew them. That was all part of my getting to know him so that we could get into his business. So how come Rose and me got together? I figure it happened when she was not herself, when she was down and lost and vulnerable and soft. And mostly, she took me because she wanted to show him she was just as good. If he'd been a nobody she'd have never gone for me.

She was quite a girl. We made each other feel good. Sometimes it was great. Had things been different she and I could have hooked together for keeps.

Maybe I was a shit, but I couldn't help it. Even when things got hot between us I couldn't be frank with her. At one time I really liked her a lot, yet still I put on an act. I kept quiet about what was going on. I never confessed to anything. It wasn't because I was trying to be mean, and it wasn't because I wanted her to think I was the good guy. It was business.

Like the time she went to Hong Kong with Charlie to see Roberta and meet with Paco the Filipino. I couldn't tell her I knew all about it. I couldn't tell her I was there too. I couldn't tell her Paco had been waiting for me there.

I flew into Hong Kong right after my meeting with Charlie at his office. He ran off to see Nappaporn, and I went straight to the airport and got to Hong Kong a couple of hours before they arrived.

It was all done in such a hurry I didn't get a chance to pack. I had no change of clothes, no shaving stuff, not even a toothbrush. I couldn't be seen anywhere near the Peninsula Hotel, so Paco fixed me an apartment on the Hong Kong side. In those days, before the building boom and all the luxury, their apartments stank. It was a grey old building without a lift, and I stayed inside with all the booze Paco had left me for company. The place was full of cockroaches and lizards and it was as hot as hell. Everything was hot except the water. I was filthy dirty, but I had to stay off the streets until Charlie was out of town. The only good thing about the joint was Paco's maid, who cooked like an angel. There was no telephone, no radio, no nothing, and on the second evening I was depressed enough to get myself as drunk as a skunk. On the third evening I was almost suicidal and then, unannounced, Paco turned up dressed like a judge. He walked in on me and pumped my hand like a long-lost brother.

'You like suit? You like tie? Mister Charlie choose me. Look gentleman. No?'

'Very pretty.'

'We go dinner, Mister Vincent,' he said, and gave me one of his disgusting smiles.

'You crazy? Someone will see us.'

'No problem. Mister Charlie play roulette other side of sea.'

'Where has he gone?'

'He take wife and daughter to Macao. Mister Charlie

like casino,' he said, like he was telling me something new. 'We go out enjoy. I know place of women . . .'

'I need a bath first,' I said.

'You no eat?'

'I shouldn't have, but I did. Your Ama cooks great, Paco.'

The shitface loved compliments, and he purred like a cat and started to show off some more. He told me how he'd taken Charlie off the case by offering to kill me himself, in Manila. He laughed proudly when he said Charlie believed every word of it.

'Mister Charlie think I am his side, Mister Vincent. Him sure. He fight for me with his life. You like, huh? What you want me do now?'

I wanted him to drop dead, but I still needed him and business comes first.

'How about getting a wash and a shave?'

'We go this place I said. It have bathrooms and hot water and woman will wash your body like new. Then eat and drink and enjoy. They wash your clothes too. Not good like Manila but good.'

'Is it on the Kowloon side?'

'What you mean?'

'Everybody knows you and everybody knows Charlie. We can't go anywhere together.'

'You and me can go easy. Safe for us. Mister Charlie never go place like that.'

What he meant was Charlie never needed to pay for women. I didn't like the way he said that, but he was right.

It wasn't anything like the Turkish bath places they have in the Orient these days. There were no mirrors or marble floors or luxury china baths or beer on tap or wide-screen TV. There was no French soap and bubbles like they have today. I hated it. It was a dump. But that was long ago and right now I figure it wasn't that bad. Take the statues and the glass window and the shiny new cars away, take the designer gowns off the girls, and you'll see it was just as good. People knock these places, but I don't. Nobody tells you you're fat or ugly or pale. Nobody looks at you like you should be ashamed of yourself being there at your age. Everybody smiles even if they don't mean it, but you believe it. Prostitution? It's bad, but what else would these girls do?

They knew the bastard there. They treated him like he was the king of the Philippines, and he got drunk very quickly and left me alone with two broads. I figure he was in no state to do anything, but I was and I did. We spent hours.

I said I wasn't going back to his apartment no matter what, and by then Paco was drunk enough to listen. I didn't care how he'd arrange the passage for me, but he said he had lots of contacts in the port. He said he knew everybody and could do anything. There was a ship to Bangkok which was leaving early in the morning. He could get me a cabin all to myself. He could get me the whole ship for myself. I found out later it was his own ship, but at the time he didn't tell me. I figure he wanted to impress me. Show me how great his influence was or something. I didn't ask because I was sick of the sight of him and wanted to get out.

He stayed with me on the dark quay until the ship sailed, and we talked. He was a spineless son of a bitch. You'd never believe he was Charlie's buddy during the war or nothing.

'You like Mister Charlie, huh?'

I didn't answer right away, and I was glad I didn't. Of course I liked Charlie, but I wasn't sure where Paco stood. Sure, he was frightened of me and that, but he was such a slimy liar you had to be careful what you said.

'What's the best way to get into Charlie's business?' I asked.

'Best way kill him, Mister Vincent.'

'No good.'

'Why no good? Him dead you take everything.'

'We need him.'

'You like him, huh, Mister Vincent?'

'He knows the business better than me. I need to learn. I want him to run it for us before we get him out.'

'I know business better. I teach Mister Charlie all business. When I meet him before the war he know only British company business. He know radio. He know electrics. He sit in office with machine and telephone and he write on paper. He never steal nothing. He know nothing. I teach him. I teach you.'

'You live in Manila, Paco.'

'I come Bangkok. I go any place for you.'

'What about all Mister Charlie's friends? We need them too. They work with him. They'll run like hell if we kill him.'

'I know all Mister Charlie friends. When he dead I come for funeral. I cry. Mister Charlie friends are there. They see. They like. I am start business many years before. They ask me be boss until you learn.'

'Let me think about that.'

'I do anything for you, Mister Vincent.'

'Sure,' I said, and I tapped his shoulder.

'You enjoy woman place, yes?'

'Sure.'

'You strong man, Mister Vincent. Woman say to me.'

I knew he was talking shit and I hated him more than ever. I had no desire to kill Charlie, not then, not ever, but I couldn't get involved either way. What happened between me and Charlie wasn't personal. My course of action depended on one thing only. How quickly he'd let us in.

'There is other way to make Mister Charlie work for you,' Paco said.

'What's that?'

'You take his woman away.'

'You crazy? Take his wife?'

'No wife. His woman. Nappaporn. He likes her more better than wife. She no just woman. She partner. She know business. You take her and hide her and . . .'

'I know what you mean, Paco . . . You don't have to

123

paint it for me.'

'You think good idea, no?'

'What about Nappaporn's daughter?'

I meant to ask who would look after her if we took Nappaporn. I didn't have to worry about that. They would soon find someone to look after her at the American school. She was popular there. But Paco didn't get my drift. The fuckface thought I suggested kidnapping her.

'Never mind daughter. Mister Charlie do nothing to get her back. He no care her. Only Nappaporn he care.'

I didn't believe any of it. The guy was only saying it. Every man loves his children. Especially a great-looking kid like that little girl was. Maybe Paco had something against the half-caste child. Maybe he was jealous. Maybe he thought that by telling me not to touch her I'd go against his word and hurt her bad.

That night I knew for sure the bastard didn't give a shit for nobody. Still, I had a job to do, and taking Nappaporn was not a bad idea. I went quiet, and I wondered what Charlie's great love was doing while he gave his money away to the gambling joints over in Macao. I would soon know.

When they called me to climb aboard, Paco offered to come with me for the ride, but I told him to stay where he was and said I'd make contact later. I remember seeing him standing there waving to me as the old steamer rolled away. He waved both hands with great excitement, and in the last moments of darkness he looked like the angel of death taking off for hell.


# CHAPTER EIGHTEEN

———■———

Today I knelt before the statue of the Lord God Buddha, and as I clasped my hands in prayer I noticed yesterday's flowers drying at his feet. I had laid the flowers down as I do every day, and the fresh ones I brought today were still dripping.

The colours were alive with red and blue and yellow, but yesterday's flowers were more beautiful. The hot sun had dried them, and they had much life in them because their leaves and the stems had the golden colour of my Mister Charlie's hair.

He has been gone for long this time, and I know he is with his other woman and his other daughter. I always thank the Lord God Buddha for sending Mister Charlie to me.

He is a good husband and father to both of us, his other woman and me, and his other daughter. I am a blessed woman.

It was money day, the day when my fishermen come to the house to settle the accounts of the week. There are always two of them, one for each of the boats I was given before Nalini went to the American school to learn how to become a Farang like Mister Charlie.

It takes but a few minutes' walk from the temple to the house, and when I arrived at my wooden gate I saw them. They sat in front of the door. They never come inside because it is my house and I am an independent businesswoman and well respected. The older one of the two got up and he clasped his hands to greet me and handed me two small baskets full of coins and notes. They were the sort of baskets people used for river shrimp-fishing years ago. They were made of woven strips of bamboo and were painted and waxed and lacquered to keep the water out, and many people have them in their houses for decoration. There was one basket for each boat.

The two men waited for me to go into the house and count the money. It was a weekly ritual. I went inside and soon I was out again, and I handed the baskets back to the men. I left enough money there for these two and everyone else who worked on the boats. I always left the distribution of it to them because they are my headmen and they expect it that way. It is a matter of position and honour.

I bade them goodbye and went into the house again.

Under the floorboards there is an old metal box Mister Charlie gave me during the war. It once belonged to Mister Charlie's country, and has the letters of the Royal Navy painted in white on both sides. I lifted the wooden plank and opened the box and placed the money inside, with the other neatly laid notes. I poured the coins into the blue-flowered jar that stands by the kitchen door. I keep enough coins there for the maid to go to market with, and for my daughter Nalini's pocket money.

Nowadays my daughter is called Nellie, and I try to call her that to her face, but for me she will always be Nalini.

Next I went to the kitchen and checked on the slow-burning stove. Mister Charlie's favourite meal of rice and vegetables was steaming in the large pots. He may or may not come to me today, but his food is always there. My own food and that of my daughter and the maid had been prepared, and now it waited in a different pot for our lunch. I lifted the lid and with one sniff I made sure all was well. After that I went outside and sat down by the door to wait for my daughter to return from school.

I looked up and I saw the clouds gathering above my garden, and I got up and went inside to close the shutters. I think there will be a thunderstorm, but only a small one. The season for the big downfall is not with us yet.

I had just settled down by the door again when my daughter came running down the path with my maid. As soon as Nellie saw me she slowed down. She walked up to the house and the smile on her face disappeared.

'Why are you always sitting there?'

'Because I want to be here to receive you.'

'You should go inside. Maybe sleep.'

'I may not hear you if I do that.'

'What do you need to hear me for?'

'To get your food for you.'

'You are not a maid. You are my mother.'

'When you have children you will understand.'

'Understand? I would hate them to think I was their

maid.'

'Mothers must serve their children.'

'No, Mother. Children must serve their mothers.'

'They are teaching you strange things at the Farang school.'

'This is not a Farang idea. Anyway, I am a Farang.'

'You are half Farang and half Thai, Nalini.'

'I am a Farang, like my father. And my name is Nellie.'

There was no point in pursuing that conversation. That was a ritual, too. Just like money day, but money day was a weekly ritual. This conversation occurs every day outside the house.

Nellie took her shoes off and handed them to the maid, who opened the door for both of us.

'Let me have some of the vegetables,' Nellie said when her food was put on the table.

'I have no vegetables today. You never eat them. You don't like vegetables. There's chicken. You love chicken. And there's fried fish . . .'

'I feel like vegetables today. And you do have some. There. I saw them in the kitchen. In that other pot.'

'You know I can't give you those. They belong to Mister Charlie. Your father.'

'He's not coming today.'

'He might.'

'That's what you say every day.'

'I'll steam some vegetables for you tomorrow.'

'I don't want vegetables tomorrow. I want some today. Now.'

'I'll steam some for you. Eat the fish first.'

'Forget it.'

'As you wish.'

'I wish you didn't behave like a slave, Mother. You are a lady.'

'Of course I am a lady.'

'Then stop being a doormat for your Mister Charlie.'

'Being someone's woman does not mean you are his

doormat.'

'If he ignores you it does.'

I am not a servile woman. Not the way my daughter thinks I am. She is young and she does not understand love. I grew up in my father's house with my brother and I am an independent woman. I tell my fishermen where to go because I know the waterways. I tell them where to sell the fish because I know the merchants, and I speak to them the way they expect me to speak and they give me respect. But when my Mister Charlie wants me to be soft and take the heat of the day off his brow, I do that. And if that means I am a maid it is because Nellie does not understand yet. One day she will be a woman and she will meet a man and if she loves him she will do as he wants her to do because she will know how to give and receive love. Now she is without experience and has learned the way of the Farang from her friends at the American school. But the Farang ways cannot be all good. Otherwise why would all Farang men have Thai wives too?

Of course, Mister Charlie wanted her to go to the American school because she would learn to speak languages and hold her head high anywhere, and she would learn about the world. I would never find her a Thai husband if she went on that way, but she is only twelve and there is time. I know she is a little confused by it all. She thinks of herself as Farang, though she is only half. I want her to be proud of being a Thai. We are an old people with an ancient kingdom and have many customs and beliefs that were there long before the Farang had their countries and their navies and their planes or even their religion. Mister Charlie often said that to me himself, and when he did I could not understand why he wanted her to go to the American school and become a Farang.

I asked him once what would happen to Nellie when she grew up. Would she not be too different, I asked; would she still live in Thailand and be happy? I am Farang, Mister Charlie said, and he smiled, and my heart melted at the sight of him. I am Farang, but am I not happy here? I asked him how would Nellie find a husband, and Mister Charlie knew the answer to that too. He said that by the time Nellie grew up it would not matter. She would be able to pick and choose any husband she wanted. She would be rich and have an education. But most of all, Mister Charlie said, she could live anywhere in the world. The world was becoming smaller every day, he said, and it was becoming more tolerant. When Nellie grows up, my Mister Charlie said, no one would worry about her background. Not if she is well educated.

Mister Charlie takes good care of us. We want for nothing. I am a rich woman with my boats and my fishing and other business deals I do with him and his friends. I only wish Mister Charlie would take some notice of Nellie and teach her about the world the way he taught me. If he did that she would not be confused about herself, because when you know what is around you and who you are and where you come from, the ground under your feet is safe and steady. When she was a little girl she always listened to me and never ever talked back to me. I know it is not her fault, and I know she would suffer if she did not talk back to me, and this is why I never scold her. I should not blame Mister Charlie, because he has had much on his mind these last few weeks. Something is troubling him, and I sometimes fear he is followed by danger. I am a blessed woman to have Mister Charlie, and when peace comes back to him I shall ask him to make time for his daughter Nellie. She will love him and that will give her the strength love has given me.

Lately I have seen people outside the house. People I do not know and have never seen before. Some are Farang and some are Thai, and they always come just before Mister Charlie comes to the house. Sometimes they come by boat along the river at the bottom of my garden, and sometimes by car on the road by my fence, and I know which boat it is and which car. Every time I see these people it is a sure sign that Mister Charlie will come to me. I have not mentioned this to him because I must be certain of it first.

I am not a helpless woman the way Nellie thinks I am. I know just the man who can help me.

He is not a Farang and not a Thai. He is not from Burma. He is from far away across the sea, from a big city called Manila in the country of the Philippines. He is a man who prays to the Farang Lord Jesus, who is also Mister Charlie's Lord. He is the oldest friend Mister Charlie has in the Orient, and he knows and cares about me and about Mister Charlie's Farang wife and family. He saw me many times. He knew about me from the time I first became Mister Charlie's woman. Apart from the ruby men he is the only man from across the sea who has been to my house after I moved to Bangkok. He is loyal to Mister Charlie, even though there was a time when I was not sure about him. The seed of suspicion about the Filipino man was planted in my mind long ago by one of the ruby merchants from Burma. He said that the man had betrayed us to Japan. That was during the war, when I first met Mister Charlie in Pataya when I was young. It happened when Mister Charlie was in my house and three Japanese officers came to the house to arrest him. But that is long past now, and my Mister Charlie always said he would vouch for him with his life, and that is enough for me. My Mister Charlie is in Hong Kong with his other woman and his daughter, and the man from the Philippines is there with them. That shows he is a trusted friend, and I shall speak to him before I tell Mister Charlie about the people who are watching us. Until that man comes to the house again I shall not say a word to anyone. I shall have to bear my worry and my fear for Mister Charlie in silence. I know these men are dangerous. I have no knowledge of them, but I know their kind. Peaceful people greet you when they pass even if they are strangers, but these men never do. They only look at me and at the house and then they speed away. I do not fear for myself, because only the Lord Buddha knows where the river will end and what the future will bring. He will always watch over Nellie because I love her and pray for her every day, as I do for my Mister Charlie.

# CHAPTER NINETEEN

Paco's old ship dropped anchor and I was rowed ashore by one of those long taxi-cab boats that used to float up and down the river. They had this pontoon right outside the Oriental Hotel, and a uniformed porter helped me off the rolling boat and smiled his charming smile. I have always been partial to friendly hotel staff, and the guy's welcoming face made me forget the lonely journey I had had. It was close to lunchtime, and I sat on the terrace and watched the river and the boats, and the waiter came over and greeted me like I had never been away at all. After days of eating steamed rice and fish on Paco's ship, I was about ready for a decent steak. Then, just as the food was served and I stuck my knife into the juicy beef, a shadow crossed behind me and a hand touched my shoulder. I was a little startled, and then I saw it was my local guy. Paco must have told him I was coming back.

'I think the woman has noticed me,' he said, and sat down like he'd been asked.

'What woman?' I didn't care much about the answer. All I worried about was having to eat cold meat.

'Nappaporn,' he said. 'You know, Mister Charlie's woman.'

'What's with her?'

'We've been watching her and the house, and I think she's noticed us.'

'What were you watching her for? I said you're to do that only when Mister Charlie's in town. Anyway, what if she did?'

'She's got very powerful friends in town.'

'Like who?'

'Like every Chinese fish merchant, every gemstone dealer, and all those others.'

'What others?'

'Mister Charlie's friends from the war. Some are big in the police and the army.'

'Are you telling me we must get rid of her?'

'Maybe.'

'That's what Paco said.'

'He should know.'

I was too tired to think of that. I am not a good sailor. My legs were not steady. I was hungry. I wanted to finish my meal in peace. I wanted to go up to my room and have a hot shower. I wanted to be by myself.

'I'll let you know,' I said, and he got up. 'You leave her house alone for now.'

'I can't do that, Vincent.'

'Why not?'

'You said we must watch her house.'

'Only when Charlie's in town.'

'Charlie is in town.'

'What? When did he . . .? Never mind, you get going right away. Let me know what is happening. And make sure no one sees you . . .'

He took off, and I dug into my steak. The meat was soft and delicious, and I was so hungry I swallowed it with hardly any chewing. One of the serving-girls came by and cleared my plate away. I turned, about to call the waiter for another round, when I saw Charlie's wife Rose walking out of the hotel towards the terrace where I sat. I could have walked away from it. She couldn't have seen me, because there were trees and plants and flowers between her and me, but I didn't move. Soon she saw me and she waved, and her steps accelerated as she came in my direction. I got up to greet her.

'I was coming to have lunch,' she said. 'Will you join me?'

'You join me,' I said, and pulled out a chair for her. 'Long time no see.'

'Yes,' she said. 'We've been away.'

I called for the waiter.

'What will you have?'

'Ham and eggs. I've had Chinese for a week.'

'I'll have the same,' I said, and I ordered. I think she was trying to get me to ask her where it was she had been, but I resisted. I didn't want her to think I was inquisitive. I knew where she'd been. I had not seen her for a good two weeks. That day there was something different about her. Her voice wasn't as loud as usual, and her movements were kind of slow.

'I'm famished,' she said.

'So am I.'

'We've been in Hong Kong and Macao.'

'Did Charlie make any money?'

'Lost his shirt. Couldn't leave the tables.'

'I know the feeling.'

'I didn't think you were a gambler, Mr Perotti.'

'Vincent, Rose, please. It's Vincent.'

'Yes. Of course it is. Well, I didn't think you gambled. Somehow you don't look the type.'

'What type do you think I am?'

'You're cosy, Vincent. I can imagine you relaxing in some living-room. Dressed in a housecoat and reading the paper, feet up. You're sort of comfortable-looking.'

'Fat-looking, you mean.'

'No. Just comfortable-looking.'

'You've never been in Macao with me,' I said, and we both laughed.

The food came and we ate and I tried to make small-talk, but she only nodded and sometimes she said 'Oh' and 'Really' and that's it. Something was upsetting her, but she wasn't letting on. This time I ate slowly and I watched her face, and with her downcast eyes she certainly wasn't herself. I remember thinking she wasn't a bad-looking broad after all. I knew she was having problems with her daughter. She talked about it often enough.

'What's the matter?' I asked. 'Roberta giving trouble?'

She nodded.

'I'm sorry,' I said. I put my hand on her arm and I smiled. 'Kids can be difficult.'

'How would you know? You're not even married, Vincent.'

'Who'd want me?' I asked, and she looked into my eyes and her face softened like she felt sorry for me.

'You simply haven't met her yet, Vincent,' she said, and she patted my hand. 'You are a strange one, aren't you?'

'Maybe I am . . . I wouldn't worry about Roberta. She'll grow out of it.'

'It's not that . . .'

'What is it, Rose? Can I do something for you?'

Her hesitating expression gave way to a sad smile. I knew she wanted to say something. I think I felt sorry for her then.

'Come on, Rosie, let's have a drink,' I said firmly, and I raised my hand for service.

'My father always called me that,' she said.

'I'm not surprised. It's a beautiful name. It suits you.'

'He's as kind as they come. He is a big chap. Like you. But he's a humble man.' Her eye was moist but she seemed happy.

'I wasn't born in a palace either,' I said. She laughed.

'You're a pet, aren't you? You could make some woman very happy. You ought to be married, you know. We should find someone for you.'

'Oh, I get to meet plenty.'

'Where? Not in the Club, surely.'

'No. Not in the Club. Here. Right here in the hotel. I live here, remember.'

'I've never been inside this hotel. What are the rooms like?'

She asked the question, and then her usual directness faltered. She drank some water and then she said something. I think she was nervous, because she went on talking fast as if I wasn't meant to listen. As if she was talking to herself. I don't remember any of it. I only remember how her face looked down at the table and at my hands. Then she stopped and she waited. Her face became quite beautiful and dreamlike with her eyes staring into the distance. I sneezed and my napkin dropped onto the ground, and I bent down under the table. I heard a shirt button pop. I crawled under and I felt the table shake to the touch of my back. With my bulk I must have created a pretty funny sight, and I was conscious of it and wanted to get back out, but then I saw her legs there. They were crossed and so close I could almost feel her skin on my face. Her dress was pulled up high along her thighs, and she parted her legs and then she rubbed her knees together slowly, and I hurried on out of there before she noticed.

When I sat on my chair again I saw her looking straight at me with this big question-mark across her face. I knew what she was asking, and I figured Charlie was with Nappaporn across the river not a mile downstream, so what the hell.

We sat there on the terrace and we looked at each other and for once we didn't talk at all. The waiter came and went and maybe we ordered drinks and things, and that was where and how it started.

It was never going to be like that again. Sure, we were going to be together many times after that. In Bangkok and Hong Kong and all over, before my people got to hurt Charlie real bad, but it was never like that first time.

# CHAPTER TWENTY

■

The Lord God Buddha will forgive me for this exclamation, but Mister Charlie's return from Hong Kong brought solutions to many problems. It was as if all the gods smiled down on me. I saw a boat speed by on the river at the end of my garden. It stopped, and then it turned and roared past again, and I felt my heart palpitate because that meant he was surely back. I went outside to hang the potted hibiscus on the gate. This was the signal for the maid that Mister Charlie was with me. She would then take Nellie out to the shops with her, and only return when the plant was gone from the gate. At the end of the street I saw that other car. It parked in the shade of a big tamarind tree whose leaves hid the windscreen, but I knew who was there. When you know where your enemy is he becomes only half as dangerous. There is nothing these evil people can ever do to me because I am too insignificant, and my fears were for Mister Charlie alone. I have been to the fish market, and I have heard a big steamer has been up the river today. I asked the people about the steamer, and I learned it was Paco, the man from the Philippines' steamer. I want to see this man to ask for his help, and before I left the fish market I asked my friends to pass a message to him. This is a doubly lucky day for me. But on that wonderful day I was not thinking of dangers because I was overcome with excitement at my man's imminent arrival.

Soon I heard his car outside the gate, and then I heard it drive off again. I recognized it instantly. I knew the purr of his car's engine better than the sound of any human voice. I heard the gate open, and I looked out through the door and saw him walk down the path, as he always did. He arrived at my terrace and he stopped. He took his shoes off at the top of my steps, and I hurried out to greet him and ushered him inside. He sat on his chair and I took a bowl of water and kneeled down to wash his feet. But he did not let me do that this time, and pulled me gently towards him and covered my face with kisses. I knew he had not spent much time in his office and had come to me almost as soon as he had arrived in the town.

He would, of course, have first made sure his other woman was safely installed in the big house he had bought for her. I had never been jealous of that because I knew we were, both of us, important to him. Each one of us had a special place in his life, a special meaning and a special duty. In his way he cared for both of us.

In Nellie's mind, accepting this makes me a weak woman or, worse, a slave to her father's whims. She is trying to confuse me, but she is not doing that with bad intention. I shall have to talk to her and explain our ways to her. Tell her that is the custom with us and has been for many generations. But I was so overcome by his presence that I didn't think of that when he held me close to him. Nellie believes this means I am a sinner. She is now a firm follower of Farang ways, and is beginning to suffer their guilt. Every day I tell myself I shall speak to her of that, but something always comes between us. I feel she is growing away from me, and if that is the will of the Lord God Buddha so be it. You cannot interfere with destiny.

There is an unspoken pact between Mister Charlie and myself. We never talk about his life with his other woman or his other daughter. It has been that way ever since my eyes first saw him many years ago during the war, before I became a woman. It is a just way for things to be. But I am a lucky woman, because I know about his other family and have seen them on the terrace of the Oriental Hotel when I have sailed past in my boat. I have also seen them coming out of his big house near the American Embassy. That day my daughter was with me, and I did not tell her whose house that was and whose family. His other family know nothing of me. It is better, because they are Farang and do not understand our custom the way Mister Charlie does.

Today he talked to me of Hong Kong. He told me he had seen Paco, the man from Manila. He didn't notice my anxiety.

'We had a little misunderstanding, Paco and I,' Mister Charlie said.

'What misunderstanding?'

'Oh, nothing, really. Just business. But it's all clear now.'

'Is Mister Paco in Bangkok too?'

'No. Why?'

'I was told his old steamer was in the river today.'

'You must be mistaken, Nappaporn.'

'My man Sumchai saw it on his way out this morning. He makes no mistakes.'

'Maybe it's come in to collect the ploughs and the whisky I've promised him.'

'Impossible. I have a shipment of nets for him. It won't be ready before next week.'

'Paco does many other things here. He's got connections in the customs house. If he's here to see me I'll have to find out why. I'd be surprised if he was. I haven't been to the office yet. I came straight here.'

My heart smiled when he said that, and the pride I felt made me too happy to worry about the sighting of Paco's boat. There must be another explanation.

He wanted to know about me and about my fishing business, and then he asked about the ruby-dealers from Burma. I said I was expecting them to come soon. Maybe next month. Maybe the month after.

'They are becoming a little expensive,' Mister Charlie said.

'They are being watched on both sides of the border. They have to pay more bribes.'

'Soon there will be no profit in it at all.'

'There is another thing. With so many new Chinese gem-cutters in town there is a shortage of rubies. The new-comers offer more money than we do.'

'Do you think we're going to lose our supply?' he asked.

'No. Not as long as our old friends from the war days

are in the mines there. They could have left us before. But we have to help them somehow. Their costs are going up and the new prices must be tempting.'

'Can we afford to pay more?'

'Not right now.'

'In that case you'd better talk to the Burmese, Nappaporn. See what you can do.'

I was proud of what he said, because he trusted my ability.

'I will,' I said, and before I said more his lips covered mine. I felt his hands touch me and my excitement throbbed out of the core of my body towards my skin. The woman of business was dying within me. He got up and his strong arms lifted me and then, with me curled around him, he walked into our room. I could feel the storm of his desire for me harden in him, but he was slow and gentle. He put me on the large bed, the one I lie in only when he is with me, his eyes looked into mine, and I felt his hands all over. Our robes fell away as if by magic, and I could hardly wait for him to come into me and bring me the pleasure of relief. And then he kissed me and I began to feel him, and all else disappeared behind our door.

# CHAPTER TWENTY-ONE

I saw Charlie's half-caste girl Nellie walk out the main gate of the American school. I had been watching her closely over the last few days to decide what to do next. Maybe she was the key to our problem. Getting to her would get us Nappaporn. That Thai woman proved to be a lot smarter than I figured. I found out she was much more than just a toy for Charlie to pass the afternoon with. Paco did say she was a great pressure-point, and I had dismissed that because I hated him. Having learned more about her, I began to think he had something. We started to make enquiries about Nappaporn, and everywhere my man downtown turned he found the local traders one hundred per cent behind her. By all accounts she is a smart cookie, and people here respect that and look forward to doing business with her. Her visits guaranteed a good haggle, even if she often came out on top. They love to haggle in this part of the world, as they do in every hot country, but in the Orient they don't do business yelling at each other. Everyone seems to be a winner and nobody ends up mad when it's over. Maybe that's why they always look like they're smiling.

Nappaporn was never alone in the markets. There were always some guys around her when she was selling fish. They were big and strong and built like stevedores, and when I went over there to see for myself I thought they were kind of guarding her. The same happened in the gold-shops of Chinatown. There were other big guys there while she was talking rubies, and I figured Charlie had been arranging protection for her, but my man didn't go for that. He said there were no robberies in Bangkok. He insisted these guys were friends and onlookers who just happened to be around when she was out trading. My man had lived there since before the war, and I had to listen to what he said. But I didn't buy any of it at all and did plenty of discreet snooping of my own.

The only time Nappaporn was on her own was when she went to pray to her Buddha.

She did that at least once a day, and she always left a bunch of flowers at his feet. And even then there was always some priest snooping around. You bet I don't believe every guy with a shaven head and an orange robe is necessarily ordained. Men of God get to go places without suspicion, and I knew plenty of hit-guys who used that disguise. Why should things be different here? Sure, when she was in her house she might be alone, but I had never seen the inside of it. Whenever someone came to see her there they talked to her on the porch or in the garden. No one ever got through that door except Nellie, the maid, and Charlie himself when he was in town. My man confirmed that too, because he had been watching her house for a long time. I don't know what she hid in there. Could be a couple of machine-guns. If she was that smart, and with Charlie being an old hand at war and a hero, anything could happen.

My man didn't believe that at all. The trouble is he didn't understand our business too good. He was a Chinese American who had lived in Bangkok forever. He used to be a schoolteacher before losing his shirt gambling, and was still a bit naive. Don't get me wrong. He'd do anything I told him to do because he needed the money. He needed it so bad he was going to learn a lot. But just then he sure knew nothing about what people would do to defend themselves.

So there I was, watching Nellie coming out the main gate and, as usual, her maid was there to take her home. It would be a cinch to grab her there, but I wasn't sure what the best thing to do was. I figured I'd watch the girl for a while and decide later.

She was as pretty as a picture of an angel. If you looked at her from a distance you could have mistaken her for a full Caucasian. Her thick, straight hair had the Oriental texture, except it did not shine and it was kind of auburn, not black like her mother's. She had high cheekbones and her face was Charlie and Nappaporn fifty-fifty. Her eyes were very slightly slanted, but only when they were closed, and their colour was sensational. I don't know how to describe it. Maybe mustard. No. They were pale burnt almond. Pale brown. Just like Charlie's eyes, but on her darker face there was more light in them. They were clear and so bright you could see them shine at you from a distance. She had her mother's figure and Charlie's height, and as she walked towards the gate she was erect and proud. Inside the school, I saw her dance around the playground with her friends, and you'd have thought she didn't have a care in the world. But as soon as she was out in the street and the maid grabbed a hold of her she'd change. Her back would stoop a little and she'd go all slow, and sometimes I noticed the maid pulling her along like she was taking her to the dentist or something.

Anyway, she walked along and I had the driver take us on ahead of them and I looked through the back window and saw them. Sometimes they got pretty close before we took off. Sometimes we let them pass and I got a good look. She didn't notice us at all. It was as if she was on another planet far away.

She walked down the street with the maid like she was dreaming. You could see the maid was saying things to her, but Nellie hardly answered, hardly talked at all. The aggressive animation I saw when she was talking with her friends was gone, and I figured she would rather have stayed at school. With all I knew I couldn't blame her one bit. Nappaporn was a high-powered businesswoman, known all over town as some tough lady. She ran a fishing business and was importing stuff and she dealt rubies for Charlie. Whenever Charlie came to see her she only had eyes for him, and had her maid take her daughter for a long walk. I reckon she didn't have any time for the girl, so why should she be happy going home?

But Paco had said her mother was crazy about her, and him being a native I had to take his word. I was getting nowhere with Charlie, and if we took Nellie away I was going to make sure nothing bad happened, and then we'd talk to Nappaporn and get to Charlie through the back door. There was nothing personal in it. Months were passing by and New York wanted results. I was the man on the spot and I was expected to deliver.

# CHAPTER TWENTY-TWO

◼

They sat akimbo on the carpet, their torsos bent around the low round table. One large Burmese and two smaller ones, all clad in white cotton. Cigar smoke floated slowly up to the ceiling, then disintegrated as it hit the fan. A half-empty whisky bottle took turns amongst the men as their hands picked uncut pink stones out of cloth bags. They lifted them towards the light and watched and talked some before placing them onto the table. There, on the black velvet mat, they lovingly watched the glow of three growing heaps of raw rubies. The room was full of laughter and reminiscent talk and mutual teasing, and then the door opened. The squat little American walked in, a broad smile cut across his wide face.

'Sounds like you guys are having a party in here.'

'You might have let me known you were coming,' Charles said. 'I am a little busy right now.'

'That's what you tell all the girls.'

'You don't own this office, Perotti.'

'Not yet we don't.'

'Would you mind waiting outside?'

'Yes I would. It's damn hot out there.'

'We are sorting rubies, Perotti; nothing that would interest you.'

'You try me, buddy. Anything that's going in here interests me.'

The room went ice-cold. The three Burmese looked up at the man. The large one directed a silent question at Charles; the others continued their work in silence.

'Ain'tcha going to introduce me?'

'This is Mr Perotti,' Charles said.

'Vincent,' the man said. 'It's Vincent.'

'This is my friend U Nan.'

The three nodded their heads. Their expression was decidedly cool. Charles mumbled something and all three rose to their feet.

'They're not going on my account?'

'We're nearly finished anyway,' the Englishman said as they all got up. Without a word, the two short Burmese smiled at Charles and followed their large friend, whose shape towered over everybody as they made for the door.

The cloth bags and the sorted stones remained where they were.

'Big guy, your U something, huh?'

'His name is U Nan. Yes. He's big.'

'Wouldn't like to meet him alone in the dark.'

'U Nan is as gentle as a lamb.'

'Doesn't look like a lamb to me.'

'I promise you he is.'

'Old friend of yours?'

'Yes. We know each other well.'

'Wartime pal?'

'You could say that.'

'You didn't have to break up on account of me.'

'They were leaving anyway.'

'Where are they going?'

'I couldn't tell you.'

Charles sat down again. It was twelve o'clock. On the table, three little pineapple-shaped pyramids projected a myriad of pink spots which quivered on the ceiling.

'Beautiful stuff, rubies.'

'Yes, aren't they.'

'Don't freeze up on me, Charlie. I'm only doing my job. Same as you do.'

'Not quite the same. Tell me, Perotti, what do you want?'

'You in a hurry?'

'As a matter of fact I am. Rose is expecting me for lunch.'

'Oh well . . .'

'What do you mean?'

'Nothing. Nothing. Isn't she in Hong Kong visiting Roberta?'

'She got back last night. Come on. What do you want?'

'Look, Charlie, you know I like you a lot. I wish you were someone else. I wish I was someone else. But it's you and me sitting here and my people want in. We don't give a damn about the rubies and all that other stuff. All we want is the morphine and penicillin you've got. But we'll take the rest on board if it makes you happy. As I see it, you can stay in here and run this for us the way you've been doing it for yourself. Alternatively, you can stick around while we learn how you run things and then split. Either way I'll see to it you come out good.'

'And if I refuse?'

'Do you want me to spell it out for you?'

'Pray do.'

'Don't push me. You're a clever guy. I hate this kind of talk. I really do. I mean it . . .'

'Don't suffer on my account. Go on, tell me.'

'There will be trouble. At first, only little trouble. No more than the usual trouble you get when you run a business. The electricity will break down . . . the telephone. The water supply. Cars will blow up . . .'

'I thought you only heard that sort of thing watching what you call B movies.'

'I know, I know. I told you I hate this kind of talk. But if we don't do a deal it'll happen for real. You'll have problems.'

'I've lived with problems for years.'

'The difference is these little problems will never go away. Then there will be other problems, big problems like you wouldn't believe. And if you still feel like keeping us out there might have to be some eliminations.'

'You mean you're going to kill me?'

'No, Charlie boy. Not you. Not as long as I'm in charge. There are other people we could eliminate before we get to you. I'm asking you to be reasonable. If it was some other guy here with you you wouldn't be talking at all. Not all of our guys are reasonable. Like I said, it's lucky for you we're friends . . . Lucky for me too, but my people will not see it this way. If my people think I'm going soft there will be no talking at all. We'd both be out of it.'

'We are not in New York, Perotti. This is the real world. I know plenty of people here. You could have an accident 'yourself, you know.'

'Don't say it. Don't even think about it. I told you . . . I told you I'm not alone in this. I'm only an agent here. If you play funny with me my people will come after you forever. Maybe you know nothing about them, but dammit, Charlie, you must have heard they are big in the revenge department. It's a family business for Chrissakes. You hit one of them and the world's not big enough for you to hide in . . . You're better off dealing with me. Remember, remember always, it's nothing personal.'

'Yes, I know. It's business.'

'That's right.'

'I need more time.'

'You're playing games.'

'No. I really do need more time.'

'I'll give you a week.'

'Three months.'

'No way.'

'Four weeks.'

'You've got it.'

Charles got up. He did not take Perotti's stretched hand. The American looked at the table and the stones.

'You're leaving all this stuff here, just like that?'

'Once you are out of this room, Perotti, the stones are as safe as the Bank of England.'

'That wasn't nice.'

'What you're trying to do isn't nice either, Perotti.'

'Your business is not that different to ours, you know. You'll see. You should think about staying in, Charlie. You'd get on fine, you and my people. You'll do great.'

'If you'll excuse me, I'd better be going.'

'Give my best to Rose.'

# CHAPTER TWENTY-THREE

He looked at her and he smiled. She was wearing an elegant white dress which showed up the healthy colour of her skin. He had been looking forward to lunch. In some inexplicable way he had felt easy with her of late. She was laughing a lot, and that old confident posture of hers seemed firmly back. She now sat on the other side of the long table and he thought she looked ravishing.

'The tennis club is doing wonders for you.'

'Thank you, darling.'

'I hardly see you these days.'

'Absence makes the heart grow fonder.'

'How was Hong Kong?'

'The usual. Did some shopping.'

'How's Roberta?'

'Same as ever. We didn't fight. Any news here?'

'Had another letter from Sam.'

'Oh yes? What is it this time?'

'This and that.'

'Still hopes you'll come out to Jamaica?'

'Yes.'

'Don't you like it here any more?'

'Of course I do.'

'So why don't you just tell him no once and for all.'

'You never know, Rose. You must never burn any bridges.'

'What are you talking about?'

'Life isn't getting any simpler.'

'Surely you can do something about it.'

'I'm trying.'

'Why don't you sell out? We can all go back to England then.'

'That's what your friend Perotti says.'

'Makes a lot of sense to me.'

'Do you really think we could live in England again?'

'We can try, can't we? Didn't you say one can live every-where with money?'

'Yes. But I'm not sure we're going to be left with much.'

'Are we going bust?'

'I didn't say that. It's just that things are difficult.'

'Maybe you should talk to Vincent, Charles. He's got a good head. And he's got connections.'

'I bet he has.'

'You keep making snide remarks about him . . .'

'I'm sorry.'

'Don't apologize to me. He's your friend, not mine.'

'Yes. Do you want to leave, Rose?'

'I don't mind either way.'

'They say Jamaica is beautiful. Lifestyle's much like it is out here.'

'Whatever you say, Charles.'

'He's a wonderful chap, you know.'

'Who?'

'Sam.'

'I hardly know him. You kept him all to yourself that time.'

'Yes. I suppose I did. He needed me.'

'Of course he did.'

'You don't seem too keen on going.'

'Look. I'll go wherever and whenever you say, darling, but weren't we going to go back to England, ultimately? If we must live in the tropics we might as well stay here. You are forgetting Roberta's school, our friends, my friends . . . I mean, I thought you loved this country . . .'

'I do . . . You know I do . . . but things change. Things can become difficult . . .'

'What's the matter, Charles? . . . tell me.'

'I don't want to bother you with that.'

'Then don't. Just let me know where we are going and when.'

He detected a new distance in the way she answered him. There was a slight hardening in her eyes. Her face perhaps. Something. Could be she had not been listening to what he was saying. If only they could talk again . . . But it was late. She had her own life now. She was right, of course. Maybe he could turn the clock back. Tell her more. Confide in her more . . . But how could he?

'Would you like a little trip somewhere? A short holiday or something?'

'I've just come back . . . I have lots to do right now. I am on two committees, you know, and there's the tennis tournament . . .'

'Shall we stay in this afternoon?'

'Didn't you say your ruby people were here?'

'We're nearly finished.'

'Who is here?'

'U Nan and two others.'

'Last time that man was here you were out for three days . . . No more entertainment?'

'I can take them out tonight . . . I'm free until then.'

'I have to go out this afternoon. See what's in the shops . . . There's the Christmas Bazaar to think of. I am sorry.'

'Don't worry about it.'

He had forgotten how assertive she had become. He wasn't sure how much he liked her independence, but he knew it was good for her. There was nothing new about it. She had always been a resolute woman, except when they first came back from the island, and now she was herself again. But why did it take him by surprise? Perhaps he wasn't paying her enough attention. Perhaps he did not notice how her insecurity had gone. Was she rejecting him? Well, maybe she was, but then she was only giving him a tiny bit of his long rejection of her. He had always wanted her to find things to do. Occupy her mind. Well, now she was doing things and she had found contentment in whatever it was she was doing. In her new space there was no room for him. Served him right. What made her look so attractive all of a sudden? Was it because she was happy? But why did her happiness confuse him so? Because he wanted it all. Because he was an insensitive, selfish bastard, that was why.

It seemed she was finally settling down to life in Bangkok. Not just settling, but liking it here. Just now that things were heating up. He wasn't going to worry her with Perotti's latest war games. The less she knew the better. Perhaps he was just tired. Perhaps it was time to go. What Perotti had to say earlier could not be misunderstood. Yet, still, he could not help thinking the man was not all bad. The American was doing his job and he was in no position to judge him or anyone else. Perotti couldn't help talking the way he did. He was taking orders from other people and they were clearly pushing him. He was risking his own skin as it was, getting close to him and his family the way he did. Under different circumstances they could have been friends.

He was definitely confused. More than that. He must be going mad. Friends? The bastard was a killer. How could he contemplate such a thing? Even his Burmese friends saw through the man. The pressure must be getting to him.

He looked at his wife and he watched her read a London magazine with obvious interest. Her eyes lingered on the pages as she turned them at a slow pace. Lucky woman, he thought to himself. Prices of country houses and the latest fashion. Who won what race and who was the latest champion. Who married whom and where. Her eyes exuded contentment.

That was the world she wanted to belong to. Not Nappaporn's, not his. But was Nappaporn's world all there was in store for him from here on? While the war was on the adventures were young. There was excitement in the air. There were dangers. She was his love. Then she became his mistress and business partner. There were adventures still, but the excitement had gone. No. Not gone. He was just weary of it all. Is that why he was in need of Rose? Was he finally sampling the taste of fear? Maybe. No. Because he'd had his fill. He was ready for a change. Perhaps there was no room for Nappaporn in the next stage of his life. He was tired. He wanted a rest, but not on his own. There was something nagging him. There was something he had to do. A solution to a problem had always come to him in the past, and it had always brought that sweet elation of success. Like winning at the tables.

There must be another world out there, Charles Paget-Brown said to himself. A place where people met and talked and worked and bought and sold and then went peacefully home to their families. On their way they watched shop windows. A place where people meant what they said and what they said did not require immediate action. Where nothing was important enough to kill for. A slow, easy-going place where there was no need to look over your shoulder. Where there was no need to think too much. Where small things mattered. Flowers. The weather. Which car to drive. A world in which stupid little knick-knacks mattered. An uncomplicated world where the lines were clear. Where you could keep what you had sweated for. Where no one was ever after something that was not his. A world which most people were supposed to be living in.

Bullshit. If such a world existed it wouldn't be for him. He was too far gone. He would never last there. Not in this life, nor the next.

His life was a drug. He was an addict.

But what if he took a break? A pause long enough to recover from this burning need of his. The ever-growing need for stimulation that could only be appeased by excitement.

Yes, but first there were things to do. And if no help was forthcoming, he'd solve things as he'd done before. All by himself.

He looked at his wife, so far across the long table, and suddenly it occurred to him that his constant fight against boredom was leading him into loneliness.

The servant brought lunch.

# CHAPTER TWENTY-FOUR

■

I saw him come out of the lobby below my verandah and walk towards the river. He was, as always, self-assured and elegant and handsome, and as he crossed the terrace people greeted him with demonstrative affection. He held a large suitcase in his hand, and they made a fuss of him. Twice I saw him refuse help from one of the waiters who offered to carry it for him. This man had it all and was genuinely loved by everybody, and though I always had a kind of complex about him, I felt I was pulling all the strings. He was like a fish caught in a tiny bowl. He could swim in all directions, but he'd never get anywhere. He could never win with us and I figured he would fight for what was his, and I knew it would all be for nothing. I had told him often how I wished we were not on opposite sides of the fence, and I meant it.

That day Charlie had asked me to give him time and I had settled for four weeks. But as soon as I came back to the Oriental Hotel to wait for Charlie's wife there was a cable from New York. The message from the family was as clear as a bell. I had horsed around long enough. I had been spending a fortune and there was nothing to show for it. The Orient deal had been my deal and I wasn't coming through. I didn't have no four weeks. They wanted action now or the whole deal was off. There was plenty of action to keep me busy right in New York.

A week before, I had summoned Paco the Filipino from Hong Kong. He was on his way, and I hoped he wouldn't turn up just then, with Charlie in the area. I had asked him to keep his boat far down the river and find a discreet way of coming into town. It was time for me to act, and I could count on Paco to do the dirty work for me.

The river was calm, and Charlie got to the long pontoon and boarded his boat. He could have been going to see his woman Nappaporn, or maybe he was going somewhere else. He did not seem relaxed, and there had been much energy and purpose in the way he had walked. No man goes to see his woman in that state. Maybe he was about to skip town. Maybe he was going to some sort of a business meeting with people we did not know of. Maybe he was going to see the Burmese I had seen in his office earlier in the day. They were living in a little house his Thai woman had near hers.

He sat erect like a king at the front of the long boat, and it took off upstream. It didn't matter where he was going. Where he went we went. Nappaporn's house was watched, and my men would catch up with him before long. One of the waiters waved at him. Charlie didn't look up. He didn't look anywhere. He didn't see me, but I know he was thinking of me. Thinking so hard I could have been sitting right there with him. The ring of confidence he was hiding in was becoming his noose. His class and his easy manner and his lifestyle were far from my reach, yet that afternoon, as I saw him float by, I felt no jealousy at all. The thought of his wife lying in my bed right then, right there behind the shutters, made me stretch with the pleasure of expectation. A guy should never knock youth. Life was good in those days.

She always made me wait outside the room while she undressed. She was, for all her strength of character, a shy woman, and never allowed me to see her in the nude. I stood there on the verandah and I thought of every delicious detail of her. Every bit of cotton as she peeled it off. Of the shower she would take and the quick strokes of the towel that would touch her body before she crawled into the sheets. I had known since early morning she was coming to see me, and knowing that had made me feel strong and generous during my visit to Charlie's office earlier.

I heard her knock on the shutters, and I knew she was ready for me. I lingered a little longer outside to give her a chance to get back into bed. Then I walked in.

She was, as always, a sight. Over the last few months, right under my nose, she had become a radiant beauty. The way women sometimes do when they're happy. Of course, she wasn't in love with me, but I knew I had made her feel good. Yes, fat little me, Vincent Perotti, the ex-nobody, was beating the great Charles Paget-Brown in his own back yard. It couldn't last. I knew that. But while it did I was living on top of the world.

I opened the shutters and walked in. The room was cool and dark, and I could make out her shape in the large bed. I pulled my silk kimono off and came closer. No words passed between us. She stretched her hand and touched mine. Her fingers felt hot. I climbed inside and I felt her strong, long body arch towards me. Her legs arrested mine and I felt the moist brush of her rub my skin and, cool as I tried to remain, the flame ate me alive. I sucked under her arms and tasted the soap, and her fingers tore at my back. I tried to kiss her but she wanted none of that. She was an impatient lover, and her shyness exploded into loud groans as soon as she touched me there and made me slip into her.

I was plunging into a city of pleasure. The buildings and the streets and the sidewalks were hot with sweat and desire. It was a place where nothing mattered except this woman who belonged to another but whose body was hungry for me alone. I was moving like the wind, and my usual breath-lessness was gone as if by magic. She gyrated and she moaned and she yelled things and all the while I thought of my forth-coming victory. He was a better man than me, but I was beating the shit out of him on every front he owned. A strange sensation of power came over me, and I felt secure and strong and so relaxed I could have gone on forever.

But she couldn't. Soon I felt her body approach the end of the road. Her movements became shorter and faster, and then she grabbed hold of my lower back and her teeth sank into my shoulder, and with the pain of it I heard her scream before her final explosion came up at me, and then she went limp and the room assumed the silence. You could hear nothing but the ceiling fan cutting the air. Then we started talk-ing. She did. She never mentioned Charlie by name, but it was him she was talking about. Her voice was steady and she sat up, straightened her hair, and covered herself before she switched the side light on.

'There's something wrong with him. I noticed it at lunch.'

'You think he suspects something?'

'Not at all. Nothing like that. He keeps talking about closing the business and getting out.'

'No kidding.'

'No kidding.'

'Why? Are things difficult?'

'So he says. I don't know. I suppose I should have asked, but I was in too much of a hurry.'

'To do what?'

'To come here. I'll ask him tonight, if he gets in early enough. There's something on his mind . . . I have no idea what. He tried to tell me but I didn't encourage him. I was selfish.'

'Everyone is selfish sometimes . . . You can be too . . . you're entitled. He wasn't always . . .'

'I know, I know,' she said, 'but if I didn't know him better I would have said he was afraid of something . . .'

'Charlie afraid? You're kidding me. Afraid of what?'

'I don't know. Maybe not afraid, maybe just nervous. For the first time in years he made me feel he needed me. And I let him down.'

'What d'you mean?'

'He wanted me to stay with him . . . He needed help. I know he did.'

'It will all be over by tonight.'

'I hope so. You know, I thought he was doing fine . . . I mean, our life hasn't changed. He hasn't said anything before. I have been spending money like mad . . . I wish he'd come out with it.'

'Must be business,' I said.

'I expect so.'

'If there's anything I can do, just whistle . . .'

'You're a darling, Vincent. You're a tower of strength. I don't know where I'd be without you.'

I knew damn well where she'd be, but I didn't say.

I was a lion that afternoon.

# CHAPTER TWENTY-FIVE

My Mister Charlie came in this afternoon unannounced. His three Burmese friends came to the house, and I gave them a meal of steamed rice and fish and fried noodles and more of the rice that is cooked with sugar and coconut, the way they cook it in Burma. They are staying at a small house Mister Charlie bought for me three years ago, just across the garden, between my house and the temple.

When Mister Charlie's driver brought them in for a late lunch they seemed contented. Their hair was still wet, and I knew they had been to a house of women. I did not ask if my Mister Charlie had gone with them because I know he would not. His Farang woman had just come back from visiting his other daughter in Hong Kong, and I knew he would spend time with her. He is a good and considerate man, and I am a blessed woman.

The Burmese U Nan and his friends came in and had their meal and then we spoke. We did not speak for a long time because they were sleepy with the pleasuring and the food they had had. But we did speak, because they were worried. They told me about a visit they had in Mister Charlie's office earlier. They said a Farang man burst into the office just as they were looking at rubies. Everyone knows that looking at precious stones is an exacting occupation and people must not be disturbed while they do it. They said the Farang was an American whose name they did not remember but whose face and effect on Mister Charlie were hard to forget. These were difficult days for the ruby-traders. Prices were going up and crossing the border was becoming difficult. There was stiff competition for goods. In their village people were beginning to wonder why they were selling goods to Mister Charlie for less than their worth. They were looking at the stones when the Farang came in. They were discussing the future of the trade. There were important decisions to be made just then, but Mister Charlie stopped the discussions dead. He would never have brought a meeting of such importance to an end. It was clear, they told me, that Mister Charlie was much disturbed by this man. Maybe even a little afraid of him.

I know my Mister Charlie is not afraid of anyone, but I did not say. The lady of the house must never contradict a guest enjoying hospitality at her table. They said they were going to speak to Mister Charlie about it. If necessary they would cut the man's throat and throw him to the sharks, they said. They would get a fishing boat to take him down the river to the sea and do it there. And I said if Mister Charlie was in danger they could count on my help. I said I would prefer to find out more about the man before anyone acted in haste. I was living in this town and I knew many people and I could find out. Perhaps we were wrong, I said. Perhaps the Farang was just a businessman with whom Mister Charlie had had a misunderstanding. I knew they did not think that, but a guest can sometimes be a prisoner of the host. They agreed to wait until I had spoken to my friends. They said they had great respect for me, and they said they would do anything for Mister Charlie, and then they went over to the little house to sleep the food off. I took a very short nap while the maid cleaned up. I knew I would not sleep because my mind was disturbed with what I had heard.

Of course, I had known about the car outside and the boat that sped past the bottom of my garden whenever Mister Charlie came to see me. But now that I had heard of the Farang I decided I would find out who he was. Perhaps he was the man who had sent the car to spy on me out there, under the tamarind tree. All manner of fears came to my mind, and I tossed and turned while the maid walked about the house. Then I heard her put her street sandals on to go out for my daughter, and I got up. I washed my face and went outside to sit on the porch and wait for Nalini. I know she hates seeing me there, but I did it all the same. With me I took a Farang picture-book Mister Charlie had left in the house long ago. It was a colour picture-book of pictures that were painted by an English Farang in England many years before. Mister Charlie loved looking at it and explaining to me where the scenes were. It showed the countryside of England and many sunsets and castles and lakes and forests. It was a beautiful book which had always calmed me down. I sat there on the porch and looked and then I saw him.

He came up from the riverside garden, dressed in an office suit and shoes. In his hands he carried a very big travelling suitcase. He walked fast. He must have come by boat because I did not hear his car. It was the first time my Mister Charlie had come to my house from the river, and that in itself should have told me something was different. He told me long ago that the riverside was my kingdom, and that he would never step on it unless we were together. I got up to run towards him, but he held his hand in the air as if to stop me, and I sat down again and waited. I knew something unusual was happening to him because he started speaking without greeting me.

'Ask our Burmese visitors to come across,' he said. His voice was calm, but there was some difference. The travelling suitcase could have meant he was going somewhere. And if he was he would have told me. He wore the wrong clothes and came from the wrong side and his voice was hurried. He knew his guests had only just gone for their rest, and yet he called for them. I had seen my Mister Charlie in difficult waters before, but I had never seen him confused. In all the times we had together with the Japanese and the war he never forgot to greet me, and his voice always sang with affection. I knew a storm was brewing behind his eyes.

I ran across the garden and on my way I saw that other car parked under the tamarind tree. I had gotten used to seeing it there and paid little attention, but something inside of me said my Mister Charlie's situation had something to do with the owners of the car. The Burmese came out as soon as I knocked on the door, as if they were expecting to be disturbed. I told them about the other car and they understood, and we all walked back to my house very slowly, as if on a country stroll.

When we got to the porch we saw him sitting on the steps. He was smoking a long Burmese cigar, and he looked at me and then at the others.

'Shall we go inside?'

'No,' my Mister Charlie snapped. 'We talk out here.'

'Every question has an answer,' U Nan the Burmese said. He was a large man who had been our friend for many years and had known my family even before I knew my Mister Charlie. 'The ship sails better on calm waters.'

'Quite right,' my Mister Charlie said, and then he turned to me and his lips smiled at me while his eyes said he was sorry. I made out nothing was wrong. A woman must not make a man feel guilty when he is down.

They all walked down and they sat by the river bank. They were talking, and I brought them some tea. When Nalini came home with the maid she saw them. She made no move and did not ask what they were doing there. I thought how much better Mister Charlie would feel if he had the love of his daughter to protect him along with mine. If he had a real family to nest in. But it was the wrong time to think about that. I had other things to do.

The Lord God Buddha never leaves me. He makes things happen just when they are needed. Only this morning some useful information came my way. My friend at the fish market told me Paco the Filipino's boat was sighted off the coast again. She was an old steamer that had sailed these parts for more than twenty years, and everyone knew who owned her. I had no idea why Paco was coming to Thailand. I was sure he was coming to see Mister Charlie, but he did not say and I did not ask. This time I was going to do something on my own. I had been planning to approach him for some time.

To ask him about the car that was always parked outside my house, under the tamarind tree across the road. To ask him about the fast boats that fly past my garden every time Mister Charlie is in my house or about to come to me. I have known Paco for many years and now, having seen my Mister Charlie the way he was today, I know I have little time left. I had made my mind up to send him a message to contact me as soon as he came to town. I have to ask him for his help. He will know who that Farang was and what he wanted with my Mister Charlie. He will know because Paco the Filipino knows all the Farang Mister Charlie has business with. He will know how best to appease him and how much to pay him and, if it is too late for that, he will know how to deal with him.

The way things are now, Paco is the only man I can trust.

I looked down at the riverside and I saw my Mister Charlie and the three Burmese. They were talking. Their conversation was animated, and Mister Charlie seemed to be explaining things. I saw the cigar smoke surrounding his head as he listened. Perhaps the Burmese were right. Perhaps he did have something to fear.

I greeted my daughter Nellie. This time she did not scold me for sitting by the porch. She looked towards the river one more time to see her father, and then she went inside for her meal.

No one will be missing me for now. I shall cross the garden into the other house. From there I shall walk down the road and find a cab to take me to the fish market. I have friends there, and some of them will know where Paco the Filipino is. I have to speak to him before tomorrow breaks.

# CHAPTER TWENTY-SIX

·

'Did you enjoy your visit to the house of pleasure?'

The three Burmese looked at him. From the corner of their eyes came a bemused expression of surprise.

'Did I say something wrong?'

'No, Mister Charlie, you did not. It's only your timing that is wrong. You know where we have been this day and you knew we would be sleeping now, yet you have burst into the house from the river. Your face is not your face. You are fully dressed. You are carrying a large suitcase; are you travelling anywhere? You didn't say you were.'

'I am not travelling anywhere.'

'Why the suitcase?'

'I'll come to that soon. I am truly sorry to have disturbed you.'

'You have no need to apologize to us. You did not come all the way here to tear us away from an afternoon rest to discuss pleasantries.'

'No. I did not.'

'We go back a long time, Mister Charlie. What did you come for?'

'I want you to take this suitcase for me.'

'What is in it?'

'Your rubies.'

'Are you not going to buy this time?'

'Of course I'm buying. I'm buying it all. In the suitcase you will find payment in full. American dollars and English pounds and gold sovereigns.'

'We did not agree a price yet.'

'I am paying you market price. It is a little more than it was last time.'

'We did not ask for an increase.'

'Nappaporn has told me what the situation is. She has talked to you about prices.'

'Yes. But nothing was agreed. We have been friends for

a long time. You must make profits too.'

'I shall. I have paid you a fair price. When you get back to the house you can count it and you will see it is all in order.'

'Then why are you returning the stones?'

'I am not returning them. I want you to keep them safely for me. I want them out of the office for a few days.'

'You do not have to pay until you have taken delivery. This is not the custom.'

'I have taken delivery. The money in the case is yours. The rubies are mine. I'm only asking you to keep them for me until I find a place. I'm working on it now. I'll take them back long before you leave this country.'

'We haven't finished sorting the stones out . . .'

'I have decided to take the whole lot. You will find the payment covers everything.'

'You need not have said that, Mister Charlie.'

'I am sorry. Of course not.'

'We have been friends for a long time, yes?'

'Of course we have.'

'We have been in the war together and have faced many dangers.'

'Of course we have.'

'Then why don't you trust us?'

'Of course I trust you. I know the rubies are good.'

'I don't mean the rubies. I mean the man who came to see you today.'

'Vincent Perotti?'

'Yes. That was his name, I think.'

'That man and his visit has nothing to do with you. He wants nothing of yours.'

'Is he the reason your office is no longer safe?'

'Yes, but this is only a precaution.'

'Has he threatened you?'

'Yes.'

'Your property or your life?'

'My property. My life is not in danger now.'

'Better to silence him before it's too late.'

'He is not alone.'

'You are not alone.'

'You don't understand. This man is very powerful.'

'We can help you.'

'You cannot. No one can. I have to deal with this myself.'

'No man is that powerful outside his own land.'

'Do you trust me?'

'You need not ask that. Of course we do, Mister Charlie.'

'Then listen to me. There is nothing we can do now. I am going to work something out. I'll let you know if I need you.'

'I am not sure your judgement is right.'

'What makes you say that?'

'You seem changed. You have never acted like this before. You have taught me to always hit the enemy before they get near you. This lesson saved my life many times during the war. We remember that well. Our families, everyone in our village remembers that.'

'This is another situation. Another enemy. Far away and all-powerful and endless.'

'No man is all-powerful and endless. Only the Lord Buddha is.'

'I didn't mean it like that. This man is not alone. He belongs to a group of people who, like an octopus, have long arms that spread far; they reach all over the world. They control companies, police forces, politicians . . .'

'There is nothing new about that. There are octopus people in our country too . . . In our country you can talk to them and sometimes pay and if you can't, you deal with them. They are only people . . . men like you and us . . . You must never allow people like that to walk over you . . . You must do something.'

'We can't act in haste this time,' Charles said. 'I'll tell you when I need you.'

'You promise?'

'I promise.'

'This will be like the old days.'

'Perhaps. Please keep Nappaporn out of this.'

'You underestimate Nappaporn, Mister Charlie. She knows something is wrong. If I were you I would talk this over with her . . .'

'If I did that she would worry.'

'I told you we feel she suspects something is wrong. She did not say anything, but she is close to you, and anyone who knows you, Mister Charlie, would suspect it. Forgive me for saying it, but you seem confused. You fly like a bird left alone over a desert. I have known Nappaporn before you met her. I have known her when she was a young girl living with her father in Pataya. She has a strong mind, and if she knows something she will worry, and if you do not talk to her about it she will act on her own. You know she will.'

'That would be dangerous.'

'That is why you must talk to her about it.'

The big U Nan looked towards the house and his hand pointed. They all looked, and they saw Nappaporn walk across the garden towards the house they had slept in. She walked very slowly, and in her hand she carried a basket of fruits. All four men smiled, and then one said:

'Nappaporn makes sure we never go hungry. There is much food in the house. I will come back home a fat man. You are blessed, Mister Charlie.'

'The Lord God Buddha smiled down at you when you met her,' said another.

The roar of an engine sliced into their conversation. A long, narrow boat flew past, then turned about and stopped dead mid-river, facing them. Two men sat in front. The engine idled and the boat rolled as it faced the strong tide. One of the men got up, his arms gesticulating as he tried to steady himself. He then grabbed the other's shoulder and a pair of binoculars appeared in his free hand, and he watched them. The afternoon sun fired bright flashes of light off the lenses. He watched them for a few moments, and then he sat down. The engine revved and the boat shot off and soon disappeared upriver.

'Someone is following you, Mister Charlie,' U Nan said. 'You have many friends in this town. You may have enemies.'

'I don't believe I have.'

'What about the American?'

'He is not from this town.'

'He lives here now.'

'He stays in a hotel. He does not live here.'

'Where did you meet him?'

'I was introduced to him by a close friend. He is a Filipino. You know him well. I am speaking of Paco. Paco the Filipino. We go back a very long time. We were partners before the war.'

'I remember him well,' U Nan said. 'He betrayed you that time in Pataya.'

'You are mistaken. It was a misunderstanding. He's a good and trusted friend.'

'Why would a good and trusted friend introduce you to an enemy?'

'He did not know. He thought the American was interested in doing business with me.'

'You trust this man, this Paco?'

'I do,' said Charles. 'Totally. You may ask Nappaporn about him. She trusts him too.'

'Maybe you should meet this man soon. Ask him for advice. He introduced you to the American. He should help you cut yourself away from him.'

'I told you he didn't know where this would lead. Paco has introduced me to many people. I still work with them today.'

'You should still talk to him.'

'I intend to. I have tried to locate him over my radio but he is not in Manila. His wife says he's at sea.'

'He could be in Hong Kong.'

'He talks to his wife every day. He knows I am looking for him. He will contact me soon.'

'How can he do that?' asked U Nan.

'He has the latest radio equipment on board his ship. I installed it there myself.'

'Then why don't you call him on his boat?'

'I have tried. Something must be wrong with it. I cannot raise him. But he will call me. I am going back to my office, and then I shall go to my house. I will wait for Paco to make contact with me. I am sure he will talk to me today or tomorrow. I shall keep trying to get him until I succeed. He might even be on his way to Bangkok. If he is, I shall try and get him to take the rubies on board his ship and out of the country. I shall send word to you about tonight. I must go now. Please take the suitcase and wait for my message in the house. You need the rest.'

The large Burmese took the case. Charles walked towards the river and waved at his boat. The engine came to life as he approached the bank. U Nan stood there and his eyes followed his friend. Charles boarded the long boat and waved. U Nan lifted his enormous hand and waved back as the other two exchanged a silent glance of doubt.

# CHAPTER TWENTY-SEVEN

■

I knew he was coming because I had ordered him to get his ass into town, but I never expected the bastard to turn up that quick. He knocked on my door within minutes of Rose leaving. These two did not get on, and though he was on our payroll I didn't want him to see her walk out of my room. You could never be sure what that shit would do with such information, especially when the reason for my wanting him in Bangkok was to get at Charlie. He stood there, his oversized shiny jacket hung over him like a half-empty sack of potatoes, his tie full of fading colour, like ice-cream melting in the sun. His teeth shone with that disgusting smile, and a ton of ash dropped from his eternal big cigar and fell straight onto the expensive carpet.

'Why didn't you call from the lobby?' I asked.

'What you mean?'

'You could have let me know you were here.'

'You know I come. You tell me come. I come.'

'Let me get dressed. Sit down and pour yourself a drink.'

'No time. We move now.'

'What the hell do you mean, no time? I decide when we move.'

'Mister Charlie's woman, Nappaporn, she know me here in Bangkok.'

'You sure?'

'If she no know now she know in one hour.'

'How come?'

'She friends all over fish market. All over river. I take water cab and I see many her friends on way. They see me. She want see me. She send me message long time.'

'What does she want to see you for?'

'Me no know, Mister Vincent. Think she want talk. Me no know what. And more problem. Mister Charlie, he want see me too. He want see me bad quick. He call my wife many time by radio. Also Mister Charlie call ship by radio, but my captain he pretend radio broke.'

'You can keep them waiting a few more days, can't you?'

'No secret on this river. No secret this town. No secret for Nappaporn. Her friends find me and then I must see her. I must talk to her.'

'Why?'

'Custom among friend, Mister Vincent. She know I in town. If I no go see her and talk to her she know something wrong. Then she tell Mister Charlie, then he know something wrong. We have no time, Mister Vincent. Can kill Mister Charlie quick quick. No more problem. You take business. I teach you how do business after people stop cry for Mister Charlie. Like we say.'

'Shit.'

'Yes, shit. Big shit, Mister Vincent. Number-one big shit.'

The taste of Rose was still with me. All over me. I knew I wasn't thinking good. I needed time to cool down. To think of what he had said. Work out how to use his rabid hatred of Charlie without hurting the limey too bad. I showed him the chair and went into the bedroom to put some clothes on. When I came out he had made himself at home with my bottle of scotch. The room was full of the white smoke of his half-chewed, stinking cigar. I went to the window and I opened it.

'We kill Mister Charlie today. . .before his woman tell him. . . before he find our plan. Your people can do?'

'Do what?'

'Kill Mister Charlie, Mister Vincent.'

'Who said anything about killing Charlie?'

'We said, remember? That time in Hong Kong when you go my ship.'

'Take it easy, will you, Paco? I need to think.'

'Better no think too long time, Mister Vincent. Better do.'

'Did anyone see you at reception?'

'You drunk, Mister Vincent. I already tell you. No one see me, sure. If I call you from lobby they see me and they talk about me. In one hour all town know I am here. Nappaporn know. Charlie know . . . No, I no call. I come straight up. Now we hurry kill Charlie like we said.'

'I didn't say that. I said I'd think about it.'

'You afraid of Mister Charlie?'

'No. We must do something else first.'

'What for?'

'We give him a big scare first. He'll play.'

'What you mean?'

'He'll give in. He'll let us have the whole goddamned business. No blood.'

'You no know Mister Charlie. He never leave. He no let you take nothing. I see Mister Charlie in war. You take no blood you get nothing.'

'Charlie's not the same man. He's older. He's got more to lose. We can get at him without killing him.'

'What you want we do?'

'We take his daughter.'

'His daughter go school Hong Kong.'

'Don't play smartass, Paco. Not that one. The other one. Nappaporn's daughter.'

'I no good for that. Your people must take her. I no get near her. Her mother know me. She know me too.'

'The girl knows you well?'

'Sure. She know me from time she little child.'

'That's great. If she knows you she'll go with you no questions asked.'

'You no think good today, Mister Vincent. If her friends see me near daughter and know I never go see Nappaporn first they understand something wrong. If daughter no come home they know and they find me and they kill me. Nappaporn know all people on this river. They kill me before I touch daughter . . . before even see daughter. You want kill Nappaporn daughter?'

'No. Take her, not kill her.'

'Double no good me do it. If she go with me and stay alive I am dead for business, Mister Vincent. Soon after she go home and she talk. Mister Charlie never trust me after. No one trust me. All plan dead.'

'You never wanted to take the girl. You said Charlie didn't care for her.'

'Is true. I tell you before but you never believe.'

'No, I don't.'

'Then you take girl. You waste time. You see. Where is Mister Charlie?'

'He's here in town. He's got visitors. Looks like he might be going somewhere.'

'You say Mister Charlie have visitors?'

'Yes.'

'You no say who. You know who?'

'Yes. Three Burmese ruby-dealers.'

'You see them?'

'Yeah, I saw them.'

'Where you see them?'

'I saw them in Charlie's office. I was there this morning. Don't ask me how I know they are ruby-dealers. I'll tell you how I know. They were sorting them out when I came in.'

'He let you come office when looking rubies?'

'I didn't ask. I came in the door.'

'You make Mister Charlie nervous?'

'Yeah. I did.'

'The Burmese . . . one man big like giant?'

'That's them. You know them?'

'I know U Nan but never meet other Burmese. Only hear them from Mister Charlie. Mister Charlie likes talk about old friends. He talk many hours when he like them. He talk so much you know them even if never see them. No, he never go when Burmese in town.'

'He's a good friend to have, our Charlie. U Nan is a lucky guy.'

'Lucky but no good. Bad man U Nan. He no like me.'

'Why not?'

'He think I friend Japanese in war.'

'Were you?'

'Never, Mister Vincent. I fight Japanese same same you.'

'I don't care about that now. I tell you, though, Charlie's quitting town.'

'Mister Charlie never go no place. Never leave visitors. He stays with U Nan. They are old friends. From wartime. He stay.'

'This afternoon he took a boat downriver. He was dressed up and packed. He had a big travelling suitcase on him. He could be going somewhere.'

'Mister Charlie no go. Suitcase is full of money. Maybe rubies.'

'I don't understand.'

'Mister Charlie number-one clever. He plan something. You say you come in office. You see rubies. He think you want rubies. He takes rubies out of office, put them somewhere else. He know something is wrong.'

'Of course he does. He don't need to suspect me. He knows I'm after his business.'

'Number-one important you find out where Mister Charlie put case. You can find out?'

'Yeah. I can find out.'

'You find out quick quick. You think Nappaporn tell Mister Charlie I'm here?'

'Nappaporn has left the house. Charlie is there with the Burmese. Alone.'

'Where Nappaporn go?'

'To the fish market. That's where she goes every day. She's in the fish business.'

'Fish market? In afternoon, Mister Vincent? No business in fish market in afternoon. If she go to fish market in afternoon already too late. This morning she know my ship is here. Now she know more. Maybe she know where I go. I told you, she ask everyone to find me. She want talk to me. Captain of my ship know she want to see me.'

'What she want you for?'

'I tell you already I no know.'

'You better keep yourself in hiding until we find out.'

'Maybe better I get out before she see me. Send message had to get out quick quick.'

'Are you scared of Nappaporn?'

'Nappaporn number-one big shot on this river. This river stomach of town. People wash themselves in river, wash clothes and take water and people talk by river. She know many people, I tell you. Small policemen, everybody. No. Not scared of Nappaporn, just careful. If she never see me this time she believe I had to get out and no problem with Mister Charlie. She never talk about me to him before she talk to me.'

'How do you know?'

'She Oriental woman. I Oriental man. I know her. She never talk to Mister Charlie because if she no see me she have no facts. Oriental woman talk only facts.'

'Nappaporn screws Charlie. She is his woman. His lover. She'll talk to him anyway.'

'You no know nothing, Mister Vincent. Nappaporn Oriental woman. They no jump with panic. She find fact first. Oriental woman never worry man for nothing.'

'Maybe you're right. Maybe I'll have to think of something else.'

I wasn't sure what it was I was going to do, and I wasn't going to tell him anyway. I wasn't sure whose side he was on when I wasn't around. I was going to give him a little fright, threaten him and tell him to watch his step, but the telephone rang. It was my man. He said Charlie had taken the boat back. He was coming upriver. He said I should see him out my window any minute now.

'Charlie's on the road again,' I said.

Paco recoiled. His face went pale.

'You think he come here? Come see you here?'

'Maybe he does and maybe he doesn't.'

'If he see me here . . .'

'He don't see you here. If he wants to see me he'll call first. Anyway, he's never been up here. He don't come up. We meet downstairs. Anyway, what you so scared about? He can see you here. He knows we do business. You introduced us, remember?'

'I know him longer than you. If he see me here he ask why I no call him first.'

I walked towards the window and pulled the curtain slightly and looked out. The river was aflame with the mid-afternoon sun. The thick glass absorbed all the sounds and the boats moved up and down the glittering water like in a silent movie. Paco took another drink. The pig could take his booze better than any man I knew. The cigar stank to high heaven. I looked out again and then I saw him.

The long boat approached the hotel's pontoon. Charlie got up and I saw him peel a note out of his wad and pay the man. I saw him clearly. He swiped his hair off his brow and put a foot out. He seemed so close I took a step back. Two waiters came towards him, but Charlie smiled at them and jumped onto the broadwalk like an athlete. He straightened his tie and his jacket and walked away. He was definitely in a hurry. He raced on under my verandah and disappeared into the hotel. If he was going to call me he would do it soon.

Paco's foul-smelling breath came flying into the back of my neck.

'Have no suitcase,' he said. The sonovabitch was right. Charlie came off the boat empty-handed.

'Yeah. What d'you think he's done with it?'

'He left with Burmese. You see, he no go no place.'

'Well, now you know.'

'What you mean?'

'Now you know where the suitcase is. What's the big deal about it? . . . Now you know. Now what?'

'Now I leave. I go my boat. I tell my captain put radio in order. You bet Mister Charlie call there again. Captain will answer him. That is good. Then I arrange everything.'

'What the hell are you saying? I don't understand you. You'll arrange something? You'll arrange what?'

'Never mind. You never understand Orient, Mister Vincent. You need me explain you someday. Or Mister Charlie explain you. He know Orient like Oriental. I go now, but before I leave country I see you one time more. You let me and you see I can do for you too. I do good for you before I leave. I make you see I work your side. Loyal only to you. I do something good for you. Something number-one big. After all quiet I come back. I work Mister Charlie business with you.'

'What's on your mind?'

'What you mean?'

'What are you going to do for me?'

'You want hurt Charlie, Mister Vincent, yes?'

'Yes. But I don't want him touched.'

'I fix. You see.'

'Paco, don't you do anything to Charlie, you understand? You touch a hair on his head and you're a dead duck. Your wife and your children too.'

'I no touch Mister Charlie. I hurt him bad, but no touch him.'

'How?'

'Leave to my hand.'

'I'll send one of my men with you to make sure.'

'He have car?'

'Yes. He's got a car. And he's coming with you.'

'You no trust me?'

'You're damn right I don't trust you. You fuck with me and your ship will fly.'

'What you mean?'

'You'll soon know what I mean.'

I picked the phone up and called my man. I told him to make sure there was enough stuff attached alongside Paco's ship to blow it out of the river if something went wrong. I said it real slow and I watched Paco's face. I didn't trust the guy at all. I didn't believe the bit about Charlie's half-caste daughter. There was something up the bastard's sleeve, and I was going to keep him in fear until I found out for myself. I picked the phone up again and I dictated a cable to Manila. I instructed my guy there to get into position outside Paco's house. Kill his wife as soon as the signal was given. The cable was in code, but I made sure the Filipino understood what it meant. His expression said he did. I wasn't taking any chances with him. I wasn't going to let him loose on Charlie. I wasn't going to let him out of my sight until everything was in place. In this business you've got to make sure everything's in place before you act. That's how you survive.

It was maybe a half-hour later that my man called from

the lobby to say he was waiting. Paco got up. He asked me to tell my man to pick him up a little way down the road, by the customs house. When he got to the door he looked at me one last time and he smiled.

'You better remember what I said, Paco. Nobody touches Charlie.'

'You wait here for me, Mister Vincent. You no move before I come back.'

# CHAPTER TWENTY-EIGHT

At the fish market they told me the Filipino was in town. He did not sail his ship all the way into the river. I know that because I had sent word to his captain and word came back Paco was not on board. In the afternoon he hired a river cab, but the captain could not say where. He could not say when he would be back. But soon my friends will tell me which one of the cabs it was. My friends know everyone along the river, and as soon as we find out whose cab it was we shall know where Paco the Filipino was taken. It is best for me to be on the spot when the information comes.

There is not much a woman in my position can do in the fish market in the late afternoon. I am a boat-owner, and by then all the night catch has been sold and all the money has changed hands. In these uncertain days many people take their paper money to the gold-shops in Chinatown to trade notes for metal. I have no business in the fish market at that time. Not even to see my own fishermen, because they are either repairing their nets or tending the boats, or they go home to sleep.

I have known the dealers in the fish market ever since I arrived in Bangkok. Even before Mister Charlie bought the fishing boats for me I knew them. I used to go there because my grandfather was a fisherman, and although my family had lived on the coast at Pataya we have many relatives in Bangkok. Most of them are still in the fish business.

The Lord God Buddha has blessed my country with long coastlines and wide rivers and our fish are plentiful. There are many types of fish, from the largest sharks to the smallest sardines. There are shrimps and lobsters and crab, and there are many fishing villages along the rivers and the coast. Of course, Siam is rich with rice and fruits and vegetables too. It has always been a country where food is available in plenty. No one need go hungry if they are healthy and are willing to work.

My father has traded the life of a fisherman for that of business, because he is a talented man. In his youth he travelled the South China Sea as a deckhand on board a Japanese cargo vessel. He learned about trade there, and he learned to master the English language. My brother too spoke that language, but I was a little girl and no one thought of teaching it to me. The Lord God Buddha must be smiling because I now have a daughter who knows English better than my father and my brother combined. But then she is half Farang and, above all, she goes to the American school where they teach in that language. She speaks it, and I know the way she speaks it is very different to her father. When he is in the house, and when she is there too, she speaks nothing but Thai.

Word of mouth floats fast along the river. By the time I reached the fish market everyone knew that I had come to hear news of Paco the Filipino. I made certain people would talk about it to each other, so that with the rumours Paco was sure to find out I was seeking him. I know he will contact me as soon as he can, and I hope he will do so before he sees my Mister Charlie. My effort will bear no fruit if he does that, because Mister Charlie will not believe he has enemies and will not know anyone is threatening him. He is a good and kind man, and he believes all people are like him. I have never seen Mister Charlie get angry at anyone. Not even during the war when he was forced to shoot to survive.

I gave the maid extra money before I left so that she may take Nellie to see a film. There is nothing Nellie likes better than watching films. I don't know why. Maybe the stories on the screen take her to faraway Farang lands. Mister Charlie, when he was young, read books of such places. This is how he left his country to come here. Maybe Nellie is like him.

I said they could stay out late. Until seven o'clock in the evening, provided my daughter completes every bit of her schoolwork. When I left the house she was already hard at it, and she was excited about going out on the town. Generally speaking there are no problems with Nellie and her work, and she sits down to it as soon as she comes home. Nellie is a very ambitious young girl, and I know she cannot wait to get out of school and start her life. I don't know what sort of a life she wants. She never talks to me about her plans. Sometimes I feel she does not wish to include me in her future. Her bitterness about me and my love for her father is strong because she thinks me his servant, but she will understand when she becomes a woman. And yet it is her father's people she wants to belong to.

She has no Thai friends at all. When she was a little girl I used to send her to Pataya to be with the children of my aunt. I preferred to stay in my house in case Mister Charlie came to see me. In those days he came to me almost every day. When Nellie learned to speak and understand more of my life she changed. She refused to go to the coast and insisted on spending her holidays in the house with me. After she started to go to the American school she began to avoid meeting members of my family who live in Bangkok. She became more and more involved with herself when she was in the house, and with her Farang friends when she was at school.

She is a very popular girl in her school, and is always invited to the house of one or another of her friends. Often she stays there overnight. There is one Farang family from America who love her most. They buy her presents and books as if she was their child. I can well afford to buy her anything she wants, but that would take away her humility and make her feel that there are no obligations in life, only rights. No one knows what the Lord God Buddha plans for us, and if she is destined to be poor I want her to know how to survive. These Farang people from America are kind. They have a daughter just Nellie's age and her name is Nina. Nina is a Farang name which comes from Russia, because Nina's mother's mother came from Russia. In America there are many Americans who came from other countries. Mister Charlie told me that all Americans came from somewhere else at one time or another. They have brought many habits and customs and recipes from all these foreign places, and that will make America a country rich in culture. But it will take them time to digest it all, Mister Charlie said. It will take time because America is a young country.

Nina's parents are going for a holiday in America this coming summer, and Nellie says they have invited her to come with them. I have not discussed it with my Mister Charlie yet because I have only heard it from Nellie. If and when Nina's mother says something to me I shall speak to him. In the meantime I am not sure. Sometimes my daughter Nellie is lost in a daydream. I know when that happens because she sits in her room and she looks out of the window and she does not talk. Not even to my maid. It could be that this invitation is a figment of her imagination. I shall not ask Nina's mother about it because I do not wish to embarrass my daughter in case she was not telling the truth. And until I know the truth I cannot talk about it with my Mister Charlie.

My daughter only tells lies when she goes into a world all of her own. And that happens to her because she is unhappy about who she is and what she is. I have not discussed this with her father yet because I want to understand her better first. It is not easy for her because, like America, she comes from two different parents, and because she is young it will take her time to accept she is different. For now she has chosen to disregard her Thai heritage entirely, and this saddens me. Ignoring my half of her blood makes her ashamed of being my daughter.

But if she had been with me today at the fish market, and if she had seen the way I was looking for clues to find Paco the Filipino in order to help her father, she would have been proud. The protection of my family is the most important thing in my life. Knowing who and what you are gives you strength. Unless you are like my Mister Charlie, who is above all that. He is an Englishman, but he considers himself a resident of the whole world and judges people by their character and not their place of birth. Maybe my daughter Nellie will learn that from him when he finds the heart to be with her.

Shortly before the hour of seven in the evening my friends found the man who took Paco the Filipino downriver. He was bought to the waterside house where I sat, sipping tea with the wife of one of my friends. His boat was new and it had a shining engine at the back, and he tied her up on one of the stilts below the room in which we were. He came up the wooden ladder. Behind him was one of my friends from the port police. The man climbed up and then he came to the door and clasped his hands as a mark of greeting and respect, and I told him he could come inside.

I am not a rude woman and would never invite a man into a house which is not mine, but I was anxious to have news about Paco, and my friend's wife understood. A large crowd of people waited outside, some on boats and rafts on the riverside and others out on the road. These were all fish-market people who had heard I was looking for someone and had helped to trace the river-cab man. Now they waited to hear what would happen.

The man came in and he told us about all the work he had done that day, and when he spoke of Paco he said he remembered him well. He remembered being hired to collect him off a big old steamer. The man who hired him was an American. Not a Farang but a Chinese American who used to be a schoolteacher and was now working in town. The river-cab man said he had never heard of him before. He said he had collected the Filipino off the gangway of the steamer and had taken him to the customs house near the Oriental Hotel pontoon. He said the Filipino was a man of authority on the big old steamer because all hands came to see him off, including the captain. He said the Filipino had paid him all he had asked for and had tipped him well. The money he was paid with was American dollars. Can anyone change that for me? the man asked at that point, and the whole assembly laughed.

I thought Paco the Filipino was going to see someone at customs in order to arrange for a shipment. He could have gone in there to bribe someone. There was nothing unusual about him visiting the customs house. He is in the business of moving merchandise all over South-East Asia, and for that a man needs contacts.

As soon as the river-cab man left I asked my friend the port policeman to find out at the customs house who Paco had gone to see. My friend is not a high-ranking officer. He is a simple policeman, but these people know other humble people, and they always discover what they set out to find. In many cases they know more about the places they work in than the owners. My other friends went over to all the buildings between the customs house and the Oriental Hotel to leave messages there for the Filipino to come to me there, in my friend's house by the river. I decided to wait until he came, even if it meant going home in the dark. I was not going to go to my house, because I knew my Mister Charlie was with his guests, and when they are together they sometimes want to be alone, or go to a house of pleasure, and my presence would make them feel uncomfortable.

With time on my hands I went over to the local temple. I sent out for flowers and laid them at the Buddha's feet and said a prayer for my daughter Nellie and her happiness, and another for my Mister Charlie. By that time my daughter and my maid would be back from the cinema. So I sent a message to my house to tell the maid to find out what my

Burmese guests wanted for their dinner if they were staying in. I also sent word ordering her to make a meal for Nellie and eat with her without waiting for me.

# CHAPTER TWENTY-NINE

They were tired. They were frustrated. Their old friend and customer Mister Charlie had left the way he had come. He clearly needed help, but they had not been able to give him any. The sunlight was pouring down on the water and the air was hot. In the garden there was no shade. They took the suitcase and they went back to the little house, and there they sat and talked until tiredness took them.

U Nan was woken by a strong knock on the door. Behind the wood he heard Nappaporn's maid calling for him. He got up and looked around the room. His friends, sprawled about the smooth wooden floorboards, were in deep sleep. The evening had come while they slept, and the air had cooled. He switched the light on and wrapped a sheet around his body. He gently tapped the head of one of his friends and shook the other's shoulder. Time to get up, he said quietly, and when he saw them move and open their eyes and stretch he went to the door.

The maid stood there and she was smiling.

'There is a man to see you,' she said. 'He is in a big car outside in our street. He says Mister Charlie has sent him here. He says Mister Charlie wishes all three of you to come with him.'

'Do you know him?'

'I never saw his face. The street is dark.'

'Did you notice his voice?'

'I have never heard his voice in this house.'

'Did he say what his name was?'

'He did not say.'

'You will have to find out who he is.'

'How shall I do that?'

'You go and tell him we want to know more.'

The girl went away and U Nan shut the door. His two friends were wide awake. He pulled his large white tunic over his head and packed his wartime pistol under his belt as the others got dressed. Soon the maid was back at the door.

'Where is Nappaporn?'

'She is out.'

'Did you leave Mister Charlie's daughter alone in the house?'

'Yes. But I can see her from here.'

'Did you get to see the man better?'

'Yes. He had a Farang voice but he is Chinese.'

'Is he one of Mister Charlie's friends?'

'He has never been in this house before.'

'Did you ask for his name?'

'I did.'

'Well?'

'He did not say, but he said you will know what his business is because of the suitcase.'

'What suitcase?'

'The suitcase Mister Charlie left with you this afternoon by the river. He sent word to say you must bring it with you when you come.'

'If he said that we need not know any more,' U Nan said. 'You may go back to him and say we are on our way.'

It was a large American car and the driver jumped out and opened the door for them. Inside, in the dark, sat a man dressed in a suit and tie. He was Chinese.

'Why the mystery?' U Nan asked. 'Mister Charlie doesn't usually play games with his friends.'

'This is a difficult moment for Mister Charlie. I had instructions to say nothing until I saw you for myself. You are the ruby-dealers from Burma?'

'Yes.'

'Mister Charlie wants you to join him aboard a ship.'

'Are we going somewhere?'

'No. Mister Charlie is. He wants you to join him there for a meal. When I left the ship Mister Charlie was not yet there. I cannot tell you any more. I don't know. I was only asked to make sure you have got Mister Charlie's suitcase. I was told we don't go anywhere until I see it.'

'We have it here. Do you expect me to give it to you now?'

'Not at all. You hand it to Mister Charlie yourself when you see him.'

'We'll do that.'

The car glided through the narrow tree-lined street.

'This is not Mister Charlie's car.'

'No. It belongs to one of his friends.'

'Where is Mister Charlie's car?'

'I can't tell you. Maybe he is using it himself this evening. I wasn't told anything. I'm only guessing, but I believe he has many arrangements to make before setting sail.'

'Does the ship belong to Mister Charlie?'

'No. It belongs to a friend of his. His name is Paco.'

'I have heard Mister Charlie speak of him. Paco the Filipino?'

'Yes.'

'You were not born in Bangkok, were you?' U Nan said.

'No. I was born in Los Angeles. My father and mother came from China.'

'What did you do before?'

'I was a schoolteacher. I taught English.'

'Teaching is a noble trade. Where is the ship anchored?' U Nan asked.

'It is a good way down the river. There is a raft waiting for you on the river bank near the ship to take you to it. It will take no less than an hour to get there. The roads are not very good, and I was told to offer you an alternative way if you prefer.'

'What is that?'

'We can cross over to the Oriental Hotel and take a river cab all the way.'

'How long will that take?'

'It all depends how quickly we find a cab.'

'That will not be necessary,' U Nan said.

'It's too cold at this time of night,' said the other.

'Too many mosquitoes,' the third Burmese said, and they all laughed.

# CHAPTER THIRTY

He knocked on the door at eleven o'clock. I had fallen asleep on the couch, but I didn't feel rested. Something was bothering me, and although I had warned my man to watch Paco like a hawk I could never be sure. I did not go with him because we could not be seen together before he'd met with Charlie or Nappaporn. I opened the door for him and he came in, a large suitcase in his hand.

'Where did you get this?' I asked.

'No mind now. I tell you later. No much time. Must go Nappaporn quick.'

'Don't give me shit, Paco, what's with the suitcase? Where did you get it?'

'Your man, the Chinaman schoolteacher, he clever man. Best number-one actor. He know when talk and when no talk.'

'Cut the crap, Paco, where did you get the suitcase from?'

'I take from Burmese.'

'You what?'

'I take from Burmese. Your Chinaman bring them to my ship.'

'What happened?'

'You want I tell you?'

'Yeah. I want you tell me.'

'Your Chinaman go to house where they stay. He say Mister Charlie waiting for them on my ship. They come.'

'They believed him?'

'Sure they believe. If no believe they no come, right? You no listen. I tell you your Chinaman number-one movie actor. Same same Charlie Chan. Chinaman tell them to bring suitcase. They believe him quick quick. No one know about suitcase so they expect Mister Charlie call them so they believe and come. They come quick quick. All rivers go into sea, Mister Vincent.'

'Then what?'

'I try tell you, Mister Vincent. They come to ship. They come by car all way. My sailors take them by raft and they come on my ship. First your Chinaman say he no invited but Burmese say he come, so they tell Mister Charlie how good man he is. He comes. They climb ladder. Big one first with suitcase, other two later. Then Chinaman. They never talk. No one talk. They never worry nothing.

'When they reach deck my captain greet them. He say Mister Charlie come soon. He say they wait until he come. He offer them whisky and they walk into bridge. I have nice bridge with big room. You remember, Mister Vincent. Burma ruby people never see my ship. I think they never be ship because ruby-mine villages in countryside. They take time standing on deck looking at water and lights on shore. U Nan the big Burmese hold suitcase and he follow my captain. He walk slowly and he look. One one the other Burmese walk into bridge room and one one they are hit on head by hammer. First U Nan fall on ground and others follow like sheep. They all lie on ground. My people and I cut their throat big. No one say nothing. Your Chinaman he pretend he feel sick. Now you know.'

'You're crazy. You've killed the poor bastards because one of them thinks you were some stool pigeon during the war?'

'No, Mister Vincent. No kill for that. Kill for business.'

'What good will that do?'

'You never understand, Mister Vincent. Mister Charlie and Burmese old friends. Specially big man U Nan. Back long time from war. When he know they dead he know you mean business. He pain bad. He great shock, Mister Vincent. You no know Mister Charlie. He loyal to friends long time. He pain much much. Then better chance you take business from him. Big pain make man think.'

'What you going to do with the suitcase?'

'I bring show you I never tell lie. You want see it?'

'No.'

'You look.'

He didn't wait for me to answer. He opened the suitcase and I looked inside. It was all there, just like the little shit had said it would be. There were pounds sterling and dollar bills and sovereigns. And there were three bundles of stones. White bundles, like small flour sacks. Three bundles, I thought to myself, one for every dead body. Killing has never worried me. It's not personal. It's business. But Paco seemed to enjoy himself. Animals kill to eat; we kill for many reasons. But that guy, he loved it. I could tell. I stood there and I looked at the loot.

'What you going to do with this stuff, Paco?'

'You take, I take, I no care. You boss. You say.'

'These damn rubies are going straight back to Charlie. I don't care what you do with the money.'

'What you say? Why you want give Mister Charlie rubies?'

'Because he's paid for them.'

'How you want to do? I say no good I go see Mister Charlie.'

'I'll give it to him myself.'

'You crazy, Mister Vincent.'

'You better learn something, Paco. When a man pays for merchandise, he gets it, you understand? This here's going to be our business, and if you work with us you better remember that. When we pay we collect, and Charlie paid.'

'But why you no care money?'

'The money belonged to those Burmese guys and they don't need it any more. You keep the money. You did the job and you get paid.'

'Mister Charlie go crazy when he know Burmese dead.'

'How is he going to know? You're going to tell him?'

'No, Mister Vincent. This your job, no me. I must see Nappaporn, but no Mister Charlie. I must put plenty time between us first, maybe one month wait before he see me. He know me. If he look my face now he know. No good he know I against him. You against him he know already, yes? You say he already know.'

'He does. He won't be surprised at anything from me. What did you do with the bodies?'

'They are in your car outside, Mister Vincent. They washed good, no blood. You take your men and you take bodies away. You find other men. Not Chinaman. He no like what he see. I think he pretend but he real sick like dog, no pretend. You get your men to take bodies. You make sure one is in Mister Charlie garden, other you put outside Mister Charlie office, and one by Nappaporn house. All body in places tonight, Mister Vincent. When you can do like that in this town far from America, Mister Charlie he think you big big number one in world organization, and he think good what he do.'

'You're sick in the head. Crazy.'

'No sick. No crazy. This good. I look your eyes. I know you think this good, Mister Vincent. You remember what Paco do for you today.'

'You bet I'll remember.'

'You want nothing?'

'You get rid of the suitcase, Paco. Burn it, don't dump it in the river.'

'You sure I keep the money?'

'Yeah, I'm sure.'

'You call man in Manila tell him go away my house?'

'Not before the rubies are back with Charlie. Then I

call.'

'But you say you give rubies back to Charlie. How I can sure?'

'You can't. If something happens to me before I do, your wife gets it.'

'Why you do so? I do big favour and you want kill my family?'

'Just pray nothing happens to me, Paco. Get someone to watch me if you like. I told you before. In my business we pay for merchandise. Security is merchandise too. You call your wife on the radio two days from now. You'll see she's OK. But if you don't do as you're told, you will never see her again.'

'You hard man, Mister Vincent.'

'And you're a choir-boy. Anyone see you come up here?'

'No.'

'Then go see Nappaporn now.'

# CHAPTER THIRTY-ONE

When Paco the Filipino came to see me it was after midnight. I have never been out of my house that late, but I had had a little nap and my wits were about me. There was a strange look across Paco's face and he had grown a lot older since I had seen him last. I asked him to sit down and the lady of the house brought a plate of peanuts and cashew nuts and roasted corn kernels. She brought beer. Paco the Filipino emptied the glass in one gulp and then he sat down.

'Thank you, Nappaporn. That was the best beer I have ever had.'

'One always feels like that when one is thirsty.'

There was something strange in his eyes. They were alive, and they looked around the room like he was searching for something. His face was exhausted.

'You look tired, Mister Paco. You look disturbed. Something wrong?'

'Yes, Nappaporn. Something is very wrong. I tell you later. First you tell me what you want to see me for?'

I do not believe in coming straight to the point, but Paco the Filipino was not a man versed in niceties. The hour was late, and I admitted to myself I would have done the same.

'Have you seen Mister Charlie yet?'

'No.'

'He is not to know about this conversation. I am an ignorant woman, but you are an old friend and there is no one else I can talk to.'

'What is it, Nappaporn?'

'Something is disturbing Mister Charlie. He is not himself. He is confused. Preoccupied. Sometimes I think maybe something is frightening him.'

'Mister Charlie is no coward.'

'I know that, but what is frightening him could be the safety of his family. Or mine.'

'Did you speak to him about it?'

'No.'

'Well, do not speak to him. It will only add to his worry. Let me find out more. Is it business?'

'No. Yes, maybe it is. I'm not sure.'

I told Paco about the car that parked every day outside my house. About the fast boat that flew past the bottom of my garden every time Mister Charlie came to the house. I told him about the short American Farang Mister Charlie had been seen with. I said the American Farang was very friendly with Mister Charlie because my friends have seen them together in many places, including the British Club. They have seen them together with Mister Charlie and his other wife. And sometimes they have seen the American Farang alone with Mister Charlie's other woman. They had to be close friends for that. I asked Paco the Filipino if he knew who the man was.

'I do,' he said. 'I know the man well.'

'Why is that?'

'I have known him for many years. I have met him after the war in Manila. He was an American soldier there. We did business together, and later I introduced him to Mister Charlie. But I regret that now because that man is evil. He threatens my family. He keeps frightening my wife. I don't know what he wants. I would not be surprised if he is giving Mister Charlie trouble. I have said to him many times we must do something, but Mister Charlie doesn't listen. Maybe he doesn't believe the American is dangerous, but he is. I know he is. I think he has sent the car. I think he's behind the boat that passes your house. But I have to find out more before I can say for sure.'

There was a moment, after Paco had spoken, when I thought he was holding something back. A hint of suspicion came into my heart, but then I remembered how my Mister Charlie had always trusted Paco.

'Can you tell me more?'

'Yes. I can tell you that I have been to see the American today. In his hotel. I was begging him to leave my family alone. He makes threats and he frightens me, but he never says what he wants. Maybe that is what he's doing to Mister Charlie.'

I knew where he'd been, and this admission put my mind at rest. I could confide in him. I said:

'Maybe you are right. Mister Charlie has been acting very strange.'

'Nothing surprises me about the American. You make sure your daughter is safe.'

'We are safe. He could do nothing to me or my daughter.'

'Don't be so sure. This is a cruel man, Nappaporn. Like a mad snake. He kill for nothing. When I saw him this evening he looked madder than ever. As if he'd done something terrible to someone. I don't know what he did. He never tells me anything. Just demands and demands and demands. I am so very sorry I have introduced him to Mister Charlie. I hope the Lord Jesus forgives me. I hope you forgive me. Mister Charlie told me about people in Pacific island who eat other people. That is what the American looked like tonight. Like he's eaten someone alive. I am afraid to think and my nerves are bad so I prefer to wait until I cool off. We can think better then.'

'Can you tell me more?'

'I would prefer to keep this to myself until I have more facts. I have a cousin in New York, and he is trying to find out for me. This will take time and I have no time at the moment. I have to leave town. One of the customs officers I am dealing with has been caught taking bribes. I will arrange it, but until everyone has been paid off I have to get away. I have no time to see Mister Charlie, and he has been looking for me. He is not involved in this transaction at all, and I am ashamed I have chosen the wrong man, but we all make mistakes. I will not be here, but I will find out what goes on and will come back soon. Before I go I shall do all I can to stop the man's car from parking outside your house. This I promise to do. I am sailing to Hong Kong tonight and will stay there until the coast is clear again. You know how it is in our business.'

I understood that and I respected Paco for being open with me.

# CHAPTER THIRTY-TWO

My mother had never stayed away from the house at dinnertime before. Until last night I could always count on her to be in the house whenever I was there. In fact she is in the house too much, and I often wish she was not. Where she goes and what she does when I am at school or when I stay with friends is not my business. Maybe she went out yesterday night because I have never, not in the last two or three years, made her feel she was needed. I always thought it would be just great to spend most of the night in the house alone with my mother's maid. Sitting up late and chatting and doing what I like. I have even dreamt of living there without my mother, and yet last night I found out I was not quite ready to be on my own.

The day started like any other day. I was taken to school. I worked. I played with my friends, especially Nina, who is my best friend and whose parents are taking her to America this summer. I keep hoping they will invite me to come with them. I feel sure they will, because Nina's mother likes me a lot and I have spent many nights in their house. I like their house better than my mother's house. They have many books there, and I spend many hours reading. I love reading. I so want to go with them to America this summer. I am almost sure Nina's mother said something to me once. Perhaps it was wishful thinking.

On the whole I tend to imagine myself as being someone else and living in all sorts of places. Nina's mother says I could be an actress. I am not sure yet what I want to do when I grow up, and my mother does not talk to me about it.

Yesterday started like any other day until I got home. As usual, my mother sat on the porch waiting for me. If only she knew how mad I get when I see her sitting there she would wait indoors. Once Nina came home for lunch with me and saw my mother sitting there, and I knew she was laughing at her. It was very embarrassing. Nina's mother never sits on the porch when she comes home. I know. I have gone to her house for lunch many times. Nina's mother trusts her completely and does not treat her like a baby.

I am not a baby. My teachers say I am advanced. Nina's mother says that too. My mother thinks I am young for my age, and that makes me mad. I cannot talk to her about my future because I believe she wants me to follow her. Become someone's woman, sit at home all day and wait for him to come home. Or maybe work in a small, dirty shop, or in the fish market like all my mother's family do.

I am different. I feel I am destined to do great things. Above all, I want to be a very famous woman one day. I want the whole world to know who I am. Especially my father. I have never shared this secret with anybody. It is very difficult for me to talk. Sometimes I want to say something and I know what it will be, but the words refuse to come out. My own feelings, and especially my secrets, I cannot talk about at all. Not even with Nina, who is my best friend, or her mother, with whom I can talk about everything. I can talk better when the words belong to someone else. Repeat things. That is why I like taking part in school plays. When I recite lines I can talk very easily.

The day started like any other until I got to the porch. My mother seemed a little nervous and definitely different. She did not try to hug me, and when I looked towards the river I saw why. My mother's Mister Charlie, who is my father, was sitting there by the water with the three Burmese who are staying in our guest-house. My mother didn't even try to push me to go and greet him as she usually does when he and I are in the house at the same time. That does not happen very often. Maybe never these days. In fact I can hardly remember the last time Mister Charlie and me were in my mother's house on the same day. That was the first different thing about yesterday.

I stood for a little on the porch and I looked at Mister Charlie and his Burmese friends. They are very nice people, and ever since they arrived they greet me every morning when I go to school. Yesterday was different. They saw me very clearly and I waved at them but they did not wave back. Maybe that happened because Mister Charlie was by the river with them.

Mister Charlie is a very strange man. My mother says I look just like him. She says the size and colour of my eyes and the texture of my hair and the shape of my face have all come from him. She says I am tall, and when I grow up I shall be as tall as a Farang woman. She talks about Farang like they were strangers, and yet the man she loves more than anything in the world, and I, her only daughter, are both Farang. I feel I am a Farang because all the things that I love are Farang things. Paintings. Books. Bible stories. The school. The way Farang people look. Everything. Everything except my father. My father is a handsome man. I know he is a war hero and a famous adventurer. But he has never come to my school and he has never met any of my friends or their parents. Not even Nina's parents, with whom I spend so much time.

I do not have a picture of my father. I am not even allowed to speak about him at school. Only at home, and only with people who know him. Such as my mother's family or my mother's sailors or her employees. Or people who work with my father, but only Oriental people. I have never been introduced to any Farang who works with my father or is his friend. At school they know I have a Farang father, but none of the teachers has ever mentioned him. I had been warned not to speak about him from the beginning. Right from my first day at the American school my mother said I must not mention him to anyone.

I see his pictures in the papers often, but I am not allowed to cut them like my mother always does. Once, not too long ago, he met with the Prime Minister and one of the royal princes and his picture was in the papers and I so wanted to show my friends that he was my father, but my mother stopped me. I did not understand why that was. Did he commit some crime? Did my mother help him? Was I to blame for that? Is he ashamed of having me as his daughter?

I know he has another, Farang family. A woman and a daughter who is at school somewhere out of the country. I think he spends much time with them, and I passed their house once. It is near the American Embassy, and I only knew it was his house because I saw my mother's face. She looked at it from the corner of her eye and then she lowered her head. I knew it was his house because my mother's expression had told me. She became servile, small, insignificant. The way she always is when he is in the house. I used to wonder why all this had to be. Why he can be seen everywhere with his other wife and daughter. Why he can live in the same house with them. Invite people for dinner, the way Nina's parents do.

I used to imagine him sometimes, in his home. I imagined him sitting around the table making small-talk. Telling jokes. Talking about children and school. Just like Nina's parents and their friends do whenever they entertain. I know. I have been to their house many times. They introduce me as Nina's best friend. They tell their friends I am good at school. They tell them I read books and am a very talented young lady. They make me feel good and important. They tell them my mother's name is Nappaporn. They tell them my mother is a big businesswoman in the fish market. A boat-owner and a trader. They tell them I live in the house by the river in the best area. But they never talk about my father. As if I haven't got one. I used to want to tell them my name is not plain Nellie Brown. My name is Nellie Paget-Brown. I know my father's family is an old family and their blood runs through me. But I have never met any one of them because they live on a big estate in England and they never go anywhere. It used to upset me a lot. Then it didn't upset me that much. I used to want my father to talk to me about his childhood and his life and what he was thinking about. Tell me how to do things. Above all I wanted him to come to school so that I could show him to my friends. I wanted him to come places with me. Take me to a picture show. Anywhere. Even to Nina's parents' house. Brag about how handsome and important and brave he is. About what a hero he was in the war. But that never happened, and whenever I asked my mother about it she'd go all sad and small and lower her head and say there are things little girls do not understand. She said I would understand it all one day. She said I must not be upset about it. She said he loved me and cared about me.

Now I don't care at all. I don't mind any of it.

My friends know I have a father somewhere, but because

they have never met him they don't ask me about him. Maybe they think he has gone away. Many of the other children at school have fathers who travel all over.

Yesterday was strange. As soon as I finished lunch my mother said she must go out. She told the maid she could take me out to see a movie in the afternoon. I knew something was different because my mother did not look servile yesterday, even though my father was down in our garden by the river. She did not fuss around him or offer him tea or anything. She did not wash his clothes or show off the food she had cooked for him the way she usually does. On the contrary. My mother put on her best street clothes and had the maid call a cab and gave the money to me and she said we could go out and stay late as long as I finished my homework. Her voice was strong. Stronger than the whisper I hear out of her when my father is in the house. Usually, when he has been in the house and is about to leave, she stands by the door and waves. Her eyes follow his car until you cannot even hear it, and even after that she stands out by the door for a very long time. Like she does when she goes to the temple or stands before her spirit house. Yesterday she did none of these things. As soon as she was ready to go she went. She did not even go down to see my father and tell him she was going. She did not even wave goodbye to him.

She walked tall, taller than I had ever seen her, and left us in the house. She took some fruit for the Burmese who are staying in the guest-house and she was gone. Even the way she walked and the way she held her head up showed strength. I was so proud of her yesterday.

The maid and I went out on the town. It is not a long way away and we walked. I saw a car drive past us a few times. I have seen that car before. Especially when I leave school and walk down the road with my mother's maid. It is a big black car with dark windows, and I imagined someone sat in there and looked at me.

I imagined I was an important princess from a faraway land. I imagined the man in the car was watching over me to make sure no harm came to me. I imagined he will come out of his car one day and take me to a country on the other side of the world where they will know me and respect me like a long-lost princess.

I did not tell my mother's maid about the car. I have never told her about that, because she would only laugh. She always laughs at me when I tell her someone we didn't know was looking at me. I have heard Nina's parents and their friends talk about me. They always say I am exotic and beautiful. I do not know if I am beautiful or exotic, but one day I will know. I know I am different. No one in the school looks like me.

The film we saw was *The Wizard of Oz*. I have seen this film many times and I still love it. I love the bit about the fairy. I always wanted a fairy like that to come and get me and take me away from here and bring me back when I am the most famous woman in the world.

I do not know where my mother went. Usually, when Mister Charlie is in the house, she does not move. She stays in the house and listens to him and she sits around while he sleeps. She feeds him and she hovers over him. Yesterday he was at the bottom of the garden and was in her sight and on her land, but she went away all the same. She has never done that before. Yesterday was different and strange.

When we came back, a man from the fish market waited for us in the house. My mother sent word to say she would not be back. My mother has many friends in the fish market and they do anything she asks. She said we must eat dinner without waiting for her. She has never done that before either.

The maid and I sat outside after we ate, and then a car came to our street and stopped. Someone called out, and the maid went to the gate. Then she went over to the guest-house, and later I saw the three Burmese leave the guest-house and go to the car. I thought it was Mister Charlie. I didn't expect him to come inside because my mother was not at home, and he never comes over just to see me. He has not seen me for so long I am not sure he would recognize me if he did.

At first I couldn't go to sleep. I thought it was because of the film. Today I know I couldn't drop off because my mother was not at home. Maybe I am still a little girl like she says. Maybe it is better if Nina's parents do not invite me to go to America after all.

Yesterday started strange and it ended the same way. I heard my mother come home. It was very late at night. It could almost have been early morning. The crickets were not singing, and I heard some boats along the river. My mother always comes into my room to check on me, and I always pretend I am asleep. But that night I was not asleep and I heard her and I wanted so much for her to come in, but she did not. Something must be disturbing her. I hope it is not me.

# CHAPTER THIRTY-THREE

◆

I wasn't going to let Paco think I was eating out of his hand. I wasn't going to deliver the bodies like he said. I was going to decide how and when to do that. But, let's face it, I'd better not kid anybody here. I'd better be honest about it. After all these years, it's best to face things the way they really were. The way they happened. Not the way you'd have liked them to have happened. You read people's auto-biographies. You read how great they were. How noble and honest and brave. How hard done by they were. And some-times, if you happen to have known them, you realize some are lying through their teeth. They only do that for posterity. They want the world to think they were tops.

I don't understand that at all. I don't really believe there's anything after this. I don't give a damn what people will think. And anyway, I have never tried to tell anyone I was a saint. If I kept secrets about my life while I was active it was only because it was safer and made business sense, not because I wanted to hide something.

What I did that time in Bangkok had nothing to do with Paco the Filipino or his plans. I wanted to save Charlie the pain. I couldn't save him from that forever, but I could postpone it. He was bound to find out what happened to his Burmese friends sooner or later, but for now I decided to go for the half-caste girl first. I didn't believe what Paco had said. I was sure he cared enough for her to protect her, and even if he didn't her mother did, and through her I was going to get to Charlie.

I don't know why the stupid man didn't give in. He could have had it all. I wasn't going to harm him one little bit. He could have gone on running his business. He had a great future with us. I didn't expect to stay in the Orient once we had Charlie's company. It was going to form a local spearhead for our operations.

People think of us as some sort of an international monster business with a single headquarters and policy. I can tell you I've never met members of other families. I am not even sure there was any connection between the family I worked for and the others. I wasn't interested in politics. I was a field man, or what they call a hit-man in those cheap movies they like to make these days. Until they discovered I had brains, I was shooting people who were supposed to die and never asked why. I was working for Don Antonio's family. His sons and his nephews were running it and making all the decisions, and I was on the fringe. The business was no sophisticated multinational at all. It was a family business, and it remained that until the boys split. Each one formed his own family, and I became a kind of go-between. They were both Don Antonio's sons, but they hated each other real bad. They were always trying to get at each other. They killed each other's employees. On one occasion they even killed each other's brothers-in-law.

It was only when it started to get real hot that we had a

meeting. They were screaming at each other and accusing each other and would have started taking shots at each other right there. But the meeting took place in one of the private rooms of a famous restaurant downtown, and they had to toe the line. I got up and I said something. I don't even remember what it was, but everybody listened. They all got up and applauded me, and there and then they decided I was going to be the referee. And that is how I got to stay alive after all these years.

I don't know why I'm thinking of that now. I must be getting old. That happened much later. At that time in Bangkok, during the Korean War, while I was trying to get into Charlie's business, the family was still united. The brothers still worked and talked together. Don Antonio was still alive and his eldest son ran the operations and they were very local. There was nothing international about it. They had plenty of dough and ambition, and their interest in Europe and the Orient only started because of me. It was I who first saw the possibilities, the money and the opportunities in the rest of the world. It was my three years with the US Army and my experiences there that brought the Orient to their attention. I figure before that Don Antonio's eldest son had never been further east than the Statue of Liberty.

Yeah. I was a soldier too and wore a uniform at the end of World War Two, but I didn't get the chance to see any fighting. Three years in the Orient gave me chances. I was doing all sorts of deals there, especially through Paco the Filipino. I didn't do a thing on my own account. As soon as there was real dough in it I turned it over to the family. The money convinced the family there was gold in them hills. New York wanted the penicillin and morphine Charlie was shipping in and out of all these Oriental ports. The crumbs he sold Paco the Filipino were small-time. They wanted it all. That's why they wanted his business. We were going to switch it to Europe, where you made fortunes out of the stuff.

He could have gone on playing with his rubies and his

fishing nets and his radios. He could have become our number-one man there. It would have given him all the power and the excitement he craved and more. I figure by the time we first met he'd had enough. Perhaps he needed some peace after the war and that. But Charlie could never stick to being a gent. It wasn't in him.

That night, as soon as Paco left the room, I called my man to come up. He looked as pale and transparent as a dead fish. I asked him to find a place to keep the bodies. His wife had a distant relative somewhere in the outskirts who ran an abattoir. They had one of those old-time room-size coolers there in which they kept carcasses. I told him to have the three Burmese packed up and shipped over there for a while. I was going to spring them on Charlie just the way Paco had said. But not when he said. Not yet. I was going to spring them when I wanted, or best not at all.

The guy stood there and looked so sick I thought he'd faint.

'They won't feel a thing,' I said. 'Don't worry about it.'

'What shall I tell my wife's relative?'

'Tell him they died in an accident or something. Tell him they're foreign. The Consulate is waiting to ship them back home. Tell him anything.'

'Why do I have to say they are bodies of people?'

'They don't look like cattle, do they, but I don't care what you tell him, as long as you get them there before morning.'

I saw he wasn't going to hold up, so I got two other guys to go with him.

When he finally got going I was dead. It had been one hell of a long day. In the morning I had been to see Charlie, then Rose came over, and then Paco. Twice. So when I got into bed I remember thinking it wasn't worth it. I figured I wouldn't get more than one hour's sleep. But I dropped off like a meteor, and then the telephone rang. I turned the light on and looked at my watch. It had stopped during the night. In those days you didn't have many battery watches. You had to wind the fuckers if you wanted to know what the time was. I tried to remember what had happened. I tried to picture it all. I only remembered my last instructions. They had to do with Charlie's half-caste kid. I remembered telling my man to start the ball rolling first thing in the morning. Make sure the kid still went to the American school. Make sure the maid still collected her. Make sure what route they took. Make sure what days she was going straight home, what days she went visiting. That sort of thing. I was more than half asleep when I noticed the phone was still ringing. It irked me. I willed it to stop, but it wouldn't. I was dog-tired. The ring was loud and maddening. I pulled the bed cover over my head. I figured I'd kill whoever it was if they persisted.

Finally I picked it up. It was Charlie.

'Did I wake you?'

'Matter of fact you did.'

'I am terribly sorry.'

'What time is it?'

'It's nearly lunchtime.'

'Shit,' I yawned.

'I'm very sorry. Had a hard day last night, did you?'

I wasn't in the best of shapes and he must have felt it. He kind of forced himself to be nice to me. I was too tired to figure out why.

'Can we meet?'

He had never suggested a meeting before. It was always me. There must have been a new development somewhere. I hadn't heard from Paco the Filipino. The bodies were safely where I had wanted them to be. The rubies were by my bedside. Everything I dreamed had happened the day before had really happened.

'Sure,' I said.

'Where?'

'Would you like to come up here for lunch?'

'No. It's too public. I'd like to see you alone.'

'You name the time and place. I'll be there.'

'My office?'
'When?'
'Half an hour?'
'You want to talk?'
'I want to talk.'
I said I was on my way and fell out of bed.

# CHAPTER THIRTY-FOUR

Up in the centre of the white ceiling the fan worked at full speed. Hot air circulated about the room. It felt like an oven. He sat at his desk, dressed in his suit. There was not a drop of sweat on his face. He had been trying to get Burma on the telephone but the lines were down. There was a typhoon, the secretary apologized. He leaned back and he stretched. There might be a simple explanation, he thought to himself as the door opened and Perotti walked in. In his hand he held an oversized lizard briefcase. The man's beaming face and his Father Christmas shape seemed almost friendly.

'You look like a proper businessman.'
'I am a proper businessman, Charlie.'
'Of course you are. Do sit down. Kind of you to come down.'
'Didn't keep you waiting too long, did I?'
Some of the poison had gone from Perotti's voice.
'No, Perotti. Of course you didn't.'
There was something softer about the Englishman's manner. His eyes smiled as they always did, but his face was down.
'What's the matter, Charlie? You look like death.'
'The Burmese have disappeared.'
'What Burmese?'
'The people you saw in this office yesterday.'
'The ruby guys?'

'Yes.'

'No kidding.'

'I'm serious, Perotti, they've gone.'

'You think they've gone back to Burma?'

'They wouldn't do that.'

'Why not? Didn't you do the deal?'

'Yes, yes. I did the deal, but we weren't finished yet.'

'You mean you didn't pay them?'

'Oh, I paid them, but . . .'

'What are you trying to say, Charlie?'

'I don't know why I bother you with this . . .'

'Maybe you think I've got something to do with it.'

'Have you?'

'I might.'

'What have you done with them?'

'Calm down, Charlie. I only said I might have something to do with it. I didn't say I have.'

'It's time we were open with each other.'

'I agree. What is it to be, Charlie? Are you staying in or getting out?'

'Seriously, Perotti. You are a man of the world. Imagine you have friends visiting you. You've done business with them for years. They come here and they sell you some rubies. You buy the whole lot. They stay in your house. You introduce them to all the girls. They see you every day. You take them out all over. Then they take off.'

'Did you pay?'

'Of course I've paid.'

'Then you're sore because they take your money and run? You want them to sit another week and eat your food, screw your local women and talk about the good old days? Is that it?'

'Maybe it is . . . I don't know any more.'

'Are you telling me everything?'

'Of course I am.'

'Well, at least you've got the rubies. I hear prices are up.'

'Are you interested in rubies?'

'Not usually, but I'm hoping you'll teach me all about it when we're partners. What I saw here in your office was fascinating.'

'I don't understand where they've gone.'

'Maybe they've gone back?'

'They wouldn't do that to me, Perotti. We're old friends, I'm telling you. Close friends. We've been through hell together.'

'Let's look at the stones, Charlie. A deal's a deal if you've done good. I bet that will cheer you up.'

The Englishman sat back. Across his face flew a flash of discovery. As if someone had just shown him something he had been looking for all his life. He looked at the American. He smiled.

'You do know something, don't you. Come on, you do want me to trust you.'

Perotti opened his briefcase. He took the three bundles out and he laid them on the table. The smile froze on Charles's face. He went pale.

'I was going to get you to admit you hadn't got the merchandise, Charlie. But seeing as you and I are going to be partners, I decided to level with you.'

The Englishman looked at the stones and remained silent.

'What's the matter, Charlie boy? I thought you'd like to have the rubies back,' Perotti said, and he laughed.

'Where the hell did you get these?'

'What does it matter?'

'Why did you bring them here?'

'If you've paid for them they're yours. I am no thief, Charlie.'

'I don't care about the stones. What have you done with the Burmese?'

'I did nothing to the Burmese. I swear it.'

'Where did you get the stones from?'

'I told you before. We have contacts all over.'

'Where are the Burmese?'

'What about our business, Charlie? Are we going to talk turkey?'

'Not until you tell me what you know.'

The American got up. He picked up the empty briefcase and went to the door.

'Where are you going?'

'I'm going back to my hotel. I thought we were going to get somewhere. You got me up for nothing.'

'That's not fair . . .'

'Why not? You bought some rubies, you've paid for them, you lost them. Now you've got them back, haven't you? What more do you want?'

'Did you hit my friends?'

'I told you before, I didn't hit anyone. I sometimes lie when I have to, but that was the truth. I swore I didn't. When we left your office yesterday you said the rubies were only safe when I was out of there. Today I bring them back to you myself, and you're accusing me of killing your friends. I don't know what you want. I'm getting out of here. I can't talk to you. You're making me mad.'

Charles tried to say something but the little man was gone.

# CHAPTER THIRTY-FIVE

I wasn't mad at him at all. I was out to confuse him, not hurt him. I left him in his office staring at the rubies and trying to guess where I got them from and what happened. I wasn't going to tell him about his friends. I was going to wait until he gave in, and then have them put into the ground somewhere. He need never know, I thought, as I walked back to the Oriental Hotel. My mind was made up. I was going after the little half-caste girl, and if that didn't do it I'd let the bodies loose on him. I hoped that would not happen. It would hit him bad, just like Paco said, but that wouldn't be my doing. He'd have had all the chances I was going to give him. From what I knew of Charlie, he'd crumble. He was no chicken, but I knew the loss of his friends would knock him hard.

I knew what I was going to do next. I had it all worked out in my mind. According to my watch it was the right time to act. I stepped into the hotel first. I wanted to drop my briefcase, but then I saw Rose walk into the lobby. She didn't see me, and I turned round and walked out. The car was parked in the little side street near the hotel. My man sat at the back. He knew where we were going. He told the driver.

The school stood along a tree-lined avenue. The asphalt was shaded and sometimes, on a cloudy day, it could almost be dark. In front of the school there were a few cars and a lot of maids waiting to take their charges home. I thought of my own school years. No one ever came to collect me.

Nappaporn's maid was not there. I had been told she was sometimes late. We parked the car a little way down and we waited.

Soon we heard the big gong go, and a few minutes later the kids began to pour out of the building. I looked back. Charlie's little girl Nellie stood by the gate with one of her friends. The girls kissed, and then the other one walked into a parked car and was gone. Nellie stood there by herself. She looked around her but the maid was nowhere to be seen. I saw her talk to a few other children. Then she shrugged her shoulders and began to walk in our direction. She didn't look unhappy. She almost danced as she walked on the grass along the road. Then she passed our car and she stopped. That was unexpected. I thought she would walk on. I wanted her to put some distance between herself and the school gate. I thought we'd drive on and stop and open the door and haul her in as we passed. But none of that happened. The girl stopped and stood there and looked straight at the dark windows of my car as if she was waiting for someone to do something.

I lowered the window and stuck my face out.

'Is there anything you want?' I asked.

She smiled. Boy, what a smile that was. It was a sad smile, and yet as it spread and made her lips curl her whole face lit up. I had seen her before, but never that close. I had either forgotten or maybe I never knew just how pretty a little girl she was. She was tall, and though she was lanky you could see the shape of the woman she would grow into. Her eyes, bright and almond-coloured, shone under her forehead, under a waterfall of thickly textured hair. There was intelligence there, and curiosity. Her eyes asked no questions. It was as if she was waiting for me to say something else. To make some move. It was as if Charlie was looking at me out of someone else's face.

'No,' she said. 'Did you want something of me?'

I was taken aback. The husky voice that came out of her mouth sounded thoughtful and mature. It was almost teasing, as if she dared me to do something. She was maybe shy, and at first she talked slowly as if she was forcing herself, but later it changed. Somehow she became more confident. Maybe because I was a stranger. She was certainly not afraid. She didn't even look over her shoulder to see where her mother's maid was.

'What d'you mean?'

'I have seen you look at me before. I was waiting for you to speak to me. Is there something you wanted? Were you going to take me somewhere?'

She had clearly noticed the car. There was no point in denying anything. She sounded almost hopeful.

'Oh no, that's not what I was going to do.' I could have sworn she looked disappointed.

'Oh,' she said.

'Not unless you want me to. No, no. I thought maybe I knew you. Or your parents. Do you like the school?'

'Oh, yes. I love it. It's a great school. Are you American?'

'Yes.'

'Where in the States do you come from?'

'New York.'

'I bet it's a beautiful city.'

'Not beautiful. Exciting, though. It never sleeps. There're people all over the place. Everybody's doing something. Going somewhere. You can always get something to eat or go to a movie or drive somewhere.'

'Have you ever been in a skyscraper?'

'Sure.'

'What's it like?'

'It's like being in a plane. You look down and the streets look narrow and long, the people look like ants, and the cars and the buses and the trucks look like toys.'

'Are there any trees in New York?'

'Sure there are. We have avenues just like here. Out of town there are forests and lakes.'

'Did you come to see someone in my school?'

'No. I have no children at all.'

'That was a stupid question to ask.'

'No it wasn't.'

'Yes it was. You would have parked outside the gate.'

'I was just driving through.'

'Why did you stop?'

'I don't know.'

'Did you stop to talk to me?'

'I don't think so. But I'm glad I did.'

'Me too.'

My Chinaman was dumbfounded by the conversation. He'd expected me to do it. I had expected me to do it. But something in the girl's face and her chatter paralysed me.

Then all of a sudden her smile died and she thought a little and then she said:

'Maybe you know my father.'

'What's his name?'

'Charles Paget-Brown.'

'I know him some.'

'He's an Englishman. That makes me English too, right?'

'I guess it does.'

'Are you a friend of his?'

'No,' I said abruptly, and I expected her to turn away and walk off. Instead, she came closer to the window.

'But you do know him?'

'Sure I know him. Everybody knows your father. Does he come collect you here sometimes?'

She went all silent. As if she'd changed her mind about talking to me about something. I didn't know what had changed her, and didn't stop to think about it. I was too charmed by her simplicity, by her haunting little face. Then her expression went sad. Her mouth contracted and she wiped her face. I thought she was going to burst into tears.

'What's the matter?' I ventured.

'Nothing.'

'Anything wrong at school today?'

'No. I love school.'

'Did I upset you?'

'No.'

'Don't you like talking to me?'

'Sure I do.'

'Did I say something wrong about your father?'

'No.'

'I'm sorry if I did. You see, we did meet a few times, but I can't say I know him.'

'That's OK.'

'Are you a sad girl?'

'Sometimes I am sad.'

'Why?'

'I don't know. Why are people sad?'

'All kinds of reasons.'

'Why did you ask if I am sad?'

'I was a sad kid myself.'

'Do you know why?'

'Yes.'

'Will you tell me?'

Right then she was ready. I could have done it then. She would have gone with me. But something was happening to me. Something I had no control over. I had never lost control before. I would have been dead years before if I had. This was no contract. No tough guy on the other side. No hit. This was a girl and she was ready to come but I was not ready to take her. I had to act then or never. I was close, but I couldn't close the deal. Words were getting ready to come out of me. Wrong words that weren't mine but out they came anyway.

'I am sure your mother's told you not to talk to strangers. Certainly not to strangers in cars. Otherwise I'd offer you a ride home.'

'She did, but I don't mind talking to you. You're nice.'

That was too much for me to take. What she said about me being nice split me in two. Worse. It screwed me up. I was a total loss. Sure, I know I'm saying all these things now, many years after the event, but I must have noticed them even then. Noticed them big. I wouldn't remember it otherwise.

OK, there was something else. Nellie reminded me of me. My old man had disappeared when I was little, and later my mother was always busy pleasing my first boss, Don Antonio, so I was a lonely kid myself. They gave me anything I wanted, and I learned to charm them out of more, but it was no fun. It don't matter much now that I am an old man, but I reckon it left a few holes in my heart. Age don't make the pain no easier.

I saw a movie once, not long ago, about a guy who kept dreaming he was falling off some roof. They suspect him of killing people. He goes to the shrink and in the end he finds out something that happened when he was a child and he gets cured. The shrink turns out to be the bad guy. Our guy becomes something big. I forget what. But that's not always true. Even if you do find out what's what it don't always mean your problem has been solved. I found out what happened to my father before I was twenty. I took care of it my way, yet still the thing pains me even now, and I am much older than he was when they killed him. Knowledge is no cure for pain.

So there I was talking to Charlie's half-caste girl, and I forgot what I was there for. My mind was blowing. It was flying all over the place, and my memory flew with it. Pictures came to me from long ago. In the face of the beautiful little girl out there I saw my own face.

I was back in my mother's apartment waiting for her to come home. There was food on the table and in the icebox there were sodas, but there was no one to talk to. Sundays were real tough. I'd go with her to Don Antonio's office and he'd give me money and then I'd walk the streets for two or three hours. Be back at five or six. Or whatever it was. And then I'd come into the office and smell the alcohol on her breath. See the messed-up make-up on her blouse, her nylons all torn as if she'd been attacked by a wild dog. I saw it all and knew no one had attacked her. She was there because she wanted to be there with him while I froze outside. She had a great smile all across her lipstick-smeared face by the time I was back. But that smile was not for me. She smiled because Don Antonio had made her feel good. It was a smile of contentment.

I didn't want to think of it, and I looked at Charlie's half-caste daughter and she tried to smile. I knew she tried hard but she failed, and instead she put on a brave, steady face. She wanted to talk but she did not. Maybe she couldn't. Maybe the words got stuck somewhere under the tears. I knew the feeling well. I felt like a schoolboy who's just crapped in his pants in front of the whole class. I failed. I wasn't going to kidnap this girl. Not now, not ever. What the fuck was I doing there digging out my past? Why did I look for my own misery in her eyes? Hot flushes sprang all around my face. I had to get out of there.

'I'd better go now. I hope we can talk together again sometimes.'

'I hope so too,' she said. She waved at me as if she was sad to see me go and turned away. Her shoulders stooped.

I wound the window up and I looked back. With her hands waving frantically, her short, fast steps hitting the soft grass, Nappaporn's maid came racing down towards us. I opened the window again.

'What's your name?'

'Nellie.'

'There's someone running up there, Nellie. Maybe she's looking for you?'

'My maid.'

'Oh.'

'Please don't tell her we had a talk.'

'No. If you don't want me to I won't. But maybe she's seen us. Maybe she will tell someone.'

'No she won't. My mother will kill her for being late.'

'Oh.'

'I like to have secrets. This will be our secret,' Charlie's half-caste daughter said, and I tapped the driver's shoulder. As we drove down I saw Nappaporn's maid catch up with the girl. She touched her as she got to her. She tried to grab her hand, but the little girl shot on ahead as if something drove her on. I saw her little hand rise above her head as though she was waving. She couldn't see me behind the tinted glass, but I waved back.

'You're friends now, Mister Vincent,' my man said with great admiration. 'Next time you can take her no questions asked.'

'Shut up.'

I must have looked at him like he was crazy. He recoiled and moved away to his side of the back seat like he'd seen a snake. He wasn't crazy at all. It was me.

# CHAPTER THIRTY-SIX

■

My dear Charles,

My son Richard has completed his studies and returned to Jamaica last week. Jean attended the graduation ceremony. She says it was something to remember. I am sure it was, and I wish I could have been there, but business is keeping me here. We are opening a new hotel on the north coast of the island. They still need me for some reason. Of course, if you were here I would be able to take some time off. What I will do with it I don't know. There is nothing I am qualified for except listening to projections about room occupancy and the cost of borrowing money. After that they expect me to bring out the magic stick and say yes or no. Jean says I should have developed some hobbies, but in my state it is difficult. Luckily the office and some old friends keep me busy. Jean insists on buying me all sorts of speaking records. These are books and stories and lectures, but I haven't started listening to any.

We are having problems finding enough qualified personnel for our hotels. The economy is booming, and even local people spend weekends in our places. My colleagues are recruiting American graduates for reception jobs and administration, and German or Swiss chefs for our kitchens. We are not able to find any French chefs. I don't know why.

I have had some unexpected news today. It should not have come as a surprise, but as you know I pay very little attention to what is going on around me. You would have expected me to have learned my lesson after 1947, but obviously I have not. In my office I am known to be quick on the uptake. Everybody wants my opinion, and I can listen to three pages of a company report and tell you whether it's worth buying or not. But in my private life, if you forgive a bad joke, I am as blind as ever. Unless people spell things out to me I notice no changes, no moods, and no difference in attitudes – nothing. The doctor says I'm going through some sort of a reaction. I did not listen to it all, so I can't tell you what I am supposed to be reacting to.

Actually I can. It's to do with why I left my village. I'll talk *to you about it sometime.*

Richard told me today he has decided to go into politics. My managers think it is good for our business, and are asking me to put money behind his coming election campaign. Jamaica will be independent one day soon, my managers say. It will be useful for us to have someone in government. You understand these things better than I do, and I suppose you would agree with my people. He is still young, and I hear he is wild. Of course, if that is what he wants to do, I shall not object, but I must tell you it is a disappointment.

Richard intends to fight for a representation of part of downtown Kingston. It is near where I lived when I first arrived. The people there are mostly poor, and I don't know how he expects to win seeing as everyone knows whose son he is. I said so, but Richard told me I don't understand politics. He is quite right.

It was kind of you to send me the Chinese table. Of course, I cannot see it, but I can touch it, and Jean says it is the most beautiful thing she has ever seen. She says it's an antique and must have cost you a fortune. I am pleased things are going well for you.

You know of course that there is always room for you on my board.

I was told about the end of the Korean War and about the growing strength of China. Does that mean Hong Kong might fall to the Communists before they have to give it back?

I think about you a lot and the wars in your area worry me greatly. My sudden knowledge of international affairs would surprise you. But I am not really interested. I have asked my public relations director to dig out anything he finds about your part of the world and talk to me about it every now and then. I suppose it gives me the feeling of being with you. That feeling has always been very good for me.

I am ashamed to admit to you that what goes on in the rest of the world still leaves me cold. Maybe I have taken the limiting boundaries of my village with me. Maybe I never really left there.

I have written so many letters to you over the years, and you have written to me. I hear what is happening to you, and you know *what goes on here. Forgive an old friend, but I often get the feeling you are not telling me everything. I hope I am wrong. I feel that we must soon meet. No one is getting any younger, and even though I cannot see you I can hold you close to me, and then I will know.*

*With best regards to Rose and Roberta and mostly to you, my dear brother,*

*Your brother Sam*

# CHAPTER THIRTY-SEVEN

I had them drive me back to the Oriental in a hurry. I was good and mad. I had failed to do anything I had planned to do. Why the hell did I hesitate?

It was all Charlie's fault. The way he treated his daughter drove me mad. How could that loving man ignore a little treasure like that one was? Was there only enough love in his heart for one daughter, that spoilt brat Roberta, who had given Rose such a rough time? It was all his fault. All Charlie's. Maybe he wasn't a loving man at all. Maybe he liked romance but only in books. He was a selfish sonovabitch who never thought of anyone but himself. They all ran to him as if he was God. All these poor stupid bastards who saw him as a saviour. The Burmese, his so-called partners, his woman Nappaporn.

I'm not kidding myself. The only reason Rose took me on was because he didn't want her. His daughter, the poor half-caste beauty I had tried to take, was going to be all screwed up. She was looking for his love. She wouldn't accept he had none to give. And Paco? Paco didn't count because Paco was only interested in himself.

I sat there in my room and I was getting madder by the minute. Why did I bother getting upset about the Filipino? He was the only man I knew who was ready to sell Charlie to anyone who would pay, but Paco would sell anyone. Paco was not strong in the loyalty department and Charlie was. And so am I. I started my career working for Don Antonio. Later I worked for the kids. But all the time it was neither him nor the kids. It was the family, and I was always loyal to the family. I have robbed and blackmailed and killed for the family. And they were good to me.

Then Charlie came into my life and my loyalty came unstuck. I fell for the limey lock, stock and barrel, even though I never admitted it to anyone. That infatuation with Charlie was close to coming between me and the family, and that couldn't happen in a million years. Loyalty is life, and losing it certain death. So I got mad at him, and then, after trying to kidnap his daughter and noticing how unhappy she was because of him, I got madder.

I don't know what came over me that day. It was the first time I was mad enough at someone to hate them. Emotions are out in my business. In any business. You don't get mad at anyone. You make sure they give you whatever you need and then you settle with them. When you're mad you make mistakes, and I was about to make one.

In the old days, the caveman was mad at his neighbour for having a pretty wife. He burst into the other guy's cave. He killed him and took his woman away. He ended up at the bottom of some river with his throat cut by one of the other guy's kids or his brothers. You must always think first. You're much better off making friends with the husband, getting him to like you, getting the wife to like you too, and then having her. I didn't expect to seduce Rose. She fell into my life while I was friends with Charlie. But I wasn't getting Charlie at all.

I had tried to be friendly with him. Make him see reason. I tried so hard and for so long I began to like the guy.

New York was giving me a hard time. Maybe they thought I was getting off the bus. They were going to start making threatening noises. And all because of Charlie.

Everywhere I looked, there he was. At the centre of

every failure. That was why I lost my nerve that day. That day I figured I had been nice long enough. I figured he didn't deserve it. I figured I could only get him the hard way. By frightening the shit out of him and getting him to move out. I should have waited. I should have taken it easy and let things follow their course. But I was mad at him that day, and I didn't wait. We all make mistakes, and what matters is the end of the story. The bottom line.

I sat on my bed and I called my man on the telephone.

'We do it tomorrow morning. First thing,' I said.

'We do what?'

'We deliver Charlie's ruby-suppliers to him. One at a time. Like we said. You get to the house nice and early. Charlie's wife leaves before him. You wait for him to have his breakfast. Then you dump the big guy in Charlie's garden. When you're through you call me.'

# CHAPTER THIRTY-EIGHT

Outside, the elements were at war. Thunder and lightning traded fire across the sky.

The electricity was cut off and the servant brought a lit candle into the library. The telephone rang. Charles picked it up. Just then a cannon-like boom exploded above the roof. Someone said something but he couldn't hear a thing.

'What did you say?'

The phone crackled. There was no one there.

'Talk quick, whoever you are. The line will be dead soon.'

Then the weather settled down for a minute, and he heard Perotti's voice.

'That you, Charlie?'

'Yes.'

'Go out into the garden.'

'You must be mad. Have you seen the rain?'

'I've seen it. Go out into the garden. Go out the dining-room french windows.'

'What for?'

'I've sent you a present.'

'I'm not in a mood for any jokes, Perotti.'

'I'm dead serious.'

The Englishman slammed the phone down and raced through the house. The sun came out for a minute, and then the clouds closed again. He opened the metal doors and looked outside. He walked over the soft, soggy ground and stepped over flower beds and his feet skated along the muddy paths. A flash of lightning lit the lake that had been the garden with the force of a million electric bulbs, and then he saw a face amongst a heap of flowers. There was a lull in the storm, and he looked. The light had gone, but the sight remained in his mind.

U Nan's eyes faced the grey, angry canopy of heaven. Thick raindrops hammered at his face. The storm continued to blow relentlessly above the swaying royal palms. More water came pouring down from the sky. The river rose and swept out of its banks and covered the lawn. A growing puddle formed around the body and lifted it, and it floated around the garden. He had been a kindly man, and even in death his face was at peace. Branches were strewn all over the garden and fallen flowers floated then settled to adorn the dead man's white tunic. He looked like Gulliver, with a million invisible little people rafting his bulk along a miniature ocean. The scene had the eerie feel of an Oriental Viking funeral. Charles felt heavy, as though a ton of lead filled his chest. He couldn't breathe.

He splashed to the ground and he hugged the cold head and looked into the open eyes. The expression on the good broad face seemed to speak to him. He wiped the large brow. It's not so bad, the face said. Not so bad.

'Yes it is,' Charles screamed. 'It is bad when it's for

nothing. It is bad when you're cold and alone and far from home. It is bad when it is not you they want but me.'

He felt a hand touch him and he looked up. The gardener stood over him.

'Where is my wife?'

'She club. I call police now?'

'You don't call no police. Go get me a rug.'

They covered the large body and they dragged it towards the house. Just then a long black car came into the drive. Perotti's driver jumped out and with an open umbrella he ushered the American towards the garden. The rain stopped. There was total silence.

'I'll fix that,' Perotti said. Another man came over and bent down over the Burmese. He touched the dead man's shoulder. The driver opened the large boot.

'He won't fit in here,' the man said.

'You go in the house and call. Tell them to send another car.'

'Yes, Mister Vincent.'

'You leave him alone,' Charlie said quietly. 'You leave him alone or I'll shoot you.'

'You're not yourself, Charlie. You let my man take care of it.'

'Not myself? What the fuck do you expect . . . You bloody murderer . . .'

'You see a dead body, you get yourself all excited.'

'This is not a body, Perotti . . . This is a man . . . was a man . . . I've seen death before. People who died with honour . . . if there is honour in death, they died with honour. Not murdered in cold blood by hit-men like yourself.'

'Here you go again. I've told you my hands did not touch this man. I mean it.'

'You're a coward and a liar and a killer . . .'

'Yes, yes and yes, but not this time. I haven't killed your friend. I'm not lying. I swear it.'

'You've got no one left to swear by, Perotti. No one. Just get the hell out of here. Get out of this house. Get out of my life.'

'You better get a hold of yourself, Charlie. You're forgetting what this is all about. I can get out of here and out of your house, but you know damn well I cannot get out of your life. Not until you give me what I'm after.'

'If you think this is going to make me give in you're wrong. All you can think of is business . . . even at such a time . . .'

'I always think of business. This is what it's all about.'

'My friend's body lies here . . . He's not cold yet.'

'Touch him, Charlie, he's as cold as ice.'

'You're a cold-blooded murderer.'

'Maybe I am and maybe I ain't. You go inside. I'll get rid of . . .'

'You don't just get rid of him. To you he's a body. To me he was a friend.'

'Stop acting like a child, Charlie . . . Just go inside and we'll talk later. Maybe this will make you see some sense.'

'What the hell do you mean?'

'Stop this crap and start handing the show over. If you're smart you'll stay with us.'

'Don't you people ever let go?'

'If I was my own boss I would. But I have people telling me what to do. My life is on the line here . . .'

'Why did you have to kill this man? What did he ever do to you? He was a kind and gentle man. A hero. He fought on our side during the war. That was your side too, Perotti. Later on he became a smuggler, the sort of people you do business with . . . Why did you . . .'

'I did not kill this man.'

'You ordered it.'

'Not exactly.'

'There you are . . . you miserable little bastard,' Charles said, and stopped in mid-sentence. He stared at Perotti. The air was silent. The wind dropped. There was no rain. The

Englishman's eyes were burning with anger and hate. 'Next you're going to admit it . . . You have to . . . I know you ordered it.'

'You've got to trust me this once.'

'Don't tell me you had nothing to do with it.'

'I am not saying that. I am saying I did not kill the man. I didn't order his death.'

'Who did, Perotti? Who killed U Nan?'

'I will not tell you. All I'll tell you is it wasn't me.'

'But it suits you, doesn't it? It just happens to bloody well suit you.'

'I'm not going to say it doesn't . . . As it happens . . .'

'Accident, right, Perotti? You get into my office the day after the Burmese disappear. You bring the rubies back. The next day you just happen to call me and tell me to look out of my door to find this man dead. And now you've got the audacity to tell me you've got nothing to do with it. What sort of a coward are you?'

'You are barking up the wrong tree, Charlie. Come on, let me take care of this.'

'You said there were going to be eliminations . . . Is this one of your eliminations? The mindless slaughter of an innocent man?'

'No one is innocent, Charlie. Certainly not you and me. But I am innocent of this man's blood. Not guilty, understand? Yes. It suits me. Yes, it was done by someone working for me. But no, I did not order it. I would have ordered it sometime. Maybe tomorrow, maybe the day after, but not today, or yesterday, or whenever this happened . . . I promise you. You've got to trust me . . .'

'I don't have to do anything. I'd shoot you right now if I could. And one day, I promise you, I'll do it. I'll shoot you.'

'I believe you.'

'Good.'

'Do you know why I believe you, Charlie?'

'Because I mean it.'

'No. Not because of that.'

'Why, then?'

'Because you said it the way you did. Quietly. Without anger, only with hate. You might do it and you might not, but I've told you before, it'll all be for nothing.'

'Not for nothing.'

'Come on, Charlie. Let me handle things. We'll talk.'

'I have nothing to talk to you about.'

'You can't help it. You gotta talk to me.'

'You'd stop at nothing.'

'That's right.'

'You're not kidding.'

'I'm not.'

'Well, neither was I, Perotti. Neither was I.'

'What weren't you kidding about, Charlie?'

'One day I'll shoot you, Perotti. I'll shoot you like a dog.'

'I bet you will, Charlie. I bet you will.'

# CHAPTER THIRTY-NINE

◼

The night before the storm was unusually quiet. The air was so still I could hear every tree in my garden as it creaked. Before dinnertime I had sent word to my fishermen to warn them not to go out to sea in the morning. Of course, I realize they know the sea better than me and would not wish to go out into a storm, but it is polite to let them know the owner of the boats is in agreement. I should have fastened the shutters in preparation, but the great heat was oppressive. I was thankful for any whiff of air that entered the house, so I left every window open. But the air that came in was hot and humid and I got very little sleep.

After breakfast I went outside and looked at the sky. I knew it was about to burst open, and I wondered whether

Nellie would get to her school before it did.

I was on my way to lay incense and fruit in the spirit house when I saw the elongated parcel by the river bank. I did not need to get too close to know what it was. I turned round and I looked at the house. I saw my daughter Nellie walking out of the house to go to school. She loves going to school, and the maid needs to be quick on her feet to keep up with her. I waved at my daughter but she did not see me. I think she was still angry with me for what I had said at breakfast.

I seldom argue with Nellie these days, but on the morning of the storm I had. The Lord God Buddha must have willed me to do that, because what I said made her cross and she did not look at me. Had she done so she might have seen the worry in my face. She might have come down to see what the matter was, and then she would have seen the dead man.

I saw my father dead and my brother and others during the war. Death is the last part of life and therefore an important part of it. Maybe the most important part. But the young should not be exposed to it too early. Death is beautiful because a person lies down and rests without worry. After death there is no pain. The human soul floats down the ever-flowing river on the way to the Buddha, and there all suffering is gone. The expression on the dead is usually one of relief. Because one life has ended and another, in another form, is about to begin. But the face of violent death is ugly because it is caused by evil men. I did not wish her to see him, and I was grateful that she was out of the way.

He was one of the small Burmese who had stayed in my guest-house with Mister Charlie's friend U Nan. He was fond of children and had spoken to Nellie and my maid and they had laughed together. I don't know what they spoke of because Nellie did not tell me.

I went closer and I looked at the body. The wind began to howl in the trees, and I knew the sky would soon open.

The force of the wind grew and it started to shriek and

I watched the stem of the large royal palm. It swayed with the wind like a mast in bad weather, but I knew it would not break because the gods have made it flexible. Some trees and some shrubs will die in the storm. Plants, like people, have a limited time on earth, and when they go under new ones come up.

I approached the body and lifted the cover from his face. At that moment lightning hit the sky and soon thunder flew past my garden and the river. The river went wild, like an animal in a cage. The brown water threatened to break over the banks, and I pulled the body all across my garden towards the guest-house. It would be good to bring the little Burmese into the house where he had slept in peace when he was alive. I am not a big woman but I am strong, and the rain came and cooled me, and I dragged the man by his arms. As we got to the guest-house, the sky cracked open. The storm that had threatened the city during the night exploded over the top of the trees above my head. I reached the door of my guest-house and I pulled the man inside. There was mud over his face and body and I washed him clean. His face had an expression of pain and I examined his head. His skull had been hit hard and his throat cut, but there was no blood. He was as cold as ice and could have floated down the river just before dawn when the water is coldest. But the water is never that cold, and I guessed he was put in my garden on purpose. Outside it was dark. The wind screamed past the house and the rain rammed the roof with the might of cannon-shells.

I covered the man's body with a clean rug and by his side I laid some clothes that were left in the house. Judging by their size they could have been his. Next I ran across to my own house to secure the shutters and wash myself and change and wait for the storm to subside.

I knew my maid would be delayed, and I cleaned the house and passed the time preparing the daily meal for my Mister Charlie and my family. I never knew when my Mister Charlie was going to grace me with a visit, but that day I was sure he would come. I kept myself busy cooking and cleaning, and all the while the relentless powers of heaven came down on my house. There was a different storm brewing inside of me. As if something great was going to happen today. I was almost afraid to think of what it might be. But we can only wait and see what the Lord God Buddha intends to put in our way. Then at length the rain stopped, and through the shutters I saw the first rays of sun crawl into the room.

I ran to the door and I opened it. My garden was submerged as the river reached halfway up my land. But the rest of it was dry. Drops of water lit up with the sun and looked like diamonds, and I knew they would soon evaporate. Up above the clouds were sailing past. The red-brick path Mister Charlie had built for me was intact. I took my mother's old paper umbrella and walked into the street.

Across the road, the tamarind tree seemed almost lonely without the car that I had seen so often, lurking underneath the generous branches. It was the absence of that car that made me realize who was behind this killing. The menacing threat had been replaced by action. It was clear to me that Mister Charlie's enemy has decided to take his war into the open. It can only be a disturbed and mean mind that kills a man's friend in order to hurt him. I had been waiting for the man Paco to bring me some more information about the American Farang I had suspected, but so far no word had come.

It would have taken no time at all for me to travel to the fish market by boat. But I knew the water was still high and no water cabs would pass my garden before the storm was truly over. This was only a lull.

I ran past the temple and across the wooden bridges, and then I got to the house of one of my friends. I told him what had happened and I asked him to send help to the house. I asked him to take the body away and hide it in a safe place until my Mister Charlie came to tell me what to do.

After that I went back to my house to await Mister

Charlie.

It was right after midday that he came. First I heard the familiar purr of his car, and I walked to the door and opened it. The sun was shining and the heat of the day was back in the air. I stood by the door and watched as my Mister Charlie walked down the red-brick path. His shoulders were stooped, and then he looked up and saw me and he smiled. I had never, never seen him look like that. Not in all the years, and through all the dangers we have lived with, have I seen him that way. His face was muddy and his clothes were wet. He smiled at me, but his smile was sad. He waved at me, and then I saw the ashen colour of his face. The expression in his eyes was one of resignation. More than that. He seemed to be lamenting. As if the world he was born into and walked in was coming to an end. He was so far away from me I could not reach him.

He came very close and I looked up at his handsome face, and what I saw shot arrows of despair into my heart. This was not the time to load him with any problems. I decided I would settle the matter of the body by myself.

I took him by his arm. He walked into the house. He forgot to take his shoes off and followed me like a child.

'I may have to go away,' my Mister Charlie said. His voice was not his voice.

'I know.'

'I have lost it . . . Everyone around me is danger. I have forgotten how to survive. The gods have left me.'

'Every mountain has a peak. Your luck will come back.'

'I cannot bear the hate.'

'It will blow away.'

'I hope it will, but I think I'd better go away until it does.'

'I understand.'

'If I go, I may be gone a very long time.'

'Where will you go?'

At that moment Mister Charlie's face contorted. I

thought he wanted to cry. I prayed he would. I have never seen him cry before, and I did not see him cry then. He fought his tears and then he looked at me. For one moment his eyes shone like they normally did, and then the life was gone from them and he said:

'Far. To the other side of the world.'

He could no longer speak. He wanted to hold me in his arms, but he did not. He just looked at me and waited. I do not know what he was waiting for. My Mister Charlie was not the same man I had known for so long. This man was someone else. I wanted to ask him to wait for Nellie, but the man who stood before me then would not have understood. I wanted to ask him to stay for his meal, but the man who stood before me then could not have eaten.

'Will you come back soon?'

'When you are safe,' my Mister Charlie said, and then he pulled his shoulders back and stretched his hand towards me. He pumped my hand like a Farang. He could not look at my face. Perhaps he was ashamed of something he had done. Or something someone had done to him. Or something he himself was about to do. Perhaps he could not bear me seeing him in that state.

And then again, all men are children at times. Maybe my Mister Charlie had a need to go back to his childhood. Maybe in his mind he was already there. I wanted to caress him and hug him, but suddenly he became remote and stiff. Into his eyes came a decisive glow, and he turned round and walked towards the door. His step was sure and even, as if the hesitation I had witnessed was over. My fear of losing him was gone. I could see why he had thought of going. I could see why the load of worry on his mind needed to explode before he could be free of it. I was pleased it had happened with me alone, with no one else to witness it. He stopped by the door and straightened his back. I saw the old spirit in his eyes. Resolution returned to his voice.

'I am not beaten yet.'

'Of course you are not.'

'I have not decided what to do.'

'May the gods put wisdom in your soul.'

'Yes . . . I hope they do. I must think clearly first. Then I shall decide.'

'I shall be here every day.'

'There are arrangements I must make if I go. You will have to help me.'

I was the proudest woman in the world when I heard that. Even when my Mister Charlie was at the bottom of his world, he knew he could rely on me. I was a strong woman that day. I did not go out to the porch to see him off. I heard the car start and drive away and I sat on the floor and I cried.

# CHAPTER FORTY

They found the body of one of the Burmese who had stayed in our guest-house. It lay under the tall royal palm at the bottom of the garden, near the river. My mother's maid said he was wrapped in a jute sack and his hair was dripping wet. But she was not in the house when they found the body. She did not see anything. My mother's maid often makes up stories. Sometimes she tells lies. Especially when she wants to impress me or when she wants to cover up for something she did not do. I could have been there. I could have seen it all myself, but in the morning I had a big fight with my mother. It started with nothing at all. Maybe my mother was in a bad mood or worried about something. She has been very worried lately, and I have seen her whispering things to people about this and that, and whenever I come near she stops whispering and she smiles at me as if nothing is wrong.

I would so like her to tell me what is on her mind when she is down. But she keeps bad things to herself because she is trying to protect me. If she talks to me I shall talk to her. I know she means well, but I do wish she would tell me because it would make me feel closer to her and part of her life.

My mother can often tell the future, like a witch. I mean a good witch, of course.

Thinking about it now I think my mother had a premonition something big was going to happen. Usually she is full of lively talk at breakfast-time, but today she kept to her side of the table and did not look up at me at all. I asked her what the matter was.

I must try to be honest. In reality, I did notice something was bothering her but I didn't care what it was. I was just bitching because she wasn't paying me any attention. That's the truth.

She did not answer, and I said something about her losing her power of speech. I said I hated her and wanted to go away. She said no one would take me, and I said I could go to Nina's house. I said they were going to take me to America with them this summer. My mother said I was lying. She said she had spoken to Nina's mother and had asked her about this. She said Nina's mother never invited me at all. She said I was a liar. I said Nina's mother would not stoop to talk to her because she was a lady and my mother was a slave. Upon hearing this my mother got up and crossed over to me and slapped my face. It was the first time she had ever done that to me. I think I was shocked, but I did not cry. I just went to my room to wait for her to go to her spirit house as she does every morning. I was not going to let her see me upset. Maybe I was not upset because I knew she was right. I was humiliated, but I was not going to admit that to her. Not ever. I waited in the room until I heard her slam the door, and then I ran out with the maid following close behind. That is why I did not see her walking towards the spirit house, which is near the river, and did not get to see the body.

No one was there except my mother. But later on the house was full of people who came and went. My mother's maid said she listened to what was said and she bragged and claimed she knew what had happened.

She said there was no blood. The river may have carried the body all the way to our house during the storm. He may have drowned. I remember one of the Burmese telling me they had never seen the sea because they live in the mountains where the rubies are found and bought and sold. They have of course seen rivers, and their people use rivers much the same as we do. Water, he said, fascinated him, but he could not swim because it is difficult to swim in the river. The water always moves fast and it can carry you away, and if there is nothing to hold on to you drown. I don't know which one of our guests he was because I did not see him. They were all cordial and nice to me and always greeted me with a smile. I should be sad about it, but I did not see any of it. I have never seen a dead person.

I hope this man was happy with what he did while he lived. I hope I become happy and famous before I die.

I am a good swimmer. I win every competition in the school. This is because I used to swim in the sea with my cousins in Pataya when I was a very little girl. In those days my mother would send me to the seaside for the summer holidays. I always stayed with my cousins, and then I was sent to the American school and became a Farang and found I had little in common with them. I started hating going there. My friend Nina knows about that and she told her mother and her mother said it was because I have seen a different world and have friends in the school, and where your friends are is where you want to be. But that is not all. The truth is I know my mother always sent me out of town because she wanted to be alone with Mister Charlie, who is my father. And that made me scared. I began to worry about my mother. I know I am rude to her and am mocking her, but I must be sure she loves me. She waits for me by the porch and I hate it, but I don't know what I would do if she did not. I am confused.

Today my mother was very upset. She said the dead

man was a good friend of Mister Charlie and also her friend. I said if Mister Charlie was a friend of the dead man he should have been here in our house. He should have come here and collected the man himself, not send my mother's fisherman to do it. Not have my mother's friend carry him all through our garden to the boat and then take him downriver. He left my mother to do all this for him. Her friends came as soon as she called for them. They did everything. They cleaned him and dressed him in dry clothes and then they took him away on the boat. I was told all that by my mother's maid, and she swore she was not lying. My father should have done it all himself and not have burdened my mother with it. I was angry about that, and I told my mother so. I said maybe her Mister Charlie was not such a great hero after all.

My mother said I did not know what I was saying, and I did not answer. She said I did not see anything and she was right because they had found the man while I was at school and all I know was told to me by the maid. I did not tell my mother the maid had told me because I have seen what happens when my mother gets angry with her maid and how she scolds her and makes her sad. This girl has been with us for many years. I don't remember how many. I don't remember my mother without her maid. When I am rich and famous I will have a maid like my mother's maid.

Mister Charlie my father has been to the house today while I was at school. When I came back he was gone. My mother was in one of her strong moods. She is often in a strong mood, but never with me. Only when she is with people who work with her or with her friends from the fish market.

She was sending messages to people and was meeting other people all inside the house. There were big discussions going on. My mother was doing all the talking. I could hear her voice and I knew everybody agreed with her, but I don't know what was said because I was outside. The maid was with me too, and she did not hear either. We did hear that one of my mother's friends has gone to Burma to the dead man's village, but no one told me what for.

It is very difficult to be alone like I am. I mean when I am not at school. In my house I have the maid, but I cannot talk to her about everything. My mother's friends respect her and so they respect me too, even though they think I am a little girl, and they bring me presents, but they tell me nothing.

There is someone who I think will be my friend. He is an American. I have seen him in his car in front of the school a few times, and one time we talked. It was very easy for me to talk to him. The words came out of me without hesitation. As if we were both other people. Maybe like actors on the screen in the cinema. He said he was from New York, and he talked to me about the city and many other things. He knows my father. I was going to ask him about that, but I think he would prefer not to talk about my father. Maybe he does not like him. Maybe he knows things about him. I think he does not talk about my father because he thinks it upsets me. One day I shall tell him he can talk to me about anything. I hope we will become friends because I trust him. I think it is because he is not a handsome man and is not full of himself like my father. I know that because he said he used to be a sad boy himself, and people who are proud never admit that. He was not too proud to tell me that, and he promised he will tell me more.

When I see him next I will tell him more and more. Even about the body. I will ask him why Mister Charlie who is my father was not in the house with my mother when the body was taken away. If he loves her the way she thinks and says he does he would have been. This man is clever and he will tell me. He is a short man and a little fat, but he is honest with me and his eyes are good and he was sad when he was little, so we have much in common.

It will be nice to talk to a Farang man. Nina's father is a Farang man, but I do not talk to him very often because when I am in Nina's house I play with Nina, and it is her mother who talks to us because her father is at work. Nina's father was a daredevil pilot during the war, and now he teaches other people how to fly at the airport. I have never been there but one day I will. On that day I will not just go there for a visit to see the planes. I will get on a plane myself and fly somewhere far away and never come back.

# CHAPTER FORTY-ONE

Time went by and, like in a dream, days were lost to me as though they never were. The city was slowly being cleared and the water had receded. The river had torn away shrubs and trees whose time to go had come, and new ones climbed up from the earth. My garden looked like it did before, as though the big storm had never happened. The time that followed the murder of our Burmese friends flew past like lightning.

Other, stranger things were occurring that week after the storm. The car that had parked outside my house under the tamarind tree never came back. The fast boat that used to patrol the river at the bottom of my garden had disappeared. I was hoping that the trouble that had threatened my Mister Charlie was over. That he will remain the way he had been during our last moments together and decide he does not need to go away at all. I went down to the temple every day to thank the Lord God Buddha for this. These dangerous people were not seen again, and I knew for sure who had helped me there. I knew it was my friend Paco who had arranged for that, as he had promised he would. He is vulgar at times, but he is a kind and modest man. He would never admit he had helped me, but I added a small prayer for him in gratitude. I was hoping he would soon come to Bangkok again so that I might offer him a gift.

After the storm, I do not remember how long after, a message came from Mister Charlie. He asked me to send for a man who lived in a mining village across the border, in the Burmese hills. He was a distant relative of Mister Charlie's giant friend U Nan, whose body was found in his garden. He asked me to have him brought to Bangkok. The only way to do that was to have one of our people go into Burma in person and find him there. We were not to tell him what had happened until he was safely in my house.

In the eyes of the gods I am a small woman and my humility is eternal. But I have been in this city for a long time, and have assembled a respectable number of people who would go anywhere for me. It fell to one of them, a city policeman who knew every path across the border villages because he was born in one of them. My father had known his father, and when he heard I had left Pataya to come to Bangkok he left his father's farm and came to the city. He arrived just when the war was over, and for some time he lived near the fish market with one of my relatives. He did not have any money, but he was a young lad who was willing to work hard. With the help of my Mister Charlie's connections we managed to find a position for him with the Bangkok police. When I asked him to go into Burma and bring the man back, he took a week off from his duties and went up-country without a murmur. We gave him a car in which to get as close to the border as the roads permitted, and within a week he was back.

It is not a simple matter to take a young man away from his family and his village and bring him across without any explanation. But he had followed my instructions to the letter. The Lord God Buddha had smiled down on my friend and put much wisdom his way. And the years he had spent with the Bangkok police had taught him about the nature of people. All the way back the young Burmese asked him for the purpose of this trip. He asked and he pestered, but my friend the policeman did not give in. He always gave the same reply. He said he had been sent at the order of Mister

Charlie, and everyone in the young man's village knew about Mister Charlie and had much respect for him and his wishes. And his wish had been to see the young man from Burma and tell him the reason for the voyage in person. And so it came about that I was able to send word to my Mister Charlie that the man had arrived in my house.

My daughter Nellie was not in the house that afternoon. She had gone to spend the day and a night with her Farang friend Nina. One side of me was happy about that because I knew the task that awaited us was hard. But the other side was sad. My Mister Charlie had said he might be going away, and he had said he did not know how long for. The way things stood he might not see his daughter until he came back.

My friend the policeman bade us goodbye. My maid and I were preparing a meal while the young Burmese washed and changed. I had told him to have a rest, and promised I would wake him when Mister Charlie came.

It was late in the afternoon, maybe it was very late, but the sun stayed up longer than usual that day. I heard the purr of Mister Charlie's car and I sent my maid to fetch our visitor. We would not have much time alone together. I knew the Burmese was anxious to hear of the purpose of his journey and would come across very quickly.

Mister Charlie walked down the path and in his hand he held a large bag. He sat down with me on the porch and he looked at my eyes. There was a river of trust in them, and it made me feel proud. In his face I saw the face of a little boy. He did not speak and I could not speak, but the light that shone from him reached me and warmed my heart. He took my hand and he said:

'I think I have decided to stay. This is my home. The people I work with are my friends. You are my partner. I shall fight. That is what my dead friend U Nan would have wanted me to do.'

'Yes,' I said. I was too overcome to say more.

'They were willing to do business with me. Even though

our competitors are willing to pay more.'

'Yes.' The Buddha was smiling at me again, but I did not dare to be happy.

Then we saw the young man come running across the garden from the guest-house. Mister Charlie got up to greet him. They clasped hands, and I opened the door for them to come inside. The meal was ready to be served, the table decorated with flowers.

The young Burmese was a brave and patient man. He must have wondered why his relative U Nan the large ruby-dealer was not there. He might have guessed something had happened to him and his friends. I could feel he was tense because he kept smiling. He looked haggard and tired. I am sure he had not slept at all. But he did not press my Mister Charlie. He smiled at him with respect and waited for him to speak.

'You want to know why I have sent for you,' Mister Charlie said.

'I can wait until you wish to speak of it,' the young man replied.

'You have waited long enough. I thank you for that.'

'You do not need to thank me, Mister Charlie. Many of the miners and dealers in my village have spoken of you. I know you will tell me when you are ready.'

I saw my Mister Charlie was in great difficulty and I said:

'Perhaps we should all eat before you talk.'

'If that is what our guest wishes,' Mister Charlie said. Only I could hear the relief in his voice.

'That is what I wish,' the young Burmese said.

The maid brought the steaming pots over and I served the food. All through the meal Mister Charlie and out guest exchanged polite conversation, and the air was subdued. The days after the storm had gone by faster than lightning, but that short afternoon meal took forever, as if time had stood still. Neither of the two men was hungry, but they ate the food with apparent delight and they complimented me on it.

They talked about the ruby mines and the jewellery trade. They talked about the difficulties in finding good stones and the hardship and the border patrols. They talked about the war years when our visitor was a boy, and they talked about the journey.

My heart went out to both of them. To the young man for not daring to ask, and to my Mister Charlie for not knowing how to answer. Maybe both thought the solution lay with me.

'After tea has been served I shall go to the temple,' I said.

'Shall I come with you?' the young Burmese asked.

'Yes. We shall say a prayer for my father and my brother and for your cousin U Nan and his friends.'

The young Burmese did not express any surprise. Mister Charlie's face fell.

He believed it was his responsibility to break the news to our guest. He knows so little about the way we feel about death. In all the years he had spent in my country, Mister Charlie did not take the way of the gods into his heart. He knew about life and about giving and taking and danger and dying, but he did not penetrate the way of our gods about death. How death is not the end. How we are like a green leaf that floats down the river and goes on floating even when all life has gone from it. How it turns yellow and then gold and still it floats until it reaches its new form. How there is beauty in every stage of this voyage and every colour. The next world is as real as this world, and I know that no man disappears forever. We all come back again and we live again, even if our shape changes.

I have been told that Farang people believe they will go to another world if they have been good in this one. I have been told there is a place for every Farang soul, but I have never met a Farang who really trusted the next world. Maybe that is why the Farang move through life with such speed. Maybe they are afraid of time, and by going through it quickly they can ignore what will happen to them when time runs out. Perhaps, if they really believed in the next dimension, they would attain peace in this one. Paco, my friend from Manila, is an Oriental Farang who believes in their Lord Jesus. He is afraid of death and has confided that to me many times. My Mister Charlie is not afraid of death for himself. I know he has defied death many times, but he is the kind of man who feels pain for other people's loss.

The young man from Burma sat quietly for a very little moment and then he said he would come to the temple with me. It could be he knew all along what had happened to his relative, but I believe he did not. He accepted what I said and the way I said it and was now waiting for Mister Charlie to tell him how and when it happened. He was not going to ask Mister Charlie to tell him why it happened, because he knew our way and the teaching of the Lord God Buddha. He knew that what had happened to U Nan had to happen.

When we came back from the temple my Mister Charlie had settled a little. From his eyes came that great sadness, as though there was no consolation left for him in the whole wide world. I knew how grateful he had been to me, even though I hated the insecurity of not knowing whether he was leaving. I hated, too, my helplessness. For once he had made his decision there would be nothing I could do. It was in the hands of the Lord God Buddha. The young man seemed resigned.

'Did my cousin U Nan enjoy his visit with you?'

'He did.'

'My cousin loved his trade. He loved the stones. He loved their colour and the way they would emerge out of the raw when cut by an expert.'

'He did.'

'He was a happy man when he set off to come and visit you, Mister Charlie. He always talked about you with great fondness.'

'Thank you for saying that. I was fond of him too.'

'You did much business together.'

'Yes. But the last time we did business I failed to pay

him.'

'How did that come about?'

'I didn't get a chance to pay him. We were in the middle of negotiation when my enemy came into the office. Your cousin and his friends left while I stayed behind. The rubies were left with me. I didn't get a chance to pay for them.'

'Do you wish me to take them back?'

'Of course not. I wish to pay you. This is the main reason I asked you to come and see me.'

With these words my Mister Charlie handed the bag to our guest. The young man did not move. His hands stayed under the table, holding on to his knees.

'I do not wish to take your money, Mister Charlie.'

'I do not understand.'

'Most of us in the village did not want to continue doing business with you. Your prices are too low. The miners were losing money. The expenses crossing the border are mounting. The couriers are losing money too. My cousin would not listen to any of it. He even went against the advice of the village elders.'

'He never said that to me.'

'He was too good a man to tell you that. And while he was in your care you did not look after him. I don't want to take your money.'

'But I have received the goods. It is the custom.'

'You keep the goods. It is in payment for all the friendship you have given my cousin U Nan and your helping my village with guns during the war. We are equal now and have no more obligation to each other. I will not take the money. My cousin died while in your care. I believe you gave the money to him when he lived. We do not wish you to pay twice. The village elders would call it blood money.'

'We must speak of this again,' Mister Charlie said. His voice was dead.

'I shall be leaving tomorrow morning.'

'I am so desperately sorry for what happened.'

'It is in the hands of the gods. No man knows when it

is time.'

'I wish I could believe so, like you do.'

'You can hear the gods tell you that . . . Through the priest in many temples.'

'I cannot hear it. My sadness is too great.'

'Maybe you live too far from your Buddha, Mister Charlie.'

'Maybe I do.'

'Maybe you should go and live nearer to your Buddha.'

Mister Charlie's eyes looked like he had been struck by an invisible arrow. He struggled to keep his wits about him. The young man was humiliating him and I wanted to punish him for that, but there was nothing I could do because the gods had put the words in the young man's mouth. For a split second I thought my Mister Charlie was going to burst into tears. His face was grey with the strain of pain. He looked at me with resignation, and then he turned to the young man and he said:

'I have been thinking along these lines myself. Maybe I should go.'

'You may be happy living near your Buddha. He will protect you and your friends.'

Mister Charlie recovered his composure. 'I will let you have the car again,' he said. 'It will take you as far as the border.'

'I thank you for that,' the young man said. 'It has been a long day for me. May I go back to the other house? I wish to sleep.'

He got up and we all clasped our hands and then he was gone.

My Mister Charlie was shattered by what the young man had said. But I knew who had made him say that. I knew the young man would leave early, before I got up. Maybe he would be gone in the middle of the night. He would not wait for Mister Charlie's car.

He may not have known how much my Mister Charlie loved my country. How he had spent so many years here and in the rest of the Orient. So many years, he had almost forgotten where his own country was. And now, in my house, he had made his decision.

Neither the threats nor the death of his friends had made his mind up for him. What had finally pushed Mister Charlie into his decision were the words he had heard in my house that day. I know that because he told me so. That was the will of the gods.

We sat together late into the night. Just Mister Charlie and me. We touched hands sometimes, and sometimes I put my head on his lap. There was no more between us.

'It is clear now,' Mister Charlie said suddenly. I knew what he meant, but I refused to accept it.

'Why? What?'

'I am going to leave here, Nappaporn.'

'But it is all over. There will be no more death.'

'My decision has nothing to do with death.'

'I know.'

'You heard what the young man said.'

'I did.'

'He said it loud and clear. He told me to go, Nappaporn. He told me to leave.'

'You did not understand him.'

'Oh, I did. Believe me I did. He said this was not my country. He told me my time was up.'

'He did not mean it.'

'Maybe he didn't, but he was right.'

I am a vain and stupid woman. I should not have put up any arguments. The gods would be angry with me if I went on fighting for Mister Charlie. The die had been cast, and you do not fight destiny. Suddenly, it all became clear. Suddenly I knew why the gods had put these words in the young man's mouth. The words that came at my Mister Charlie were words he wanted to hear. Needed to hear. They had stressed the guilt that was plaguing him. They were all he needed to make his mind up. The gods wanted my Mister Charlie to leave, and no man's will is stronger than that of the gods.

We did not talk any more after that, and later, when Mister Charlie got up from the floor and left, I heard the drums of distant doom. The Lord God Buddha had put that thump of pain into me to prepare me, and I went numb. I stood by the door and listened to the purr of his car. I knew great changes were coming to our life. This time I did not cry at all because there was nothing I could do. There were no more doubts.

# CHAPTER FORTY-TWO

Suddenly he was in one hell of a hurry to let me have my way. It all happened just like I had wanted it to happen, but it didn't make me happy. Every time I think of that day I go a little funny. I feel a little lump of something up my throat. I don't know why. After all, there was no big deal. No big drama. It was all quiet and civilized, but it was the end of a great slice in my life.

I had come through the war and was lucky enough to find myself in the Orient. Unlike most other guys, I was in no tearing hurry to get back home. There was only my mother there. By then she was always home and wanted me there, but I could not face her too good. Sure, I did sit with her and I hung around New York for a while and saw the same faces and the same places. The family were going to give me my old job back, but there was no fun in it any more. I was yearning for what I had seen in the Orient. I decided to take a few months off.

At that time my old boss Don Antonio was still in charge, and he said it was OK. Maybe he did not want me around because I reminded him of my mother, and he had dumped her years before. So as soon as I could I packed my stuff and went back to Manila and met Paco again. In no time at all I realized there was plenty of dough to be made in the area. I stuck around and hit gold. I was about to have the time of my life. The life and style of every one of the guys I had met or worked with would have been a hit in the movies. Paco, my man in Bangkok, and of course Charles Paget-Brown. When my battle with him was over I knew the family would be pleased with me. After all, it was all my idea. I got them into the place and they were going to make a fortune out of it. These were great times.

I did spend lots of time with Charlie, and a bit of him must have slipped through into me. More than just my constant aping the way he talked. I had become a bit of a romantic. Or maybe I was just young. Maybe that's why I get the blues every time I think of that last day.

The great storm was over, but the water that had poured down from the sky refused to leave. Bits of plants and dead animals and furniture floated all over town. The place smelt like hell. Half-naked people worked their butts off trying to clear the garbage. You had to go everywhere by boat. Especially if you were living along the river. The streets leading to the Oriental were flooded. My man had dropped me on the corner where a guy from the hotel waited for any stranded guests. He took me in a small wooden boat and rowed me all the way to the staircase. The reception area was totally submerged. I held my shoes in my hand and my pants were rolled up to my knee the knickerbocker way.

On my table there were three messages from Charlie. I don't know how he got them there. The telephone lines were down. From my verandah I saw the river. I saw the brown water break the banks and expand into a lake. It reached the front terrace. It was hot again, so hot you would have thought the storm had never happened. Children swam happily in the water, and up above the sun shone as brightly as it ever did. The temple tops across the water glittered like coloured gemstones.

'I need to see you. I'm calling it a day,' all his messages read. He didn't even try to use a code. I guessed he was in a state of shock after he found out what happened to the Burmese. I had the feeling a change was around the corner. I had figured he would want to talk. But I didn't figure he'd want to get out of my life like a rocket. My heart thumped through my chest as if it wanted to get out of my body. I had been told once that palpitation meant nothing serious. Just nerves.

I took a stiff swig out of the bottle and sat down on my bed to think. Something big was going to happen. I should have known what it was, but I was too excited. I had planned it that way. I wanted Charlie frightened. So maybe at last he was frightened. I don't know why my emotions played such hell with me.

I was about to take another shot of scotch when the door opened. He stood there, fully dressed. His tall frame filled the door, and he was soaked.

'You didn't knock.'

'I am terribly sorry,' he said, and he smiled. His voice was steady. He was not frightened at all. 'It seems none of us knock any more. You're making me lose my manners.'

'Come on in, Charlie. Take your shoes off.'

'Yes. I think I will.'

He went into the bathroom and helped himself to a towel. He then sat down and took his shoes and his pants off and walked out to the terrace and laid his wet stuff on the table; then he walked in again. Slowly, in his shorts, with his long athletic legs, he walked to the bar and pulled a glass out and poured himself a drink. He raised it towards the window as if he was toasting someone, and then he came over and sat down at the table.

'Here we are,' I said. I was as nervous as shit but he was calm.

'Yes.'

'What can I do for you, Charlie?'

'Oh, you've done all you are going to do for me, Perotti. It's my turn to do things.'

'I don't know what you're talking about.'

'Of course you do, but it doesn't matter anyway. Look, I've had an offer from a friend of mine to join his business in Jamaica. You know about the man. I have told you about him.'

'Sam Baker?'

'That's right. I have decided to join him. His operation has nothing whatever to do with mine, so I won't be competing with you. I want you to leave us alone. My family, my friends, all of us.'

'You're going into the hotel business, Charlie?'

'Yes.'

'You don't need to go at all.'

'Don't kid yourself, Perotti. I'm not going because of you.'

'You misunderstood me.'

'I did not misunderstand a thing, Perotti.'

'I want you to stay. I need you.'

'I don't care what you want. I don't care what you need. I'm sticking to my end of the bargain; I expect you to do the same. I am leaving here and that's all there is to it.'

'But your whole life is here. Your family . . . Your friends . . .'

'My family will be with me, Perotti. Friends? Well, you know how it is. New places, new faces . . . I'll make new friends.'

'You're going to hate the hotel business.'

'I think not.'

'What about the excitement . . . the adventure . . .'

'I've had enough excitement to last me. I am tired. I want a quiet life now.'

'Just like that?'

'Just like that.'

He held the glass in his hand, then he put it on the table. He hadn't touched the scotch yet. He leaned back and his arms dangled down his sides. He looked at me and smiled politely as if we'd just been introduced. There was such innocence in his face he almost looked like a child. In his whole posture he was at such peace he might have seen God.

'You are a man of many faces, Charlie.'

'Whatever you say . . .'

'I'll tell you what I mean . . .'

'Please don't bother.'

'Well, if you don't want to talk, what do you want?'

'I told you. I want out. I need a few days.'

'You've got a couple of weeks yet.'

'I don't want a couple of weeks. I need to settle a few things.'

'You need cash?'

'No, thank you. I can deal with that myself, if you don't mind. I have emptied the kitty. I just want you off my back. I'd like to remember Bangkok without you.'

'That's not a nice thing to say.'

'Yes . . . well, I've got to be going now. When I've made my arrangements I'll let you know. You can have the stock at cost. You can have my desk, my chair, my ventilator fan. You can have the whole bloody lot. Some of my staff will stay with you for a month after I've gone. Longer if you treat them right.'

'Charlie . . . How do you expect me to take the show over without you?'

'You'll make the grade yet, Perotti. You're a smart fellow. New York is counting on you. You office boys never leave a thing to chance. You'll find a way. I'm quite sure you've got a whole new battalion lined up in the shade, ready to pounce. You know what I buy and where and for how much. Your people know damn well where to sell the stuff. You'll soon have things under control.'

'I know very little.'

'My heart bleeds for you.'

'You're being cynical.'

'I shouldn't worry about that . . . I'll soon be out of your hair.'

'Will I see you again before you leave?'

'Not if I can help it. I'll send you a note.'

'I reckon I'll owe you some money.'

'Yes. I'll let you know where to send it.'

He got up and stood there in his shorts. His things were probably still wet. But he got up and he went outside and dressed himself right there on the verandah. He took his time about it. He checked himself in the large glass window. I saw him wave to someone below. Then he came back. On his way to the door he stopped by the table and put a few bucks under the glass. The bastard was not drinking my liquor, but he was paying for it.

He straightened his tie and then, demonstrably, he did his fly button up, as if he'd just taken a leak. The bastard had done that on purpose, but I did not react. It seemed too vulgar, too out of character for him, and, momentarily, I did not accept any of it. I reckon I was in a state of shock. Dismay at the way it had all ended. The talks, the friendship, the waiting, the chance of being with a guy you admired, were all about to disappear. The best part of my life maybe.

I did not say a thing. I had lost the power of speech. I was about to experience an amputation. But I looked at him and I waited for him to say something. Even goodbye. But his expression told me the audience was over. What had gone between us never existed. What he'd listened to from me was all he was going to hear, and what he had said was all he was going to say.

I should have known why he had come. He had told me all about that long before. Or not so long before. I don't remember when it was, but I remember what he had said. About why Sam had gone back to his village. Something about a parting of the ways. About a man coming to see someone before leaving them for good. He saw me, but he did not shake my hand. He just looked mockingly in my direction, and what he saw I couldn't say. I know what he thought.

He stood there for an eternity. His face was focused on me, as were his eyes, but they looked through me like I was made of glass. As if I wasn't there. As if I didn't exist.

Charlie had done it again. In the last act of this movie he got the last word. The bastard had lost the war and I, the all-out winner, remained a nobody. I might as well have been dead.

# CHAPTER FORTY-THREE

—■—

She phoned, almost apologetically, and said she happened to be around the corner in some store. Would it be possible for her to come and see me? I said come on up.

She had always announced her visits that way. As if she was just passing by. The tone of her voice was remote and official. Like she was making an appointment with her dentist or something. The way she'd behave when she first came up never ceased to amaze me, but there was nothing strange about it. She was a shy woman, and never, ever did she come straight to the point. But once she was in my suite and in my bed and under the covers she'd unleash that passion and make me forget how distant she had been before. Maybe that is how women are when they're having something they shouldn't be having. She wasn't at all the way my mother was when I was little, but then my mother wasn't half the woman Rose is.

Her call came at the usual time, in the early afternoon, which used to give me a chance to have a little nap after lunch. She had not been up for over a week. I was happy she was coming. She knocked on the door and I said come in it's open like I always did.

She was dressed to kill in some new outfit, and the scent of her perfume busted the room as soon as she shut the door behind her. I would usually have hung the 'Do not disturb' sign on the knob outside, but when I saw her face I figured something was different. This wasn't going to be one of those visits. There was no smile. She did not sit on the couch. She didn't take her shoes off or ask for a glass of water the way she always did. She came over to the table and pulled out a chair for herself and waited for me to finish what I was doing.

I had been sorting out shipment plans and price quotations for New York to pass on to Europe. The family was hot for the ball to start rolling. Charlie's sources of penicillin and morphine were going to make them a bomb. I was busy looking for people to come and work. Drivers, shippers, inspectors and such. I had yet to figure out a way to bring Paco the Filipino in.

I folded the papers and pushed them over to one side.

'Would you like a drink, Rosie?'

'No, thank you. There isn't much time.'

'Where's the fire?'

'I've got a million and one things to do. You know we are leaving here?'

'Yes. Charlie told me.'

'I'm closing the house. There's packing to supervise. There's the furniture to cover up. A thousand goodbyes to say. I'm keeping two of the staff on.'

'Isn't that a little expensive?'

'Maybe, but I'd like the house in shape for when I come back.'

'I guess so.'

She was nervous. She kept looking at her watch. As if she couldn't wait to get out of the place. There was a tiny hint of guilt in her eyes, or regret. Or maybe it was sadness. And yet from time to time she looked at me with that old clue of expectation in her eyes. As if she had waited for me to say something personal. Something tender. But there was nothing I could say. I was the reason for her departure. She was never coming back, but she didn't know it. If there was any remorse for what I had done I could not afford to feel it then. I could not come out with the truth and tell her I was sorry. I was playing the ancient rule of secrecy. I had no idea what Charlie had told her about his sudden decision to leave. I had to wait for her to talk, but as the moments ticked away she became stiffer. None of the expected thaw was coming my way. All of a sudden we were strangers. I was thinking hard of something to say. Then my control blew and it came out without warning.

'I'm going to miss you, Rosie.'

She didn't answer. She just sat across the table from me and her eyes bored a hole into mine as though she'd tried to make sure I was telling the truth. I figured I was.

'Do you really mean it, Vincent?'

'Sure I do. Do you need to ask?'

'Sorry, I am so confused. So unhappy.'

For one moment the old magic was back. I got up and walked towards her. I stroked her head and she looked up at me. That soft, vulnerable look in her eye returned. A melt-down was around the corner. I was aroused and she knew it. I bent down to kiss her, and then the telephone rang and I raced to grab it. I knew who it was going to be.

'Hello,' I said. 'Yes. This is Perotti.'

'Mister Vincent, I come tomorrow.'

'Don't be crazy. You better wait.'

'Ready for start work. Family stay in Manila until you happy. Then come Bangkok.'

'You better put it on hold until I call you.'

'When I can work?'

'I'll have to think about a good way to plant you there.'

'You no can talk?'

'You're right.'

'I call again later.'

'Fine.'

'OK.'

'Where are you?'

'Hong Kong.'

'What for?'

'I must meet with Mister Charlie.'

'Is he there?'

'Yes. You want I finish him?'

'I have told you before. Don't even think of it.'

'But if he dead I can do like I said. Come help run his business quick quick. His friends see me sad. See me cry.

You remember how I said?'

'I remember it all, but it's all too late now. Things are different.'

The line went dead for a moment and I apologized to her. She nodded, and then she got up and went out to the balcony. She had never dared do that before. She leaned on the rail as if she didn't care who saw her. Then Paco's voice came back.

'If I kill him nothing different. We can do as I plan.'

'No. No. No. Do you understand? No. This part of the deal is over. You do that and I'll come looking for you, understand?'

'You must clean deck good. If Mister Charlie live he big trouble for you.'

'You leave that to me.'

'Yes, Mister Vincent.'

'Remember, you do nothing.'

'No talk to him even?'

'Sure you talk. You be nice, or else you never talk again.'

'Yes, Mister Vincent.'

'I'll let you know when you can come here so we start work.'

'They no want me in Mister Charlie business after him go.'

'Things ain't the same way now.'

'My way more better. Him dead they like me better.'

'We'll find a way to get you in. You leave that to me.'

'Yes, Mister Vincent.'

'Goodbye.'

I got up and I walked towards the verandah. I knocked on the big glass like I used to do from the outside when she was visiting. All that seemed to have been a million years ago. She came in and sat down again, and there was silence between us. All the while she sat there I was looking at her, and I took another swig and tried to smile but she was serious and her skin was taut and her eyes were hard. Something resembling a deep-rooted anger was about to come to the surface. She was fighting it. I knew she was. By the time I shoved a third drink down my throat she was composed. Her eyes assumed an expression of indifference. The magic was gone.

'I'm sorry about the telephone,' I said.

'Never mind.'

'Business is a frustrating thing sometimes.'

'Yes.'

'When is Charlie leaving?'

'Oh, he's gone.'

'Is he stopping in England on the way?'

'No. He's gone to Hong Kong,' she said. 'Maybe he's still there. He's saying goodbye to everybody. It's strange. He's behaving as though we were never coming back.'

'Yeah. I kind of wondered about it myself. It was all very sudden.'

'It was.'

'It sure was.'

'He is then going to Manila, Los Angeles, New York and Miami and so on. He won't get to Kingston for at least two weeks.'

'He's taking the long way round.'

'Yes. You'd think he was trying to avoid England at all costs. He has sisters there, you know. They live on a big estate. Charles was born there.'

'Didn't you tell me once he had signed it all away?'

'Oh, yes. He did that all right, but he could have gone to see the old place again.'

'Maybe he didn't want to see his sisters. Not that it matters. From what I remember the joint was going to come back to him once they were gone.'

'No it won't. It's going to some cousin of his. A chap who lives in Australia.'

'You never know. Maybe after that.'

'Not a chance. There are plenty of children there, Vincent. I'm afraid Charles will never inherit.'

'Yeah, but that's how he wanted it.'

'Yes. That's how he wanted it.'

'He's been doing good on his own anyway.'

'He was. He was, Vincent. But he's going into something new again now.'

'Charlie isn't the kind of guy to sit in one place for long.'

'He isn't.'

'Adventure is in his blood.'

'Yes. I'm afraid it is.'

That was where it ended. Before Paco's call came through there was a moment, a chance for that old passion to revive, but I'd blown it. Our hesitation was gone and with it the tenderness. It was all over. We sat there and we talked about Charlie like two kids talking about a favourite baseball coach. Or a movie star. The fan club was open again, and words flew to and fro without any problems. The conversation ran like a clock. Charlie, my victim, was over in Hong Kong on his way to Jamaica, and his wife, who had been my mistress, was in my room, and all we could do was talk and all we could talk about was him. Maybe it was better that way.

# CHAPTER FORTY-FOUR

He was so tired he could have slept for a week. He lay on his bed that afternoon and he thought of the week that had passed. A whirlwind of a trip to tie up loose ends.

Words and meals and homes and restaurants and names and faces flew incessantly through his mind. With them came the odours and sounds of the city he had once known and loved and was now destined to leave. There were smells of soy and fish and salty air and steaming rice. And sounds of car-horns and ship-horns and music and engines and hoofs and screeching wheels. And memories of long-dead friends and carefree moonlit junk-rides in the bay and endless conversations. And scents of thinly clad beauties crossing countless ballrooms and the sound of dance music and more. Thirty years of a dream-come-true life in a great city which never slept and never stopped growing or changing were all in the room with him.

The visit to all his old haunts went without a hitch. He had come to see the city one more time. Feel it and smell it and touch it and taste it. Like Sam did with his village.

So many things had happened to him here. The pain of his imminent parting throbbed through him every hour of the day. He saw each one of his friends. He told them all he was leaving the Orient for good.

Asking for permission to leave, he thought. No. He was no Sam Baker. He was not leaving the Orient. He was deserting it.

The reactions were all the same. He had seen and spoken to many over a million lunches and dinners and drinks. The conversations that followed the food and the drinks were exchanges of words between old friends, and now he compounded them in his mind and he listened. There were questions and answers and they were identical.

Why did he want to leave now? Just when he was at the pinnacle of success?

Wasn't that the best time to get out, when one is on top?

Maybe it was, but why do it? The place was growing like crazy. Goods were needed. Buildings were going up like mushrooms. There were fortunes to be made.

Then others can make them. He was more or less retiring from business. He was going into partnership with an old friend. Hotel business in the Caribbean.

Did he need the money?

No. Something to do.

Christ, that was boring, wasn't it? Wasn't he too young for a desk job?

He'd had his fill of excitement.

He'd change his mind. He'd be back.

No, he was not going to change his mind. Sure, he loved the Orient and especially Hong Kong, but thirty years was a lifetime. He needed some peace and quiet. See his daughter marry. Have grandchildren.

They didn't know he had it in him, they said.

Of course he had. Doesn't everyone?

But why so sudden a change? His business was thriving. Everyone knew that.

Yes, he agreed it was a surprising turn, but that was how he functioned best. Swift, quick decisions. Didn't they remember when he had left Hong Kong for the first time, just before the war, when he went to live on that island.

Of course they remembered. How could anyone forget the party? There hadn't been one like that before or since. Well, they were going to miss him. The old colourful characters were in short supply. The daring flyers and the captains and the naughty, naughty boys whose stories made your hair stand on end; their philandering, their deals, the best gossip. Where had they gone?

Some died and others retired and only a few of us are around now. We'll miss you like hell, old boy.

Sure. He was going to miss them too. But in the end they were all going to meet in England again, weren't they? Wasn't England where everybody ended up for the final bit? Didn't everybody go back to England when the course was done?

No. We'll stay until the bitter end. Couldn't face the weather again, old boy.

Now, after a week, he had seen them all and had listened to what they had said and he had agreed with every word of it. And he nodded and smiled and all the while he thought they were blind, but maybe they were not. The fact was he never told them the truth.

Sure, he should have stayed. Sure, he should have thought about coming back as soon as he got tired of the leisurely life that awaited him in Jamaica.

But then he alone knew the truth. Knew he could never come back. A return was impossible. The people he had visited had lived in this part of the world for many years, and had they known the facts they would have understood. In the Orient you can have adventures. You can make money and you can lose money, but there is one thing you can never do. You cannot lose face. There is no way back after that. They might not have known the circumstances of his departure, but sooner or later they would find out. He was running away to save his skin. He had lost his honour and all the years would count for nothing.

What was more, in a final put-down, he was *told* to leave. A simple bystander, hurt by his stupidity and greed, had said so very clearly. He was no longer wanted here. That was why he had to go.

He got up and drew the curtains. The Hong Kong side loomed on the other side of the bay. It was a hazy day, and he saw the shapes of ferry-boats crossing the water. There were destroyers whose great grey hulls came into view every time the patchy mist lifted. He saw a few proud old junks sail out to sea, and he thought of that same bay the way it was years before. Before the war. Before the Japanese occupation. Before the hustle and the bustle of the oncoming prosperity everyone was talking about. Before he was asked to leave.

He paced the room. There was still much to do here, but he was tired. The fun had gone out of it. That was the truth.

Funny, Charles thought to himself. It all started in this very hotel. Here he had met Sam Baker, and here he had spent many days with him. This was where their friendship had been forged. And even though they hadn't see each other since, that friendship was as strong as ever. And now he was going to Jamaica to call for his note. That note of obligation Sam had signed for him years ago, when he needed him. He was going to collect an old debt of honour.

Or was he? Maybe Sam really needed him there?

There was no sense in deliberating that. He'd have to see what the score was when he got there. For now he could sit here and ponder how to cut himself off from his past. So far, so good.

Roberta was back in Bangkok with Rose. They were going to England first. They were going to stay in one of the fashionable London hotels until he was ready for them. Everything had been organized. All his debts settled.

There was Nappaporn, but he must not become morose and guilt-ridden. He had thought that one out until he could think no more. He must not get sentimental about it. He had done the right thing by her. She was, like the Orient, a part of his life that was now over. To have taken her away from her country and her friends and family would have been impractical.

There he was again. Take her away? How arrogant could a man be? Nappaporn was no paper doll. She was no potted plant you move about the garden. She had strong roots. There was nothing helpless about her. By feeling bitter about leaving her he was putting her down. He was only feeling sorry for himself for losing a partner and a friend.

She was a proud and talented woman who could hold her own anywhere. She was a born trader, and with what had now been left to her she would want for nothing. She had always known their life together could not possibly last. She was going to find him out in the end. His weaknesses, his flippancy, his addiction to excitement, his greed. She had always accepted his other life, his other woman. But then it was not his other life that had called him away. Nothing is forever.

And her daughter would be fine. She would be much better off without him. As long as he was out of the picture she would never be considered illegitimate. She'd have the best education available and enough money to buy her a place in any family. He had done all he could do under the circumstances. He had sacrificed himself. By going away he was protecting them from Perotti. The bastard would have no use for them now. She had a strong will of her own and an independent spirit. Stronger than his.

He looked out of the window, and it occurred to him that he had a soft spot for strong women. One day he'd try and work out why, but not now. He might unearth a storm.

This was the real world. And in the real world he had one more thing to worry about. There was Paco the Filipino. He had asked Paco to come to Hong Kong to meet him. And now he was not sure what he could tell him. Paco was no Nappaporn. He did not have her strength. Her tenacity. Like himself, Paco was rootless. He was too much of a vagabond to form a base, to forge loyal friendships. Paco shouldn't have gotten himself mixed up with Perotti. He shouldn't have put his family in jeopardy for a few dollars.

A few dollars? Paco needed the business. He had no idea what working with Perotti would lead to. Paco was a trader. He bought and sold, and Perotti had been there in Manila with the army that liberated the Philippines. He had started off as Paco's hero. He was a simple man. A slum-boy who made good. He was kind, too. He only introduced the American to him because he thought he was helping him. But he, Charles Paget-Brown, he should have known better. What he had done was worse than careless. He only got what was coming to him. And now he was running from it, and Paco would lose out. How did one terminate a loyal friend and partner, a man who had brought you opportunities and riches? How did you tell him you were about to ditch him?

If Perotti was capable of doing what he did to him, what was he capable of doing to the Filipino? He would have to find a way to compensate him. An apology would never be enough. Paco was not going anywhere. He was being left behind, to face the wolves all on his own. His cowardice had created one last obligation.

He lay on his bed. He was too tired to think any more. All he could do now was wait.

Later there was a knock on the door, and Charles Paget-

Brown awoke. How long he had slept he was not sure. He had been dreaming, but he forgot what the dream was about.

'Come in,' he said, and he rubbed his eyes as Paco the Filipino walked in. The man wore his usual smile, and both his arms were stretched forward as he came closer. Charles got up. They hugged.

'You sleep, Mister Charlie?'

'Just dozed off a little. When did you get into town?'

'One hour before now.'

'Nice of you to come straight up.'

'What you mean?'

'I mean you must have better things to do here. You could have had a rest.'

'You said you want see me. I said I come Bangkok. You said no Bangkok. So I come Hong Kong see you. No other things to do. You want talk to me. We old friends from wartime. I always come where you ask. Where you want. Anytime.'

'Yes.'

'You say you have urgent business talk? You say what you need, Mister Charlie. I arrange quick quick. Something last delivery?'

'No, Paco. The last delivery is fine. I have brought the money with me.'

'I know you bring. You pay good. Why you need me so quick quick?'

'I am going to come straight to the point, Paco.'

'What you mean?'

'I am leaving Bangkok.'

'You move back Hong Kong? You want apartment?'

'No. Not Hong Kong.'

'You move back island?'

'No. I am leaving the Orient. Going away.'

'You go England?'

'No. I am going far away.'

'More far than England?'

'Yes.'

'When you back, Mister Charlie?'

'I am not coming back. Not ever.'

'You make big joke. Let me take drink. Very funny, Mister Charlie.'

'I am not joking at all. I have never been more serious in all my life. I am going away. I am leaving my business and closing the house. I have taken Roberta out of school. We are going to live somewhere else.'

'Where somewhere else?'

'We are going to Jamaica. It is an island in the Caribbean.'

'Why you go?'

'I am not going to bore you with that. I have caused you enough trouble, Paco.'

'You no make trouble. You only make good me. Why you go?'

'Our friend Perotti is forcing me out. You know he wanted my business. He put pressure on me. Big pressure, Paco. He won. I cannot stay.'

'What happen business, Mister Charlie? What about people work for you. You always say you never close business because your people them there.'

'Yes, I said that, but the pressure was too high. They will all be in danger if I stay. Even you, Paco.'

'What Mister Vincent do?'

'Believe me, Paco, you're better off not knowing. You'll find out anyway.'

'Anything you want me do, Mister Charlie?'

'No. There is nothing you can do. Just try to keep out of Perotti's way. I have told you he is a dangerous man.'

'All my fault.'

'No, Paco. Not your fault.'

'I introduce you. I stupid man. I never look.'

'No, Paco. You may have introduced us, but it was my stupidity that led to this. My curiosity. My greed. My need for adventure.'

'If I never introduce you you never leave us.'

'Not so, Paco. You had no choice. The man threatened your family. He was going to kill your wife. You had to introduce us. I won't hold that against you.'

'Yes, Mister Charlie.'

'But I did not have to do anything. I could have met him once and then gone away. I could have said there was nothing I would do for him. Even later, I could have said my supplies were finished. I could have refused to have had anything to do with him, but I did not. On the contrary. I went far, Paco. Much further than you. I took Perotti in. I introduced him to all my friends. My wife. He came to see me every day. I could have kicked him out, but I did not. I was too curious to find out what he wanted. His manner excited me. I thought we could do things together. Now that the war was over Perotti was the most refreshing thing that had happened to me. There was adventure, excitement . . . There was my youth again . . .'

'What you mean?'

'Quite so, Paco. I'm sorry. I talk too much. You ask what I mean. I don't know what I mean. I mean you are not to blame for Perotti and what happened. It's nothing to do with you. Only me.'

'You no thinking, Mister Charlie.'

'Oh yes I am, Paco. I have been doing nothing but thinking for the longest time.'

'What can I do?'

'Nothing much.'

'Why you give him business?'

'That was his plan all the time. I told you that last time we met here. But I thought I could deal with him. Reason with him. Now he's beaten me. And I know this man now. He will never let go. He will never go away. Only by giving in can we hope he will leave us alone. I am leaving. I am running away.'

'You never run away, Mister Charlie.'

'Yes I am.'

'I no believe you. Tell me truth.'

'The truth? I told you the truth.'

'Not this truth. The other truth. Why you go away, Mister Charlie? I never believe you run. Why you go?'

'Because this is no longer my home.'

'Sure is your home.'

'No. I am no longer wanted. No longer needed here.'

'I want you here. I need you, Mister Charlie.'

'Thank you for that.'

'Who tell you to go? I kill him today.'

'It is time, Paco. It really is. Perhaps I should have realized all that before. I was blind and I was greedy. Perhaps I was stupid. Perotti is only an instrument. Only a detail in a process of departure.'

'What you mean?'

'It's time to go, Paco, that's what I mean. The only regret I have is that I am leaving you here to face Perotti by yourself. You and all the people who are working with me in the business. I cannot help you there, but I expect he won't do any more harm to anyone. Not now. He's got what he wanted.'

'I can help, Mister Charlie.'

'How?'

'I go Bangkok. I watch. I look your people. All your people.'

'How would you do that?'

'I stay Bangkok forever.'

'Leave Manila? Uproot yourself? Why should you do that?'

'You and I same same. You like change. I love change too, Mister Charlie. I live in Manila but never stay there. I sail many seas many years. You and me and also me alone. You remember. Have friends and business many places. You know. No matter where live. I want go too. I like Bangkok. Same same Manila. Same fish and fruit and Oriental people like same family. Your friends my friends. I trust them like family. If go Bangkok I bring my wife and father and childrens and I work like before and see your business every day and watch what happen.'

'You're too kind, Paco, but I'd never expect you to do that. I'd never allow it. You're a true and trusted friend. This is very kind of you, but I can't have it.'

'Mister Charlie, you tired tired, you no think. I go Bangkok good for your people, good for me, good for Mister Vincent. I help him in business and he happy so he good to people, yes? He never treat people bad if business OK. I like Bangkok. I love Bangkok. Good for everyone. Good for you too, Mister Charlie.'

'Let me think about it, Paco.'

'What you do? How long you stay Hong Kong?'

'I'm off to Macao tomorrow.'

'Play money?'

'Yes.'

'Never play money when angry. You lose.'

'Maybe.'

'You want go woman place?'

'No, thank you. You go.'

# CHAPTER FORTY-FIVE

I had just come back from the temple when my friend from Manila came to see me. He had come up from the river, through my garden, and I saw him just as I reached my porch. I had not expected to see him so soon after Mister Charlie had left, and the surprise must have shown in my face. Our friend Paco is a strange man. Like many Chinese people who live outside China, Paco is always on the move. Sometimes he makes me feel strange. He is an Oriental who dresses like a Farang, but his silk suits are always too shiny and his crocodile shoes and golden teeth make him look like a gangster. He is not attractive, but he is a good man who has been a friend to my Mister Charlie and to me. When he told me why he had come all my doubts dispersed.

My daughter Nellie was in the house. I called her to come and greet my friend from Manila, but she pretended she did not hear me. Or else she was doing her homework. I ordered the maid to make Paco a cup of tea and some lime juice and bring out a plate of coconut sweets.

He sat with me on the porch and he smoked his cigar and the smell reminded me of my Mister Charlie.

'I am sad Mister Charlie is not with us here,' he said.

I nodded. I knew he meant what he said, and because I felt the same and more I had to contain myself. It is not becoming for a lady to show her emotions, even to a friend. The lady of the house must never load her pain on her guests.

'I saw Mister Charlie in Hong Kong,' he said.

'When was that?'

'Three weeks ago. Maybe four.'

'Was he well?'

'It is difficult to say. Mister Charlie is not a man to complain. He smiled and he talked like he always did, but there was something missing.'

'I understand.'

'Are you asking for my opinion?'

'If you wish to give it I am.'

'He was a shadow of himself. He was devastated. All he could talk about was his life in your country and you and the years you have been together. All he could hope for was the day he will come back and be with you.'

'I understand,' I said, and I fought my tears.

'I begged him to change his mind but he was like a rock. He did not move. He was going because he was afraid for his friends, for you. He was so upset about the murder of his friends from Burma . . .'

'That was not why he decided to go.'

'Maybe not. Maybe I will never understand why he left, but I respect him too much to pry into his reasons.'

'I understand.'

'We must go on with life, Nappaporn. We must take it

up where he left and continue.'

'You are right.'

'Mister Charlie has been my friend for many years. We have been through a lot together, and we did business and met people and shared pleasure and danger, but last time I saw him in Hong Kong he had done something he had never done before. That is why I think he has reached a serious crossing-point in his life.'

'What did he do?'

'He asked for my help, Nappaporn. For my help.'

'And did you give it to him?'

'This is what I have come here for. To talk to you about it. You are his closest friend. You know all about his connections and his friends and the places he went to and the people who came to see him and who sold goods to him.'

What Paco said should have made me suspicious, but this man was not an educated man. He had struggled to come up in the world by his wits, and sometimes he said things he did not mean to say. He was flattering me as was his way. He was a child and I was vulnerable, but I am a mature woman and I had to hear him out.

'Did you help him?'

'I will try to. I don't know how to do that. I have come to you for advice. He trusted you more than anyone, and I know you will give me good advice. You will know what he meant better than me. I am a simple man.'

'You are not a simple man.'

'I understand yes. I understand no. I know people who pay and people who don't pay. I know people I like and people I don't like. But I don't understand when people make me guess what they mean. I am bad at guessing.'

'Why do you say that? Mister Charlie always spoke clearly, didn't he?'

'Yes, he did, but the last time I saw him he wasn't clear at all. He wanted my help. He asked for it. But he didn't say how I was to help him. He told me to give you a letter, but only after you explain to me what to do.'

'You have a letter from Mister Charlie for me?'

'Yes. But I can only give you the letter after we talk. When I understand.'

'Mister Charlie said that?'

'Mister Charlie said that.'

'What is it you do not understand?'

'Mister Charlie told me he was leaving the Orient for good. But his heart, he said to me, was not going with him. He said he was not going to be happy anywhere in the world unless he knew that you and his friends in his business were safe. He said only I could help him make sure. I asked him how, and he said he wanted to know if I was ready to help him. I said he knew I would do anything for him and all he needed to do was tell me. Then he asked if I was going to Bangkok. I said I would go anywhere. Then he asked how long I could go for. I said as long as he wished. Then he said good, and he sat down and wrote this letter for you and another for his secretary at the office and gave them to me. He said to tell you about everything.'

'And you don't understand what he meant?'

'No.'

'I think he wanted you to move to Bangkok, Paco. Move to this city and look after things.'

'You mean pretend to work with Mister Vincent?'

'Yes. I think that.'

'Pretend I am with him? Pretend I want to help him?'

'I think that.'

'Why did Mister Charlie not say that to me himself?'

'Because Mister Charlie is a shy and modest man. He would never ask you to do something for him unless you really wanted to. Unless you suggested it yourself. Unless it was good for you too. Do you want to work in his office? Do you want to live in this city?'

'I would do anything for Mister Charlie.'

'I know. But would you like to?'

'I would like to do anything for Mister Charlie. Anything I can do for him will make me happy.'

'Then I shall speak to all his friends. I shall talk to all my friends too. They will help you. I shall make sure you can work with the American Farang without fear of revenge from anyone. The people at Mister Charlie's office will give you respect.'

'I will go and visit Perotti tomorrow. I will offer my services to him.'

'Don't do that. I want to make it safe for you. Let me talk to my friends first.'

'Thank you so very much, Nappaporn. If only I could bring Mister Charlie back again.'

'That is in the hand of the gods.'

'After he wrote the letter we parted and he went to Macao to play the tables. I think he wants to damage himself. I am afraid he will lose much.'

'That is in the hands of the gods too.'

'I shall give you the letter now.'

'Thank you. Would you like my maid to serve some food?'

'I could not eat now.'

'Is your ship in the river?'

'Yes, it is.'

'Are you staying on board?'

'No. Mister Charlie said it wasn't safe to do that until I saw you.'

'Where are you staying?'

'I have an old friend in the customs office. I sleep in his house.'

'The man who got into trouble last time you were here?'

'The same man.'

'Has everything cleared up for him?'

'Yes.'

'I am glad. I will send a message to your ship when all is ready. Come and see me when you get it.'

He got up and we clasped hands and he left.

Perhaps I was rude to Mister Paco that day. But he had brought news from my Mister Charlie and I wanted to be by myself when I read his letter.

*My dearest Nappaporn,*
*I have gone away like a thief in the night. I could bear threats and I could bear death and torture as long as they were directed against my person. Not against my friends or my family. There is no telling what the other side would have done next. I don't even want to contemplate it. But all that would have only made me want to fight back. And the war would have lasted for a long time, maybe forever. Many people would have suffered. Many would have died. That is because the other side is backed by many people and they have no end. And even that would not have made me leave. I could have taken my family away and sent you somewhere safe and come back myself to fight.*

*You know all that well. You know it was not the danger. You know well what made my mind up. It was the young Burmese that last afternoon I came to the house. He opened my eyes. I am a child playing with fire. As long as the fire only burned my own hands I could go on playing. But I have grown up now, and I know there are no more games. The young Burmese told me to go away and live with my own people, with my own Buddha. I do not have a Buddha anywhere, but there are people I know and love and I shall attempt to do what the young Burmese said. I should have said that to myself a long time ago. I should have seen my time here was over. I should have seen the damage I was inflicting by my refusal to grow up. To you, to your daughter, to my wife and Roberta, and to my friends here who trusted me.*

*I never needed to pretend when we were together. You have been my best friend and comrade and partner and lover. You have always been the stronger one. Subconsciously I might have used you. Some of the happiest moments in my life have been with you. I thank you for that, and ask your forgiveness for this late hour of maturity.*

*My friend Paco the Filipino will bring you this letter. He will give it to you after he has told you of his kind offer to help me out. I hope you will make sure our people at the office and in the field will give him all the assistance he will require. It is a hard task he is offering. He will have to be accepted by them and trusted by your enemy all at the same time. He will have to work with Perotti, and there must be no revenge. I know you are a wise woman and will help him achieve that.*

*I am enclosing a deed of ownership for you. In it I have included seven more boats, all I have left. They are yours from now on. I have instructed my bank to give you access to my safe. There you will find some money and gems to help you set up a new trading operation if you so wish. Separately, I have also left three bags of rubies and a briefcase with cash in it. The stones are those U Nan sold me. The money in the briefcase is full payment for the rubies, and I ask you to try and pay the Burmese off for them. Otherwise use the contents of the safe in any way you see fit. You are a talented and beautiful woman, and you will do well whatever you decide to do.*

*Make sure Nalini gets the best education money can buy. Never stop her from doing anything she wants to do as long as it will widen her knowledge and her vision. When the time comes I know you will see she meets and marries the right kind of person. It is arrogant of me to say this, and I apologize to you for saying it. I know you are better aware of it than I.*

*Writing this is as difficult for me as it is for you to read it. I hope we shall see each other again. I hope the river of time will slow down for us one day, and until then I embrace you.*

*Yours, Charles*

There is nothing final about death. You can become anything in the next world. A horse or an insect or anything. If you are a good person and you have pleased the gods you may come back a man. But whichever form the gods choose for my reincarnation, I know I shall see my Mister Charlie again in the next world. Or in the one after that. Even the Buddha endured five hundred reincarnations before he came back as himself.

The gods were smiling down on me that day. My Mister Charlie had gone to live closer to his Buddha, but he was still on this earth. There was time enough for us to see each other in our present form, even if we were to become old first. This was not the end. I thought I would go to the temple first thing in the morning to thank the gods for what they had given me. For the trust and the love and care they had sent me through my Mister Charlie. I was a rich woman, and I was going to be a richer woman. My Mister Charlie had made sure my daughter and myself would want for nothing. And even so it was not all over yet.

I went into the house and into the big bedroom in which I had slept only when Mister Charlie was with me. I closed the door behind me as if he was there on the bed waiting for me. I could smell the sweet smell of his body and feel the soft touch of his skin. I remained in there all night. I could hear my daughter and my maid calling for me, but I did not open the door. That night I wanted to be alone with my memories. I did not cry at all. I lay down on the bed and I was eighteen years old again, and I stayed that way until morning came.

# CHAPTER FORTY-SIX

I think I have decided finally to give up on my mother. I can no longer make her out. Her moods swing from one extreme to the other. Nothing I do is good enough. Nothing I do makes her happy. I have tried so very hard to please her since Mister Charlie left. He was so important to her, and I knew her world had fallen apart, and I did try hard. Honestly I did. I stopped staying nights with my friend Nina. I stopped going out with my mother's maid. I have not been on the town or seen any of the new films. All I did was go to school and come home and do my homework and try to be nice to her and talk to her and humour her. I have not been successful.

Two weeks ago I won a prize for the best essay. We

were asked to write about our home life, and I wrote all about it. Mostly I wrote about my mother. About how beautiful she is and how she works and how she looks after the house and how she prays daily at the temple. I know little about my mother's religion, but I asked her maid to explain it to me. I wrote about my mother's spirit house at the bottom of the garden. I even wrote about the fish market. I described it in detail, and I wrote about my mother's friends there. I wrote about the river. I did not mention my father at all.

The teachers liked the essay so much they made me read it to the whole school at assembly-time. There was applause. The headmistress said everybody knew I could act, but my expressing myself so well in writing was something that should be nurtured.

The whole school talked about that for days. Maybe I will be a famous writer one day.

I sat down with my maid and I translated the essay into Thai. I wanted to read it to my mother. She would hear for herself how much I appreciated what she had done for me. I wanted her to see how much I needed her.

I chose the time very carefully. Usually my mother likes the morning best. After she has had a good night's sleep and before the business worries of the day hit her she can be easy, and she laughs a lot.

I waited for a long time. One afternoon my mother's friend Paco the Filipino came to her house. I don't like him very much. I shouldn't say that because we have known him for ages, and he often came to my mother's house, even when my father was not there. I should not like or dislike people because of the way they look. He is always dressed very loudly, and I have never seen him clean-shaven. He has a mouthful of gold teeth and he always brings me a present, yet still I don't like him. He has been my father's best friend for many years. Maybe that is why I do not trust him. But I know my mother does trust him, and his visits always make her happy, and that is how I wanted her to be.

I was listening to what he said. He said he had seen my
father and had brought her a letter from him. I knew that
would make my mother very happy. I decided to read the
essay to her on the morning of the next day. I sat down all
that afternoon, while Paco and my mother were on the
porch. I stopped listening to their conversation. I locked
myself up in my room and I went over the essay again. I
cannot write in Thai, and I had written the translation in the
Latin alphabet. I had to make sure it was all right. I heard
my mother call for me, but I did not answer. I was too busy
working on my essay. I worked for many hours and then,
after everyone went to bed, I called the maid in. I whispered
the whole essay to her one more time, and she said it was
fine.

My mother had shut herself away in her room and the
maid said she was reading Mister Charlie's letter. She said
my mother was very happy. That meant she would have a
good night. I was so excited I think I did not sleep much at
all.

At breakfast-time the next day I took the paper out. I
asked my mother to listen. The maid's face lit up in expectation. I read the whole essay in one go. Not too quietly and
not too loud. I read it slowly, in Thai, and all the while my
eyes stuck to the paper because I was afraid to look at her in
case what I said was embarrassing to her. My mother likes
to be loved, but you cannot give her compliments.

When I finished reading there was silence. My mother
did not say anything. The maid looked at her, and then she
looked at me. I think she wanted to cry. I hate people feeling
sorry for me.

'What do you think?' I asked my mother.

'You said nothing about your father.'

'You said I must never mention him at school.'

'You tell too much. You must not let people know how
you feel.'

That was all I could take. I wasn't going to let her see
me cry. I did not have breakfast, and I jumped up and took

my books and ran out of the house. I was so quick, and my going that early was so unexpected, the maid didn't get a chance to follow me. I ran and I ran and I did not look back, but I knew the maid would never catch me up.

It was too early to get into the school. The gates were still shut. I had started to walk down the avenue when I saw the big black car slow down behind me. I knew who he was. I had seen him before, and one time we spoke and I think I liked him. Now there was nothing to worry about. He was no longer a stranger. I stopped and the car stopped and the American lowered his window and his head came out and he smiled.

'You're early. Can't you sleep?'

'I like getting up in the morning.'

'You're lucky. I hate it.'

'Maybe you go to sleep too late.'

'Maybe I do.'

'Do you have bad dreams?'

'Maybe. I can never remember what I dream about.'

'Neither can I.'

'Then we have one thing in common.'

'We have two things in common.'

'What is the second?'

'You said you were a sad kid.'

'Did I say that?'

'You said that. Did you lie?'

'I never lie to pretty little girls.'

'I am not a little girl. I am thirteen. And I am tall for my age.'

'Sure you are. I'm not very good at telling children's ages. I don't have any.'

'Where you really a sad boy?'

'Why d'you ask?'

'You said that to me once.'

'If I said that to you I was.'

'Where are you going?'

'To my office.'

'Where is your office?'

'It's near the Oriental Hotel.'

'But that is the other way.'

'I like to take a ride in the morning.'

'My father's office was near the Oriental Hotel too.'

'Was?'

'Yes. He's gone.'

'Oh, yes. I've heard something about it.'

He then went silent. I don't know what happened to him at that moment. He lowered his eyes as if he didn't want to look at me. I looked at his face. It was a broad face. My mother always said broad-faced people are kind, and his really was. It was chubby and sweet and soft. I could see what he had looked like when he was a sad kid and I wanted him to talk more, but he remained silent. As if he waited for me to say something.

'You said you have heard about my father.'

'You like talking about your father, right?'

'No. I don't.'

'What do you like talking about?'

'My friend Nina. My maid. The school.'

'Tell me about school.'

'I wrote an essay.'

'What about?'

'About my home.'

'Was it good?'

'I thought so.'

'You don't think so now?'

'I am not sure.'

'Why aren't you sure?'

'I don't know. My mother didn't like it.'

'Did the teachers like it?'

'Oh, yes. They liked it a lot. I read it out loud to everybody.'

'Will you read it to me?'

'OK.'

I stood there by the side of the car. I took the book out

and I leaned against the door away from him. I read the essay out. I read it fast. When I finished reading I was still afraid to look at him. Maybe I didn't want to disappoint him. He had been a sad kid and this was a happy essay. Then he started clapping his hands and I turned round. His face beamed.

'You like it?'

'I love it. You are a talented girl.'

I did not know what to say or what to do. I should have been happy to hear what he had said, but I think I wanted to cry.

He looked at me and he said:

'You write good. You read good, too.'

'That's what the headmistress said.'

'She was right. I don't understand why your mother didn't like it. It's a great story.'

'It's an essay.'

'Sure. It's a great essay. But it's so good it could be a story.'

'You like stories?'

'Sure. But I have a friend who likes stories better than I do. He liked books. He always read books, and he read so many he became a dreamer.'

'Who is this friend?'

'Oh, he lives far away.'

'Did you like him?'

'I liked him, very much.'

'Then I am sorry he is so far away.'

'So am I.'

'Would I like him?'

'I don't know.'

Again his face fell. The sad kid came back into his face. I felt sorry for him. I think I wanted to stroke his head. I think I liked him then. This was very embarrassing. I turned round and I saw that the gates of the school were open.

'I'd better go now.'

'I hope we'll talk again. I always pass here at this time of the morning.'

'I hope so too,' I said, and I ran off. I didn't want him to change his mind. I wish I did not have to live with my mother. I must find a way to leave home. But where can I go?

# CHAPTER FORTY-SEVEN

Charlie always did have the last word. Even after he had scrammed bang out of my life he remained in control like some ghost. With him out of town the whole deal was worthless. You can't run a show like his without goodwill. Sure, he had made the business over to me and I sat in his office under his fan. Sure, I knew where he got all that morphine and penicillin and I knew how much he was paying for it. For the first month after Charlie had left everything went great. Just like he said. I was being good to Charlie's guys and I gave tips and time off and stuff. I thought we were sitting pretty, and then the month was up and things became kind of slack. His people started screwing me with delaying tactics, and every time I asked what the problem was I got one of their dumb smiles and some excuse, but nothing changed. The ruby guys from across the border were sending crappy stuff that made us look like assholes when my guys tried to offer it to the local gem-cutters. My social life did not exist. Zilch. Kaput. There were no more clubs, no nothing, and even though Charlie's friends knew nothing, they shunned me like I was dirt. I was living in a desert, working my butt off. There was no fun at all. I began to hate the place. It was as if the Orient went sour on me once Charlie was out of it.

The only good thing about my life at that time was Charlie's little half-caste daughter. The more I saw of her the more of her I wanted. I would pass her school deliberately, but she was not always there. Sometimes I was too early and sometimes I was too late. I couldn't be seen there too often because Charlie's friends might have noticed me talking to her. They might call the police, and they were the last people I needed then. But when I did manage to see her and talk to her it set me up good for the rest of the day. And even that bit was Charlie's. Not mine. He controlled me there too, because I could not talk too much about him. The kid was as smart as a whip. She'd see through me in a second. I couldn't get too close to her, like inviting her over to the office. Somehow she would find out I was in her father's office, and then what? So Charlie was in charge of my socializing, and he was behind every bit of crap I was eating in his office. Things were not good there at all. I could see us losing money in no time. The shit would soon hit the fan unless I did something radical.

The family was going to ask questions any minute now, and I was putting my own money on top of our payments to cover up. I couldn't go on doing that forever. Any small-time accountant would find me out, and if they were going to send someone out they wouldn't send a jerk. I couldn't tell New York what my problem was. I knew what they were going to say. You couldn't just waste everybody in this town because their heart wasn't in it. Everybody knows I am no administrator, but I wasn't going to go back home a failure. Not after all the time and effort and cash we'd spent. I wasn't going back to any number games or contract shooting or collecting protection money. The alternative was getting lost, and the world wasn't big enough for that. I didn't know then what I know today, so I needed to hold on regardless.

The problems in the office became public knowledge. Everybody started saying Charlie was right to sell out and get going when he did. They said he foresaw what was coming. They said I was some son of a rich guy from the States whose father needed to get him away. I didn't really care what they said because no one said it to me. I was mad at the way I fucked up with Charlie. I should have made him stay.

Only after he had left I realized it had nothing to do with me. I didn't get the credit for his departure at all. I didn't even see him after that time in my hotel. He didn't bother to contact me or say goodbye. He just sent me a message. He had scribbled it on the back of a used office memo sheet of paper. 'Come and get it, Perotti', the message said. He said he had finally decided he was going, and I was not to think it was because of me. He said the locals had convinced him his time was up. I didn't know what the hell he meant. I've often tried to work it out, but I couldn't make any sense out of it.

But during that period I had no time to find out why Charlie had left. I was looking for ways out of the mess I was in. Funds were running low, and soon I wouldn't be able to pay bills without an injection from New York. When Charlie wrote me a note of where he was at in Jamaica I ignored it. He was after the money I owed him, but I reckoned I did not owe him a thing. Not while the business he had left me was in trouble. Besides, when you owe a guy money he'll sure stay in touch with you.

We had been keeping Paco the Filipino out of Bangkok while we figured out a way to bring him in without arousing suspicion. Having him work with us in the current climate would have been the last blow of death. Any one of Charlie's friends seen with me would have been treated like a leper. I needed him more than ever before. He would have been the right guy to show us the ropes. In desperation I began to think he had a point when he suggested we should get rid of Charlie, and have him come in like the people's saviour. I was young in those days and I thought I knew it all and, besides, I had done a deal with Charlie and I was going to run with it. The troubles he was giving me only made me admire him more. But I caught myself thinking of Paco almost every morning. Then one day the shitface himself turned up. I was sitting in Charlie's office when he came in, dressed like a tie salesman, smiling that sickening gold-tooth smile of his.

'Has anyone seen you in the general office?'

'What you mean?'

'I'm having a rough time with the bastards. They are not cooperating.'

'You no make money?'

'You kidding? I'm losing money like crazy.'

'Why? Mister Charlie he rich with this place.'

'I can't get his people to move.'

'They will do good now, Mister Vincent. They do just as you say.'

'How you think you're going to get them to do that?'

'You say to me and I say to them.'

'If they find out you're here they'll kill you, Paco.'

'Kill me, Mister Vincent? Office people kill me?'

'They have friends. Tough guys from the fish market. Nappaporn's friends.'

'Nappaporn my side.'

'Your side? You're crazy. I haven't made any arrangement for you yet. You should have waited. You better get out before someone sees you.'

'They see me, Mister Vincent. They see me and they greet me like lost baby.'

'What the hell do you mean?'

'Mister Charlie he want me come. He write letter to his people. Another to Nappaporn. He ask them look me as friend. He say I be like him. Like Mister Charlie himself. If you speak me and I speak them I be Mister Charlie. That how they make good.'

'You're lying.'

'No lie.'

'If you're not lying you're crazy.'

'You try. You see.'

I had nothing to lose. I almost wished he was going to be proved wrong. That would have given me a reason to get rid of him once and for all. But he was right. One week into the new deal and things began to run like they did when Charlie was boss.

That was how our operation in the Orient started. They call it the Far East now, but to me it will always be the Orient. I have spent many years there, running what started as Charlie's old business and what became a great money-maker for the family. Of course, I didn't stay there to see the computers and the accountants and the clever guys come in. But I did make the money that made it all possible.

I worked with Paco the Filipino and every one of Charlie's old staff. In time they began to accept me as though I had always been there.

There were changes, but these didn't happen in Bangkok. Two years after Paco's return the old man, my first boss Don Antonio, died. As I see it, the brothers only waited to have him out of the way before they split up. It was a question of the family honour. Still, there wasn't much honour around after he went. The family was split in two, and they divided the operations in New York and Europe between themselves. We were only a small family, and in the larger picture we didn't amount to much. I'm not even sure anyone had ever heard of us, but we were there and we were doing good. Even after the split.

In a funny way, the only common piece of property they had was me and the operation I had set up for them in the Orient. And because they hardly spoke to each other except when someone was born, got married or got buried, I was the only guy both brothers were on talking terms with. I was the only one they trusted. That put me in a very strong position for later on, but I am racing. When you get old you prefer thinking of the good things that happened.

This place is a peach at springtime, and Nellie Brown is here. We saw each other yesterday. I've seen Charlie too, but she didn't. I promised her I'd fix it for her to see him, but I'm not too sure these two should get together after all these years. She moves in different circles now. But I hope I'll catch another glimpse of the girl before I go. The concierge will let me know where she's at and when. Everyone knows everyone in Cannes. This is a small town.

The guy from reception says to get ready. The limousine has arrived, he says, and if you want to make San Remo by three o'clock you better come down. I haven't been to a funeral since one of the brothers bought it five years ago. It was a big affair, like in the movies. There were many limos there too, stretching a couple of blocks. There were flowers and messages and police. The guy was younger than me, but he drank and smoked too much and chased too many women and finally his heart gave in. With his past he should never have died in bed, but that's life. His son is running that side now and we get along fine. He calls me Uncle Vincent.

I didn't mind that funeral. They say funerals make you think of when your own time comes, but that don't bother me.

# BOOK THREE

## CHAPTER FORTY-EIGHT

———■———

I never thought I would be writing a diary. This is certainly not meant to be the story of my husband's life. They have written many articles about his career in the local papers. About how he had arrived, a penniless Arab who had found a niche for his talents, and how he's become a millionaire. On occasion, I would read some of those to him and he'd dismiss them out of hand. Nothing to it, he would say. It was a dream and an adventure. And it's not over yet. He didn't mean to come to Jamaica at all. He was going to America. We always laughed when he said that, because it didn't end there. I would say, Why don't you go to America. Do what the boys from Abu Hanna's coffee house did. And he would say he no longer needed to go because he already had me, and that was the best America could have given him.

These notes are meant to record the thoughts and feelings of a man named Sam Baker. A man who in mid-life suffered the trauma of blindness. They are not too long. My dear husband Sam talks little.

A friend of mine who is also his doctor has suggested that I talk to Sam and that I put his thoughts and feelings down on paper. That way we could monitor whether or not the depression that struck him a few years ago shows any signs of creeping back.

At first I resisted. I thought it would be an intrusion on my husband's innermost self, a betrayal of private emotions revealed to me alone. And then the doctor suggested that I make these notes with Sam's knowledge and consent, that I share these notes with him. He said I should encourage Sam to participate. Talking freely about his days, his thoughts and his feelings would help Sam understand himself better.

The doctor admitted that this was an unusual therapy, and that to the best of his knowledge it had not been tried before. Not scientifically.

Sam has a very close friend. They'd met in Hong Kong years ago, when Sam first lost his sight. Discussing him comes easy to Sam, and the doctor agreed we should concentrate our notes on him. As long as his friend lived in the Orient that was impossible, because all we could talk about were letters. But now that Charles Paget-Brown, the man from Bangkok as I like to call him, is here on the island, my husband has plenty of opportunity to meet with him and talk to him and observe him. He has been living here for a few years now and there is, therefore, much to discuss and take note of. These notes belong to the two of us. We talk, and then I write down what we talked about and read it back to him for his comments. At first I used to blot out what he did not like, and then I asked him if he minded my keeping my own thoughts intact, even if he does not agree. Sam said my thoughts were my own and they must stay on this pad.

My family came from the Middle East. Much the same way as Sam did. They too dreamt of a better life, and they found it in their success. My grandfather started in the market-place. He had the same accent Sam has. I am a New Yorker through and through, though my father still had plenty of the old country in him. He loved the food and the old customs and he tried to be the patriarch. He was very fond of Sam, and he was as happy as a child when I decided to marry him. There were oceans between us when we first met, and these persisted well into our married life. It was not always easy. I came to this beautiful island a very brash young woman. I was independent, and more than just a little pampered. My interests were varied and I needed the hustle and bustle of a big city. I loved the theatre and the museums. The society I was going to live in was very British, and I knew little of the local customs. I understood my husband's background and tried to rebel against his traditions the way my father did. But I did not succeed and stuck to him because I love my husband. Sam was and will always be the most wonderful man in the world. He is kind and considerate, and even though, in our early days, he was the undisputed head of the house, he always allowed me to be my own woman.

We are no longer young. Our son Richard has left the house and I have settled into a social routine that keeps me busy while Sam is in business or at his club. In recent years there has been a real danger of a rift between us. But this will not happen. These joint sessions of ours have done wonders for our marriage. We learned to talk all over again. They have brought us closer together. The vast sea that separated us when we first met has slimmed down into a lake and is now no more than a trickle of water. These notes help me show Sam what he is. Perhaps that knowledge will protect him from sinking again.

The time Sam was down was difficult for me. Watching the man you have known and loved suffer the way he did was torture. At first I did not know what it was. It could have been the death of Sam's mother that had triggered his breakdown. He had felt responsible for her life. Sam was born out of wedlock, and because of that his mother was unable ever to marry and have a normal life. That, rightly or wrongly, made Sam feel responsible for her. She had no friends and never learned to speak English. He was very attached to her. Even though she never left the house and sat in her apartment at the top of our house, he went up to see her every day. They would talk. Later, when she had lost her power of speech, he still came to see her every day. He'd talk, but she did not answer. When she died he missed her greatly, and the depression he suffered came a few months after her death.

And then there's the business of why Sam left his village. I am happy about it because we would never have met otherwise. I'm almost sure he's hiding something, but I can wait. In one of these sessions he might reveal it all.

There could be another reason. Our son Richard.

Shortly after Sam's mother's death, Richard phoned him and told him he was going into politics. Sam always wanted our son to take his company over, and when they talked that time and the boy told Sam to forget all about it he got a bit of a shock. That could have triggered the problem too, the doctor said. It may be we shall never know. What is important is to make sure it does not happen again.

Here was an energetic, kind and considerate man who suddenly changed. He became lethargic and detached from everything around him. The work he had devoted his life to, his friends and his family, were all brushed aside as if they didn't matter. He simply lost interest in them. All he did was stay in his bed; he refused to see anyone or talk to anyone. And we all felt hurt because we did not know. There was nothing I could do. There was nothing he wanted me to do. Of course, I looked for a share in the blame. I finally managed to get the doctor to see him. But then I do not wish to talk about this now. I am sure this will never happen again. Not now that Sam has got the man from Bangkok by his side.

Charlie's decision to sell his company and come and join us was the best thing that had ever happened to my husband. Charlie is blessed with ingenuity, inventiveness, and an inexhaustible energy rare in a man his age. At the time of his arrival he must have been well into his forties, with the rich and colourful past of one who had lived the life of ten others. I did not know much about him until he arrived.

That first day in Hong Kong I was in no condition to assess anyone else's character. I was, all of a sudden, married to a blind man in a place I had never been to, far away from anything I had known before. Instead of being allowed to deal with my husband's problem, I was forced to pass it over to Charlie. That was how Sam had wanted it. With vigorous obstinacy he insisted on spending his days in Charlie's room. At nights we were together, and I was not aware of what had been tormenting him because he seemed so normal. So strong. They spent days and days together, and I resented that. When Sam began to improve, my resentment changed into jealousy, but I was wrong. Today, with the luxury of hindsight, I know that I was sure of Charlie even then. Sure about his humanity and generosity and compassion. I was pleased Sam was able to offer him something on this island. It was only a small return for having saved my husband's life. When we first met, the giving was all his. And for this I have always encouraged their friendship and will always love him like a brother. Of course, we still argue about Charlie's reasons for coming here at all. I say he's had problems in the Orient and Sam says never. I say he was forced out and Sam says no way. But I am a great believer in time. Only time can tell what the truth is. We'll wait and see.

Whatever it was that brought Charlie over, Sam was the proudest man in Jamaica when he introduced him to his board of directors. Of course, human nature being what it is, there were jealousies. You wouldn't expect people who had worked with Sam for many years to accept a total stranger without questions. Not when this man was put in charge of the company, answerable only to Sam himself. I suspect they had made their own enquiries about him. About his exploits during the war and the life he had led in the Orient. What they found out was not all that good.

There were rumours about him. During the first weeks after his arrival, they said the ugliest things about him. They said he had been a smuggler, a buccaneer who broke the law of every country in the Orient. They said he had many wives and a string of outside children all over the South China Sea. They said he owed money everywhere. They said he'd arrived almost penniless.

Maybe my current misgivings about Charles originated then.

Socially, of course, he was a thundering success. Gossip is an important element in the social life here, as it is in any small community. Kingston was a very British city in those days. There was a shortage of war heroes. The mystery attached to Charlie's past, his adventurous wartime career, and above all the stories connected with his love of women, made him an extremely desirable guest at most parties. The funny thing was he never confirmed any of it, nor did he deny.

He would simply beam that disarming smile of his and turn the conversation over to another subject. If he was a war hero, he certainly did not talk about it. But people loved having him around. He was invited everywhere.

He was proposed, and was accepted, into every important club in Kingston. He was interesting, he was handsome and powerful, and he was English. When you listened to him talk, you would have thought he had never left that estate he was born on. No one knew where it was, but everyone talked about it.

His wife, Rose, became a pillar of the local English circle. We could soon see what she was made of. She worked ceaselessly on every charitable committee there was. At that time, a few short years before Jamaica's independence, there were still a lot of English people living on the island. I had only known her very slightly, because when we were in Hong Kong I had my own problems. I was looking around the shops for antiques. I was seeing the sights and spending time with Richard, my son. I did all that because Sam didn't really want me around. He spent every available moment in Hong Kong with Charles. They lived in Bangkok, and she only came over for a short time. Later, of course, we exchanged Christmas cards and birthday greetings, but that was all. She was only mentioned in passing in the lengthy exchange of letters that came and went between the two over the years. I thought things were not too good between them then, but Sam dismissed that out of hand. When they finally came out here, Charlie was where I had expected him to be, at the centre of things, and Rose seemed a fitting and contented spouse for him.

At the office, behind his back, they said many things about him. They soon realized Sam was not going to listen to any of it. He was told his people believed he was under

Charlie's spell. They said he had borrowed money from him. They said he was blackmailing him. Of course, we laughed about it a lot, and Sam always said it would all go once they realized what a capable man Charlie was. The fact was no one doubted his ability. Even before they succumbed to his charm, they had to admit he was a force to reckon with. Not two months after his arrival he announced a plan that was to make us a lot of money.

Sam fretted about it when we were alone. He said he wasn't too sure about Charlie's ideas. Not at first.

'Well, why don't you stop him?'

'I have given him my word. He can do as he sees fit, Jean.'

'Do you trust him, Sam?'

'Of course I do. Totally.'

'Then let him get on with it. And don't worry.'

'All we can lose is money.'

'What is it he wants to do?'

'He wants to form a trading company. Bring in air-conditioners from the States. Sell them to the general public. Not just our hotels.'

'Sounds like a great idea to me.'

'That's what I think. But this isn't like bringing in food-stuffs, Jean. Foodstuffs I understand. It's part of our business. I have never been a great one for international business. I don't understand it.'

'Don't do it, then.'

'I have to. International business is all Charles under-stands. I have asked him to come here. I have to let him try it out.'

'I understand.'

'It's only that bringing in equipment is a new thing alto-gether. It's not just buying and selling. You need a whole organization for that. You need a repair shop, spare parts, warehouses; you need new salesmen. We've never been in this business before. The manufacturers insist we pay in advance.'

'Do you have the cash for that?'

'No. But Charles wants us to go to the banks.'

'Will they give it to you?'

'Of course they will. Charles talked to all of them. They are competing between themselves. They all want to give us the money.'

'Well, where's the problem?'

'You are naive, Jean. You know we have never borrowed money. We've always lived on what we've earned.'

'What are the others saying?'

'They say Charles is mad.'

'What do you think?'

'He is not mad.'

'What are you going to do, Sam?'

'I am going to let him do it. I gave him my word before he came here. He can have a free hand.'

'Then you've got no choice, Sam.'

'That's right.'

'Why are we talking about it?'

'Didn't the doctor say we should talk?'

'Yes, Sam. He said we should.'

'That's why we are talking about it.'


Sam was right to have put his trust in Charlie. Within six months of the first unit being installed, the profit made by the trading company reached a tenth of the total income of the hotels. A year later the trading company Charles had started brought in a quarter of our income.

And then something strange happened. Sam should have expected it, but he told me it came as a surprise. At the end of four years, with Charlie's trading company adding a third of the total to our profit, Charles instructed the board to find someone else to run it. He had, he said, brought the new company as far as he could. It now needed new blood. He, Charlie announced, would look for something else inside the group.

Sam was bewildered and confused. He did not understand why Charles had decided to get out. He did not object. He couldn't. He said he had given Charlie a free hand and the choice must remain his.

I myself thought our friend Charlie was simply bored. Perhaps he wanted to make a bit of cash for himself. I was the daughter of an independent trader and have married another. I never thought Charlie was the type of man who would be happy working for other people for the rest of his life.

# CHAPTER FORTY-NINE

He looked at the postcard again and again. The old Hong Kong skyline he had known so well was replaced by new tall buildings. But the shoreline and the bay and the mountains were still there. The handwriting and the style and tone of it were familiar. So familiar he could hear the permanently hoarse staccato voice behind the words come at him.

> *Mister Charlie*
> *Life good Bangkok. All friends OK. Make much money no spend. Try lose in Macao but bad luck. Play play. Make more. Go New York first. Soon come visit you Jamaica. You face me face see. If need buy visa America.*
> *Paco*

A smile crept over his lips. Even if he didn't know the right people he'd find a way to get into the island. And he was coming just at the right time, too.

Rose looked up over the *Daily Gleaner* and saw his bemused face.

'What's funny?'

'Paco is planning to pay us a visit?'

'Paco the Filipino?'

'The one and only.'

'Really? And you intend to see him?'

'Of course I do.'

'What will people say?'

'What do you mean?'

'This is not Bangkok, Charles. You have to be careful who you're seen with.'

'I don't care what people will say. I'll be glad to be seen with him anywhere.'

'The way he dresses they won't let him into any hotel.'

'I am a director of the biggest hotel chain on the island, remember.'

'And you will recommend him?'

'Sure I will. Unless you prefer him to stay here with us.'

'What's he coming for?'

'To see us, what else?'

'Are you going to work with him again?'

'I am in a different business now, Rose.'

'Thank God for that.'

'Yes.'

'You'd better tell him the old days are over.'

'What do you mean?'

'All that other way of life . . . The smuggling, you know . . .'

'Oh, he knows.'

'Then if it's not business, why is he coming?'

'I expect the poor chap is bored.'

'Don't tell me you are bored too.'

'I won't tell you.'

The servant poured some more coffee into his cup. Bored, Charles thought to himself. That's what it was. That was the key to it all. And if you're bored with what you do you won't be successful at it.

'I am thinking of joining in a syndicate at Keymanas,' she said.

'You mean buy a share in a racehorse?'

'Yes.'

'Isn't that expensive?'

'Are we poor?'

'No. Not poor . . . But we're not rich any more.'

'How come?'

'I'm not in business for myself, Rose. I get a great salary, but it's not the same.'

'What happened to it all?'

'To what all?'

'All our money . . . your money.'

'I've lost it, Rose. Lost it when I had to get out of Bangkok . . . What was left after that I lost playing the tables in Macao.'

'You never told me why, did you . . . For years I thought you wanted to get away because I was happy there; was that it?'

'Of course not. I tried to tell you about it back then, in Bangkok.'

'Yes. You did. I should have listened. My fault.'

'Not your fault, darling. All mine. I've lost it. Not you.'

'I should have listened anyway.'

'It wouldn't have made much difference.'

'It might have done. I could have advised you . . . I could have . . .'

'No, darling. I was in it too deep by then. There was nothing anyone could have done.'

'Do you think . . .. Never mind.'

'Do I think I'll ever make it again? I can't tell you. We've only been here a few years. I'm looking around.'

'I hope you won't get yourself involved with Paco again.'

'I don't expect I shall. But it wouldn't be a bad idea.'

'You're quite mad, darling.'

'I've always made money with him.'

'Are we penniless?'

'Not exactly.'

'Are we poor?'

'Relatively speaking, yes, I suppose we are.'

'Do we own this house?'

'Of course we do. That took care of most of what I had.'

'What about the rest?'

'I'm investing it in St Hilda's at Brownstown.'

'It's a great school. Roberta loves it.'

'Of course she does. But it's expensive.'

'What about the boat? Can't you get rid of it?'

'It's the only luxury I have. I'd go mad if I couldn't go out to sea from time to time. Besides, what would your smart friends say if we didn't have one? We'd have to resign from the Yacht Club.'

'Can't you talk to Sam?' she asked.

'Of course not. Not about money.'

'Why not?'

'He'd feel guilty about it.'

'What's wrong with that?'

'When you feel guilty about people who work for you, you get rid of them.'

'What do you mean?'

'Nothing irks one more than one's own conscience. When someone in your organization irks you, you feel unpleasant when they are around. Even if it's not your fault. Sam thinks I have come here for him. He thinks I came with my money intact. If he finds out what the position is, he'll feel guilty.'

'Maybe you're right,' she said. 'Yes. Maybe you are . . . But surely Sam is different.'

'I've caused him enough trouble with his board . . . He put me on top without asking anyone.'

'And so he should have . . . You came here for him.'

'I did not come here for him. I came here because I was running away.'

'You never said that to me before.'

'We've never talked about that before.'

'Are you going to tell me what happened?'

'One of these days.'

'Why not this afternoon?'

'I'm overdue at the Club. There's a poker game on.'

'You hate clubs.'

'That's quite true.'

'Why did you bother to join?' she asked.

'It's the done thing here. It's expected of one.'

'I never thought you'd care about what is done and what isn't. You've always done what you wanted . . . Social graces didn't matter.'

'They do now.'

'Why is that?'

'I'm not rich enough to ignore them.'

'What are you doing about it, Charles?'

'I'm looking around.'

He *was* looking around. The trouble was their new circle of friends was too legitimate. Old-established companies. Sugar estates and great houses and parties. British education. British law and order. Jamaica was a paradise for millionaires because taxes were low and the place was safe. There was not one exciting loophole in sight. Maybe he was missing something, but Paco was coming and he was sure to find a corner he could get his teeth into. Something he could get excited about. There was so little of that in his life now.

He spent his days in a civilized office, with a civilized secretary who smiled at him and offered him the proverbial cup of Blue Mountain coffee. His suppliers supplied on time and his customers paid their bills. Afternoons and weekends he spent in the clubs with people who were gentlefolk. There were tennis clubs and the Yacht Club and horse-racing and there were poker games. There were excursions to the country. Visits to someone's sugar estate. Trips to the north coast. There was nothing wrong with anyone. They were gentlefolk. They were decent and kind and set in their ways. Some were English; others came from long lines of old families who had made good on the island. They liked music and dancing and good food. It was a close-knit society and they took him in. The same people he did business with came fishing with him, and their wives played cards with Rose.

Now that he had been accepted there were no more challenges. He could suggest anything, offer anything, and they would agree because he was one of them. He was yearning to get to do some real, demanding work.

At the beginning, there was some mystery to the place. There used to be a little excitement around because of the suspicion that came at him. There were stories about him and people had tried to discredit him, and at board meetings they voted against his ideas. That was stimulating because he had to use his brain to make them see his way. And he did. He convinced people that his thoughts were valid and he got through, even without Sam's casting vote, which always backed him to the hilt.

This was a conservative, very British society. People sent their children to schools and universities in England. There were pounds, shillings and pence under the tropical skies. New ideas were hard to establish, but he had managed it. And now that he had been successful, there was the office and the Club and the same faces. Luckily, there was the boat. She was a sleek fifty-footer with a large sundeck, but the drinking aboard stopped him from exploring the coast. He enjoyed fishing, but the weekends were too short. Rose was having a better time of it. Kingston was an enlargement of the British Club she so loved. She was going great guns.

He was now where the young man had told him to live. Near his own people and near his own Buddha. But that wasn't making him happy. There had to be something he was missing. Something that stared at him right there. Yes, Paco would do him good. He would identify the island's weaknesses and hiding-places and darker corners as soon as he landed. The rascal knew a deal when he saw one. He needed to make some money, but it wasn't just that. The managerial mask he was wearing was cutting into his skin. He only felt half alive. Out there, he thought to himself, was the promising prospect of boredom. The drive out. The office. The endless mass of paper to look at and agree to and sign. The Club. All those nice people. The gossip-laced conversations over lunch. The drive home.

He got up and walked across to his wife. He kissed her cheek and left the house.

He got into the car and started the engine. Outside, over the ornamented fence, an overgrown hibiscus poured bright rays of red which reached the asphalt. Into his mind came the little potted plant Nappaporn had hung over her gate whenever he came to her. For a moment he was overtaken by an inexplicable desire to see her. Talk to her. Listen to her advice. To race his car across town and across the river to her house. He must be hallucinating. Nappaporn was far away. On the other side of the world. As he joined the slow-moving traffic, Charles thought of dreams. A man can afford anything in a dream. To go back to the past. Live again through days long gone. To fly. To be wherever he wants with whomever he wants.

The Filipino had written and was coming. Something was about to happen. Things always happened when Paco was around. Ever since Hong Kong before the war. It was Paco who had started him off. It was Paco who had introduced him to Perotti. Paco was Nappaporn's friend. It must have been the thought of Paco's visit that made him think of her. A chance of a return to that dream. No. Not a dream. He did have another life when they were together, he and Nappaporn. She was probably the richest woman in Bangkok by now. He had not thought of her for a long time. As if she had been a part of someone else's world. Someone else's life.

Her daughter Nellie must be a big girl. She was the same age as Roberta, or older. He couldn't remember. But there was nothing to worry about. Not about the girl. Nappaporn was a careful woman. If he'd stayed they would have starved. Or worse. At that time he was no good for anyone, washed out. His luck had run out on him. Good thing he'd left Nappaporn on her own. Maybe Paco would bring his old luck back again. No, no. He'd done the right thing by them. The best thing he'd ever done. Somewhere far away there was a part of him that had no share in his failure. A part of him best forgotten. The young Burmese had done them all a great service. The woman and her daughter were better off without him there.

# CHAPTER FIFTY

If my mother finds out she'll die. Nina promised people would never recognize me because my face would be covered by a veil. There is no one in my house I can be frank and open with. I have not decided yet what to do. Nina is pushing me to make my mind up. She says I will be a great success and will make lots of money.

Nina is only interested in making money. And she does make a lot of it, but as soon as she gets it she spends it. I didn't know on what, and I was too scared to ask. Things between us are not the way they used to be. Of course, we can talk and stuff and we laugh, but I know we are both pretending.

I don't know why our friendship changed so much. Maybe it is because Nina changed. Her mother certainly did. She used to be such a good friend to me. She had patience, and you could talk to her about everything. When Nina's father first moved to Hong Kong I used to come to their house almost every day. They were lonely, especially Nina's mother. It became so I spent more time there than at home. My mother didn't mind because she saw I was happy. On the contrary, when I got into trouble with Nina's mother, she even came to the house herself and tried to talk to Nina's mother.

I don't want to think of that time at all. It is far too painful.

Sometimes I think it is sad we have to grow up. Nina is eighteen and I am seventeen and a half, but Nina said I should go ahead and do it because I look older. The people she is working with are all rich. They come to collect her from school in big American cars, and they give her money to go to the cinema and for clothes, and the work she is doing only takes a few hours every week. She said I'd be great at it.

Weeks ago, when she first showed me the postcards, I giggled. I thought she had got them somewhere from one of the shops that sell dirty books. I had seen things like that before when I was younger. Some of the girls took them from their brothers, and we all had a good snigger looking at them. Once we were caught by one of the teachers, and I was sent home for two days with a note for my mother. But my mother does not know how to read English, so I told her it was a mid-term certificate and I got her to sign it without any problems. I was quite surprised at myself and how easy it was to lie. But afterwards I felt bad about it, and I swore I would never do it again.

The postcard Nina showed me was just like the one we got into trouble over. I looked at it and I gave it back to her in a hurry. Then she showed it to me again and I recognized it. It was Nina's picture, and she was stark naked. You could just make the shape of her head out, and that was only because she has a very short haircut. Almost like a boy. Her face was in the dark, but I saw it clearly, and what I saw I didn't like. The expression she had in the picture was mature and new to me. She was smiling, but it wasn't the smile of a young girl. If anything, it was sad, and there was a question in it. As if she was pleading with you, or offering you something. I couldn't say what. Nina asked me what I thought about it, but I was so shocked I could not talk. Then the bell went and we had to get back to the classroom.

That day we walked home together. No one disturbed us. Nina's mother didn't come for her any more. And my maid only came for me whenever I wanted her to. I'd give her a few baht and tell her where to wait. This way my mother never found out where I was going and with whom.

We walked down the road and we talked.

'What do you think?'

'I'd rather not talk about it.'

'It makes money for me.'

'I hate dirty postcards.'

'This isn't a dirty postcard. It's art.'

'Who told you that?'

'The guy who took it. He says this is only the beginning.'

'I bet it is. Next thing they will ask you to sell yourself.'

'You're crazy, Nellie.'

'I don't want to talk about it.'

'Don't you want to be an actress?'

'Yes.'

'Don't you want to be famous?'

'Yes.'

'How do you think you're going to get there?'

'Not posing in the nude.'

'But that's exactly where you're wrong. They love me. I am becoming famous.'

'How come?'

'The postcards are sold to tourists. But most of them go to New York. They sell them there to collectors. People who like to look at beautiful things. Beautiful bodies. Soon they will want to know who I am. Soon someone in Hollywood will see one of them and ask who I am and he'll send for me.'

'You're crazy.'

'Crazy? Didn't you always talk about being an actress? How someone will discover you and take you away? Did you forget? How do you think anyone will discover you here. Who? Where? In the fish market? In your mother's house?'

'Leave my mother out of it.'

'OK, but think, Nellie.'

'Think of what?'

'Think of me. I don't want to be a star. I can't even act.'

'Why are you doing it?'

'I need the money.'

'What for?'

'I need it for my mother.'

'I can get money for you.'

'I know. You'll give me every bit of your pocket money
. . .'

'I can get more than that . . . My mother is rich.'

'Sure. Your father is rich too. That's where she gets her money from.'

'What she's got she's made herself. My father went away a long time ago.'

'So did mine.'

'Let's quit talking about that.'

'Fine by me.'

'I'll get you money.'

'Not enough, you won't. My mother spends a fortune.'

'What does she spend it on?'

'I don't want to talk about it.'

'Well, what do you want to talk about?'

'I want you to let them take your picture. You're the most beautiful girl in the school. In the whole of Bangkok. You'll be a great success. You'll be famous.'

'I don't need the money.'

'Then do it for me. I need money.'

We got to Nina's gate. We stood there. I knew she wanted me to come in with her, but I couldn't. Not since the big fight I had had with her mother. That was many months ago. Maybe a year.

We used to be good friends, Nina's mother and I. We could always talk about everything. I was in the house one afternoon. Nina and I were doing our homework when her mother came in. I had never seen her look like that before. She was beautifully dressed and her make-up was impeccable. But the smell of whisky flew into the room before she even came in. Her eyes were red. She looked at me with hatred in her eyes and said:

'What's the Chink doing here?'

'Mother . . .' Nina whispered. I couldn't believe my ears.

'Get the fucking Chink out of my house.'

'Mother . . .'

I got up.

'What is it?' I asked. 'What have I done?'

'What have you done? You should know what you've done. You've taken my husband away, you whore.'

'Me?'

'You, someone else, what's the difference . . . You Chink whores are all the same.'

I burst into tears, and Nina grabbed me by the hand and dragged me out. I didn't go to school the next day. I locked myself inside my room. I did not come out for any meals. I didn't leave until Nina came over herself and begged me to forgive her mother. She told me her mother had been drinking for months. It was all because her father shacked up with some air stewardess in Hong Kong. She hated all Orientals. She knew I was really a Farang, but my mother is an Oriental. She said her mother didn't mean it. She said her mother loved me. She spoke to my mother and she apologized to her. She begged both of us not to tell anyone.

I went back to school that day and told everyone I had had a cold. I swore to myself I would never go into Nina's house again.

Nina had told me my mother had gone to her house. She had tried to see Nina's mother, but she wouldn't come out of her room. Nina told me how my mother stood there for hours and how she talked to her and calmed her down and how she said I was not to blame. She said my mother fought for me. She said she wished my mother was her mother. I don't know why my mother never told me of this visit. Perhaps she did not like to admit she had failed. I kept my word. I never went to Nina's house after that.

We stood by the gate and Nina said:

'Will you at least come to the studio with me? See what it's all about? I am not sure they will let me work after that. Not after they see you.'

Maybe I go soft when someone pays me a compliment. I know I did what Nina had asked because she told me how beautiful and talented and kind I was. How I'd help her and her mother, and weren't we friends forever?

I'd do anything for a good word. It is a bad thing, but I do crave attention and kindness. I am willing to give everything for it. Vince has it all for me, but he asks for nothing in return. He has been a very good friend to me. The way things are going between Nina and me, he will soon be my best friend. I did not want him to know what we were doing. And then I had to tell him because I needed help.

I did not ask Vince for a meeting for almost three months after I started posing. He is such a good guy. I know he worries about me, but he never pesters me and he never insists. We met only at my request. I did feel he was watching over me. I saw his car pass in front of the school many times during that period, but he never tried to talk to me. He never even slowed down.

The place where they took the pictures was over a shoemaker's store in Silom Road downtown. We were picked up by car after school and brought there. There were three photographers there and many costumes. No one made a pass at me. It was all very professional. They allowed us to choose the dress we would wear, and then they took the pictures. There was always a picture of something behind us. The seaside or a palm forest or a terrace or a moonlit night aboard a great liner. There were background pictures of foreign cities. Skyscrapers. Airports. Looking at them after the shots were taken, I could imagine I was really there.

We used to go to the studio three times a week. I must have been a success because they started taking more pictures of me. But I never kept the money. I don't even know how much it was. I gave all the cheques to Nina. Her mother has a friend who works in a travel agency and he cashed them for her.

All through that time I did not see Vincent. Until a week ago when I left him a message to come and see me after school. I only had a few minutes, and all I managed to tell him was that I was OK and that I'd explain. When he said he was going to New York, I said we'd see each other once more the day before he left. That day was today.

Yesterday morning Nina did not come to school. The teacher said she had called the house and was told no one knew where she was. I said I was her best friend. I said I would go to her house to find out. I didn't like going there because of what Nina's mother had said, but I went all the same.

Nina's mother was lying on her bed and she was crying. She was in no shape to speak. She didn't know what time of the day it was. She did not recognize me. I think she was drunk, but there were no bottles in the room at all. There was a sharp smell of something burning. Maybe old wood. I did not stay to find out. On the floor there was a cheque. One of the cheques they used to give Nina at the end of each session. A green piece of paper with a New York address at the top. I took the cheque and I left.

Outside the house I hailed a taxi. I went to Silom Road and I burst into the shoemaker's store. They all had blank faces and no one stopped me. I ran up the stairs to the studio, but there was no one there. On the wall there was a background picture. The Golden Gate Bridge. Other than that the room was empty. I ran out of there. The shoemaker and his son looked up at me as if I was a ghost. No one said a thing.

I didn't dare go back to school without an answer. Everyone saw me go. I knew they were all waiting. I took another cab and I went to Nina's house. I told the driver to wait for me. I went inside. Her mother was still where I had seen her last. The same way I had seen her last. This time I went upstairs to Nina's room. The door was locked. I knocked on it and a man shouted something. I knocked again. After a little while Nina opened the door. She was stark naked. Just like in the postcards we had been making. The room reeked of whisky. I tried to look inside, but Nina didn't let me. The man whose voice I had heard was nowhere to be seen. Nina was laughing out loud. I knew she was drunk because her voice was vulgar and hoarse and she sounded just like her mother did the day she screamed at me. She even looked like her mother. She didn't look like a young girl at all. She looked at me and tried to talk but nothing came. I did not want to see any more.

I ran out of the house and jumped into the cab and went back to school. I told the teacher everything was OK. I can't remember exactly what it was I said. I said Nina was sick, that's all. Time of the month, I said. Nothing serious. The teacher thanked me for my help and I went back to my desk and sat down. I must have looked as calm as anything because no one asked any questions, but inside I was bursting. I put on the best performance of the week. I had just seen my best friend in her shame, but I was feeling great. Not because of Nina's trouble. I wasn't happy about that. I was just feeling great. I don't know why, but I feel best when I'm not myself. When I'm acting.

That is why I do so well in school plays.

Later that evening I sat at table with my mother. At first I felt good about being with her. She was a good woman. She was strong. She would never have cursed anyone the way Nina's mother had. She was steady, and her love and care made me feel safe. Even the time she'd wait for me like a maid at the porch had paid off because I felt wanted. I will never end up like Nina. I wanted to share my feelings with my mother last night, and I told her about it. Not about Nina and what happened. Just about my acting. I asked her why it was I felt so good about myself when I played someone else. I should never have bothered. All my mother said was people who pretend to be other people and enjoy it are people who hate themselves. Every time I open up to her she disappoints me.

I made a decision last night. I shall never confide in my mother again.

All I could do now was try and meet with Vince. He was going to New York the next day. I decided to give him the cheque and find out who the people in New York are.

Yesterday after school I left an envelope in the hotel and I waited all night for morning to come. I promised myself I'd be on time. I couldn't sleep at all. I think I was excited about seeing him again. I left the house just after my mother went to the temple, and that's early. I got to our meeting-place by our tree ten minutes before 6.30. Soon after that he showed up. He looked out to make sure I wanted to see him still. He always does that, because once we did make a date but I was too upset to talk to him. I don't remember why, but I know he had been hurt. As soon as I nodded he smiled at me, and then he told his driver to leave us. He opened the door and I came in.

He did not tell me off for not making contact for so long. For doing it only when I needed something. He was patient and kind, and he never tried to push me. I couldn't tell him about Nina. I knew where she was, but I couldn't tell him. I asked him to find out who the people Nina and I worked for were. I didn't tell him what I wanted the information for, and he did not ask. As always, he just said he'd do it. He never asks for anything in return. I wish he was my father. He is the only man in the world who really likes me and who listens to me. My mother is in no condition to listen to anyone unless they are a priest. She has gone far too religious.

# CHAPTER FIFTY-ONE

I had been visiting New York for my mother's birthday. The old lady had turned eighty years old. I had put her in one of those homes for the elderly ever since she quit being able to look after herself. Her memory was shot, and I don't figure she knew who I was. It made no difference to me. I sat there in the big, sunny room and she sat on her chair and we looked at each other, but we didn't talk at all. I watched her old, crumpled face and her thick, long socks and I tried to remember how pretty she used to be. Oh, yes, she was a beautiful woman when she was young, and she had a great figure. I know she had, because people used to whistle when we walked together down the street. She used to sit for hours at home and paint her nails and do her long black hair, and she never went out in the sun because she liked her skin white like alabaster. I tried to think of all that, but all I could remember was how she never liked doing the house and how it was always in a mess and how she never cooked unless she had to. There were some good times too, and I did try to remember them and the way she looked when she dressed up. The way my schoolfriends said she was the prettiest mom any boy could have. But all I saw was this old lady who constantly fell asleep. She probably didn't even know I was there. The nurse came and straightened my mother's hair, and then she looked at me.

'She's such a pleasant lady.'

'Yeah.'

'She's got a great bone structure. Must have been some looker.'

'She was.'

'Shame you don't come more often. You live overseas?'

'Yes, I do.'

'She must miss you a lot.'

'Does she say so?'

'No. She doesn't talk at all. But sometimes, just before I wheel her out, I comb her hair and she smiles for me. A kind of sad smile of anticipation. As if she was going out to meet someone very dear to her. Are you her only son, Mr Perotti?'

'Yes, ma'am. I'm all she's got.'

'Then it must be you she's thinking of.'

'Must be.'

The nurse took my mother's hand and stroked it and then

she left. I sat there, and on my lap I had a box of chocolates and a bunch of flowers. I wanted to tell her things. I wanted to ask her why the hell she cheated on my father. I wanted to ask her why she made him leave the house. I figured she was to blame for the way he ended up, wet and cold and floating face up in the river. I was very young then, maybe ten, but I had heard them fight. My old man never drank before. He only got deep into booze later. When he found out what she was doing while he was out on the road selling stuff out of a suitcase. Socks, soap, ties, shoestrings and toothbrushes door to door.

I knew Don Antonio was her friend. Before my old man left she used to go see him weekday afternoons, and sometimes she'd take me with her. But I was little then, and I reckoned they were like schoolfriends, if you know what I mean. Nothing more. In those days I didn't know about what boys do with girls.

At first, for a long time, I liked going to Don Antonio's office. He was a dark, tall guy with a big moustache, and he looked kind of like a movie star called Ramon Navarro who was all the rage then. Don Antonio was always nice to me, even though I was a little scared of him. Not scared. I had lots of respect for him because he had a big office and a big car and was always dressed nice and his face smelt good. I liked the way he used to give me candy and a few dimes. He'd let me look at his gun and play with it. They never sent me out on the streets by myself then. Don Antonio always had one of his henchmen go with me. We'd go to a soda fountain and have a couple of ice-creams or see a movie and then we'd go back. I did not know what she was doing there, and she said I had to keep quiet about it because it was a surprise for my dad. Some surprise it turned out to be.

I'm not sure if my old man ever knew who her lover was. I remember her screaming at him about us not having a nice home or a car. About her not having nice things to eat and me going to a bad school. I remember how he cried and said he'd get it all for her.

What happened was he did get the dough. He borrowed

it from one of the loan sharks. He never did buy the house or the car for her. I don't know what he did with the cash. I figure he lost it gambling and then they got rid of him.

Years later I was in a position to find out who they were and I got even.

So there I was, sitting with her and thinking I wished she had never been my mother. I was getting angry with her. Then I felt sorry for myself. Then I calmed down. I never asked her a thing. I figured even if she did understand what I wanted to ask she wouldn't remember the answers. She looked so old and so frail, but I didn't feel sorry for her. I didn't give a shit. Then the nurse came and took the flowers and the chocolates and wheeled the old lady away. I didn't say goodbye.

The whole visit was a farce, but the family said it was the right thing to do. They had been trying to get me to come back to the States for a long time, and I figured they were using my mother's birthday as a bait. There was no need for that at all. I had plenty of work here in New York, and there was Nellie's problem, too. By that time Charlie's half-caste daughter was the reason behind almost everything I did outside business.

Nellie had requested a meeting with me the day before I left for New York. She made it for 6.30 in the morning, half an hour before school started. We had worked out a system for that. Whenever she wanted to meet she'd call at the Oriental Hotel and leave an envelope addressed to me with the concierge. If she wanted to see me the next day the envelope would be empty. Otherwise she'd put a note in with the day and the hour. We either saw each other before classes, or after. The option was hers. The meeting-place was always the same. Down the road from her school, where we had first started. I would drive down there and wait. She was always on time. The concierge must have known how eager I was for her notes. Every time one arrived he'd call me at the office and tell me about it. And me? Knowing I was going to meet with her set me up for the day in the good mood department. I'd give big tips. I'd walk around and whistle. I'd cancel whatever else there was just for the pleasure of having five minutes with her.

We had become firm friends, Nellie and I. She talked to me about everything. That last meeting of ours was strained. I think she wanted to tell me more.

It was, as usual, a sunny day. Early mornings in the tropics are beautiful. The heat of the day is not running your life yet and you can hear the birds and smell the flowers. There is no dust. The traffic is light and the air is clean. She was waiting by the usual tree when I got there. When I first saw her, years before, she was a beautiful child. Now she was a stunning young woman. She had the shape of a Rita Hayworth, the face of an angel, and the smile of a goddess, all squeezed into a drab school uniform. She was taller than me, and though she was young and inexperienced I was putty in her hands, because her vulnerability remained intact. She was still in need of much understanding and patience and love. She could ask me for anything.

We had to be very careful about it. Our meetings were a secret. Whenever I gave her a present I'd always give her a story with which to explain it. Don't get me wrong. There was no sex in it. Not a bit of it. Certainly not in my mind. Nellie Brown was no woman in my eyes. She was a child. Even later, when things got rough for her because of the way she looked, she was still a child to me.

I lowered the window to make sure the meet was still on, and she nodded. I told the driver to go take a walk, and she came inside.

'Thanks for coming.'

'Any time.'

'I'm sorry it had to be early.'

'No problem.'

'You hate getting up in the morning.'

'Not for you.'

'Thanks, Vince. You're a champ.'

'What's the problem, Nellie?'

'I don't know how to tell you.'

'Take your time.'

'I really don't know how to tell you. I've been thinking of it all night. I don't know what to do.'

'You're getting me all worked up.'

'That's why I don't know how to start. I know how much you worry. I don't want you to.'

'Just start talking. From the top.'

'I'm trying.'

'Is it your mother?'

'No.'

'School?'

'School is fine.'

'You need anything?'

'Yes.'

'What?'

'Advice.'

'D'you want me to guess?'

'No, Vince, I don't want you to guess. It's just that I can't find the right words.'

'I can wait.'

'I know. I know,' she said. 'I should have thought more about it before asking to meet you. But you said last week you were going away.'

'Yes. Tomorrow.'

'New York?'

'Yeah. It's my mother's birthday. She's eighty.'

'I wish I was going there with you.'

'Same here.'

'There is an address in New York I want you to check for me.'

'Sure. What is it?'

'I haven't got it yet. But I'll have it later.'

'I can come back.'

'You don't need to.'

'It's going to be a pleasure.'

'I don't know how long I'll be. We have a rehearsal after school. I'm in the new play.'

'Big part?'

'Yes.'

'You know your lines?'

'Yes. Almost . . . I wish you could be there and see me. Don't you?'

'You bet.'

'You can find a way. You can do anything.'

'We've been through all that. There's no way.'

'I know.'

'I will be thinking of you. You'll be the greatest star.'

'You really think so?'

'I really think so. What about that address in New York?'

'I'll leave it in an envelope at the hotel.'

'That's fine. Right, let's say I've arrived in New York. Let's say I've found the place. What do I do next?'

'You go in there and find out who's in charge.'

'Who's in charge of what?'

'I don't know,' she said.

'What am I looking for?'

'That's just it. I don't know. It could be anything.'

'What d'you mean anything? A restaurant? A beauty parlour?'

'Yes. Anything. Maybe they are working under cover. But you will find they have some connection with Bangkok.'

'Where did you see the address?'

'On a cheque.'

'A cheque? Whose cheque?'

'It's Nina's.'

'Where is it?'

'In my locker at school.'

'Are you going to give it to me?'

'Sure. I said I'd leave it for you later.'

'What are they paying her for?'

'I can't tell you'.

'I promised.'

'Well, it's none of my business anyway. All you want me to do is find out what they do and who's in charge, right?'

'That's right. Don't get upset, Vince, I'll tell you about it soon.'

'Whenever you're ready, doll.'

She looked at the watch I had given her last Christmas. I knew she wanted to go, and I pushed the door open.

'I'm so proud you're wearing it, Nellie.'

'I don't know what I'd do without you, Vince.'

'You don't have to know that. It'll never happen.'

'I love you.'

'I love you too.'

She got out and waved to me and ran up the road to her school. The driver came back, but I did not go back to my office. I went to the Alien Registration office instead. I had a guy there working for us. He was fixing work permits and things for our people. We paid him plenty for that. I went to his office to see him. I spent a good two hours with him. I asked a lot of questions and he gave me all the answers.

When I left I had all the low-down on Nellie's friend Nina and her family.

I went back to the office and got my local man to do some more snooping. It was my last day in Bangkok for a long while, and I had plenty to do. By the time that day came to an end I knew exactly what the problem was.

The source of the trouble was Nellie's friend Nina. She had been her best friend ever since they were little, and what was happening in Nina's family could screw things up for Nellie. They had lived in Bangkok for years and her father was a pilot. In the last few years he had not been at home too much because he'd joined some new airline in Hong Kong. There he took up with some young Eurasian chick who was a stewardess or something. At first the girl's mother did not hear about it, but when she did she started fooling around herself. I don't know the details, but after hearing all about it I remembered having seen Nina's mother around. She used to go to all these joints down in Patpong and pick young men up. She wasn't choosy, neither. She got GIs on leave from Korea and young salesmen and Filipino musicians and sailors and so forth. I had heard she was even paying them for it. I reckon she was giving it back to her husband.

My guy found out the girl's mother got herself hooked on some stuff. It wasn't the sort of junk they have now. It was more like some Oriental drug they smoked. A paste made out of a plant related to opium or something. Whatever it was it cost a fortune. The police knew about it, but no one did a thing. I figured the girl Nina was paying them off and Nellie, generous as her father was, must have given her money too.

The situation was a big problem for the girl Nina. I was an expert at that, having been in the same soup myself when I was a kid. But I was a boy, and that was different. Nina was a foreign broad smack in the middle of a great Oriental town, and anything could happen. She was Nellie's best friend, and her influence was not good. Not good at all. I had to do something about it.

Nellie was as good as her word. That evening, when I got back to the hotel, I found an envelope from her with the concierge. I had Nina's cheque in my wallet.

The girls were being very stupid. I am not sure what it was they were doing. Maybe dealing dope. The fact was they were making money, and I was going to find out how and get Nellie out of it. Maybe it was Nina who had started it first, but that didn't matter a damn. What mattered was they were in the shit. I figured someone had made them do it.

My man in Bangkok had said the centre of the operation was right here in New York, and I was going to find out where they were at and what they were selling.

But there were other things I had to do first. I was working on a deal that could change everything.

And there was Paco's trip to Jamaica to watch.

# CHAPTER FIFTY-TWO

He drove down the narrow strip of the Palisados Road to the airport. He was alone in the car. As he approached the palm-lined road to the main building, he could hardly contain his excitement. New expectations and old hopes and memories ran through his mind and refused to leave. The old sounds and smells of the Orient were back with him. Years had gone by since he had delivered Paco's first junk to him. Years that saw him man and boy. Years that witnessed his slow but steady move into the periphery of underhand dealing. Rose had been right. Paco and he were breaking the law but, man, those were the days. They were having the time of their lives. A war had been fought and won and he had made fortunes and had lost them. But he had had fun. Now Paco was coming and he was going to bring it all back.

As he turned into an empty parking-spot, he looked at himself in the mirror. There were deep lines along his cheeks and grey patches had appeared across his hair. You're kidding yourself, old boy, he whispered to his own reflection; you are not the same man.

And what would his friends say when they met the Filipino. Can't be trusted. Not one of us. What does Paget-Brown think he is doing.

Paco had said he was coming for a visit. Perhaps he had fallen out with Perotti. Perhaps life was too quiet for him. Years go by everywhere, even in Bangkok. Maybe the Filipino was coming to him in search of his youth? Even Paco could not cheat time. The whole business must have changed over there. There were new, younger people in it now. It could all turn out to be quite conventional, he thought to himself, but his tension hammered on at him. He was almost desperate. He wanted to jump out of the car and run. But that wouldn't bring Paco out of Immigration any faster. He sat back and he tried to calm himself. He turned the ignition off and got out of the car. He saw the Pan American jet making the final approach in the distance, over the water. He'd soon know.

In the arrivals hall he sat down. He listened to the announcements. He looked at the indicator slots for all the airlines. There were uniforms all over. Air hostesses, pilots, policemen and customs officials. In between the khaki and the blue he saw the usual sights of people. Some going away, uttering words of parting or indulging in a last embrace. Others coming in, pale faces clad in winter clothes, arms carting heavy luggage. Some waiting patiently for their loved ones, others searching nervously for a familiar face to appear through the sliding doors. There were unaware, sleeping infants in their mothers' arms.

And there were his favourites, those inevitable first-time sightseers sitting in quiet awe of an intimidating international atmosphere. He loved watching them best. Their respectful eyes following every change, their hesitating fingers pointing everywhere. He knew how they felt, embarking on a voyage to a faraway world they would never see. On an adventure that would never happen. No. He must never feel bored. He had been lucky. He had read books which had ignited his imagination, but he had followed the pages. He had seen the sights. He had done it all. He had no call to feel sorry for himself.

And then he saw Paco walk out, a heavy coat weighing him down. Behind him, a porter carried a crocodile suitcase.

Charles got up. He walked towards the Filipino. He walked fast and he called his name out, and then Paco saw him and ran to him and they embraced.

'Good to see you, Paco.'

'Me you too, Mister Charlie.'

'You haven't changed a bit.'

'You too, Mister Charlie.'

'Rubbish. I'm an old man now.'

'You lie me, Mister Charlie.'

'You're dressed to kill.'

'New York cold like ice. Buy many things. Buy coat.

You like?'

'Come, let me help you carry it.'

In the car, Paco lit a cigar. He opened the window to let the smoke out.

'Nice car, Mister Charlie. American?'

'No. German, actually.'

'Benz, yes?'

'Yes.'

'You do OK, Mister Charlie? You happy here?'

'Yes.'

'Looks nice place. Same same Manila.'

'Yes.'

'You make plenty money?'

'Well . . . I do all right.'

'No can make money this place?'

'I am working for someone now, Paco.'

'But boss give you piece of business, no?'

'No.'

'You salaryman?'

'I suppose I am.'

'Your big boss, he have son, no?'

'Yes. Sam has a son.'

'Why your daughter no marry boss son?'

Charles laughed.

'You're a card, Paco.'

'What you mean?'

'Roberta is still at school.'

'But she pretty girl, no?'

'Yes. She's a pretty girl.'

'Why not marry boss son?'

'It don't go so.'

'What you mean?'

'That's a local expression. It means things aren't that simple. Not out here.'

'Why you no leave?'

'I like it here.'

'You make no money. Your daughter no marry boss son. Why you like here?'

'It's a quiet life. It's safe.'

'You like safe, Mister Charlie?'

'You get used to it.'

'You never like safe before. No danger, no good time after.'

'You have a point.'

'No monkey business?'

'Not that I know of.'

'Monkey business every place, Mister Charlie. All world have monkey business. People like. Monkey business keep you young. Monkey business best money-maker.'

'You have a point.'

'You say already. This island, what they have?'

'They have rum, wood, bauxite for aluminium. They have coffee. They have sugar. Bananas.'

'Have many pirates here old days. Where they go?'

'Hollywood.'

'Never worry, Mister Charlie. I find something.'

Paco's talk brought mischievous, wild thoughts. Into his mind's eye came a recollection of faraway ports and paper lanterns and junks being unloaded in the dark. Rows of drying fish hanging on lines. Sounds of wheeling and dealing and good-natured arguments over payment terms.

'What do you mean?'

'I say later. Family fine?'

'Yes. They're fine. How about yours?'

'My father dead . . .'

'I'm sorry to hear that. What happened?'

'Him sick.'

'Did he suffer much?'

'No suffer. He die Bangkok quiet. I take him bury Manila.'

'You still live in Bangkok?'

'Yes. I rent old house same same you rent. Gardener same same.'

'How are people in the office?'

'OK. Many new people come. Many paper, many machine. Mister Vincent him same. He make trip many times. He soon go back America. New boss come soon. Me no know who.'

'Will you stay there?'

'I stay. I give word in Hong Kong. I stay for you. People no work if I go. All remember you good.'

'Yes.'

'Mister Vincent never get my father.'

Paco looked around with great intensity. He watched the cars and the people and he smiled his lecherous smile at the way the women walked. Music pulsated out of little huts along the road. People huddled over wooden tables. Eating, buying, selling, working, drinking. There were colourful signposts.

'Happy people here, Mister Charlie. All look like dancing.'

'Yes. They're happy.'

'Many banks. Big boards tell so. Many, many banks.'

'I hadn't noticed, but you're right.'

'Canada banks, England banks, America banks.'

'You've a sharp eye, Paco.'

'Plenty money this place.'

'Yes. Some have plenty of money.'

'Why you no get some, Mister Charlie?'

'You want me to simply walk in and ask for it? I don't suppose they'd just give it to me, do you?'

'You no ask. You make. You take.'

'Rob a bank?'

'No rob bank. More better way. I tell you later.'

'You do that, Paco.'

When they got to the hotel, Paco didn't wait for Charles to usher him in. He jumped out of the car and marched towards the reception desk as if he owned the place. Perhaps he had been a gentleman for too long,

Charles thought. Why should the Filipino not know his way? He'd been travelling the world for years. He knew all the tricks of the trade. He was an adventurer. He had charm. There was nothing unusual about the way Paco asked for a room. Nothing unusual about the way he tipped the clerk before being told there was just one room available. A last-minute cancellation.

He'd been here too long. Among people who did things by the book.

'You needn't have done that, Paco. There was a room booked for you already.'

'Not booked.'

'My secretary must have booked it in my name.'

'No need secretary. Me can book room any place.'

'I am a director of this company. I can get . . .'

'No worry, Mister Charlie. I like come new place see new faces. Make tip, make friends.'

'Shall I collect you tonight, Paco?'

'You no worry.'

'I would like to make some arrangements for you . . . Some . . .'

'You no worry. I look. I see. I call you after I see.'

'When shall I call you?'

'No worry. I call you.'

'I'll give you the number.'

'No worry. You director this company. My friend reception know where find you. He give me number. I like be alone. I look. I ask. I make more friends. I call you after.'

# CHAPTER FIFTY-THREE

The rugged surface of the cockpit country was ascending towards them. Up where they were the island looked smaller than Charles had imagined it to be. The blue, cloudless sky stretched all the way to the horizon, where it touched the emerald mass that was the Caribbean. The little plane circled above rocks, hills, sugar plantations and endless royal palms. There were great white houses and bordered estates. There were a few roads and rivers, but the people seemed to have gone into hiding somewhere inside a world dominated by green.

How quickly Paco found his feet did not stop amazing him. After three days of scouting the countryside, he knew where to charter planes, boats and cars. He knew about prices, politics, and about people Charles had never heard of before.

'Any minute now,' the pilot said, speaking at the top of his voice through the roar of the engine. 'Perfect day for flying, eh, gentlemen?'

'So it is.'

They had taken off from Kingston some thirty minutes before. Due north, the pretty town of Port Antonio and Errol Flynn's island were taking their first lazy glimpse of Sunday. It was not to be coffee on his terrace with a copy of the *Gleaner*. Nor the spot of fishing he'd promised himself. He had no idea where they were going or why. All Paco had said was it was going to be a surprise.

The pilot looked about him and consulted his map one more time before pushing the stick forward. The plane began to descend. Dead ahead, Charles saw a black tower of smoke rising at them, some halfway along a straight stretch of dirt road that lifted towards them from nowhere.

'This is it,' the pilot said. 'We're going in. It'll be a little bumpy, but nothing to worry about.'

Charles consulted his watch. With a little luck this

wouldn't last too long. He might still be able to take the boat out and make dinner at Sam's house. It would be nice to know what to expect, he thought to himself as the wheels hit the jumpy earth. The tractor-like grind of the engine grew louder. Through the dust, he saw two camouflaged wooden buildings under the trees on the side of the strip. Then he saw the people.

There were five of them. All dressed in city suits and ties, all holding briefcases, they looked totally out of place there. The plane crawled closer and then it came to a stop and the engine coughed and died. Two of the men came forward. One opened the door.

'Good morning, Mr Paget-Brown,' the man said. He wore metal-framed sunglasses and had the sombre expression of an insurance salesman.

'Good morning,' Charles answered. Behind him, he heard Paco's feet thump into the ground.

'Nice of you to come down.'

'Since I have no idea what I'm here for, I'll reserve my answer for later.'

The man behind smiled.

'Why the formality?'

'You appear to have known I was coming. You know my name. I don't share the same privilege.'

'Come now, Mr Paget-Brown. Everybody on the island knows who you are.'

'Should I know you?'

'All this is too serious for me.'

'Mister Charlie number-one serious man,' Paco said.

'You've kept me in the dark long enough, Paco. It's time you told me what this was about.'

'You soon see. You like surprise, no?'

'This surprise has been going on all morning. What are we doing here?'

The serious-faced man came forward.

'Our friend Paco told us you may be interested in negotiating with us.'

'Negotiating what?'

'The purchase and export of ganja, Mr Brown.'

'I should have guessed. Paco never ceases to amaze me.'

'We grow the best grass this side of paradise. Welcome to our little farming enterprise, Mr Brown.'

'How many men do you employ up here?'

The speed at which he rose to the occasion, the authority and strength of his words, startled him.

'At this plantation, only three. But this is a small one. You might call this operation a sort of cooperative. Over ninety per cent of the grass comes from outside suppliers who grow exclusively for us. As you may know, this is still a cottage industry. Most people only grow this on the side, to supplement other crops. They use it themselves and only sell for pocket money. It's all done on a very small scale. We are proud of what we've been able to build here. We are a very specialized organization. We do nothing but ganja; we sell only the best and our people only work for us.'

'Can you trust them?'

'Yes . . . But actually we don't need to. We pay cash, you know. We are talking about a whole group of small growers who deliver . . .'

'If I am to have anything to do with this, your suppliers will stop delivering right away. No one is to come near the place. We collect.'

'Good point, but there's no need. None of them has ever been up here. You can either fly into this location or you walk. Difficult to find from the ground. They bring the bales to the road down there. You can't see it from here. That's where we left our cars. They are so well hidden you wouldn't even see them from the air. And none of the growers have wings . . .'

'And you don't think someone's ever tried to find out where this place is?'

'I don't. There is a truck down there, and we load it and pay and they leave. The fetching is done by our personnel. All three of them. They trek it up to this point.'

'From now on you collect. Right from where it's grown.'

'It's dangerous. Some of the growing is done far away. All over the island.'

'In that case you designate a central point a short but safe distance from here. They deliver there. You pay. You change the central collecting point every week or so.'

'This will take money.'

'If I go in with you, you'll let me worry about money.'

'You've done this before, Mr Brown.'

'No. But I've been in business before. I take it this is a packing station, right? You don't really grow much up here, do you?'

'You've hit the nail on the head. It's packed here and sold here. Customers fly in and take out.'

'That's not bad, but you should split the risk. Find a few more collecting places for your customers. You find a few strips closer to the coast. You alternate. When a small business becomes big, people talk. Never have the same customer come here twice in a row, understand? You might find yourself under attack if you do.'

'Isn't that expensive?'

'Cheaper than getting caught.'

'Good idea.'

'Unless, of course, you only sell to one customer.'

'What do you mean?'

'What I say. You get one man to buy the lot. You check him out first. You make sure he buys only from you. You make sure he can pay. You get all the stuff collected. You make sure it gets here. You inspect it and then you let this customer know the stuff is ready for him. Only this one customer. He flies in. He pays. No one else is involved.'

'Am I to understand we're in business?'

'You're to understand no such thing. I'll let you know.'

'But all the hints you gave us. All the advice . . .'

'If I come in, these hints will become regulations. If I don't, use them with my compliments. I'll let you have my decision within a week.'

'But you don't know how to find us.'

'Paco knows. That's enough for now.'

'You're quite some character, aren't you, Mr Brown?'

'Mister Charlie number-one character.'

'Come on, Paco, I've got a boat waiting.'

'You like, Mister Charlie, I know you like.'

'Would you like a drink, Mr Paget-Brown?'

'No, thank you.'

'You want me tell you name of people now?'

'I don't think that will be necessary for now, do you, gentlemen?'

'You never believe Mister Charlie number one,' said Paco. 'Now believe, yes?'


On the flight back they did not talk. The Filipino's usual effervescence gave way to silence. Perhaps he was planning something. It was best to keep quiet. He had talked too much, Charles thought to himself. Far too much. He did not understand what had come over him. He had talked well out of turn. His enthusiasm must have taken over. This was too good to be true. He was fantasizing. He must have gone soft in the head when he talked about the one customer they were going to have. He'd made no secret of his interest. It was clear to one and all he had meant himself. No. Not soft in the head. It was what he wanted. What he had been craving for these past few months. Longer. He had caught himself dreaming during dinner parties and meetings. He had become lethargic. Maybe he wasn't cut out for this life. And Paco, Paco didn't volunteer anything. Was he going to join him in this? There was a market for the goods. He knew that. But that market was out of Jamaica, and he wasn't about to leave in search of customers. He couldn't. He was mad. But he was as happy as he had been in a long time. He was going to stay right where he was. Do two jobs. Live a double life. But would Paco work with him? He could not prod him. If Paco was silent, there was a reason. Perhaps things had gone too far too fast. Perhaps he wanted to think about it. Perhaps he worried about what Perotti would say to him, what he would do to him? He was, after all, working for the American. Was he going to use this as a way out? But the market for what grew up on the hills was in the States, and Paco had no connections there. Hold it. Yes, he had. He had a cousin in New York. Charles looked at the Filipino, but the other man's face was glued to the window. He had kept his posture all through their descent and landing. His silence continued until they got into the car.

'You like go boat now, Mister Charlie?'

'Yes. It's Sunday. You want to come with me?'

'We fish?'

'We fish.'

'Only you me fish?'

'No. I've got a man down there.'

'No have boat suit. No have swimsuit.'

'We'll find something on board. Someone always leaves one behind.'

'Same same size me?'

'I expect so.'

'How long drive to boat?'

'Twenty minutes.'

'You like my friends, Mister Charlie?'

'Interesting.'

'You like work with them?'

'Could be.'

'You like.'

'Yes. There are possibilities. But what about you?'

'I like.'

'You know most buyers are in the States.'

'Yes. New York and Florida.'

'Someone needs to be there for it. Someone we can trust.'

'You leave my hand, Mister Charlie.'

'What are you going to do about Perotti?'

'Never mind Mister Vincent. You leave him my hand. First you give answer. You want do business like you see? Like you say? You say yes or no. No good you say maybe.'

'I'll do it.'

'You sure?'

'Sure.'

'You no change mind?'

'I'll do it.'

'You shake?'

'I shake.'

'Then take me to hotel. I no go fishing today. I leave. Plane to New York leave four o'clock.'

'How do you know?'

'I know. I go today.'

'Hold on, Paco. Tell me more.'

'No more tell now. First fix everything. You trust long time. You trust now. I come back quick quick.'

'You're leaving me here without telling me anything?'

'Why you say? I introduce you to people like big brother. You talk, me no talk. They listen you. Now they do what you like. You think new ideas. I think new ideas. We need buyer. I go New York to fix. Then come back quick quick.'

'Fine. I'll wait for you at the hotel while you get your things. I'll drive you to the airport.'

'No, Mister Charlie. You go boat. More better you relax good time. I take taxi.'

'You might not find one that easily.'

'You no worry. I find. Porter find. You go boat.'

'When do I hear from you?'

'You no worry. You hear soon. Same same old days. Me happy man today.'

'Me too.'

The doorman raced towards his car as he approached. He opened the door for Paco and smiled at him and greeted him like a long-lost relative. The Filipino turned and winked and pumped his hand one last time, and then he was gone. The doorman ushered him inside.

A strange emptiness descended upon him as he started the engine. The mountain of energy that had taken him all morning had exploded and left him wanting. Then the answer came. What he had felt was the peace of mind a man gets when he knows what to expect. The excitement that was coming his way again had calmed him down.

He had not felt like that in a very long time. He'd have to plan. To do some real thinking. To watch what he said and did and who he was going to be seen with. Paco had brought him his freedom again. Life would not be the same after today. On his way to the Yacht Club he whistled a happy tune.

# CHAPTER FIFTY-FOUR

◼

The address Nellie had given me was on a small street off Lexington. It was a printing company that specialized in picture postcards and posters. I had someone case the joint for a few days. I demanded clear photographs of everything that moved in and out. I requested the guys to get someone in there and find out what was really going on. I was promised prompt action, and I was going to collect the information and act on it. But when I finally got in there myself they hit me with the biggest surprise of my life.

I got an introduction to the manager through one of our contacts who packed fruit. His labels were printed by these guys, and I walked in there making out I was looking for someone to print stuff for me. The guy was pleasant enough, and he took me into the boardroom. The table there was as big as an airport, and we sat there and talked. When I said I had spent years in the Orient, he suggested we went into his office. He had something to show me, he said. He sure did.

When I got in there I saw Nellie's face smiling at me from every wall. She posed up against a great white yacht or in an open car or on top of some building. She was dressed in everything from elegant evening gowns to tennis stuff and bathing-suits. Some were nude, but there was nothing cheap about the pictures. Nothing glitzy. Nothing sordid or dirty. Not a hint of a woman for hire. She was beautiful. Her smile, her skin and her flying hair were haunting. And from under her forehead, she looked down on the room with Charlie's smiling eyes.

So that was what she was doing. That was what they were making her do. I was getting apprehensive. I knew I'd soon get mad, but I kept quiet.

'What d'you think?' the man said proudly, as if he owned her.

'Beautiful girl. Who is she?'

'She's our top money-spinner.'

'I'm not surprised.'

'She sells calendars, motor cars, furniture. You name it. The beauty of it is she doesn't know. Our people say she's as timid and naive as a child. She's got something, wouldn't you say?'

'Yeah. But how long for? These girls get used up and thrown to the dogs, don't they? In a couple of years it's all over. First they sell pictures, then they sell their bodies.'

'You're crazy.'

'Isn't that what happens?'

'To some, yes. But not this one. Never.'

'Why not? What's the difference?'

'Star quality. That's the difference. That's what she's got. Yes, sir. Class. She's going places.'

'You think selling furniture will do it for her?'

'You bet it will. I only hope she'll stick with us when she gets where she's going.'

'Ever met her?'

'No. We've been building her up as a mystery.'

'What d'you mean?'

'People want to know who she is. Where she comes from. What her name is. We keep it quiet. We whet their appetite. We feed them a few crumbs from time to time. We tell them she's South American Indian mixed with European royalty. We call her The Princess.'

'She'll get a big head.'

'Are you kidding? She don't even know how well she's doing. It's all part of the programme. She knows nothing of the build-up, the sales, the name people call her. Nothing. She's a schoolgirl now. A kid. But she's a good kid. She's decent. Our people in the Orient love her. She's as clean as a whistle.'

'Let's hope she stays that way.'

'She will. She's no pauper, you know. She's got money. Her mother is a ship-owner.'

'Who is her father?'

'Who knows. Some GI maybe. Or a missionary. I don't know. It doesn't matter. When you look like that, nobody asks. They believe what they want to believe. And we tell them what they think they want to hear. She'll do great.'

My doubts took off. It was comforting to listen to what the guy had said. There was no need for me to interfere. She was safe. What they had in mind was good for everyone, especially her. He would never know, but I was going to watch his investment for him and even help some, in my own way.

I said I'd take samples of their work and come back to them. He said he'd be pleased to work with me. He said they were not the cheapest, but they were good. They didn't really need any business. They were doing great as it was. But seeing as I was a connoisseur, they'd be delighted. I thanked him and said he'd hear from me, and I left.

Back at the office the news was Paco the Filipino was flying into town. I had this deal coming up and he was going to help me start it off. I could have used one of the other guys for that, but I didn't rate them too high with foreign business or foreign people. Paco was mine. He had worked with me in Bangkok ever since we took Charlie's joint away from him. He was good. I didn't trust him, but he was good. He got the dirty jobs too, but there wasn't much of that any more. He was a kind of go-between. Whenever I wanted something special from the staff, he got it. They trusted the bastard completely. It was all because of the letter Charlie had sent to Nappaporn that time. Telling her Paco was the cat's whiskers. At the beginning they were all loyal to Charlie, and what he said was the law.

I'd kind of grown used to having Paco around. Of course, I could never talk to him for any length of time. He knew nothing except business. I had to watch him like a hawk every time we started something new, but he couldn't go far. His father had died and his wife and children had settled into Charlie's old house, and they loved living in Bangkok. He had a couple of local women he kept in two shacks, each in a different part of town. He knew everybody, and was very useful to me there. I thought his sparkle had gone a little, but that could have been the good life. He had settled down and become quite conservative, and had sold his old steamer. His roaming days seemed over. He was quite happy sitting in Bangkok.

And then I figured out a way of bringing Charlie into the camp again. The deal was my invention, and I needed Paco in New York to get it going.

I had him come over here, and he stayed in town for a week while we discussed his trip to Jamaica. It was a new experience for me. I had never seen a guy from the tropics fall for New York the way this guy had. He was frozen in his thin silk suits and his light lizard shoes. All we did was go shopping for winter clothes for him. But that wasn't all he bought. He went crazy with the stores. He bought shoes and ties and shirts. He bought socks and boots and a walking-stick and three gold watches. He bought cigarette lighters and nylon stockings and two radios and a record-player and God knows what else. He would have bought the whole damn town if he could. I tried to talk him out of some of it. I told him he was living in the tropics. I told him he wouldn't have any use for half the heavy junk he'd bought. I told him he was never coming back here except to report on his visit with Charlie, but he said he could use the stuff somewhere else and if not he could sell it.

I didn't tell anyone why I had Paco come to New York. The family thought I was giving him a bonus for the years he served with us. I did try to arrange some socializing for him. We went to a couple of shows and to Coney Island and the Empire State Building.

I introduced him to some of our guys, but no one took him seriously on account of his funny talk. The boss did have lunch with him, in memory of that meeting the two had had many years before in Hong Kong, when Paco first mentioned Charlie. That time the two nearly came to blows, but here they got on like brothers. The boss treated him with great respect, and even arranged for a hooker to spend nights with Paco in his hotel. She was a big blonde broad, two heads taller than Paco, and the guy loved it. With the broad and the shops he would have stayed forever, but I wanted him over on the island. There was money to be made there, and I wanted Paco to go see if Charlie would play ball with us. I couldn't be the one to go see him. He wouldn't trust me, but I figured he would listen to Paco.

The Filipino had a ball here, and in between we worked out what he should do once he got to Jamaica. Talking about Charlie and what we had in mind brought happy memories. I had not heard a thing from the limey ever since he had left Bangkok. I missed him, sure I did, but seeing as I had never sent him his money I figured he'd be sore.

It was best to wait and see what he could do for me once I decided to pay him. You never know how useful people can be unless you owe them something. Now that Paco was over on the island I began to worry how he would do. He was a long way from home, and maybe he had become lazy, but he had talent. If I knew anything about Charlie, I knew he could not resist the deal I had for him.

The Filipino was only gone for a week, but I was having a rough time waiting for his return. I was tense. What if Charlie didn't buy the deal? I knew nothing about him these days. I knew nothing about his life. What if he'd gotten used to living off the fat of the land? Maybe he liked the quiet life. I became neurotic. I had to fight the impulse to talk to Paco while he was still there. I had to assume Charlie was watching everything Paco was doing, people he was making contact with, the works. And then, four days into his trip, Paco sent the cable I had prepared for him. It arrived, as arranged, in the hotel flower-shop, asking for a dozen red roses to be delivered to some broad in Manhattan. The same blonde broad who shacked up with the Filipino when he was there. The date of the flower delivery was the date he was arriving. The flower-shop passed the message to the office.

It would have been better to have had him collected by someone. Seeing me there would give Paco a big head. He might feel he was so special he could run my life. But now that he was coming early, my curiosity was killing me, so I went to the airport myself, much against my better judgement.

It was a very cold day. All the way, tucked back in the big limousine the family had provided for me, I was nervous. I was not sure what my own score was. The deal I had cooked up with Paco had possibilities. It would mean spending a big chunk of my time in New York.

I didn't mind that too much because the work was becoming monotonous. There were many people in the Bangkok office, all sent by New York to deal with the growing shipments. There was plenty of business, and mostly it was legit. I was no more than a glorified office boy now, and except for Nellie there was nothing left for me in the Orient. I wanted something new. The family must have known I was bored. They treated me with respect because I did good in the Orient and because I was thick with both sides. Maybe they wanted me to retire, but I had something new to offer. Something big, closer to home. They would make plenty of dough if it worked, but I wasn't saying anything.

The traffic was light, and I watched the grey afternoon and tried to be honest with myself. Was I making excuses? Did I want the deal to go through to make more money for the family, or did I want it because I'd be working with Charlie. The chance of that confused me like hell. I was being childish. I didn't even know if there was a deal, and here I was driving myself crazy about why I wanted to do it. By the time we got to the airport, I felt so stupid I decided to stop thinking about it altogether.

I made it in good time. In those happy late fifties you didn't have too much hassle waiting for someone outside the arrivals hall. Here I go again. Happy this and happy that. When you start feeling nostalgic about the good old days, don't worry about it. It happens to everybody. You're getting old; you think everything about the past was great and, believe me, you're not all that wrong. Maybe things were better. You didn't hear about old people being mugged. You didn't hear people using foul language in public. Maybe life was slower. Maybe it was sweeter. Maybe they took more care about the food, about the way people dressed, the way people talked to each other, I don't know. No one wants to remember the shit, but there sure was plenty of that in the old days too. Still, the bit about the airport is true. No one came barking at you to get the hell out of there the minute you arrived. They let you stick around for a little where the cabs were, and when the police talked to you they were polite. Maybe it was because there were not so many people travelling. Or perhaps because there was no hijacking and no bombs.

Anyway, the guy parked and I got out and went inside, and within minutes I saw Paco. He came down the hallway running. He always ran when he was happy. He pulled his brown crocodile case behind him, like a dog. He stopped

dead in front of me. He tapped my shoulders and he hugged
me.

'Mister Vincent. Mister Vincent.'

'That's me.'

'Mister Vincent, you come bring me city?'

'I didn't come up here to wait for the bus.'

'Mister Charlie, he come for me too.'

'Everybody loves you.'

'What you mean?'

We went outside. It was bitterly cold, but the Filipino
didn't notice it. I suggested he put on that expensive winter
coat he had bought, but he said he'd packed it. We got into
the car. The driver closed the glass partition. Paco sat up like
a proud cock.

'Me VIP, yes, Mister Vincent? Same same you.'

'How's Charlie?'

'You no ask how are you, Paco. You no ask did you
have good time, Paco.'

'How are you, Paco? Did you have a good time?'

'Better time New York.'

'How's Charlie?'

'My woman . . . She wait me?'

'Sure she's waiting, Paco. She's dying for you. How's
Charlie?'

'Mister Charlie he big man Jamaica. Big director hotel
company. Big director import company. No same same
import we do. All legal. All official licence paper. All pay by
bank. He member important clubs. His wife member
important clubs. He know all people. He famous. Even chief
of police friend.'

'What's new about that? He was the same in Hong
Kong.'

'No same. Mister Charlie he change. He more old. He
more slow.'

'You're no spring chicken either, Paco. Is he well?'

'He well. But his eye tired. He get up late every morning. He never hurry go office. He go club, but he no like.

He go club because better than office. He never take me club. He say people no my type. He like spend time on boat fishing, no work. Yes. He well but not plenty well. After see me he better.'

'He likes the deal?'

'He like.'

'You explained it all to him?'

'Mister Charlie he clever. No need explain nothing.'

'He wants in?'

'I tell you he like. He want. He think deal is he and me.'

'Did he ask about me?'

'He worry about you.'

'That's nice. You should have told him I'm OK.'

'No. He no worry you healthy. He worry what you do to me if he and me work marijuana together.'

'You mean you didn't tell him it was my deal?'

'No can do.'

'Why not? He's going to find out.'

'He find out, sure. But not now.'

'What are you talking about?'

'Mister Charlie do work of office boss. He look at letters and he write letters and he sign paper. He go to club. He play cards. He like go boat but have no time. Too busy sit in office talk telephone. Island Jamaica same same Philippines. Many party. Many drinking. Everybody have time. All slow. When I see Mister Charlie first day he slow too. After I show him place in mountain he change. He want run. He become same like before. Up there Mister Charlie talk marijuana people like number-one boss old time. They like him quick quick. Like him plenty. But he clever. He never say nothing. He say goodbye and we fly back. All way fly back I pretend. I stay quiet like dead fish. I look him. He change. He have colour back in face. Life back in eyes. He wait like clock bomb before explode. But he wait until we land Kingston and we talk in car. He say he like. He so happy work monkey business again he look happy like childrens. Talk like childrens. Now you want me tell him you in deal,

Mister Vincent, yes? We kill change. We kill happiness. If I tell is you make deal with us I make him forget deal. He change mind. He go back his office quick quick. He become more slow, more old, more dead. Like before I come. He become no good for nothing. No good for deal. So I no tell him is your deal.'

'So what did you tell him?'

'Mister Charlie clever. He know must buyer for marijuana in America. He no live America. I no live America. He ask how we arrange buyer.'

'That was your chance. You could have suggested me as a prospective buyer.'

'You deaf. You know me long time, Mister Vincent, but you never listen. If I tell buyer is you he drops quick quick. No chance, no nothing. He never trust me again never never. Deal dead.'

'Well, you must have said something.'

'Sure I say. I do slow slow, like in Orient. Quick quick never catch butterfly. Mister Charlie, he know. Sure I say. I say I go New York to fix. I say I fix then come back.'

'You ran from it, didn't you?'

'I run, Mister Vincent.'

'You're sure he wants in?'

'You no listen. Sure I'm sure. You no hear I say Mister Charlie go crazy like childrens when I talk deal?'

'I heard you. What do we do now?'

'No we do. You do, Mister Vincent. You go Jamaica. You explain him. If you afraid I go with you.'

'I'm not afraid.'

'Sure, you never afraid, Mister Vincent. You know how make people talk. You know how make people afraid good. You make Mister Charlie run before. He run from you like dolphin from net. You make him afraid easy. Little fish nervous when big fish come. They confused and afraid and they run to net. You make him talk you now.'

'You're over-selling it, Paco.'

'You me go Jamaica together. Better no make Mister

Charlie afraid. I fix.'

'No you don't, Paco. I'll go see Charlie myself. You go back to Bangkok. The boys over there need you real bad.'

'You need me too, Mister Vincent. You need me help you see Mister Charlie. Make him feel relax.'

'Who the hell do you think you are? My mother? I'm a big boy now. I even go to the toilet by myself.'

'Why you talk me mad, Mister Vincent? I only want help you speak . . .'

'I know that too, Paco. I speak real good. You go back to Bangkok.'

'You want I go today?'

'As soon as possible.'

'Can stay couple days in city. Visit Mister Charlie make tired. Drink rum. No sleep.'

'I don't care. The boys will arrange a flight for you. They'll tell you when it's all booked. You go when they say.'

'When you go see Mister Charlie?'

'None of your business.'

'When you come Bangkok, Mister Vincent?'

'When you see me you'll know.'

He was stepping on my toe. He was going to tell me how to talk to Charlie. He was making out like I'd enjoyed making Charlie run. I should have had the fuckface wasted that day. But I was mad and I was taking it personal. There's no room for personal feelings in this business. So I sat back and stopped listening to him. Soon I was calm again. Had I been a prophet, I would have done him for sure. We were on my back yard and an accident would have been the easiest thing in the world to arrange. But I didn't have a crystal ball, and Paco got himself a few more years.

# CHAPTER FIFTY-FIVE

He yawned. Coffee was being served, and everybody got up to go into the games room. They would talk a little and then they would have a game of cards. They were all nice and decent people, but he had very little in common with them. He had tried to say something about Richard's election campaign but no one was interested.

The talk that day was about a Canadian member of the Club who was about to leave his wife and children for a younger, half-Chinese woman. He had been living on the island for twenty years and had a big job with one of the banks.

'He's gone mad.'

'Everything is fair in love and war.'

'He's risking everything. His pension, his friends.'

'He loves the woman. Says she's crazy about him.'

'She is years younger. Could be his daughter.'

'There's no fool like an old fool.'

'She's a China royal. Wife hasn't got a chance.'

'No wonder we haven't seen him here lately.'

'Pity, that. He's damn good at snooker.'

'Quite right.'

'Where is he these days, anyway?'

'In Toronto. Consultation with head office.'

'How d'you know?'

'My wife saw him at the airport last week.'

'Was she going out of town?'

'No, man. Her mother is visiting. Anyway, she saw him and he told her where he was going.'

'Storm in a tea cup. Who's dealing?'

Charles looked at them and he listened and he thought to himself it was either that or reading memoranda at the office. Then the waiter came over.

'There was a call for you, Mister Charles.'

'What was it?'

'The man didn't say, sir.'

'Who was the caller?'

'I don't know, sir.'

'Why didn't you call me?'

'You were having lunch, Mister Charles.'

'Did the caller leave a number?'

'Yes, sir. He left a number and a room number but no name. Here's the note.'

'Thank you.'

He got up and excused himself. One of his friends looked up.

'Not a moment's peace, what?'

'I'm afraid not.'

The message gave a Kingston number, and he went into the reading-room, asked for a line and dialled it himself. When the girl answered, he realized he had called one of his company's hotels.

'Room 123,' he said. 'Could you give me the guest's family name, please?'

'Sorry, I can't. We don't like putting people through unless they tell us who they wish to speak to, sir.'

'Is that something new?'

'I couldn't tell you, sir.'

'My name is Paget-Brown. I am a director of the hotel.'

'I am sorry, sir, I'm new here.'

'Don't apologize, miss. You're only doing what you've been instructed to do, and that's commendable. I am sorry to have caused you a problem.'

'That's all right, sir.'

'Would you please put me through to reception?'

They knew who he was, and they told him the name of the guest was Perotti, Mr Vincent Perotti of New York. He was about to put the phone down, but the reception chief knew who he was. Having made the man break the rule, he couldn't just turn off now. He held on. He panted. The obvious question came next.

'Would you like me to have you put through, Mr Paget-Brown?'

'Thank you.'

He sat there and he waited, and he felt his blood curdle. Perotti on the island. Must be a direct result of Paco's visit. The poor bastard was caught out. He must have run into Perotti in New York. He was never good at keeping his mouth shut. He'd give the Filipino a piece of his mind when he saw him next. If he saw him next. Christ, what a fool he had been to let the fellow loose in New York on his own. Then Perotti's voice came through. It was crisp and clear and confident. He could almost see the vile smile on the man's face. It made him feel strange. He thought he'd feel sick, but he didn't. If anything he felt angry. Excited and angry.

'That you, Charlie? Long time no see.'

'Not long enough as far as I'm concerned. What brings you here?'

'Business.'

'Not much of that around, Perotti. I've got nothing to sell. I'm an employed man now. You're not thinking of going into the hotel business, are you?'

'No way. No. I've come to settle with you.'

'Settle?'

'Yeah. You do remember I owe you money?'

'Oh yes, that.'

'Yeah, that.'

'You could have sent me a cheque. We do have banks here.'

'Banks is for the good guys, Charlie. I don't deal in cheques.'

'No. I suppose you don't.'

'How's Rose?'

'She's well, thank you.'

'Roberta?'

'She's well too.'

'Maybe we should talk things over. I can't leave you the cash at reception, can I?'

'I suppose you can't.'

His reaction made no sense to him. The inexplicable was happening. All of a sudden he was seized by a desire to see the American. It was only curiosity, he thought. Couldn't be anything else.

'How long has it been? Five years? Six?'

'I couldn't tell you, Charlie. Something like that.'

The man must have aged. Perhaps he'd mellowed. Not a chance. Not a chance. He hoped the little man hadn't changed. He didn't want him to. You couldn't despise an old, benevolent Perotti. He wouldn't be fun. He'd be a bore.

'You there, Charlie?'

'Yes.'

'Do you want your money or not?'

'Of course I want my money.'

'Well, are you coming over?'

'I'm on my way.'


His adrenalin soared. Powerful emotions were pushing him. He had to stop himself from racing back to the table. He felt his thumping pulse rock his body, and he stopped at the bar and asked for a whisky. He gulped it down. His throat was on fire. He walked slowly across to the games room. The stack of cards was intact. They had kept his seat for him.

'Are you in, Paget-Brown?'

'I'm afraid I've got to go.'

'Duty calls, eh?'

'Something like that.'

'Sam works you too hard.'

'You'd better speak to him for me.'

'He won't listen. He needs money badly these days . . . to get his boy elected.'

'Rubbish. Richard will get in on his own.'

'Sit down, man. You can tell us all about it while you deal.'

'I really have to go . . .'

'You look flushed, Paget-Brown. Got a hot date?'

'That's right. Mum's the word.'

'You can count on us, you lucky man. See you for lunch tomorrow?'

'Yes.'

He had to weigh himself down or he'd take off. He stood around for a moment and lit a cigar. He shrugged his shoulders and waved at the others, and then he walked out slowly. His mind was racing. He had plain forgotten all about the money. He should have remembered. It would come in handy. It was a tidy sum. He'd try to get the American to pay interest. He'd find a good use for cash now. He'd be able to finance a few shipments himself. Maybe the visit had nothing to do with Paco the Filipino. Perhaps Perotti was told to pay up. These people had a strange code of honour. Things were definitely looking up. Some excitement would help him survive the office and the Club and the races. Life would be bearable with a little something on the side.

He got to the car and tried to watch his speed as he drove out. On the road he lost control of himself. He raced down through the district of Half Way Tree. Perhaps the visit had nothing to do with Paco. The hotel Perotti was staying in was not the same. That meant nothing. He'd soon find out. He was dying to find out. Suddenly there was something to look forward to. Where the hell had he been buried that long? His tyres shrieked as he broke through traffic lights. He did not notice a thing on the road, and then he found himself in front of the hotel and slammed on the brakes. The porter opened the car door and saluted. Charles got out, took a deep breath, and walked into the lobby. He didn't acknowledge the uniformed bellboy by the elevator as he slipped inside.

He knocked on the door. Then it opened and Perotti stood there. The old squat shape of Edward G. Robinson was still there, inside a beige three-piece suit. The smile, friendly and open as ever, shone at him from the man's clean-shaven face. He had put on a little weight.

'You look great, Charlie.'

'You do too.'

'Life must be good down here.'

'It is.'

'Why are we standing by the door like strangers? We're old friends, right?'

Charles went inside. He pulled out a chair and sat down. He looked at Perotti's beaming face. He felt he was back on some hunting-ground he had known all his life. He had not seen the American in years, yet his shape and his voice were so familiar and cosy they could have been embossed on his very soul. As if he had no other life, no memories of his own. As if he had lived with Perotti in this room and had seen him every day. As if this was home. He was comfortable. All his anger had evaporated. He must be mad. No, he was not. This man was a killer. What of it? Everyone kills. He had killed too. In the line of duty. But the venom had gone. It was like old times again.

On the table there was a basket of fruit and drinks. A gilt-edged card with the hotel logo had the American's name printed under the 'Compliments of the house' bit. It was the result of one of his own suggestions. It hadn't all been bad, he thought. He felt hungry. He could eat a horse.

'How about a drink, Charlie?'

'Would you mind if I had a bit of fruit first?'

# CHAPTER FIFTY-SIX

As soon as he sat down and started unzipping his banana I knew he was mine. He ate slowly, as though he was savouring every sticky bit. He did not talk, but his face said it all. He was tense, but not disinterested. He was unsure of what he had come for, but he wanted to listen. I looked into his face and tried to see behind his skin. I searched for the hate he had once felt. The accusations he had made. I didn't see any. I thought about the last time I had seen him, at my hotel room by the river in Bangkok. About the way he had humiliated me. About how he had spoiled my moment of victory. There was none of that arrogant superiority he had had that last day. He was on fire, but there was no anger in his face, no desire for revenge in his eyes, and he had plenty of reasons for both. All I saw was a man eating at my table. A man who had come to see me because he had wanted to come to see me and listen to what I had to say. It wasn't only the money I owed him. He could have met me somewhere else. Or just have come to the door and grabbed it and got out. He could have invented a million other ways to collect, but he came in person and sat down and took his time because he was as curious as hell. Not about Bangkok, or Nappaporn, or his own daughter Nellie. I could have told him about her. About the great future she was going to have. He would have been proud. Or maybe not. Maybe he didn't care, or maybe he'd forgotten all about her. I didn't know. I did know he wasn't about to ask. He was burning. He was only interested in what I had come to see him about.

And I? I had forgotten how he used to make me feel like nothing. Within seconds of his being in the room with me, I had forgotten his selfish treatment of Nellie. I had forgotten how his ghost haunted me in his old office. On every Oriental street corner. All I could think about was the excitement, the stories, the stimulating conversations we had had. I didn't even think about the deal. I didn't care. I was happy just to have him there, eating at my table.

After he called me from his club, I got so excited I had a couple of stiff drinks while I waited for him to turn up. I had them in secret, in the bedroom, like a schoolboy. I poured a ton of mouthwash into myself and I gargled. Now that he sat there and munched at the fruit, he pretended to relax and he gave a convincing performance, but he didn't fool me. He was just as excited as I was. He made that banana last forever. He was waiting for me to say something. To get him out of the corner he had put himself into and start him off. He was ready for anything. He was just like I had remembered him, just like I had admired him. I was still on a high as I waited for him to come out with it. I had forgotten how much I used to like this man. How much I had missed him.

'We've been a naughty boy, haven't we, Perotti?'

'Why?'

'I thought your word meant something to you people. Honour and all that. You never paid me, did you? My money is earning interest in your pocket. Are you in the banking business now?'

'You're still a funny guy, Charlie.'

'Must be quite a packet you have for me.'

'Yeah. It's a lot of dough.'

'Good. I could use a bit of money.'

'What are you going to use it for?'

'That's my business.'

'It's a pity you feel like that. I'd like to talk business with you.'

'I'd like to see the cash first.'

'Suppose I gave it to you . . .'

'Suppose you do.'

I got up and went into the bedroom. I brought a suitcase out and I opened it there and then. It contained a couple of hundred thousand dollars and some change. I had the whole bunch computed good, including the interest. I had a slip of paper to prove it.

'Count it, Charlie.'

'I don't think that's necessary. You wouldn't cheat me now.'

'Why not?'

'There's something you want of me. Besides, you told me goods must always be paid for.'

'You remembered.'

'Yes. Did you declare the money when you came in?'

'No.'

'Good. Can I keep the case?'

'Sure.'

He got up calmly and picked up the phone. In his best voice he asked for reception to send someone to my room right away. For one moment there I lost my nerve. I thought he was going crazy. I didn't know what he was doing. I didn't know whether it was legal or illegal to bring cash in without telling anyone about it. I was on his pad. Paco did say he knew everybody here, including the Chief of Police. If it was against the law, he could have me put inside. It would be weeks before anyone found me. Months. I hadn't told anyone where I was going. This was going to be a new business deal. Another surprise for the boys. I was going to show them I wasn't a wash-out yet. I must have been crazy to think it was going to be easy. He had me just where he wanted me and I, with all my experience, I fell for it like a sucker. I could never play poker with Charlie. My face must have betrayed my feelings, but he didn't take any notice.

There was a knock on the door and Charlie said come in and some guy came in. He was dressed in a suit and tie, and he showed great respect for Charlie. It was Mr Paget-Brown this and Mr Paget-Brown that. He didn't even look in my direction. I felt small. I felt cornered. Charlie gave the guy a set of keys and picked the case up and told him to take it away and put it in his car. The guy said certainly, Mr Paget-Brown, and was out the door before I could say a word. My heartbeat ran faster than the fan.

Charlie looked at me as if nothing had happened.

'May I have another banana?'

I nodded. The bastard knew damn well what he'd done, but I couldn't bring myself to hate him for it. I figured I wouldn't have been as generous as he was.

'What's on your mind, Perotti?'

'What d'you mean?'

'You said you wanted to talk to me about something.'

I was so confused I plain forgot. Charlie was gaining the upper hand.

'I'm thinking of going into business here.'

'What are you selling?'

'I want to buy.'

'We've got rum. We have a little mahogany. We've got hotel spaces. Beach properties . . .'

'No, Charlie. Don't make out you're dumb. You know damn well that's not what I'm looking for. I'm after some grass.'

'We've got that too.'

'I'll say you have. And good stuff, too.'

'The best.'

'Problem is delivery. You guys here do things the local way. Everybody's got time. I need speed. Quantities. Reliable supplies. Constant quality.'

'You can leave that to me.'

'I figured I could.'

'I suppose you're here because of Paco.'

'Something like that.'

'It's not like last time, Perotti. I don't work for you. I sell. You buy.'

'Exclusive?'

'Yes. As long as you pay on time, I won't sell to anyone else.'

'Suits me fine.'

'Good.'

'Nice to see you again, Charlie.'

'Yes.'

'Can I be open with you?'

'If we're going to work together you'd better be.'

'It's going to be great. I have been drying up back in your old office in Bangkok. Little to do and too much time.'

'I know the feeling.'

'I love it.'

'What is it you love, Perotti?'

'Having you as a partner.'

'Supplier.'

'OK. I love having you as a supplier. Us two working together again.'

'We've never worked together, Perotti. You bought my shop, that's all.'

'It was business.'

'Let's not talk about it any more.'

'Fine by me.'

He got up, and from his face I saw the interview was over.

'When do we talk turkey, Charlie?'

'I'll come pick you up after breakfast.'

He lingered by the door and he smiled at me. He held his hand out and I got up and took it. The wild light was back in his eyes. I wanted him to stay.

'I'd like to invite you for dinner tonight.'

'Let's leave the social side for later. See how we get on.'


# CHAPTER FIFTY-SEVEN

Election fever had seized the city and time raced on. Socially it was a season no one forgot. There were parties, speeches, and excitement in the air. Sam said he had not seen Charles for five days. Of course, in his position he did not have to sit in the office all the time, but he did come up to the house almost every day. For the first time in five years there was no contact. I don't remember how long for. Someone told me they saw Charles at Montego Bay airport, on the other side of the island. And then, one evening, he turned up at the door. When the servant said he was not coming in I went down there myself to see what was up.

'Hello, Jean. Just passed by to see how Sam is. Can't stop now.'

'Why not?'

'I've got a friend in the car. I didn't get a chance to warn you.'

'You bring your friend right in, Charlie.'

'I'd rather not. Not tonight. Does Sam know I am here?'

'No. But he'll find out.'

He mumbled something and apologized. I insisted. He shrugged his shoulders and went down the steps. Within minutes he was back. Behind him stood a short, squat man I had never seen before. He was dressed very formally in a three-piece pinstriped suit.

'I'm Jean Baker,' I said.

The man stepped forward and held his hand out.

'Perotti,' he said, 'Vincent Perotti.'

'You're an American.'

'Yeah. You too.'

'Yes. Why don't we go in?'

'Why not,' he said, and we walked inside. I didn't understand what the connection was. He and Charlie were so different it wasn't funny. But Charlie had said he was his friend.

'You known each other long, Mr Perotti?'

'Yeah. Years and years. We met in Hong Kong after the war.'

'Everybody met Charlie in Hong Kong after the war.'

'So it seems. It was a small place then,' Charlie said.

'You met him first, though,' Perotti said.

'Are you sure?'

'Yeah, I'm sure. I've heard much about you. I reckon your husband is Charlie's favourite subject.'

'And mine,' I said, and the ice melted. After years on this island I had forgotten how New Yorkers are. He wasn't rude. He was just open. I suppose I used to be like that years ago.

'I have been looking forward to meeting your husband. I know so much about him I'd recognize him in the street.'

We went inside. I was going to describe to Sam what Perotti looked like. I've been doing that for years. We had made a little game of it whenever someone new came into the house. Sam would tell me what he thought the person looked like and I would agree or disagree. Sam was usually reserved with new voices. He wouldn't talk much. He'd listen and concentrate and work out the man behind the voice, but he was much more relaxed with Perotti. Perhaps because he was Charlie's friend.

'Charles must be happy to have you with him.'

'I sure hope so.'

'You like living in the Orient?'

'It was a very exciting place when Charlie and I first knew each other.'

'Life is very different out here.'

'It's a beautiful island.'

'Yes. But it's slow. Charles is used to a different rhythm, Mr Perotti.'

'Vince. Please call me Vince.'

It was a request Sam had heard before but always ignored.

The conversation ran smoothly until Sam asked what Perotti was doing for a living. The little man hesitated. He looked at Charles and Charles looked at me and finally he said:

'I was in international trade. Import-export. Finance. I'm more or less retired now.'

'Are you in good health, Mr Perotti?'

'Yeah. I reckon I am.'

'You should find something to do. Your voice has the power of youth.'

'Thanks.'

'Don't let Perotti fool you, Sam,' Charlie ventured. 'He's come here to look for something to buy. Or something to sell.'

'Then you're a trader, like me. You'll find something.'

'I hope I will. Meantime I'm going to look around a bit. Have a little holiday. Relax.'

He didn't look like anyone on holiday, I thought, but that was man-talk, and I was going to think about it all before I decided what he was about.

They left after about an hour, and then Sam and I had

some hot chocolate and we talked. He guessed Perotti's looks to a tooth.

'You're not very taken with him, are you, Jean?'

'I don't know . . . He's a bit secretive . . .'

'International businessmen are a little like that . . . I found him refreshing. He didn't boast much about having seen the world . . . He is sensitive and polite and he's an old friend of Charles. He must be proper . . . He wouldn't have brought him to see me otherwise.'

'Well, that famous Filipino has never come back.'

'He lives in Bangkok. It's a long way away.'

'Come to think of it, I've never met any of his friends.'

'I have. When we were in Hong Kong, Charles brought many of his friends into his room to meet me. They were all very decent.'

'That was a long time ago.'

'What is it you are trying to say, Jean?'

'Nothing. I'm just a little tired, that's all.'

'You're too suspicious.'

'We girls are naturally careful.'

Sam laughed and then yawned and said he was going to bed. I was too excited to settle down yet, and I stayed in the living-room. I sat on the couch and listened to music. I may have dozed off for a little, and then footsteps woke me. I looked up and I saw my son Richard standing over me. Ever since his election campaign we hardly saw him in the house. He ate and slept in a small office in his constituency downtown. He sat down and he hugged me.

'Good to see you, stranger. I thought you had forgotten the old lady.'

'You'll never be old, Mother. You're as pretty as a flower.'

'Thank you, dear. Save it for all these young women we hear about.'

'Gossip, Mother. Just gossip.'

'Take care you don't get yourself into trouble. You're a public figure, Richard. How is the campaign going?'

'I didn't come here to discuss that.'

'Well . . . your father has gone to bed.'

'I know. I came to talk to you.'

'You look so serious, Richard. What is it?'

'I hear Dad's friend is getting himself into whole heaps of trouble.'

'You mean your Uncle Charles?'

'I mean him. And he's no uncle of mine.'

'What's the matter, Richard? You sound angry.'

'I am angry. The man could ruin us all. Father, you and me.'

'What is it?'

'There's talk, Mother. Bad talk. I have been denying it, but I believe he's up to no good.'

'What has he done?'

'He's been seen in all sorts of places. Places he has no business to be in. With people he has no business being with. People with police records. Something smells, Mother. The trouble is I have no time to deal with it myself. I can't get the police involved because if he gets caught by them it will be too late. I won't be able to do anything. I am worried about Father.'

'Who told you?'

'There are people in my constituency who move about in dark corners.'

'Criminals?'

'They hear things.'

'And you trust them?'

'Not always. But they know what goes on.'

'What are you going to do?'

'Right now there's an election coming. I can do nothing. But if you want to help, please drop in to see me sometime soon.'

'What can I do?'

'I'm about to tell you, Mother. You come and see me and I'll fill you in. Then you go and see Charlie. Confront him point blank with what we've heard. If he admits to any of it, you tell him to start behaving himself or his career on this island is over.'

'Your poor father.'

'Quite right. But that is why I have come to see you. I don't want Father to know any of it. You must give me your word.'

'Of course, Richard.'

'Good.'

'What next?'

'Come and see me downtown.'

'When?'

'It'll have to be after the election. I'll let you know.'

He embraced me one more time and left.

What Richard had said was shocking. I decided to put my judgement of Charlie on hold until I found out what was going on.

This part of my notes will remain private.

# CHAPTER FIFTY-EIGHT

My mother has taken to ignoring me totally. In the old days she used to watch me day and night, and now I have become invisible. It was probably my fault. When I was young I did not understand what being the centre of her life meant. Now I started wishing I could turn the clock back. I would have loved to have shown my friends how she waited for me under the porch. How she made sure I ate and slept. None of their parents ever did. I know I used to hate her doing that, but when she stopped I realized how much I really needed her. Not to have her sitting there, smiling at me under the porch as I walk in, makes me feel unwanted. I don't know where all that affection and love have gone. She used to know what I needed and when I needed it, but her sensitivity is no more. She's either running her business or praying at the temple.

Weeks go by and not one word is exchanged between us. When we are at home together, I am too scared to say anything to her in case I make her mad. Ever since she stopped initiating conversations the house has fallen silent. It is like a tomb. The only human voice around is the maid's. And she is getting old and her chatter has become monotonous and boring.

There is so much for her to be proud of. I am becoming very successful in the school plays and everyone knows me. Everyone, teachers and pupils alike, know my name. They show me a lot of respect. They think I will have a great future. I am almost famous. And not just here in Thailand.

After I saw the man in Nina's room, she stopped coming to school and I found myself alone. Nina was my best friend, and now that she has left school there is no one I can really talk to. Be myself with. Sure, many of the girls like to be seen with me and they come to my house, but they idolize me like a star, and that makes closer friendships difficult because I have to pretend all the time. My friendship with Nina was the only reality I had at school. I have given her all the money I have earned and still do. I used to ask my mother for money, and I got my maid to drop it at Nina's house. Now I have money of my own to give her. I know she is spending it and I am happy, because in spite of the difficult time we are having I still love her. I have been giving her money, but I have not tried to speak to her. I feel so bad. Maybe she stopped coming to school because I saw the man in the room, but I would never have told on her. I should go and see her, because friendship should be all about forgiving, but I do not know how. Vincent has been away for many months and with my mother ignoring me completely I have nobody to help me find the right way. I crave adult company. Someone I can share secrets with and ask for advice. Someone who would see how well I have done. Someone who would praise me. Was Vince staying away on purpose? Does everyone I love have to go away? Is there something repellent about me?

One afternoon as I walked out of school I saw an American car parked by the gate. I recognized it instantly. It was the car the photographers used when they came to collect us. I stood there and I waited to see who they had come for. Then the back door opened and a man walked out. He was the photographer who had taken all those pictures of me and always said nice things about me. He came up to me, and I said Nina was not there, and he said he knew she was not there. He had not come to see her. He had come to see me. Not Nina. He told me they had moved away from Silom Road. He said they now had a beautiful new studio in a private house near the American Embassy. They did not want Nina any more, but they wanted me. They said I could name my own price. The photographs they had taken of me were becoming very well known and were sought after. People were collecting them. People were asking who I was. He told me the company who printed them was now rich.

I asked the photographer why they did not want Nina any more.

'Have you seen her lately, Nellie?'

'No.'

'She is no longer what she was. She smokes and she drinks and she takes heavy stuff.'

'This is because she is a very unhappy girl.'

'She is no girl. She was sleeping with everybody. She even tried to seduce me.'

'I do not believe that.'

'It's true.'

'And you refused her?'

'She's sick. She even infected the manager.'

'Infected the manager?'

'Yes. She has a disease.'

'She got it because of you . . . Until she started to work she was a virgin.'

'Maybe she was. She isn't now.'

'Maybe if you hire her again she'll change.'

'She's no good to us. The girls we want must look young and innocent. That is what people want. You can

photograph every whore in Bangkok, but you won't sell
one.'

'You can try her again. Get her to a good doctor . . .'

'She isn't strong like you, Nellie. She could not take the
temptations.'

'What makes you think I will be any different?'

'You are strong, Nellie. Nothing can touch you. You
will be a great star one day. You are made of different material. You're not just beautiful. You've got class.'

The photographer took me to see the house. It was beautiful. Like a palace. The furniture was all imported and there
was marble in the bathroom. The studio itself was much
larger than the one in Silom Road. It was sunny and light
and full of house-plants and Italian antiques. On the walls
there were many pictures of me. They were enlarged to the
size of paintings and were gilt-framed.

'You see what I mean?' the photographer asked. 'These
are not pictures of a cheap woman. This is art.'

'That was what Nina said. She understood that, too.
You can try her again.'

'She could have been successful, but she does not have
the character. To succeed you need a strong character. You
need to be single-minded. You need to be intelligent. You
need steady nerves. You need ambition. Sure, you look at
yourself. You are the most beautiful young woman I have
ever seen, but I wouldn't dream of touching you.'

'Why not?'

'Because you are remote. You are unattainable, like a
princess. Like royalty. People yearn for you but only for your
vision, not your body. To admire and worship you like a
goddess. No one can possess a goddess.'

What the man said flattered me no end. My mother has
never come to see me on the stage. All she cared about were
my grades. She did not talk to me. She did not encourage
me. Here was a man who hardly knew me but had seen
greatness in me. I saw no reason to refuse him. I would be

making a lot of money, and with the money I would help Nina. It was on the same street my father had lived on when he lived in Bangkok. My mother's friend Paco the Filipino was now living there with his wife. But the studio was far enough from the house for me to be safe.

That was how I started to have my pictures taken again. They came and collected me three times a week. Sometimes four. They were paying me a lot. The most important thing for me was to make sure my mother never found out. If she did it would kill her. Of course, I was going to be a very famous woman one day, and then she would be proud of me and agree with what I had done and why. There are many ways to reach the top of a mountain and I was on my way. Until I got there she must not find out.

# CHAPTER FIFTY-NINE

—————■—————

My daughter Nellie was growing up so quickly I had to learn to stop myself from doing things I did when she was small. Every habit I had as a loving mother had to change. She was now a young woman, and when I was a young woman I was my mother's best friend. The fact of the matter is we were almost estranged. Before asking the Lord God Buddha for help I am going to search my own soul for answers. All the gods in heaven will be my witnesses. I had always done my best for her, but I am only a fallible human being and could have overlooked matters of importance. Matters that weakened my resolve to bring her up the way I had intended and caused her to go the way she chose for herself.

I cannot think where it was I went wrong; when she gave up speaking to me. Perhaps it was when she began to leave me notes on my bed. She was always asking for money. I did not know what she needed all that money for, and therefore I only gave her a quarter of what she asked for. I did that because all I had belongs to my Mister Charlie and he was her father, but he was far away and I had to do what I thought was right. I had always told her she could have whatever she wanted provided she told me what it was for. I told her everybody needs to explain their needs when they depend on someone else, but she sulked. Maybe I had made a mistake. Maybe I should have treated her like an independent woman, but I saw her as a girl. Yes, even then I relented and I gave her some of the money. I am a rich woman and could have easily given her all she asked for. Then she stopped leaving me any notes. I knew she was not short because she bought her own clothes and sometimes her purse was full of big bills. I am ashamed of myself for having spied on her, but unless I knew what she was doing I would not be able to help her.

I have heard today that Nellie has been taking pictures of herself in the nude for gainful purposes. My friends in the fish market have known that for a long while, but no one dared tell me for fear of hurting me.

The people in the fish market have found one of these postcards for me. It is said to have been stolen from a Farang who stayed in a small hotel downtown. Until they showed it to me I refused to believe what was said.

Perhaps I am a failure as a mother. Perhaps I gave too much of my time to my Mister Charlie when Nellie was a little girl. All this I know to be true, and maybe it was wrong. Perhaps I spent too much time at the temple worshipping the gods. That is what Nellie used to scold me for when we still talked together. This I know to be true too, but I cannot find fault in it. A human being must praise the gods and pray to them at all times, because they are eternal and we only stay in our current form for a very short while. It is the gods who guide us, and through the priest in the temple I have tried to be a pious woman. If my daughter Nellie does not understand this now she may never understand it, and I can only lament for her. To live without belief will take her direction away from her and ultimately make her an unhappy woman.

I have decided to try one more time to speak to her before going to the temple to pray for help. It is not becoming for a human being to rely entirely on the mercy of the gods without first trying to solve the problem for himself.

This morning, when one of my friends produced the postcard for me, he apologized for doing it. He told me where they got it from and added he was only trying to protect me. He said I was known to be a strong woman and, having talked about it with all my other friends, they agreed I ought to know. This morning I would have preferred to have been thought of as frail.

But I would have found out sooner or later, and even though every one of my friends knew about it, and soon the whole town would know about it, I had to think about Nellie and how I could help her.

I did not go home. My company has a small house around the corner from the fish market. We use it for private negotiations and for guests. Like the guest-house I have near my home, but simpler and smaller. My fishermen sometimes bring their families from out of town to stay there. The house is empty at the moment, so I went there to be on my own. I sat there and my mind was on Nellie. Where did I go wrong? Was she right when she accused me of treating her like a child? Did I not notice how she had grown into a young woman?

When she was a little girl, she used to be embarrassed by what I did. By the way I fussed over her. By my waiting for her under the porch at the entrance to my house. It was not easy for me to let go, but I wanted to please her. I stopped sitting under the porch a few years ago. Nellie had become more popular because of her acting in the plays they put on at school, and many of her friends came to visit. I kept myself away because I think she was ashamed of me.

Perhaps I was wrong. Perhaps I should have persisted. But as long as she was behaving like any other growing girl, it did not matter. I knew the Lord God Buddha was watching over us, and I prayed to him every day. But now I know something is very wrong. And before I consult the gods, I must try and find out what it is. Now that I am older I know how difficult it is not to have a man in the house. But I must not feel sorry for myself.

I would go to her friend Nina's house. She knew my daughter better than anyone, and she would help me. I had not been in their house for a long time. Ever since Nellie had an argument with Nina's mother. At that time I never got to see the lady, but Nina was very kind to me. She took her time speaking to me, and she explained what had happened. She said her mother was under strain. She said it would all pass. She thanked me for coming and told me Nellie was lucky to have me for a mother. I had not seen her in my house for more than a year, but when she used to visit she was always gentle and polite and I could talk to her.

I was about to ask one of my friends to drive me across the river to Nina's house. He was a retired sea captain who had travelled in many countries and could speak English. He was now the owner of six fishing trawlers and a restaurant. He was a pleasant gentleman who always had plenty of time on his hands. He was not a young man any longer, and I knew he would not gossip about what he was going to hear.

I was about to get into my friend's car when I saw Paco the Filipino's big American car stop right behind us. I knew he had been away. He had told me he would try and see my Mister Charlie.

Paco had been living in Bangkok ever since my Mister Charlie left. He sometimes came to see me in my house, and sometimes he ate at my table. I never asked him about his work, because he was working for that American Farang, Mister Vincent, who is a bad man. He was now living in Mister Charlie's house and drove Mister Charlie's car. Sometimes, when he came to the house, I would listen to the purr of his engine and imagine Mister Charlie was back.

I came out and Paco saw me. We clasped hands in greeting.

'You look well, Nappaporn.'

'I thank you.'

'I have been on a very long trip. I saw America. I saw many Farang countries.'

'Did you enjoy your trip?'

'The shops in New York are most amazing.'

'Do they have a fish market there?'

'They must have but I did not see it.'

'What brings you here?'

'I wanted to see you. I have seen Mister Charlie.'

'We shall talk about it, but not today.'

When he heard what I said, Paco went silent. He had been in my house and he saw how I cooked a meal for my Mister Charlie every day, and my dismissal surprised him. I was yearning to hear all about my Mister Charlie and his life, but I was on my way to Nina's house. I may have neglected my daughter because of Mister Charlie before, but I was not going to do that again.

'Where are you going, Nappaporn?'

'Into town.'

'You can come in my car. We can talk.'

'It is better we talk in my house, Paco.'

'When should I come to see you?'

'Any time you like, but not today.'

Paco the Filipino and I clasped our hands for the parting, and I got into my friend's car. I turned back and saw him go into the fish market.

I stood in front of the door with my friend the retired sea captain. It was Nina's mother herself who opened the door for me. She was dressed in a housecoat and in her hand she held a glass of wine. From the corner of her mouth a thin cloud of white smoke climbed into her eyes, and she blinked. She took the cigarette out and she looked at me.

'We don't need anyone for the house.'

My friend the retired sea captain told me what she had said and then he told her what my answer was.

'I did not come for a job.'

'We are not buying anything today.'

'Don't you remember me?'

'I've never seen you before.'

'I am Nellie's mother.'

'Nellie's mother?'

'Yes. Nina's friend.'

'Who's the man with you?'

The sea captain told Nina's mother who he was and why he had come.

'Oh, yes. Come in. Please come in. Both of you. I was just having a little drink. Would you care to join me?'

'Thank you.'

'I never know whether that means yes or no.'

'We will take tea with you.'

'Come into the kitchen.'

Nina's mother was extremely kind to me. Not every Farang person would allow a pair of strangers into their kitchen. Especially since the place was so dirty and neglected it looked almost derelict. I felt ashamed for Nina's mother. I wanted to offer her some help in cleaning it, but that would only humiliate her. It was best to pretend nothing was wrong. We sat down and we sipped tea while Nina's mother drank her wine and smoked. She did not mind us there at all. She was quite cheerful.

'What can I do for you?'

'I am having problems with my daughter.'

'Tell me about it.'

Nina's mother had given me permission to speak about my private problems, but her face did not appear interested because her eyes wandered all around the kitchen. Perhaps she did not mean what she had said. Perhaps the sea captain did not understand, but I looked at him and he nodded and I talked about Nellie. She became agitated. Perhaps she did not understand everything. I was talking slowly, and she got up in mid-sentence and poured herself another glass. I waited for her to come back and I continued. Then she got up again and wiped the table. It was clear she was not in a state to listen to me. I really wanted to speak to Nina herself, but evidently she was not at home.

Suddenly Nina's mother got up and went into the other room. The sea captain and I exchanged glances. Loud Farang music broke the silence. Nina's mother came back inside, and this time she held her arms up as if she was embracing someone. Her body moved like she was dancing, and she sang with the music.

I know a woman must expect loneliness because men go to the Buddha first. They are of his kind, and while they are on earth they can never be alone because they, like children, always need playmates. And then they go and their women are left alone.

I had my friends and my business and one day I will have my daughter back. I looked at the poor woman and my heart went out to her. She danced and she sang and she drank. As if the world she lived in now was the last and only world for her.

We got up and we clasped our hands to her to show our respect. She did not notice what we did. She did not walk us to the door.

All the way back, inside the car, the sea captain and I were quiet. The Lord God Buddha never stops teaching us. I learned again that day what a fortunate woman I was.

# CHAPTER SIXTY

Whatever it is that is putting pressure on Charlie is taking a great toll on him. He had been out of the country while the elections were on. He did not come to the big celebration party at our house. I knew he was back, but he had not come to see Sam yet. No one had seen him out on his boat. There was the usual gossip, but nothing concrete. When I tackled

Rose at the Club, she said there was something wrong with him. She thought someone was blackmailing him. He was being tormented by something. He worked too hard and was always tired. He was impossible to live with. And yet, Rose said, he claimed he had never been happier. Maybe he was going through a male change of life. I did not tell Sam any of it. He'd worry too much. Anything like that might bring another depression on. Especially if what I'd been told was true. I could no longer share all my information with Sam.

This part, too, will have to stay private. I am marking the bits I'm going to keep for myself in red. To make sure I won't read any of it out to him by mistake. This makes him feel I am betraying him, but if I told him what I know I might damage him. His trust in Charlie is unshakable. But the fact is there are rumours about him. About some illegal operations he's involved in. About people he meets outside the office. People who have nothing to do with the company. People nobody heard of. Every time I hear these stories I think of the American man who came to our house that night. There was something very strange about him.

Now that Richard was in the Government, he had access to all sorts of information, and what he had told me was in confidence. He waited until he was elected before calling me. Maybe I was acting in haste, but my son did ask me to see if I could make Charlie see sense. He warned me to be wary of Charlie. He said the man was the best actor in the world. He said I was doing the country a great service. Otherwise he would be forced to act, and that would damage his father. What he had told me was strictly off the record. I was his mother, he said, and he could trust me. I was flattered.

I had not been to the office in a long time. This was not a social visit and I had misgivings. As the chauffeur opened the door for me, the secretary in reception came running towards me. She hugged me against her large frame and she stroked my hair. She had been with us for many, many years. Perhaps twenty. She used to be Sam's private secretary and then she retired, but she came back when her husband and son were killed in a car crash. We used to talk over the phone in the old days, and at that time I knew everything that went on there. She was the kind of woman you'd go to if you were in trouble. She always had something good to say. Sam worshipped her.

'So good to see you, Mrs Baker,' she said, and her generous smile shined. You would never have realized how lonely this woman was after office hours. 'Did you come to see me?'

'Of course, my dear, but I would like to see Mr Paget-Brown first.'

'You're a lucky girl today, Mrs Baker. He is actually in.'

'What do you mean?'

'We don't see much of Mr Paget-Brown in here these days.'

I did not make a comment and she did not expect one. She picked the phone up and told Charlie's secretary I was here to see him. Soon he came down the corridor himself. He held my hands and kissed me on both cheeks as he usually did.

'Come in, come in, my dear Jean. What a pleasant surprise.'

Sam had always been frugal about decoration, but in contrast Charlie's office was plush. There were Chinese cabinets and Japanese prints and old English maps and prints of horses. There was a big bronze Sukotai Buddha by the window. There were rows and rows of leather-bound books. There were two deep wine-coloured Chesterfield couches and three leather chairs. His desk was French, and his old-time gilt telephone completed the picture. Whoever decorated Charlie's office had impeccable taste.

He showed me to the Chesterfield.

'Do you mind if I light up?'

'Go right ahead. I like the smell of cigar.'

'Thank you. What can I do for you?'

'I have come about a delicate matter.'

'What is it, Jean? Is it Sam? Is he OK?'

'He's fine. No. This is not about Sam. It's about you.'

One of his irresistible childlike smiles came flying out of his face.

'There is nothing delicate about me.'

'May I be frank with you?'

'How long have we known each other?'

'Why do you ask that?'

'Why do you ask whether or not you might be frank with me?'

'I don't know where to start.'

'Are you looking for funds for Richard's campaign?'

'No, Charles. Richard's campaign has been fought and won.'

'Of course. I'm sorry. I've been out of the island for months. Silly of me.'

'You went to New York?'

'Yes. And Miami and Los Angeles.'

'Sam told me about it. Was your trip successful?'

'It was not a business trip. I took a holiday.'

'I see.'

'You did not come here to talk about my holiday, did you, Jean? If you don't know where to start, I suggest you start at the beginning.'

'Fine. Look, Charlie. You know how highly Sam rates you. How close he feels to you . . .'

'Of course I do.'

'He does not know of this visit. I really feel like a cheat, but what I have to say must not reach him.'

'I cannot promise you that. Sam and I have no secrets from each other.'

'Are you sure?'

'Of course I am sure, Jean. What is it?'

'I have heard some disturbing rumours.'

'Such as?'

'I have heard you dabble in the illegal export of marijuana.'

The wild, open laugh that boomed out of him was almost infectious. He looked at me with his innocent eyes and he continued laughing as if he had heard the funniest joke ever.

'Why would I do that?'

'That was what I was going to ask you.'

'Well you did . . .'

'You did not answer me.'

'I don't. I mean, I don't really know what you are saying or why you are saying it or who might have put such an idea in your head. I suggest we talk about it to Sam.'

'I would rather he was kept out of it.'

'Sorry, Jean, no can do. If I, a key man in his organization, am rumoured to be involved with something shady, he ought to know about it.'

'He won't believe it.'

'Of course he won't, but he should know such rumours circulate.'

'These are not exactly rumours.'

'What do you mean?'

'I have it from a very serious source.'

'The Chief of Police?'

'No. Not him.'

'Who?'

'I cannot tell you that.'

He got up and walked to his desk. Not once did he lose his cool. He picked the phone up and he asked to be connected to the house. I looked at my watch. Sam would be in the garden at this time. He would be playing backgammon with his oldest friend on the island, Phillip. He would shake the dice in his cup and Phillip's little grandson would move the stones on the board for him. Phillip would tell him how the board stood. Sam was lucky at backgammon, even though he could not see. His instructions were always accurate. He must have been immersed in it. He did not come to the phone.

'I see,' Charlie said. 'Would you have him call me as

soon as he's back in the house?' He put the phone down and looked at me.

'Sorry about that, Jean, but I'd rather nip this one in the bud.'

'You shouldn't involve Sam in this, Charlie.'

'Oh, but I should. Sam's trust is very important to me.'

'I wouldn't worry about that. He trusts you completely.'

'He shouldn't. Not if I keep this from him.'

'What if it's true? Don't you think he'll be hurt? It could lead to bad things, Charlie. I don't want him to be sick again.'

'Nor do I.'

'Look, Charlie. What you do in your spare time is your business. But you do have responsibilities toward us. Toward Sam. I must protect him from anxiety. If you get caught he'll stand by you and he'll lose face.'

'I agree. I'm just surprised you believe this.'

'Do you think my son is a liar?'

I regretted that as soon as I said it, but it was too late.

'Richard? Richard thinks I'm involved in ganja?'

'He does not think you are. He says he knows you are.'

'I suppose he can prove it?'

'Only a guilty man would say that.'

'You're watching too many films, Jean.'

He was being rude. I couldn't blame him for that. I was so shaken by his demeanour I did not notice he never really denied a thing. I had allowed Richard's name to slip out and I was regretting it. I was out of order. I had accused my husband's best friend of a crime. What if Richard's information was wrong? What if Charlie was innocent? I had to make peace with him again.

'I'm sorry, Charlie. Maybe I spoke out of turn. I'm going through a bad patch.'

He got up again and came towards me. He smiled. He was a very handsome man, and I wanted to believe him. He came over and he spoke to me. His voice was soft and his eyes were kind.

'What is it, Jean? If it's Sam's health, don't worry. He's

made of tough old wood.'

'We'll talk about that some other time, Charlie. Please listen to me. I don't care what you do as long as Sam doesn't get to hear of it. If I am right, please stop this right away. If you can't, be careful or leave the company. If I am wrong, I beg you in all sincerity to please forgive me. But whatever happens, I ask you not to talk to Sam about it.'

'I hear you. But I cannot promise anything.'

There was nothing more I could say. I got up and he kissed me on both my cheeks as if nothing had happened, and I walked out the door. He did not walk with me. I reckoned he was angry. If he was innocent, he had good reason to be. I felt stupid.

As I passed the reception desk the secretary was busy on the phone. I waved at her and she blew me a kiss and her eyes apologized. The chauffeur opened the door for me and we walked out into the merciless heat. When we got to the car, I told him to take me over to Richard's office.

I have never liked government buildings. People walk around as if they have nothing to do. As if all that taxpayers' money is spent on coffees and electricity and useless telephone calls. I walked towards his door, and some young woman came chasing after me. She caught up with me and grabbed me by the arm.

'Who are you?' I shouted.

'I am Mr Baker's secretary. You can't go in there.'

'I have never seen you before. I am his mother.'

'I know who you are, Mrs Baker . . . But you can't go in there.'

'Try and stop me,' I said. The poor girl was so shocked she let go of me and I burst through the door. Inside, I saw my son Richard behind his desk. On his lap sat some blonde woman. There were clothes on the floor. Her legs and bare back were all over the place. They were locked in a long, passionate embrace. They looked up and saw me. I recognized her. She was the wife of one of Sam's younger directors. I had heard the gossip about Richard many times, but I never believed it. Now I saw it for myself.

'Get out of here,' Richard said. 'How dare you?'

For a moment I just stood there, speechless. Then I looked both of them straight in the face and said:

'You should be ashamed of yourselves.'

'I'm sorry, Mother . . . I wasn't thinking.'

'You're damn right you weren't thinking. If you were you'd take your whore somewhere else. Go pay for a hotel room. This is taxpayers' property, Mr Baker.'

'How dare you?' He was good and mad, but so was I.

'Next time you send me on an errand you better check your facts.'

'What the hell do you mean?'

'You have no respect, Richard. Not for your father, not for me, not for this whore's husband, and not for your father's best friend. You better clean up your own act before you point your finger at others. Don't you ever talk to me about him again.'

'What are you saying, Mother?'

'The man's denied it,' I said, and I walked out. All politicians are liars, I thought to myself as I stormed through the general office. My son included.

I went straight back to Charlie's office. My friend the secretary was sitting at her desk. She got up and came over to me. I was abrupt. I said I had to see Charlie that very second, and she wasn't to ask any questions. She must have seen the desperation in my eyes. She said he was in his office and I walked through. I knocked on his door and I came in. I must have looked a sight. He was charming and composed. He asked me what the matter was. I had hoped he'd scream and shout. I deserved it. But his voice was gentle and understanding, as though I had not been there earlier. As though I had never accused him of anything. It made my position worse. I wished he'd be rude, but he was compassionate and concerned. I repeated my thoughts to him and I apologized.

I ate humble pie, but he was generous with me.

'Think nothing of it, Jean. We all make mistakes. Me more than most.'

'Not you, Charlie. I am so very sorry. I feel so stupid.'

'I know the feeling. Believe me.'

There was humility in his eyes, and I believed him. I was relieved. I was never going to upset him again. He was the man who'd saved Sam's life for me. How could I have doubted him? My son Richard was not half the man Charlie was. I would have believed anything he said at that moment.

'You won't mention this to Sam, will you?'

'Only if you make it worth my while,' he said, and he winked.

'How much for your silence?'

'Expensive. A kiss.'

His eyes laughed as he collected his ransom. That time I laughed too.

# CHAPTER SIXTY-ONE

Today I want to die. Soon there will be no one left for me to love. I know I am feeling sorry for myself and I know this is bad, but I am a human being and I need friends. I may be on my way to fame. I may be popular and have people invite me to their homes. But the truth is I have always been uncomfortable in the company of strangers. Maybe it is because I don't believe in myself at all. People flatter me and I like it and I do what is asked of me, but other than with Vince and my mother and Nina I never felt at ease with anyone. Maybe that is why I feel so good in front of the camera or on the stage. I can pretend to be anyone I want.

Today was the most terrible day of my life. The headmistress came into the classroom and she spoke to the teacher, and then she walked up to me and asked me to come outside with her. Her face was sombre and her voice serene. We walked outside. The others looked on.

'You must be strong, Nellie,' she said as soon as we were outside.

'What happened? What happened?'

'Your friend Nina. She is dead.'

'Why? How? When?'

'We don't really know, my child. We don't really know. It's just that you were her best friend when she was in this school. I thought you ought to know. I am so sorry.'

'I want to go home.'

'Of course.'

I ran all the way. There was only my mother now. Vince was in America. He was spending most of his time there now, although we did see each other every time he came to Bangkok. We'd always meet in his car. Never in a public place. I could never introduce him to anyone. He could never see my shows. But when he was here we could talk, and I could say anything I wanted. Today I needed him, but he won't be back for another month.

I ran all the way. I could hardly speak when I got to the house. My mother was not there. The maid said she was either at the temple or in the fish market.

I ordered her to go and look for my mother, and I locked myself in my room.

I lay on my bed and I thought about Nina. About how we used to play and talk and walk together. About her father and her mother, the way they were when we were little. About my dreams of being asked to go to America with them.

I had been helping her all this time. I used to bring the money to her house myself. Leave it in an envelope on the kitchen table when her mother was drunk. Nina was hardly ever at home, and when she was she refused to see me. Where did I go wrong? Could I have done more for her? Why is everyone I love leaving? I decided to send Vince a message.

Maybe he is back in town. I decided to ask my father Mister Charlie to come back and help. I decided to go to Nina's house and live there with her mother. I was so confused. Where was that stupid maid?

I got out of bed and I went out to the porch. I looked at the river, and I saw all these people going up and down. Small boats and water buses and tourists. The sun was shining and everyone was happy. Why am I not happy? I have everything a person would wish for except for someone to talk to. I went into my room again. I tried to cry, but I could not.

Then at last my mother came home. She tiptoed into my room as if she was scared of me, Perhaps she was. I had not been too good with her lately. She was hesitating. She touched my shoulder, and then she removed her hand. I sat up and I put my arms around her. She is such a small woman. I had forgotten how small. She did not ask me what the matter was or why I had come home. She squeezed me until it hurt, and I rested my head on her shoulder and I felt so good I wanted to cry.

'Nina is dead,' I said into my mother's body.

'The poor girl. The poor, poor girl.'

'Yes.'

'What happened?'

'I don't know. No one knows.'

'We will find out,' my mother said with her strong voice. 'I will go out and find out what happened.'

'I want to go with you.'

'Of course you'll go with me.'

My mother's car was parked outside, and we went to the fish market. I had not been there since I was a little girl. I used to resent going there because people pointed at me and talked about me behind my back. Today I did not mind. I was too upset to pay any attention to the people or what they said. Small as she was, my mother walked about erect, like a queen. People greeted her. They wanted to speak to her, but she held onto my hand and acknowledged their greetings but did not stop. Everyone showed her a lot of respect, and I basked in that.

I had forgotten how much power my mother had. I wouldn't have believed what my mother was able to achieve in such a short time had I not seen it for myself. My mother has a friend with the port police. A few years ago he volunteered to go to Burma for her. That was when my father's Burmese friend was found dead in our garden. My mother summoned him to the fish market and asked him to find out what had happened to Nina.

We sat down to wait inside a small house which belonged to my mother's company. One of my mother's employees, the wife of a fisherman, served us tea, and then food was brought. I did not want to eat, but as a mark of respect for what was being done for us I did. There was a lot of noise outside, and when my mother noticed how tired I was she went to the door. The place went quiet as if by magic even before she came back inside. I lay down on the mattress and fell asleep. I don't know how long for. My mother sat by my side to watch over me. Then she woke me up. Her friend the policeman was back. She said she wanted me to hear what he had to report.

Poor Nina's body was found in her own room. She hanged herself early in the morning after coming back from a night out. Her mother told the police she had no idea where Nina had slept. While she was interviewed, she appeared to be sober. She said Nina had been spending nights out of the house for a long time, and there was nothing unusual about last night. The post mortem report said Nina had had a recent abortion. There was a high concentration of alcohol in her blood. The police said it was a tragedy. There was going to be a piece about it in the newspapers, but not before her father was informed. The Hong Kong airline he flew for said he was on his way back from Formosa. They would try to inform him of what had happened.

I listened to what was said. I cannot write Thai but I can speak it pretty well. With every bit of bad news that unfolded, I became more numb. All the while my mother held my hand. When her friend the policeman had finished he said he was sorry, and they clasped hands and he left.

My mother turned to me and whispered:

'I am sorry you had to hear that, but Nina used to be your best friend, and it is proper that you should know about how she has gone to her Buddha.'

I could not speak, but I held her hand and looked at her. I did not want her to feel sorry for me. She had been a tower of strength, and I wanted to tell her that. I had asked her to find out, and I was eighteen years old and ready to take bad news as well as good.

'Would you like to stay here?'

'No. I would like to go to Nina's mother.'

'She will not know you today. We must leave her with her sorrow.'

'Tomorrow?'

'Perhaps. Shall we stay here?'

'No. I think I would like to go back to my school now.'

'The school will be over soon. It is late.'

I looked at the watch Vince had given me. There was one more hour to go. After that there was a rehearsal for a play I was in. I was playing the lead.

I fell silent again. I could not tell her why I wanted to go back. She would not understand why I wanted to stand on the stage and read out words, dish out feelings that were not my own. She would not understand how comfortable I was when I pretended to be someone else. If we stayed there for any length of time, just the two of us, she would read me like a book. When I was a child she always knew what I was thinking. I could never pretend to her. That was why I used to lock myself in my room or run off whenever I had something to hide. What she had said about Nina's mother was true for me too. I wanted to be with my sorrow and my loneliness at school, on the stage. While reading other people's lines I could do that.

She got up and held her hand to me and pulled me onto

my feet.

'Let us go, then.'

When we got to the school gate the driver stopped and I got out. As I walked through the gate I looked back and saw Vincent's car as it crawled along. The back passenger window was open, and I saw his face there, hidden behind an open magazine.

# CHAPTER SIXTY-TWO

My heart missed a beat when I saw her. She had grown even more beautiful in the months that had passed since my last visit. There was a new maturity in her swan-like glide down the path. I had driven past the school gate in the hope of catching her eye when she came out. Instead, I saw her walk through the gate, and soon she disappeared inside the big building. I had the driver take me around the block. We passed the school gate many times, but there was no sign of her. I was not sure whether she had seen me. After an hour of cruising around like a policeman, I told the driver to take me back to the hotel. As I walked into the lobby, the concierge handed me an envelope. I knew it came from her, and I gave him a heavy tip. I tore the envelope open. The paper had only one line on it. It said simply eight o'clock by our tree. She didn't even scribble her usual three Xs. She must have been in a hurry, or else she was mad at me for having been away so long. I went up to my room and I sat on my bed. There were a lot of papers to look through. I had stopped in Hong Kong on the way over and slept the trip off in Charlie's old haunt, the Peninsula Hotel. I had picked up the pearl necklace I had ordered for Nellie on the way out. I had also bought her a new gold watch and a small camera.

Staying away from her was becoming more and more

difficult. There wasn't much for me to do in this town any more. But I couldn't give Nellie up. I had worked out a plan, and that evening I would tell her what it was. I'd have to be gentle about it. If I made it a take it or leave it proposition, I might give her a fright. I had already spoken to Paco and ordered him to make the arrangements. Now I sat in my room and counted the minutes. They took hours.

The business in Jamaica was running good, but I needed to be in New York to make sure Charlie wasn't getting into any trouble. He was doing great. He had turned the whole grass-supply system upside down. Small growers from all over the place were supplying an intricate chain of people who knew nothing about each other. They carted the stuff to central points which changed weekly and turned it over to collectors. The collectors paid the growers, and they delivered to packing stations. From the packing stations they sent radio messages to the transport offices. From the transport offices word went to Charlie to say the goods were ready to go. Charlie settled all the payments and informed us in New York when to collect. The shipments went out by sea and by air. They went to Miami and New York. Everyone knew what their job was and everyone was good.

At the top of it all there was this tight little group of people who dealt directly with Charlie. Their loyalty to him was supreme. It was the Orient all over again. They loved him, they admired him, and they were proud to have this very British gentleman in their midst. The difference was they could not really talk about him, and that presented problems. People in the Caribbean are friendly, and they like a good gossip. It was only a question of time before the identity of the man who had evaded the police for so long would be revealed. And there was Richard Baker, now a big shot in the newly independent Government of Jamaica.

You'd have thought Richard would have been an admirer of Charlie. After all, with everything Charlie did for his father, he should have been. But that wasn't so. Richard hated Charlie. Charlie told me Richard once tried to get his own mother to extract a confession out of him. It was a close shave, but he was lucky. It all fell through because Jean found Richard screwing someone else's wife in his office in the middle of the day. The story was the talk of the clubs for weeks. But no one objected. The guy was important, he was in the Government, and if he was a bit of a womanizer, good luck to him. The spirit of the macho was very much alive, and Richard, with his father's money, his famous escape through the desert in Palestine, and his irresistible charm, was everybody's hero. I figure he hated Charlie because he was a fake hero and the limey was for real. Anyway, I had to watch the situation. Richard was after Charlie and would have had him deported if he could have proved anything, but Charlie got away with it.

He was living a double life and, boy, did he love it. He took incredible chances sometimes. Just like during the war. He used to turn up when deliveries were made, when the stuff was packed, when payments were collected. Once he even took a trip on a small grass-loaded boat all the way to Miami. No one knew when to expect him, so no one cheated on us. The shipments were assembled and despatched like clockwork. I often thought about his life on the island during World War Two. About how he had the whole place working like a machine. He was the best organizer in the business. My customers were satisfied and so was everyone else. Especially the family. They were making tons of dough and I got plenty of credit for it. Life was good.

I used to go down to the island once a month. That was the time Charlie and I almost became friends. His energy was stimulating to watch. He was having the time of his life. He often told me I had saved him from drowning in a sea of boredom. He took me out fishing on his boat. I was introduced to some of his friends and I came to his house and I saw Rose.

The thing she and me had in Bangkok was still there with us. Rose was on a million committees and had a big social life and yet, every time we met, I knew what she was thinking. I wasn't sure what she would have done if we'd had a chance. To tell the truth, I figured she'd want to forget all about it. But the looks she gave me and the few words she said in private moments showed me I was wrong. Anyway, Charlie was always there, and she didn't travel much unless it was with him. I saw Charlie a hell of a lot, and we were taking trips together. He was working very hard because he did all these jobs at the same time, and I figured he didn't play around any more.

He used to sit in his club and listen to his high and mighty friends talk about the growth in the ganja industry. About fabulous amounts of money changing hands. About secret runways and small farmers and boat-owners who were now dollar millionaires. About how they had homes in Miami and private planes. About the fame Jamaican grass was achieving overseas. About how just a fraction of the money could solve the shortage of foreign currency in the country.

Above all, there were constant bets and sporting guesses about who the big boss was. Names were thrown about over countless lunches and card games. There were rumours and counter-rumours. On one occasion it was said the big ganja guy was an Australian priest who worked in the country. Once, the finger of gossip pointed at the Chief of Police himself, no less. Whenever Charlie told me about that, he roared with laughter. I suggested caution. I said when people start looking real good they always find something. The trick is to make sure they don't look.

But he said there was no problem. He said the whole Japanese Navy had failed to get him, so what could a couple of underpaid policemen do. I said Richard was not underpaid, and judging by his tenacity he wouldn't stop until he found some dirt. All politicians needed dirt to stay in office. Charlie said not to worry. He said he was as safe as the Bank of England. With his other hat as Sam's right-hand man, Charlie was more legit than anyone. Jamaica needed visitors, and the tourists who stayed in his hotels brought fortunes into the country. He worked harder than ever for his friend. He was inventing a new business every week. He took care to tell me that his brain worked better because of me. Because my deal made him free again. Enabled him to breathe fresh air and smell danger. That, he said, had given him the stamina and desire to create.

He had opened to me. I figure that was the time we nearly became buddies. But with all that, and all our time together and our frank talks, he never mentioned the Orient or his half-caste daughter.

Now I sat in my Bangkok hotel room waiting for the evening to come. I didn't dare take a nap in case I overslept. I was meeting Nellie, and I looked at my watch every second. I don't know how I managed to pass the time, but at seven o'clock I went down, got into the car, and drove myself to the school. The traffic was bad. Not as bad as it is these days, but bad. I got to the tree with five minutes to spare. Soon she was there. As beautiful as an angel. Prettier than all the pictures I had seen in New York. The Princess, I thought, and I opened the door and she came into the car.

'It's great to see you again, doll.'

'I was afraid you wouldn't be here.'

'I wouldn't have missed it for the world.'

'You shouldn't keep away from me that much. I needed you here.'

'I will always be there when you need me.'

'Then why don't you stop all this travelling?'

'I'm a working man, Nellie.'

'You never talk about your work.'

'You wouldn't be interested. I get bored by it myself.'

'My poor Vincent.'

'How much time have we got?'

'As long as you like,' she said. 'Let's drive.'

She told me about Nina. She told me about the studio.

Of course, I knew most of that from the printing guys in New York. I knew she was doing great, but I let her tell me all about it, and I made out how surprised and pleased I was, et cetera.

'You're swell,' I said. 'I always knew you'd come through. Didn't I tell you so, even when you were little?'

'You did.'

'I said you were going to be a big star. And you will be. I only hope you'll still talk to me when you're up there . . .'

'Take that back . . .'

'I was only kidding.'

'I don't want to hear that again. It's not funny. You are my best friend. My only friend now. I could have done something for Nina, but I didn't.'

'Sure you did. Didn't you tell me you were helping her with money?'

'Yes,' she said. 'But we didn't talk. I tried to, but she never wanted to see me. I don't know why. I hope it wasn't because she was jealous . . . I tried to get them to give her jobs again but they wouldn't hear of it. Why did she stop seeing me, Vince; what happened?'

'Some people can't take help. Learn something, doll. Learn something about human nature. If you want to help a weak person, do it without them knowing about it. Otherwise they might end up hating you.'

'You think Nina hated me?'

'Of course not, doll. She needed you and that embarrassed her. When someone makes you feel that way, you don't want to see them, do you?'

'You're right. You are always right. I wish I could be with you more often.'

'It's not impossible.'

'What do you mean, Vince?'

'What I mean is you're eighteen going on nineteen. You could go to college in the States. Or get into some drama school. You could work as a model while you're studying. The company I work for have connections. Somebody could sponsor you . . . get you a scholarship. I could try and talk to someone.'

'A scholarship to the States? How?'

'There are many ways, doll. There are manufacturers who would do that. Say someone makes bathing-suits or shoes or hats. I don't know. They sponsor you. They get you a scholarship. In return you take pictures for them for a couple of years. You understand?'

'Yes. I understand. Could you really do that for me?'

'I could try.'

'That would be great, Vince. But where? Where would I go?'

'I got some information about that. I thought the best place would be Florida. The weather is beautiful and the people are nice and slow. They have good drama schools there and plenty of modelling jobs. With the climate and the work, you'll have a great time . . . and I'll come see you there very often.'

'What about my mother?'

'You can send for her later. You'll make enough money for that.'

'It's not the money. I don't think she'll ever go.'

'Maybe we should drop it. Maybe it's not such a good idea.'

'Oh it is, Vince, it is.'

'You sure?'

'Of course I'm sure. It's like a dream come true. I always wanted to go. I used to dream someone would pick me up and take me away to some country far, far away . . .'

'Honest? You dreamed that?'

'Yes. Someone would take me and make me a princess.'

'Well, you'll be a princess for sure . . . And you're taking off all by yourself . . . like a bird leaving the nest for the first time . . . flapping her own wings.'

'I have to grow up sometime. You had dreams too, Vince, didn't you?'

'What makes you say that?'

'You told me you were a sad kid. Every sad kid has dreams.'

'Yeah.'

'Nina had dreams too. How come she never made them come true?'

'Only strong people manage that, doll. The rest fail, or grow old and forget.'

'Did you have dreams?'

'I suppose I did.'

'Were you going to become a prince?'

'No. Not a prince. We had no princes in New York when I was a kid.'

'What did you dream of becoming?'

'I was going to be a big man with a gun.'

'Oh yes, Vince. Yes. I can just see that. A big man with a gun. Protecting all the sad kids in the world. Killing all the bad people, right? You were going to be like Batman or Superman or some famous policeman.'

'Yeah. Something like that.'

# CHAPTER SIXTY-THREE

I am now in a place called Miami. It has long beaches of white sand like in Pataya where I was born. There are palm trees planted along the roads and hundreds of very tall buildings along the water. This is a town in America, and I have seen the map and know that the island where my Mister Charlie lives is near. Does the Lord God Buddha intend for me to see him again, in spite of what Paco said? I have come here to help my daughter settle down to her new life. There is reason for everything that happens on this earth, and Nellie's move must be one. My daughter received a scholarship from a company in America. Ever since my visit to Nina's mother's house, a few months before the poor girl was found dead, I have accepted Nellie's career. She wants to be an actress, and having her pictures taken is part of her learning. Now that I have seen how happy she is in her work, I know I was mistaken. If the Lord God Buddha wished her to stop she would not have come this far.

The Farang live very different lives to us. They are more open and they are less shy than we are. People you have not been introduced to start talking to you in the street. They are most friendly. They are curious to find out where you come from and what you do and how long you will stay. They are very much taken with Nellie. She can speak English just like they do, but they keep asking her where she is from.

The people Nellie is working for have told her never to say she is Thai. At first I did not understand this, but Nellie said the people needed a mystery. To the Farang, a person about whom nothing is known is so much more desirable and interesting. They are thrilled by surprises and they fret about the future. I have been to the cinema house with Nellie, and I saw how excited the audience becomes when they see creatures from another world, or when someone is killed and no one knows who the killer is. We take life as it comes because we believe there is little we can do to influence the gods. Only they know where the future will lead us, and we should not try to guess it, much less attempt to change it. The Farang take destiny into their own hands. Maybe that is why the Farang are so much more successful in this life. I saw this in everything. Even the palm trees that decorated the avenues were put there by people, not the gods. This whole town was built on swamps that have been diverted to make room for streets and well-managed canals. My Mister Charlie always defied the will of the gods. If he had sailed with the current he might still have lived where he wanted to live.

I know all about his life on the island of Jamaica. Paco the Filipino came to see me before I left and he told me. Now that I am near to where my Mister Charlie lives, I think about my last encounter with Paco.

It was while Nellie was making all the arrangements for our trip. There were forms to fill and documents to find. There were visits to the hospital and injections to have. Mister Charlie always said the American school would teach her about the world, and he was right. She really does know much of the world, and all she knew before we came here came from books. This is why she took to her new life as easily as she did. The passages were arranged by Paco. He was very kind about it, and although he is a friend of long standing, I must think of a way of showing my gratitude.

We were both in the house the evening he came. Nellie was about to go out somewhere. I had long given up asking her where she was going. Paco came inside and we offered him some beer. He said he had heard in the town that Nellie and I were going to America. He said he was a seasoned traveller. He said he had already been to America. He suggested he would make the arrangements for tickets and hotels for us. I said he would have to ask Nellie about that. I said I was only accompanying her. I was very surprised to hear Nellie's reaction. She said she would be very pleased to let him do it for her. They spoke a few words in English, and then she shook his hand like a Farang and went out. That was when he started talking about my Mister Charlie.

'I have been in America, but not in Miami.'

'I have never been away from Thailand at all.'

'You are going to be very near Mister Charlie, Nappaporn.'

'I know. I have looked at the map.'

'You are not thinking of going to Jamaica to see him, are you?'

'No.'

'That is good.'

'Maybe it is good and maybe it is bad. The gods know. If the gods want me to go and see Mister Charlie they will have caused him to ask me.'

'He will not ask you.'

'Then the gods do not wish me to see him.'

'No. He won't ask you because he is happy where he is. He never talked about you at all. Or Nellie.'

'I am very pleased to hear that. He must have found peace.'

'He could have asked me about you. He knows we live in the same city.'

'If Mister Charlie did that he would never be at peace. A man cannot sail one sea and dream of fishing in another.'

'I am not of your faith. I know he couldn't help leaving, but he could show some interest in you . . . in Nellie, his own flesh and blood. I was angry with him.'

'How did he look?'

'The same, just a little older.'

'Like all of us.'

'Like all of us. I miss him very much, Nappaporn. Sometimes I think of the times we had when we worked together and I cry.'

'You cry because you were young.'

'I so wish I had never introduced him to that American.'

'That was what the gods wanted. It was not up to you.'

'I hope you are right. I wish I had your faith. I wish I could accept everything the way you do.'

'It is not easy to accept.'

'Mister Charlie does not know what he has lost.'

'Mister Charlie has not lost anything.'

'He could have been here with you. Aren't you ever angry with him, Nappaporn? The way he made you live here by yourself . . . Look after Nellie by yourself?'

'How could I be angry with him. He does not have the power to decide his own destiny. No man has. Angry? The gods sent him to me and gave me many years of happiness with him. He did not leave me destitute. And the Lord God Buddha helped me with my daughter.'

'He could have sent for you. Brought you to his island.'

I knew how Paco had loved my Mister Charlie. He was only a man. He only said that to me because he was lonely. Perhaps he thought we might become close if I believed

Mister Charlie would never come back to me, even if he could. I said:

'That was not in the minds of the gods.'

'The way of your gods has nothing to do with Mister Charlie. He has made his life. He decided to leave his country and come out here. He decided to join up with me before the war. He decided to go to the island and later come to this city and make you his partner. And the mother of his daughter. Mister Charlie believes in taking his luck in his own hands. In making his own future.'

'And you think Mister Charlie did it all by himself? Without someone putting thoughts in his head?'

'Someone? Who?'

'The gods, Paco.'

'Your gods had nothing to do with it. Mister Charlie believes in making his own future. He does not believe in the Buddha or the way of the gods.'

'He may not believe in the way of the gods, but he is only a man. His life will force him to follow it.'

'I don't understand that, Nappaporn.'

'Do you always follow your will?'

'Yes.'

'Do you go out in a typhoon?'

'No.'

'Then you do understand, Paco. You do follow. No matter what you believe about who makes the big wind blow, it's the typhoon that will decide when you leave your house. Not you.'

Here in Miami the sun shines every day. The flowers and the trees and some of the fruits are the same as ours. Nellie has rented a small house on the top of a tall building overlooking the water. She goes to her school every day, just like she did when she was a small girl. She works too. The Farang company that gave her the scholarship are very generous with her. Since we have been in Miami we have eaten out in many different restaurants, and sometimes I cook for her. She works very hard on her acting. There are many pictures of Nellie in the magazines. No one ever says exactly who she is and where she comes from. They say she is the daughter of a dancing-woman from Rio in Brazil and a Farang prince from Europe. We laughed a lot when she read that to me. Nellie said it was part of the mystery the Farang were creating for her to make her desirable. Even though the time was fast approaching for me to go back to my house and my life, I was pleased we had found each other again.

Yesterday Nellie came home very excitedly. She said she was going to take part in a film. I asked her what the film was, and she said there was no name for it yet, but she was going to play a half-French, half-Vietnamese girl who falls in love with an American prisoner of war.

They were going to make a part of the film in Thailand, and that would mean that she would come with me when I leave, if only for a little while. The Lord God Buddha never stops surprising me. She said she hoped I was proud of her. When I asked her who had given her the part, she said she did not ask. It was not important because she always knew she would be a famous woman. It did not matter who the people who had discovered her were. The main thing was she got it, and finally she was going to do what she always wanted to do. It was her destiny, she said.

She smiled when she said that, and I was proud of her because some of my belief in the way of the gods had taken root in her heart after all.

# CHAPTER SIXTY-FOUR

The doctors told me Sam was unwell, and I went over to the States to make arrangements for him to go in for a check-up at the Mayo. Now that Richard is an important man I went in style. I had a police escort to take me through Immigration and onto the plane. My week in Boston gave me much hope.

With me on the flight back was Vincent Perotti, who had been to our house one evening with Charlie. During the flight we exchanged a few pleasantries, but I was in no mood to talk much because I was worried about Sam. I knew he must not get himself too excited. Not just because of the possibility of a depression, which always hung over his head. He had complained he was short of breath, and the doctors were talking about a by-pass operation. This is a new way to revive the supply of blood into the heart. All the way back I prayed he would be strong enough for it.

When we landed in Kingston I noticed Charles Paget-Brown waiting in the arrivals hall. It occurred to me he had come to collect Vincent Perotti. He did not see me, and I had no time to stop for a chat. I was in no mood to ask myself why Charlie had come down to the airport himself when he was such a busy man. I was collected by a government official who drove me straight home. He told me Mr Baker's father was poorly. When I got back to the house Sam was not there to welcome me, and I knew something was wrong. Sam had been informed of my arrival, and I had expected him to be downstairs, the way he always was. The servant told me he was in his bed and wanted to see no one.

I raced up the stairs and stopped in front of his door to get my breath back. I straightened my hair and walked in. Sam was sitting up in bed.

'What is it, darling?' I asked.

'It's Richard.'

'Is there anything wrong? Did anything happen to him?'

'No. Not that. He was here today. Just an hour ago.'

'What is it, then?'

'He said some things about Charles. I did not understand it all. But apparently Charles is in some sort of trouble. With some big American group. You know them . . . I mean, you know one of them. The man who came here with him once.'

'You mean Vincent Perotti.'

'Yes. I forgot his name. Yes, him.'

'He was on the plane with me.'

'Is he on the island?'

'Yes. At least I think so. Why?'

'I need to see him, Jean. I need to see him urgently.'

'What did Richard say?'

'He didn't say much. He said Charles might have to leave Jamaica.'

'Did he say why?'

'It seems they are after him for something. I cannot imagine what. I'd like to see this man . . . This Mr Perotti.'

'I can call the office and find out where he is staying.'

'Charlie must not know about this.'

'Leave it to me, Sam. Leave it to me.'

'Thank you,' he said. 'I'm sorry. How was your trip?'

'Great. They have a new treatment in the States. I've found out everything about it. We'll need a couple of check-ups here first, though.'

'We'll talk about it tomorrow. Let me know when you've found the American.'

'Sure thing, darling. What do I tell him when I find him?'

'Invite him over to the house. Either now or this evening. As long as he comes today. Tell him I would like to talk to him. Tell him he must come alone.'

'You make it sound serious.'

'I am sorry, but it is. There is another thing.'

'What is it, Sam?'

'Please don't mention any of it to Richard.'

'I'll try. But he'll find out.'

'As long as I see Mr Perotti first, it doesn't matter.'


It proved to be a simple matter. My friend the reception-ist at Sam's office had told me where Perotti was staying. When I called, he was just about to go for a swim. I told him Sam wanted to see him privately. No one must know. I offered to send a car for him, but he declined. He said he couldn't make it before tonight. Charles was coming for him in an hour. They had some business to discuss, and he couldn't put that off. But he could get out of dinner. He could tell him he was too tired.

'Will you dine with us, Mr Perotti?'

'I don't think so. Have you seen my size?'

'Drinks, then.'

'Yeah. Let me make a note of the address, Mrs Baker.'

'Just tell the cab driver it's Mr Baker's house.'

'It wouldn't be much of a secret then, would it, Mrs Baker?'

The man was certainly all there. I gave him the address. He said he'd be here at around seven.


I spent all afternoon going over my correspondence. But my mind was not on it. I wondered what it was Richard had told Sam. Perhaps he did find some proof of something. Sam's memory was faltering, but the doctor had said it would all clear up once he's had his heart seen to. But I had a feeling of foreboding that got me down, and I couldn't get rid of it.

At seven o'clock on the dot, Vincent Perotti walked in. I opened the door for him myself. He offered me a bunch of flowers and pumped my hand.

'You shouldn't have done it.'

'It's my pleasure, Mrs Baker.'

'Did you have any trouble getting here?'

'Not if you discount the walk.'

'You walked it?'

'Nah. I had the guy drop me a couple of houses down the road. We want to keep this secret, don't we.'

I thought he was a very astute man and I said so.

'I do my best,' he said with a broad smile. I took his arm and we walked inside. Sam was waiting for him in the upper drawing-room which overlooked the city. Even after all these years, the magnificent view of a sprawling Kingston mesmerized me. When they sat down I excused myself. I wasn't going to miss any of it. Crouching where I did, behind an antique Chinese screen by the door, I felt like an intruder.

Sam was going to come straight to the point, but Perotti insisted on talking of the past. He asked Sam where and when he'd first met Charlie, and Sam told him. He talked incessantly. As if he was running out of time. He talked of Charles and how they had met and why it was he considered him his brother. I knew about most of what he said. I was just about ready to tiptoe out of my hiding-place when Sam started saying things that took my breath away. Perotti himself was so quiet I knew he was hearing it for the first time. My Sam was pouring his feelings out in a way I didn't imagine possible. Are there things a man can only reveal to another man?

He told Perotti about how close to despair he had been. How he had thought of killing himself in Hong Kong. How Charlie had brought him back to life. My Sam did not hide a thing. There was so much humility in him that night, I was fighting my tears. My big, strong patriarch was admitting his fallibility. He did not pretend to be a hero. He admitted how vulnerable he had been. How close to giving up. I had never known about that. I had not realized how much Charlie had done for him. How I wished my son Richard had been there with me, listening.

Vincent Perotti's reaction was one of complete surprise. When Sam said he would go to any lengths to help Charles, Perotti said he'd see what he could do. I am not sure what he meant by that. There was something in his voice that worried me. I couldn't put my finger on it. I had the impression Perotti had no idea what Sam was talking about. He was obviously very fond of Charlie. But in the way his voice had cracked I detected disappointment. As though what he had heard meant something totally different to him. As though he was no longer sure of Charlie. As though Charlie had let him down and was doomed for it. I did not know how he was going to help. I did not even know if he wanted to. The tone of his voice and the uncharacteristic slowness of it almost sounded like he wouldn't help Charlie even if he could.

Yet all the while there was something else there. The

way my husband spoke, the way he got under Perotti's skin by opening to him. The way he prodded about what Perotti should or should not do for Charlie. I should have known then he was leading Perotti somewhere else, away from the scent. I should have recognized the astute intelligence Sam was blessed with. The way he found things out. But my discovery of what went on in his mind when he came into my room in Hong Kong had demolished my common sense.

I slipped away from there and went to my room. I was overcome. All I could think of was what Sam had said. How blind I had been. How insensitive. I went down on my knees and I looked up and swore that if God gave me more time with Sam I'd change. I telephoned Richard's office, but he was in a meeting. His secretary told me off the record that he had asked Charles Paget-Brown to come to see him. He couldn't be disturbed.

My eyes were dry when I came down. I controlled my voice. Sam thanked Perotti for the help he was going to give Charlie, and said he hoped his stay on the island would be pleasant. Perotti said he was going boating with Charles early in the morning. You'd better get some sleep, Sam said, and they laughed and then Sam excused himself. I called the chauffeur up and told him to take Perotti back to his hotel.

As we stood by the door, Perotti turned to me and said:

'Some people have all the luck.'

'What do you mean?'

'Friendship is a great thing.'

'Yes.'

'You've got quite a man in there, Mrs Baker. It's a privilege to know him.'

'Does one person ever know another?'

'I kid myself I do.'

'And you've never been surprised? Never disappointed?'

'Always,' he said.

# CHAPTER SIXTY-FIVE

■

'Sit down, Mr Paget-Brown.'

'You make my name sound like a curse, Richard.'

'Mr Baker to you. And a curse you are.'

'What has come over you?'

'You. You have come over me.'

'I don't know what you're talking about.'

'Look, man, you don't fool me. You never have. I am not my mother. I am not my father . . .'

'You're quite right about that, Minister.'

'I am not speaking to you in any official capacity. I am simply Sam's son.'

'Congratulations. At last you remember you have a father. They can vote you out as easily as they voted you in, you know. Anyway, it's your father and I who've made the money to get you here. Ever since you got this job you've behaved like a pig. You talk to me like you're some innocent child. You screw every woman in sight.'

'Don't you lecture me on morals.'

'Lecture you, oh great leader? Who am I to do that?'

'Sarcasm doesn't become you, you son of a bitch.'

'Who the fuck do you think you are, talking down to me like this. On the phone you said this was going to be a personal conversation. We are in your office. This is a government building, so don't use taxpayers' electricity to insult me. Whatever you want to say to me, you can say anywhere. And don't lose your temper, Richard.'

'Look. Leave the personal bit out of this.'

'Only if you do the same.'

'OK. Let's not turn this into a Third World War. I am trying to minimize the damage you have caused. It's not easy. I am trying to have a private conversation with you. We have known each other for many years. I love my father, and it's because I love him that I've asked you here. I want you to sell up, pack your bags and leave the island. Your game is up, Paget-Brown. We both know what you've been doing under my father's roof and on his time, and with his money and reputation. You have used all your talents to build up a shameful trade. Farmers make so much money out of you they've stopped growing food. Your planes sneak in and out with false documentation you print in my father's office. You break every currency regulation in the book. You . . .'

'All right, Richard. You've said enough. I hope you've kept this to yourself. Your father . . .'

'You don't give a shit for my father. My father knows nothing of this. If I wanted to hurt him I'd have you thrown inside today. I have enough proof for that. You should rot in jail forever, but I can't have you arrested without getting involved. Without getting my father involved. This has got to be settled now, between us. My father trusted you, but the day you started selling ganja you betrayed his trust. When you embarked on the dark road of crime, you forfeited your right to live on this island, whose reputation you are trying to destroy . . .'

'You'd do well to reserve your eloquent gibberish for the next elections. Keep this short, Richard. Get to the point.'

'Fine by me. I want you to get out and never come back. If you don't I'll throw the book at you and damn the consequences. I give you one week. Is that short enough for you?'

'Yes, thank you.'


Outside it was dark. He felt alone. He didn't want to go home. Great changes were about to descend on him. How was he going to explain it all to Rose? How could he ever face Sam? He had done it again. Managed to get himself uprooted. But this time he was not alone. Perotti owed him. Perotti would know what to do. He'd find a way to blow this nightmare up. He drove to his office and sat behind his desk. He tried to phone the American in his hotel but the man was out. No one knew where he'd gone. Yes, he did take a cab, but it wasn't one of the regular drivers. Did Mr

Paget-Brown wish to leave a message? No, thank you. He'd try again later. He looked through some papers and called his house. Roberta was in Canada visiting her boyfriend's parents. Rose was out on some committee. He tried to get through to Perotti again. Finally, close to midnight, the other man's voice answered. He sounded tired.

'Where have you been?'

'Out.'

'Yes, but where?'

'Mind your own business, Charlie.'

'I didn't mean to upset you.'

'It's OK. I'm just tired, that's all. I've had a long day. Aren't we going boating tomorrow?'

'I'll come for you at seven.'

'Make it later.'

'Nine o'clock, then. But there won't be any fish left at that time.'

'I don't care for fishing. We can cruise around a little. And Charlie . . .'

'Yes?'

'Come by yourself. I've got things to say to you.'

'Let's talk about it now. I can come over now.'

'I have to think about it first.'

'See you tomorrow.'

'Goodnight.'

The boat rocketed through the calm emerald water. They sat on the bridge. Behind the white, rupturing wake the hills and the city of Kingston drew back into the haze.

'You haven't said a word all morning, Perotti.'

'What's there to say? You've said it all, Charlie. You've put us in the shit.'

'These things happen.'

'Happen? Are you crazy? Things don't happen, they are caused. You've been careless. A show like this needs a tight leash. I told you a million times to watch Richard.'

'You can't be everywhere all the time.'

'You have no business doing this job if you can't.'

'Are you telling me it's over?'

'You want me to paint it for you, Charlie? You know it's over. You're a dead pigeon. Any minute now they'll be burning our merchandise. Pushing ploughs through the runways. Arresting our guys. There will be nothing left.'

'They don't know everything. I only spoke to Richard. He could be bluffing.'

'Bluffing? You watch the son of a bitch. He knows. He's got to have someone right inside the organization. You've screwed up. They are probably watching us now. Any one of these boats out there could be watching us. You haven't been careful enough, Charlie . . . But wait a minute. Hold it . . . Maybe there's a chance . . . Maybe all is not lost.'

'What are you trying to say?'

'You say Richard is the only one who knows?'

'Yes. I believe he is. He wanted to settle this quietly, between the two of us.'

'I can have him taken care of. It will be expensive, but it can be done.'

'Forget it. In his way he is being kind to me. He has a job to do . . .'

'Same as you, Charlie boy . . . We have a conflict here, and if there's no deal you've got to take the other side out. I can take a contract out on him. An outside contract. The family must never find out. We can bring in a couple of guys from Miami . . .'

'I said forget it, Perotti. He is Sam's son.'

'Get out of here. I don't care whose son the bastard is . . .'

'I care whose son he is, Perotti. Forget it. Don't even think of it.'

'That's my line, Charlie.'

'Yes . . . All the same, let's not talk of it any more. Give me your word you won't.'

'My word? I'm a villain, remember?'

'I trust you.'

'You're talking a funeral here, Charlie . . . your funeral. You're crazy. At least think about it.'

'I don't need to think about it. Give me your word.'

'Give me a break, will you, Charlie? I can do it. Give you a second chance here. It'll all be over inside one week. Two weeks tops. Then it's business as usual again.'

'No.'

'Is this final?'

'Yes, it is.'

'Are you saying this is a definite, wall-to-wall negative, Charlie; the big no?'

'Yes, the big no. Give me your word.'

'You got it.'

'Thank you.'

'Don't thank me, Charlie, this is the end of the line. You're washed up. Finished.'

'What do I do now? Lie down and die? There must be something we can do together.'

'No, Charlie. There's nothing. You're through. Oh Yoo Tee. Thanks to you we're busted. We could save the situation, but you refuse to let me do anything about it . . . New York won't like this at all.'

'I can go there and explain.'

'Are you out of your mind? There's no such thing as a failure. It don't exist, understand? I'm going to have enough trouble taking the rap myself. If they find out you are the problem they'd expect me to get rid of you.'

'Find out? Of course they'll find out.'

'No they won't. You're covered.'

'What do you mean?'

'I've never told them about you. You are as free as a bird. You are a lucky man. No one knows you're in this with us. You can get out. Disappear. All they know about you is that you sold us your operation in Bangkok. You are yesterday's news, Charlie. I've never mentioned you since then. Only Paco knows, and I can deal with him.'

'You don't need to do that. He won't talk. Not if it's

going to damage me.'

'Don't be a dope, Charlie. You don't know Paco.'

'Oh, but I do. He's an old friend of mine.'

'I'd rather not talk about that.'

'Why not?'

'I don't want to upset you.'

'What is it?'

'Really, Charlie. You're in enough shit as it is.'

'Go on. Tell me.'

'Paco hates your guts.'

'You're full of shit.'

'Full of shit, huh? You never trusted me, did you Charlie?'

'I wouldn't say that.'

'Do you trust me?'

'Yes.'

'Then please believe me. Paco is no friend of yours. Nor mine neither.'

'What are you trying to say?'

'You really want me to tell you?'

'Yes.'

'It was Paco who killed your Burmese friends. Himself. In Person. In cold blood, Charlie. It was his idea. I never knew about it until after it happened. Oh, I admit I used it, but I didn't do it.'

Charles sat there. He did not answer. His face went pale. He pushed the throttle forward. The bow lifted into the air as the boat flew.

'I suppose this is the end of an era,' he shouted into the wind.

'Yeah.'

'Will I see you again?'

'I don't think so, Charlie. I'm going to be a busy guy. There's one gynormous mess to clear up here. I don't know where I'll be.'

'I can always find you in New York.'

'Don't do that, Charlie. Don't even try. It's much better

for both of us, believe me. Much safer. After today it's over. The numbers will be changed.'

'I can come and see you in Bangkok.'

'I'm quitting Bangkok. This is too serious a deal for remote control. Nothing is going to be where it was. You best forget all about me . . . Don't look so hurt, Charlie, it's not the end of the world. You're damn lucky, considering. I've never known anyone come out of this business alive. You are a lucky guy, Charlie. Once you get involved in this you're in for life. But I've told you, you're covered. I've protected you . . . The family know nothing of your involvement. You're in the clear. We must never be seen together again. No place. After today there's nothing you and I can do together. I wish there was.'

'I understand. You're right, of course. I wouldn't be any good for you.'

'I wish you were. I like you a lot, Charlie. You must know that.'

'Yes, yes. I'm sorry this has happened.'

'You're sorry, huh? So am I, buddy. So am I. More than you know. But things are worse for you . . .'

'Yes, well, we'd better get back now. I've got arrangements to make. I'm becoming quite an expert at leaving places in a hurry . . .'

'Did Sam's kid give you a time limit?'

'Yes. One week.'

'Where will you go?'

'England.'

'You got money?'

'Some.'

'I thought you were loaded?'

'I might be once I sell the house and the boat. I've got a little cash in New York. I'll manage.' He didn't sound too convincing.

'What is Rose going to say about all this?' Perotti asked.

'I'll soon find out.'

'Where are you going to go? Back to the farm?'

'No way. I cannot go there. I'm going to live in London.'

'I hear it's a great town.'

'I heard that too.'

Charles took a deep breath. He pulled the throttle back and switched off the engines. The boat slowed down, then stopped. There was total silence. He leaned back and lit a cigar. He scanned Perotti's face.

'You're not a bad sort, Vincent.'

'Why did you wait so long to call me that? Why on the last day?'

'I thought we would go on forever.'

'I thought that too, Charlie . . . Yeah . . . Till death do us part, that shit, remember?'

'Yes, well, I'd like to thank you for everything you did. For saving my life, for . . . you know . . . for being a friend.'

'I think you mean it. Your face says so.'

'I do. Now, can the condemned man make a final request?'

'Sure you can.'

'It's not an easy one, Vincent.'

'I could never refuse you. Much less now that we're on a first-names basis. What is it you need?'

'Square things up with Paco, Vincent.'

'You mean, eliminate him?'

'You know what I mean.'

'Say it then, Charlie. Say it.'

'I want you to kill Paco for me, Vincent.'

# CHAPTER SIXTY-SIX

I did not see Charlie again after that. Not until yesterday.

I know very little about his life in London. That city is one of the places I have always wanted to visit but never did. I managed to get some bits and pieces of information second-hand from Jamaica. When you hear things that way, you've got to deduct the element of gossip and then the element of wishful thinking, and what you're left with is more or less what there is.

My guys in Jamaica had idolized Charlie while he was running things. But his being kicked out had caused them plenty of headaches, and I suppose they felt sore at him for that. As though he had deserted them on purpose. The whole organization had to be rebuilt after his fall. That bastard Richard had the police comb every corner of the island. Finding and destroying our operation got top priority. Jamaicans have a great sense of humour, especially those so-called simple guys from the country. People said the police were so busy looking for Charlie's business, the thieves and the robbers had the time of their lives.

Richard wasn't satisfied with Charlie's expulsion. He had made it his business to see that nothing that smelt of Charlie was left behind. He got the authorities to hold up the sale of Charlie's house while enquiries were in progress. He made sure they lasted forever. The house wasn't worth much by the time someone bought it. The Jamaican dollar had sunk to the bottom of the ocean. He made it impossible for the lawyers to send any of the money out of the island. In short, Charlie never saw a dime. It was all very legal and discreet, but it was a vendetta all the same. In his crusade to destroy Charlie's reputation, Richard used the oldest tricks in the world. He said publicly that Charlie was the people's enemy. He said Charlie had deceived his family. He said he had vowed to stop the ganja trade once and for all. He said it put an ugly blot on the island. Lots of people made money out of it, but he was going to get rid of it. He said he was going to succeed because he was incorruptible. He reminded the people he did not need the money. He didn't care a shit about what all this was doing to his father.

For a long time I couldn't make it out. The reason for Richard's hate was staring me smack in the face, but I was blind. Now I know what it was. It was the oldest reason in the world. It was jealousy. Richard couldn't stand the affection his father felt for Charlie. The loyalty, the love. His success had gone to his head. Like any showman, he was eaten with complexes. In his book, he had saved his father's life by leading him out of Palestine through the desert. He deserved all the glory and expected it, but once they hit Hong Kong, Sam met Charlie and from then on he was pushed aside. Sam spent days in Charlie's room and refused to see anyone else. Then Charlie came to Jamaica and thrived there, and that was too much. Richard couldn't stand the competition.

Charlie never took the credit for anything. He had plenty to brag about, but underneath it all he was modest. He gave all the praise to Richard. He never told me what he had done for Sam. I only heard it from the old man himself the time I went to see him.

The operation in Jamaica became a mess. The guys who ran it went underground or left the island. There was a lack of leadership. For a few months we were losing buckets of cash, but in the end they got their act together. One of my guys got himself a job in Sam's company. He became financial director. He didn't do that because he needed money. He had Jamaican dollars coming out of his ears. The job put him into the exchange business. It gave him a chance to sell every greenback the hotels earned on the black market. American dollars were in very short supply, and businessmen were paying fortunes for them. Plenty over the bank rate. Even that was an idea Charlie had thought of, but he never got a chance to use it. Anyway, with direct access to Sam and his people, this guy knew what was going on inside. He filled me in on Charlie's life in London.

When they got back to England it was a far cry from what Rose had imagined. She used to tell me what they were going to do and how they were going to live. But for that they needed plenty of dough, and Charlie had none. He couldn't get settled to anything. I hear he tried to get himself in with some trading houses, but he was brushed aside. They told him they couldn't use him because he was over-qualified. That's a polite way of telling a guy he's too old. I figure he was demoralized as hell. Who wouldn't be? I mean, he had come up twice in his life and twice he fell down. I am responsible for the first, and I hang the second on Richard Baker. But maybe it was his destiny. I don't know.

Anyway, the story went Charlie gave every last penny he had in New York to Rose. I was not surprised because you'd have expected that from him. She did try to get him to start something, but the fight was gone from him. It wasn't going to be the sort of life she had expected. There wasn't going to be any Wimbledon or Ascot. No dinner parties, no nothing. Then one day she picked herself up and went back to nurse her old father right where she had started, in that place called Streatham. Roberta married a Canadian insurance executive and lives in Vancouver.

As for Charlie, Charlie found himself a woman. He always did have something women liked. Especially when he was helpless or in danger. I heard she was a Thai or a Filipino broad of some forty years of age. They lived in the wrong end of Chelsea, whatever that means. He started a business boiling rice for Chinese restaurants. He was small-time. I don't know how much of that is true, but that's what I've heard. I don't like thinking about this much. Maybe I feel guilty. To think of Charlie, the gentleman, the adventurer, the hero, standing over steamed aluminium pots drives me crazy.

I was upset about him, but I didn't worry. I always had great faith in him. He was a great survivor. A man like Charlie would never settle for skid row. All he needed was another opportunity to get close enough to a deal. I knew he would grab it and pull himself up again. It was only a question of time with him. I would always listen to a proposition from Charlie, now that I was retired.

I may have been out of active service, but I had plenty on my hands. In a way, I was busier than ever. I had taken a remote-control charge of Nellie's life but she never knew about it. I had built a net of great contacts in the entertainment business, and I was collecting plenty of favours. Mind you, none of them ever regretted it. Charlie's half-caste daughter was one hell of an asset.

You couldn't put a finger on when it was, exactly, that Nellie became a star. From the start of her meteoric rise to fame she grabbed the imagination of the guys who printed the papers and of those who read them. She looked foreign, but she spoke American just like the girl next door. Men adored her, and women recognized the sadness in her eyes and did not hate her for being gorgeous. She wasn't seen in fashionable restaurants. She wasn't named as anybody's other woman. Her exotic looks were explained by stories that set your imagination running. These publicity people fought to outdo each other. It was said she was the daughter of an Indian princess and an English diplomat. The daughter of a White Russian admiral and a Chinese circus artist. She was always quiet. Always alone. She was mysterious. They wrote she was a savage Greta Garbo. They wrote so much crap I forgot half of it, but it did the trick. They hid her from the public until they thought she was ready. That was when she got a real break.

I watched it all from afar. We only met once or twice a year when I found an excuse to go down to Florida. By then she was so busy she did not ask me to stick around. She didn't ask me why it was we saw each other so rarely. I suppose she got used to it.

Anyway, when that movie part came up I told my guys to make sure she got it. The producers were told the story was perfect for her. They were told she had the looks and the talent and she'd make a success of it. They were told they'd make a fortune with her in it. Everybody agreed. After all, she was no beginner. Her face had stared at people from every magazine in the country. With a little bit of gentle persuasion she was picked for the part. I shouldn't claim too much credit here. They didn't need much pressure. Whatever it was I did or didn't do for her, she never knew about it.

The story took place in Vietnam, and because of the war they filmed it in Thailand. I didn't go there, but I did meet Nellie in Switzerland once. I ran into her accidentally on purpose in Zurich. In the movie, she and her American prisoner lived there for a little while, running away from their pursuers. From what I heard, she was doing great at it.

I have been coming to Cannes for many years. Mainly to get away from the family and to relax. It is amazing how you can take it easy when you don't speak the lingo. You don't get involved in anything too deep and people leave you alone. I like it. And now that they were going to screen Nellie's movie in the film festival, I was here again. Of course, I was not going to go to the main show. I wouldn't have dreamed of embarrassing her with my presence. I would go watch it in the movie theatre like everybody else.

Cannes is a great little place, and this year it offered me a double bill. There was the thrill of watching Nellie in her hour of glory, and the chance of seeing Charlie again. I heard he was on his way down here, and that was great. Knowing the place as well as I do, I'd find him in no time. At first I didn't plan on meeting him face to face. I thought, I'd just watch him from a distance and see how I felt. Maybe get a chance to do something for him if he still needed it. Whatever happened, it was great to know we were all going to be in the same place again.

I knew when he was coming and where he was going to stay. It was all Sam's idea. He wasn't doing very good in the health department, and had to take it real slow. He came into the office only once a month. He had refused a by-pass operation. He was telling close friends he wasn't going to live much longer. He said he wanted to see his old friend and brother one more time. Since Jean had always wanted to see the South of France, Sam fixed it to organize the meet here.

And so he got my guy the financial director to arrange for the tickets to be sent to Charlie in London. It was all done very quietly. His own son Richard had no idea why he was going. Only Jean and the financial director knew about it, and he told me. They paid for his hotel in Cannes in advance. They even sent him some pocket money. With Charlie's pride I couldn't imagine how they managed to do all that, but I didn't ask. My guy the financial director is not big in the psychology department. And as far as his sensitivity to others is concerned, forget it.

Of course, with the way people talk, it did not remain a secret for long. He told me how worried everybody was when they heard about the plan. How they feared he'd never manage to fly all that way to the South of France. It was going to be one hell of a long haul for him, and I hoped he'd make it. He wanted to talk to his old friend again. If the trip didn't kill him, finding out where Charlie was at these days surely would. No one understood why Sam didn't organize the meet closer to home. New York or Miami, someplace like that. I figure he wanted to be near the Mediterranean again. Near the sea that took him on his first voyage away from his village. I sound like Charlie speaking at his romantic best. I didn't know why Sam wanted to go to Cannes. Maybe he wanted to get as far away as he could from his son Richard. I don't know. I was sorry to hear about Sam's health. He deserved better. I was more than fond of the man. There was a hell of a lot to him, and I hardly knew the half. There are so many guys walking around who should be buried. But who says there's justice? I never forgot that evening I spent with him. The night before I went out boating with Charlie.

Look on the bright side. Out here the sun was shining every single day. The view from my terrace was great. The flowers were in full bloom and the sea was blue and calm. It was the best time of year, not too cold and not too hot. I was as excited as hell by the prospect of seeing Charlie again. I was excited about Nellie. We were in the month of May, when the film festival was on. I was so full of life and energy I could have danced for joy. Even the guys in the hotel commented on the constant high I was on. I forgot my backache and every other ache you get when you've survived this long. To have them both in the same town was like watching a real-life thriller. A movie I had scripted and directed myself. OK, I can claim some credit for Nellie being here. But I didn't write the piece about Charlie. That was all Sam's doing.

And then at last he flew into town.

He was early, because Sam wasn't due for another couple of days. That meant I had him all to myself. From the first day he stuck himself into a routine, and I made sure I was with him all the way. I was never a great one for walking, but I could not see him good from the car, so I'd park myself across the boulevard and watch. He used to go down to the same terrace coffee-shop every day. He'd turn up at, oh, eleven o'clock, and sit for a couple of hours reading the papers. Then he'd go somewhere cheap for lunch. At three in the afternoon, like clockwork, he'd come back and sit down again. I reckon he didn't like his hotel room, and at that time in the afternoon you always find a front-line seat. He'd read another paper. I figure it would be the London papers, which usually arrived just after lunch. I wondered why he'd taken to reading the papers. I had never seen him do that when we worked together. Not even in Bangkok. I suppose there was nothing else to do, and since Sam had not arrived yet he was bored.

Anyway, Charlie would read the paper cover to cover and have maybe four coffees. Then he'd just sit there and look at the sea. His eyes had lost their lustre. He looked like a guy waiting for something to turn up, but he didn't seem to have the energy to grab at anything even if it came his way. His movements were slow. None of the old agility was there. Maybe he was in some sort of pain. His face was sure strained. But whenever the waiter came towards him, he'd put his old smile on again. The guy must have been charmed by him. He was always hovering around Charlie's table, and sometimes they would talk.

I saw an old lady, shabbily dressed in mauve, singing hoarse ballads to an embarrassed German couple who were sipping Pernod. She had a broad-rimmed hat with faded cloth flowers all over. Charlie smiled at her and got up and bowed and gave her a coin. She looked at him like Jeanette MacDonald would look at Nelson Eddy, and sang that *Maytime* song 'Sweetheart' for him. There was no traffic, and I heard every word. 'Do you remember the day when we were happy in May,' she croaked, and he loved it. I smiled to myself, standing across the road behind my palm. It was thick enough to hide me. I always put on weight in this town, but at my age, who cares?

It was sheer torture just to look at him. I had to fight real hard not to walk up to him and sit down with him, but I was biding my time. I watched him through a set of binoculars and saw it all. He was a sad sight now. I knew he had very little cash. They had cleaned him out before they kicked him out of Jamaica. He had lost a lot of weight, and his hair had gone almost white. Over his thick suit he always wore a shabby raincoat which was miles too big for him. He'd always take it off just before he sat down and put it on the chair next to him, as if he didn't want anyone to join him.

I looked at him and saw every expression on his face. My binoculars were strong. He seemed so close I could have touched him. I could almost smell him. But I wasn't really taking any of it in. I saw him for two solid days. He never changed his clothes. I cased the joint he was staying in, and I hated it. It was too pitiful, and I wanted to remember him the way he used to be.

# CHAPTER SIXTY-SEVEN

This was going to be her big day. And mine, because I had waited for it for many years. I had tried to help her the best way I could. Hers was the only success that counted now. I sat in my room and I hesitated. Charlie was in town and my mind was on him. I had seen the shit state he was in, and I thought of a thousand ways to help him. I figured something would occur to me, but Sam was arriving the next day and Charlie would go see him. It was a big day for them, too. If Sam survived the meeting, he'd help. Even if he didn't notice how low Charlie had sunk, Jean would tell him. From what I remembered, she was quite a girl. Sam was a very wealthy man, and he owed Charlie because of the extra dough the limey had made for him with the importing business and that. I was sure he would do something. And he was sensitive enough to know how to help Charlie without offending him. I wished I was a fly on Sam's wall. I wished I knew what went on, but I knew I'd find out one way or another.

So I sat in my room. It was late. On my bedside table I keep a framed postcard with Nellie's picture on it. She gave it to me a few years back. I took it out and looked at it. It came alive in my hand, and I missed her like crazy. I could hear her voice whispering those shy declarations of affection. I couldn't stand it any longer and I picked the phone up. I called her and said I was in town. She didn't express any surprise. As though she had expected me to be around. As if she was thinking of me that very minute. From her voice I knew she was the happiest she'd ever been. The conversation went something like this.

'I knew you'd be here, Vince. Why didn't you call me before?'

'What's the difference, Nellie? You were busy. They love you there in Florida. They'll be crazy about you here.'

'But you love me everywhere, don't you, Vince.'

I think there was a little tear in my eye when she said

that. For a second I lost my power of speech.

'Are you OK?'

'Sure I'm OK.'

She put on her little kitten voice.

'You and me is still our secret?'

'You bet it is.'

'I want you to come over now.'

'It's late.'

'You always have some excuse.'

'You know the rules.'

'Sure I do. We must never meet in public. Why is it? Are you ashamed of me?'

'You must be crazy, darling. There's nothing I'd like better.'

'Then why don't we? Do you know I have never seen you unless we are alone? I want to show you off. I'm so proud of you.'

'It's bad for your image.'

'You always say that. You make me mad.'

'It's true.'

'It's not.'

'It is. I have a bad name.'

'You couldn't have a bad name. You're the best man in the world.'

'Plenty wouldn't agree with you.'

'You always run yourself down.'

'It's true. Look, we'll meet tomorrow. I'll call tomorrow and fix it.'

'It's always tomorrow, never today. I'm so lonely for you, Vince.'

'With all your fans and admirers?'

'You are family, Vince.'

I was, at that, but I had to fight my tears then. I was becoming sentimental.

'Every time I say something nice to you you go silent.'

'I am overcome.'

'You are making fun of me.'

'I'm dead serious,' I said. 'Honest.'

'Then come over here now.'

'I'll see you tomorrow.'

'Where are you staying?'

'At the Martinez.'

'It's two minutes away. I'm coming over. You can't stop me.'

'You'll be mobbed.'

'We're in France, Vince. No one knows me here.'

'Tomorrow they will.'

'You think they'll like me?'

'They'll love you, doll.'

'I can come over now. I have no make-up on. I'll put some rags on . . .'

'This is a decent establishment, Nellie. They won't let you in.'

'You've got a woman there.'

'No I haven't.'

'I'm on my way,' she said, and that was all she said. She put the phone down. I put my jacket on and I looked at my overblown self in the mirror. All this good food was playing tricks with me. I was so fat I could hardly breathe. I could not do my jacket up. I combed my hair and then I heard her knock. I opened the door and she fell into my arms. She was a head taller than me. She rested her face on my shoulder. It was heaven.

'What are you doing with a fat old man?'

'You're the love of my life. And you never change. You look the same as you did when I was at school.'

'I wish.'

'I have a wish too.'

'What is it, doll?'

'I wish my father could see me . . .'

'What made you think of him?'

'I don't know. I have been thinking of him these past three months. All through the filming I thought how I might make a success, and how he'd be proud of what I am doing.'

'I can fix that,' I said, and I regretted it.

'You must not do this to me. I'm a sensitive girl. Especially tonight. Don't tell lies. You've never lied to me before.'

'I am not lying. I can fix it.'

'Fix it for me to see my father? Next thing you'll say is you'll bring my mother over too.'

'I won't say that. Your mother is far away. She's in Bangkok.'

'I know that, Vince . . . Where's Mister Charlie?'

'Did you call your mother yet?'

'Yes.'

'Is she OK?'

'She's OK. I just spoke to her. Not an hour ago. She'd been to the temple. She's praying for me. That's all she does these days. Prays and cooks lunch for Mister Charlie. The priest says he'll pray too. So will our old maid.'

'Then nothing can go wrong. You've got God on your ticket.'

'Where is Mister Charlie, Vincent?'

I must have been crazy to mention it but it was too late now.

'Your father is here in town, Nellie. In Cannes.'

'You know where he's staying?'

'Yes.'

'Why didn't you tell me?'

'You didn't ask.'

'I'm asking.'

'I won't tell you, doll. I don't want you racing all over town breaking into people's rooms. Your father hasn't seen you in many years. He'll get the shock of his life.'

'No he won't. He never cared.'

'You don't know that.'

'Do you?'

'No. But I'm sure he does. I can fix it, but not tonight. I know where he goes in the day. I know where he sits. I'll take you there tomorrow.'

'What time?'

'Four in the afternoon.'

'I have an hour at four. The screening is at five.'

'Five-thirty.'

'You know everything.'

'Everything that's good for you, doll.'

Was this going to be good for her? I must have been crazy. Once she met with Charlie I'd had it with her.

Or maybe not. If she met with him I'd meet with him. We'd be friends again. Maybe we'd do things again. We were older and wiser now. We'd go places. All three of us.

She looked at me with those impossible eyes.

'You'll call me?'

'You bet.'

'You promise?'

'I promise.'

'Cross your heart and hope to die?'

'Yes.'

# CHAPTER SIXTY-EIGHT

∎

A stretch of blue water skated backward along the runway as we landed. Somewhere near, I knew of enchanted bays, picturesque old ports, and red-roofed houses. Along the coast there were fashionable hotels and down the slopes of the hills there were vineyards. There were fabulously dressed women, jewellery shops and restaurants, casinos and galleries and museums. Knowing what I had come to see excited me. My recent anxiety was invaded by healing rays of expectation.

I lived in an island paradise, renowned for palm forests and beaches and clear, beautiful waters. Sam's main business was to cater for sun-worshippers from the cold East Coast. But I had always wanted to see the South of France. The names Nice and Cannes and Monte Carlo rang with romance, with history, with art and sophistication. During my college years, I spent a summer in England, and we crossed the channel over to France for a gloriously cultured week in Paris. I have been back to Europe one more time since then. We went to Greece and England and Paris again, but that was the year in which tragedy hit Sam. After that there were no more European trips, and my travelling was limited to shuttling to and from the United States visiting an ever-aging family.

I had dropped hints about my wishes for a long time, but my husband took no notice. His health had been poor for a long time, and of late it had deteriorated alarmingly. He wouldn't hear of any trip to the States to see a specialist. He said the Jamaican doctors were just as good, and if it was time for him to go no operation could stop it. I fought and I argued, but he remained adamant. On such occasions Sam's attitude seemed to be reverting to what it was in our early years. He said I was younger and stronger, but he was still a man. If he was no longer the head of the family, he was, at the very least, in charge of his own body. I did not persist.

I had always suspected there was a connection between Sam's well-being and Charlie's presence on the island. He was never a man who enjoyed a tease or a joke, but he could laugh and he liked the company of others. Once Charlie was gone, even that changed. He stayed at home more. We were still entertaining a little, but he always excused himself immediately after dinner. He was not a great one for small-talk himself, but he used to enjoy listening to it. And then he gave that up, too. He stopped playing backgammon with his friends and concentrated on managing his business from his bedroom. I was always afraid he would slip into a depression again, but that never happened. He was still kind and considerate to me. He never forgot my birthday and always gave me wonderful presents, and never forgot to ask about my family in America. He wanted to be alone more than before, and he encouraged me to go to New York as often as I wanted.

I had given up our joint therapy. Given up talking about

his feelings and thoughts. The experiment of writing things down and discussing them with him was over. He said he no longer had any patience for that.

These notes are now for me alone. I keep a diary after all.

He did not talk about Charlie any more, but I am sure he never stopped thinking of him. His secretary came up to the house every day, and he might have written to him, but I never found out. One thing I was certain of: he never knew what it was that forced Charlie to leave. At the time, the papers were full of it, but Sam never had the papers read to him. I had confronted Richard on more than one occasion, and I asked him directly. Richard swore to me that he never did tell his father of his ultimatum. Sam, my son insisted, had believed Charlie had fallen foul of some company he was doing business with. I suppose he meant Vincent Perotti, who didn't return to Jamaica after Charlie's departure. At least, not to my knowledge.

And then one day, not one month ago, Sam announced we were going to the South of France. He said it was by way of an anniversary present for me. Our wedding day fell on my birthday, and he said he was giving a present to himself, too. He wanted to see his friend and brother Charles Paget-Brown again. He said it was all arranged. He asked me to get all my old guidebooks out and find out about museums and the galleries in every town along the coast from St Tropez to Monaco. My worries about Sam's health had dimmed my old enthusiasm for the South of France, and I said so. He insisted he was going to feel better once he had seen Charles again. In a funny way, I believed that myself. I began to look forward to meeting the rogue again.

Sam was in a hurry to get there. We stopped in New York and in London, but we stayed in airport hotels. He said he had no interest in visiting these two cities again.

And then we flew into Nice, drove to Cannes, and settled at the Carlton Hotel.

This was a beautiful old place, and I was enchanted by

the style and quality and class the decor exuded. As soon as we'd got to our room, Sam asked me to contact Charles. He gave me the name of the hotel the Englishman was staying at. I did as he asked, and Sam sat down on the chair by the window and smiled.

'I can smell the sea,' he said. 'It's the Mediterranean. It was my sea once.'

'Mare Nostrum,' I said. 'Our sea. That's what the Romans called it.'

'You're a very educated girl,' Sam said, and I looked at him. 'I am so proud of you . . . I . . .' He gasped. His face went pale. He stretched his arm towards me, and then he clenched his fist and hammered at his chest.

'What's the matter, darling?'

'I'm a little short of breath.'

'Let me call Charles. I'll tell him to come later.'

'No, no. It will go in a minute.'

I went to him and I took his arm and led him to the bedroom. I picked up the phone and called reception. I asked for a doctor. Sam did not object.

I had never been to Cannes before. I did not know where Charlie's hotel was, and I did not ask anyone. I prayed it was far.

The doctor came, and within minutes there was a nurse in the room and an oxygen tank, and then there was a knock on the door.

'Tell the gentleman to wait,' I said to the nurse. 'Tell him we won't be long.'

Sam sat up. His face contorted.

'You do no such thing,' he said. His voice was strong, almost fierce. I got up and opened the door. I prayed it was someone else. It could have been anyone. But in the door stood Sam's old friend Charles Paget-Brown. He did not say a word. I don't know how Sam knew it was him, but he did.

'Come in, Charles,' Sam said. His face had softened. He smiled. He tapped the space by his side. 'Come sit with me.'

Our friend from Bangkok had changed. More than that. He looked positively sloppy. He wore an old grey raincoat over a thick woollen suit. His shoes were worn. His elegance had disappeared. The old mischievous light had gone from his eyes. His hair was totally grey, and he had a little limp. The rambling, flowering plant he was when I knew him had reverted back into the confinement of a pot. For the first time since Hong Kong I was pleased Sam was blind. But his ear was as sharp as a whip.

'Anything wrong with your foot?'

'I kicked a stone on the beach yesterday.'

'You went swimming? That's good.'

'I didn't swim. Just walked barefoot on the beach.'

'I'd like that.'

'I'll go with you.'

'Is life good for you, Charles?'

'Very good. Excellent in fact.'

'That's good. I am so happy to be with you again.'

'It's very decent of you to invite me over. Under the circumstances.'

'What circumstances?' The blood had returned to Sam's face. The doctor looked at me and then at Sam. He shrugged his shoulders and said he'd look in in an hour.

'The gentleman seems better,' he said. 'The nurse can stay here if you like.'

'That will not be necessary,' Sam said.

I walked them to the door. Sam and Charles held hands in silence. On my way back Charlie looked at me. His eyes were begging something of me. With his free hand he pointed at his clothes and his shoes. He shook his head. I understood and I nodded.

'What circumstances, Charles?'

'The circumstances of my departure.'

'I don't understand. You said you had to go. You said there were problems in England that needed your attention. What is so unusual about that?'

'No one told you anything?'

'What should they have told me?'

'I didn't exactly treat you well, did I?'

'What do you mean?'

'I left in rather a hurry.'

'No you didn't. You came to say goodbye, remember?'

'I didn't. I called you on the telephone.'

'What's the difference, Charles?'

'The difference is I did not come in person. I didn't explain.'

'Of course you did. You said you had to go. A man must respect other people's wishes. You said your sister was gravely ill and you were needed in England.'

'I lied. I'd like to come clean with you now.'

'Come clean?'

I shook my head like mad. I couldn't have that. If he told Sam what had happened he would surely be sick again. He'd never talk to Richard. But Charlie didn't pay any attention.

'Yes. I didn't leave because of my sister. We haven't been on speaking terms for thirty years. I knew nothing of her. I used her as an excuse. I lied to you.'

'I know that, Charles. I know.'

'What do you mean?'

'I knew the truth, Charles. I knew all the time.'

'You knew everything?'

'Yes. Everything.'

I could no longer keep quiet.

'Did Richard tell you what happened?'

'No, Jean. Not Richard.'

I was relieved. Perhaps he did not know it all. And then Sam took Charlie's hand and said:

'I knew about the ganja, Charles. I knew about the shipments and the organization. I knew as soon as your Filipino friend came. I knew what he was doing. Where he went and who he saw. I knew about it long before Richard knew. Long before you started . . . Long before you knew you were going to get involved . . .'

'Why didn't you say something, Sam? Why didn't you stop me?'

'I had no right.'

'I don't understand any of it, Sam. There I was, breaking the law under your own roof, putting you at risk, and you say you had no right?'

The sun broke into the room. The chandelier lit up in a myriad of reflections. The colours of the furniture and the flowers and the wallpaper grew sharper. I held my breath.

'Forgive me for saying it, but I have always thought you had some growing up to do, Charles. You were a warrior. An adventurer. All adventurers are children at heart.'

'What I did was against the law. It was a crime.'

'In some parts of the world what you did was no crime. Where I was born people smoked hasheesh for many years. Centuries maybe.'

'That doesn't exonerate me, Sam. You are being too easy on me.'

'I'm only being easy on myself, Charles.'

'On yourself?'

'Yes. I was protected by walls and a roof; you were out in the cold. You were having a rough time adjusting to life in Jamaica. This was still a very traditional society, locked inside rules and regulations and habits you were free of in the Orient. Your life before you joined me was very different. Working with me was too much of a change. The dullness of an ordinary, disciplined life suffocated you. When a man suffocates, he fights to save himself. He grasps for air. Battles for a way to breathe. This sort of struggle makes a man blind to what goes on around him. He loses sight of everything. He doesn't know right from wrong . . . That was happening to you. You needed help . . . You needed someone to throw you a line . . . Your Filipino friend did . . . It might have been the wrong line, but it was the only one . . . You were drowning . . . You could not think. You grabbed hold of it because to you it was a lifesaver . . . How could I stop you from saving yourself? No, my dear brother, I had no right to judge you then. I have no right to judge you now.'

'You understood all that?'

'Of course I did. I've been there myself . . . Years ago, after Palestine . . .'

'But you adjusted.'

'Maybe I did, but that, again, was only because I was fortunate. I had you to help me understand my new surroundings, my new situation . . . my blindness . . . my new self. You were my lifesaver . . . my line . . . I would have done anything you suggested. You could have used me, Charles, but you did not. You were compassionate and patient, and you took your time with me . . . And when your turn came you didn't have a man like you to help you. I neglected to do what you would have done . . . what you did . . .'

'What I did was betray your trust.'

'It was I who betrayed you, Charles . . . I let you down. I did nothing to help you. I left you to go under . . . all alone. That is one cross I shall have to bear. And there is more. Much more I must answer for . . .'

'You're a noble soul, Sam. I know what you are trying to do, but what I did was a crime against society. A crime is punishable by law. Richard was lenient on me because of you. I deserved to rot in jail for years.'

'You don't understand, do you? I saw what was happening to you but I didn't move a muscle to help. You see, my friend, I didn't have it in me. I had too many doubts. Maybe I was born in a cage. Maybe I was born too old. Too many obligations, all inside my head. I was too busy making good to hide the truth, to compensate for deeper passions that were buried within me. My past was my prison. You need to be free to help others to freedom. You need strength to overcome your own preoccupation with yourself. I couldn't help you the way you were able to help me. And then, Charlie, then you took the only way available and got into trouble . . .'

'But I committed a crime . . .'

'You are not the only one, Charles.'

'In this room I am.'

'I am trying to tell you I committed a crime too. Against society and God.'

'A crime? You?'

'Yes, Charles. Me. I don't know how much time I have. Maybe very little. I've tried to tell you about it before . . . in a letter. It is a dark secret. I have never talked about my guilt to anyone, Charles. Not even to my wife . . .'

'Guilt? Whatever would you be guilty of?'

'Murder, Charles, murder.'

'You are tired, Sam . . . We'll talk of it some other time . . .'

'I may not be able to, Charles . . . I want to talk of it. I must, like you said . . . I must come clean . . . If I stop now I'll never do it. I won't have the courage . . .'

'Then don't. Some things are better left unsaid.'

'Not this, I promise you. I have to talk of it if I want to find some peace . . .'

'What is it, Sam?'

'I am a murderer. I murdered my father. He was a Turkish soldier . . .'

'I know about that, Sam. But wasn't it your grandfather?'

'You heard all that from me . . . I made you believe it was my grandfather, but I lied to you. It was me.'

'You had the right. He . . . He raped your mother.'

'He did, but he was my father, Charles, my own father.'

'That makes no difference. The man was scum.'

'He might have been that, but who was I to judge him? I am not God . . .'

'Quite right, you're not. You're only a man. It was a human thing to do. He violated your mother and . . .'

'By violating her he became my father. I became his son. And I killed him.'

'You can't call that murder, Sam . . . It was what the French call a crime of passion . . . When you saw him you lost your mind . . . Temporary insanity.'

'Temporary nothing, Charles. It was premeditated murder. I thought of nothing else for years. I planned nothing else. I waited for a chance and then it came. I knew he was coming because they were all running from the British. He couldn't resist it. He came to see me, his son. He was bound to pass the village one more time and I waited . . .'

'You don't need to talk of this now, Sam.'

'I waited for him. I used to cross the grove on the way home from the bakery, and I waited for him to come. He was hungry and thirsty, and he passed the village olive grove and sat down to rest. It was early in the morning. My grandfather always left before me, and I stayed behind to clear up. He saw me and I saw him. I ran to him and he looked up. "My son," he said, and he asked for water. His face was drawn and old and his eyes were pitiful. The man who fathered me was a weak, caged animal, but I showed no compassion. I was ashamed of him, Charles. He knew who I was. He only came back because he wanted to see me and I denied him. I can't even tell you whether I killed him because of what he did to my mother or because I was ashamed of him. I grabbed a thick stick from the ground and I fell on him and pressed the wood against his throat. He just looked at me with those eyes and then he died . . . That is why I left my village, Charles. Not America. Not my mother's disgrace . . . The whole community believed it was my grandfather who did that, but he knew. You see, Charles, after I told him what I had done he forgave me for being a bastard . . . For a little time we were close . . . as close as I could get to him. He was a strict, traditional, old-fashioned man. And then he died in the fire and I took his place at the bakery. Much as I wanted to, I could never stay in the village. The guilt. The passion created by guilt and shame. I never forgot it . . . It drove me all my life. I worked like a dog to forget, but I never could forget. That was my addiction, Charles, and my guilt . . . Guilt for a crime far greater than yours . . . Perhaps the greatest crime a man can commit.'

'You had the right . . .'

'God moves in mysterious ways. He enabled me to live with myself in spite of my guilt . . . and do you know why?'

'No.'

'Good things always come out of bad. You came to Jamaica because you were forced to . . . I met Jean because I killed my father. I survived because I have been punished. They kicked you out of Jamaica. That was a punishment society inflicted on you. But the real punishment, the one that really counts, the one that might help you repent, is the punishment you inflict on yourself. That was why I left my village and why I went back . . . I was punishing myself, Charles.'

'Did your mother find out?'

'I told her. I told her the year before she died. But I doubt if she understood what I said. You see, toward the end she did not communicate. You never knew if she . . .'

I sat there. I was dumbfounded. I held back my tears. Charlie looked at me, then he wiped the sweat off Sam's brow and said:

'You did what you had to do, Sam. I would have done the same.'

'I hope life never puts you to this test, my brother. I lied to you twice, and I ask your forgiveness. This is the other cross I had to bear . . . After all these years I have got the courage to tell you . . . That is why I insisted. Not just for you, but for me, too. Maybe only for me. If there is any more time left I can have peace . . .'

It couldn't be true. I felt he had only said that to appease his friend. To make him feel good. Or was it the truth? Was his father's death the reason for our meeting? Did he live with that nightmare all these years? When Charlie left I would know. Or maybe not. Sam looked relieved but pale. He held his hand to his chest, and I knew he was having problems breathing. I must not make him talk about it. If it was the truth, it must be allowed to rest. If it wasn't, I would never know.

Sam said:

'I owe you some money, you know.'

'You don't owe me anything.'

'You made a lot of changes in my company. Our profit increased because of you.'

'That was what I was paid for.'

'Not enough.'

'I don't need any money. I have plenty. Crime pays sometimes.'

'No one is too rich, Charles.'

'We'll talk about it some more. You get a rest, Sam.'

'Do I look that bad?'

'You must be tired.'

'When shall I see you? What is the time, Charles?'

'I've left my watch at the hotel. It's about two-thirty, maybe three.'

'Are you going for a walk on the beach?'

'No. I'll go and have a coffee. Read the English papers. They arrive about now.'

'Aren't you going to be lonely?'

'Oh, no. I've made friends with a young Australian waiter. A very amusing chap. A graduate student on a world tour. It's fun sitting down there.'

'I'll go with you, but not before tomorrow. I should have a little rest. Let's have dinner tonight. We can have it right in the room. If I go out, Jean will get upset with me.'

'What time would you like me to come?'

'What do you think, Jean?'

I was still shocked at what I had heard. Twice I have heard Sam talk of himself in depth, and twice what he said has shattered me. My husband's humanity was almost unbearable. I wasn't too quick on the draw that afternoon. Sam must have understood, because he didn't push for an answer. He was pale and drawn and I feared for him. Charlie's gaunt face reflected total confusion.

'Eight o'clock,' I said at last.

# CHAPTER SIXTY-NINE

The Australian waiter was there again. His presence added a measure of familiarity to the place. He had turned the chairs over on Charles's table to keep it for him. He had no need to do that. There were hardly any people on the terrace at this time of day. Charles peeled his coat off and sat down. He spread the overseas edition of *The Times* open and tried to read. Letters and words and sentences flew past but refused to be absorbed. Sam's monologue had drained him. There were no secrets. Everything had come out. His friend had known all the time. Maybe that was why he had made it so easy for him to leave. And then he thought about the Turkish soldier and the olive grove and the haunting confession Sam had made.

Perotti had said it once, long ago. At the time he had dismissed it, but the American knew. He understood Sam better than he did. Could that quiet, kindly man have been a killer? There was so much to think of before tonight. He'd sit here and think about it. No. It was all too new. Unless he let it sink in first, he would never understand. He had time until dinner. He must let other, lighter thoughts enter his mind.

It was nice of the old boy to invite him down here. Now that everything was out he, too, would be his old self again. He'd be in funds. He could give him the money back out of the Jamaican dollars he still had in his Kingston bank account. Proceeds of the sale of his house and the boat. The money was worthless outside the island, but it would cover this little outing. He would certainly not accept any more from Sam. His thoughts wandered to the woman in London. He had not called her because there was no telephone in the flat. He could have called one of the customers, but restaurants are always busy and he was out of the hotel most of the time. It didn't matter anyway. He was not going to stay very long. He did not need a holiday, and he had left a few irons in the fire back in London. One of his friends, an old Hong Kong hand, was being forced into retirement by his company. He had told Charles he wasn't quite ready to throw in the towel. He had a bit of money put aside and planned on starting a small consulting business. He had asked Charles to join him.

He stretched. He could put these past few years of isolation down to a well-deserved rest. A readjustment. Something. There were people around who still remembered him. He could still contribute. Do something useful. Make it one more time and keep it. That was it. That was the most important bit. Make it big again and above all keep it. No more poverty, however genteel.

'You all right?' the Australian voice asked. He nodded. He put the paper down. He had no patience for reading. He looked at the water across the wide boulevard. Two bikini-clad young women ran through the green-lit pedestrian crossing. He heard men whistle.

'They go topless in St Tropez,' the waiter said. 'They'd get themselves arrested for that back home. Would you like your coffee now?'

'Yes, thank you.'

'You don't have to order anything if you don't want to.'

'I'll have it, thank you.'

'Is there anything wrong?'

'No, no. Why?'

'I don't know. You look down in the dumps. Had bad news?'

'Good news, actually.'

'If that's what good news does, what happens when bad news hits you?'

'You are funny, young man. You'd better go get the coffee.'

A white Rolls-Royce stopped by the kerb. A grey-uniformed chauffeur stepped out and opened the back door. A young girl got out.

'Things are looking up,' the Australian waiter said. 'Just

take a look at that.'

The girl looked at her watch and said something to the chauffeur. He touched his cap. The girl started for the terrace. She seemed to be gliding. She came straight towards Charles's table and then she stood over him. He looked up. She said:

'May I sit down?'

He didn't answer. The waiter put the cup down on the table. He looked at the girl.

'You're Nellie Brown, aren't you?'

She didn't answer. She stood there, and then the waiter took Charles's raincoat and put it on the other chair.

'May I join you, Father?'

'Father?' the waiter exclaimed. 'You are Nellie Brown's father?'

It might be. It couldn't be. It was.

Through the fog that had assembled on his brain, Charles recognized her face. It hadn't changed much. Must be years since he had seen her that close. He was hot. His palpitation rose. He took his jacket off. He pulled at the knot in his tie and loosened it, then unbuttoned his shirt. He was sweating. A sadness fell on him for a split second, and then it went as quickly as it had come. The girl still stood there. She did not speak but her eyes were on fire. The waiter watched her with blatant admiration. Why didn't he go away? He gasped for air. What other surprises were there in store for him? He felt light-hearted. He wanted to laugh. Then he felt cold again, and he put his jacket on and a strange sense of peace descended on him. No more mysteries.

'You'd better sit down,' he said. His lips were dry. The waiter regained his composure.

'What will you have?'

'A glass of water.'

'Me too, please,' Charles said.

'This is a very private moment,' Nellie said. 'Please leave us alone.'

'Sure,' the waiter said.

'You needn't talk to him like that,' Charles said. 'He's been very good to me.'

'You've always preferred others to your own. You are a selfish man.'

'You're quite right.'

'Do you know how much pain you've caused?'

'Seems to me you have done well.' His voice was weak.

'You don't sound too convinced.'

'I've had a few surprises today,' he said, and cleared his throat.

'You surprised others all your life, Mister Charlie, didn't you? Why did you leave my mother?'

'There were other people involved.'

'What other people?'

'It's too complicated. It all happened many years ago. I can't think of it now.'

'You've got to think of it. I want to . . . I must know who caused all the misery.'

'I did. Me.'

'No, Mister Charlie. You're not being let off this easy.'

'Ask your mother. She knows.'

'Ask your mother . . . I am asking you. Why don't you take a stand? You're a weak, debilitated man, aren't you?'

'Yes. I am.'

'You're no great shakes, are you?'

'No, Nalini. I am not.'

'You remember my name.'

'Of course I do.'

'Why did you ignore me, then?'

'I am a bad omen, Nalini. I bring bad luck to people. Done it all my life.'

'You're feeling sorry for yourself.'

'It's true. No one who ever lived with me amounted to much. Some died because of me.'

'What did you do?'

'I suppose it's what I didn't do. I was too selfish. I

wanted adventure. Success.'

'Were you successful?'

'Yes. Successful at creating failure, misery and death.'

'What a terrible admission to make.'

'It's a terrible affliction to have.'

'You're good with words. I am good with words too. When I quit acting I'll try to be a writer.'

'You'll make it.'

'You promise?'

'You mustn't ask me that. I'm the king of broken promises, Nalini. You'll make it if you want to make it.'

'You don't believe a word I say, do you?'

'Of course I do. So you are an actress now?'

'Yes. Ask the waiter. He knows. Lots of people know.'

'Are you famous?'

'Not yet.'

'Your mother said you wanted to be famous.'

'She said that?'

'I think so.'

'You think so.'

'I don't remember.'

'That's the trouble with you. Your memory. You never remembered you had a daughter, did you? You didn't care. I had to do it all myself . . .'

'I'm a curse. You would have achieved nothing had I been there with you. No one ever did.'

'My mother did OK. She is respected. She's rich.'

'Only because I've gone away, I assure you.'

'She cooked food for you every day of her life. She still does. Did you know that?'

'No.'

'You are not aware, are you? You aren't worth any of it.'

'That is right.'

'Nothing touches you . . . You're as cold as a fish . . . Why are you so miserable?'

'Anyone would be . . . when . . . when made to face

failures.'

'I am not a failure.'

'I don't expect you are . . . You are one of my successes. The only one.'

'You mean that?'

'Of course I do.'

'You could sound a little more enthusiastic.'

The Australian waiter came back with their drinks. He looked down at them and shrugged his shoulders, mumbled something under his breath, then left. Nellie sipped at her water.

'Are you happy to see me?'

'Are you?'

'I don't know.'

'I am so desperately sorry . . .'

'I don't believe a word you say.'

'I can't blame you.'

'I wanted so much for you to be proud of me . . . to see how you'd react when I got there . . . These were lonely years, Father, or should I say Mister Charlie?'

'If you had known me when I was Mister Charlie, really known me, you wouldn't have liked me. You would have wanted . . .'

'How do you know what I wanted? You were always such a secret . . . I wanted someone to flaunt . . . Be known as your daughter . . .'

'Be known as illegitimate? Is that what you wanted? Be a laughing-stock in that school? I kept out of your way. I was trying to protect you from that. Give you respectability . . .'

'Don't make excuses . . . No one cares about that . . .'

'They don't now, but they did then.'

'Respectability? Try again, Father . . . What about . . . I don't know . . . Yes. What about love . . . I wanted love . . .'

'Love? Everyone I ever loved is far away from me now. Doesn't that tell you something about me? Love? I could not afford that . . . I didn't deserve . . .'

'You talk like a child. You make me sick.'

'You might as well hear all of it. . .'

'There's more?'

'There is more . . . I was a dreamer . . .'

'Everybody dreams.'

'Yes, they do, but they wake up. I never did. And that's dangerous . . . I thrived on my search for excitement, on getting into trouble and working out a way to survive . . . And while looking for answers I was drunk with it . . . Had no eyes for love or anything else . . . I was irresponsible. I was feeding my habit . . . Like any addict in need of a fix, you understand? I have an addiction to adventure. To excitement . . . When it takes me over I am useless at things.'

'We were not things . . . We were a family. You are making excuses again.'

'I'm not very good with family. Never have been. Not reliable enough . . . There wasn't much love in my family . . . Maybe there was, but no one showed it. I don't know . . . Maybe that is why I don't know how . . . how to . . . to love. I didn't get on with them . . . Not even with my sisters.'

'You had a mother and a father . . .'

'A father, mostly . . .'

'You must have had a mother too. You must have loved your mother.'

'I must have. I don't remember. She left us when I was a boy. My sisters said she left because of me . . . I believed them.'

'You believed them? Why didn't you ask?'

'She was gone . . . I think she died.'

'You think? Don't you know? Weren't you told?'

'I was away at school . . . My father and I didn't talk much.'

'Were you good at school?'

'I was far too interested in going out to see the world.'

'Escape?'

'Yes. I suppose so. Yes . . . you are right. Escape.'

'Same as me.'

'We've done it, haven't we? We're both watching the world now.' He sounded nonchalant.

'I know why you're not excited about me.'

'Why is that?'

'You don't believe me. You don't believe I'm going to be famous. More famous than you.'

'I am not famous, Nalini.'

'Why did you leave Bangkok? Were you tired of my mother?'

'I left Bangkok because I was made to leave.'

'Forced to leave?'

'Yes. In a way I was.'

'Who made you?'

'A man. It's not important now. I was kicked out of other places too . . . Bangkok was not the only one.'

'Don't . . . Please don't lie, Father. Not now that we're being open with each other . . . Now that we're getting somewhere . . . A man made you leave? Who would have dared do that to you? Weren't you a hero?'

'No. I was not a hero. A selfish adventurer, a dealer . . . I don't know what I was . . . But I assure you I was not a hero.'

'Who was the man?'

'Oh, just a man. Wouldn't mean a thing to you . . . His name was Vincent Perotti.'

She recoiled. As if something had stung her. Her aggressive energy evaporated into nothing. She held her hand to her throat, and then she picked up the glass and gulped her water down. Silence followed.

'You're lying, Mister Charlie,' she said at last. Pain fuelled the anger in her voice.

'I am not lying. You can ask your mother.'

'I've got to go now. I'm late.'

She went very quiet. There was a faraway gaze in her eyes. She looked at him and through him as if he wasn't there. He did not know what to say. Then she got up. The white Rolls-Royce sailed up to the kerb. The chauffeur came out and opened the back door. She pointed at the car.

'I've got to go now.'

He did not answer. She looked at him once more. He was confused. He wanted her to stay, to talk more. What she had forced out of him was new and strange, and it evoked things inside of him. He wasn't sure what. The heat became almost oppressive. He'd have to ask for some more water or he'd die of thirst.

She didn't wait. She walked proudly towards the road and he thought she walked like a swan, and his eyes followed her until she disappeared inside the long white machine. Then the door slammed shut and the car rolled off majestically to join the growing traffic.

# CHAPTER SEVENTY

—————◆—————

I stood behind my thick tree and I saw everything. I saw how she came, how she sat, how they talked, and how she left. At the beginning they were both as careful as hell. His movements were slow, her expression was blank. I wish they'd invented sound-binoculars. I was dying to know what was said, but it couldn't have been much. At one point she even looked disappointed. This was surely not the old Charlie I had known. He used to be an exciting guy. People loved listening to him. Or maybe it was only me. Anyway, the waiter came and she sent him away. She had been so curious the night before. She had made me promise twice I'd get her to see her father. It took some organizing because I did it all on the phone. From a booth across from the café. I called to alert her immediately after he left Sam's hotel, and then I called again to say he was at his table.

Maybe he was tired. Maybe she was tired. He had just

seen Sam, and I guess she didn't sleep a wink. Maybe Sam had told him something shattering. Maybe Sam had died. Charlie had walked funny before he first sat down. And then he went all passive. He didn't change much when Nellie turned up. I don't know what was said, but she did stand around a little before he motioned her to sit. He didn't look too interested. Maybe he didn't know who she was. He must have done. If not at the beginning he knew later, because she would have told him. Yes. He knew. From time to time she had an accusing expression, and whenever that happened Charlie's face became strained. He'd go all lethargic and then he'd talk, and I could swear he was doing some explaining.

Whatever he said didn't seem to satisfy her. She kept prodding him for more. I wanted her to leave him alone. I wanted him to pay her some attention. The whole deal didn't last long, maybe half an hour, and during a good bit of that they both looked bored. Like they'd rather be somewhere else.

All the while I kept thinking about the way he used to be. How she'd have reacted if she had known him then. How much she would have admired him. How impossible it would have been for me to have taken her away from him. What I would have missed. Then I became remote. I detached myself from it as if I was watching some picture show. Charlie was down. Very down. Nothing stirred him. Not even Nellie's presence and all the questions he was made to answer.

I thought of the last time we spoke. He was down in the dumps then too, but he had resources. He was capable of plenty when he was down. I remembered sitting with him on the boat in Jamaica. With him looking at me with a serious face. What he had said to me then needed strength and concentration. I thought of how he was then. How he called me, for the first time ever, by my first name. How he'd said, for the first time ever, that we were friends. That he'd trusted me. I remembered all that and, above all, I remembered his last request. His sincere, out-of-character, top-of-the-list request regarding Paco the Filipino. It was a request I had heard a thousand times in my life. But I never expected to hear it from him. But in spite of his predicament he had the courage to change. Kill the man, he had said, and he needed much courage and clear thinking to say that then. I couldn't equate that with Charlie, but I knew he'd meant it.

I sure had plenty of chances to get rid of Paco. I could do that any time. He even came to this town to see me once, I forget why, but I kept him going. I kept putting it off.

Wasting him was too sweet a deal to rush. It was something to savour. Like a bar of chocolate you suck at sparingly and slowly to make it last.

I thought that and I kept watching. I saw Nellie and I saw the Rolls come for her. I looked at my watch and I knew she had a few minutes to spare, but then something happened. She asked something and Charlie answered and she jumped like she'd seen a ghost. I forgot the past and everything. The slow-motion movie started racing forward like a roller-ball. Her face was numb and she said something and got up and ran to the car. She didn't even stop to say goodbye. He had shocked her, and I'd have given plenty to have known what it was.

After she left he just sat there. He looked everywhere like a judge in a ping-pong game. His eyes ploughed through the countryside, and then he looked in my direction. I had to get myself away. If he saw me now, I'd had it. I wasn't ready for him. Maybe I was wrong. I hoped I was. He would only see my head, and my face was mostly covered with these big binoculars. I tried to tear myself away, but something kept me right where I was. Maybe I should acknowledge him. Go across and talk with him. Be friends again. Do something for him. For me. I waited.

# CHAPTER SEVENTY-ONE

First came excruciating pain, and then he drowned in the sweet exhaustion of relief.

Like a birth, he thought, and smiled faintly as he waited for exhilaration to surface. He devoured the water and asked for more, and all the while he thought of what had happened. There were no more lies. The decks had been swept clean. Perhaps it was only a dream. Dreams are clear and they are honest. Everything is a dream. He had never been as open as that. Not even with himself. Had he really said all that he had said? Had he revealed his innermost thoughts and feelings and fears to Nappaporn's daughter? Could he change things now that he'd been truthful with her, now that she knew?

Life came back to the terrace, and all around him there was the chatter of people. There was gossip and complaints and whistles of admiration. The Croisette brimmed over with the grating rumble of cars. But he did not hear the engines. Didn't smell the fumes. He got up on his feet and faltered, and he pulled at his chair and lowered himself down. He just sat there and looked about him and saw nothing. He wasn't sure how long he sat there, and then his eyes sailed across to the sea and landed on the short, squat shape of Vincent Perotti.

He must be hallucinating. He strained his eyes and saw him again. There was no mistake. No illusion. He got up again. His feet were steady. Nothing was going to surprise him from here on. He was a magician, he thought, and he laughed. He could have the world. All he needed to do was to think of someone and they'd materialize. The American held something to his eyes. Yes. He saw it clearly. It was a pair of binoculars.

'I see you,' he chanted to no one. 'I see you.' His eyes were young again.

Yes. It had all happened, he thought. Sam had happened and Nalini had happened and now Perotti was happening. He was so happy he could sing. He could start all over. Life had not deserted him. There, on the other side of the wide, wide road, stood the only man who could get him out of the rut. Lift him away from all this and take him back to the big open spaces. Together they would fly again. Go back to those faraway places. Exotica and beyond.

There was power in him now he had forgotten existed. He kept looking at Perotti, and he put his coat on and turned to the street. He dropped a few coins on the table and waved goodbye. On his side of the road there was the endless peace of silence. The sun hit the sea and the water caught fire. There was magic. He was a magician.

He'd make amends. He had found a daughter, and this time he would keep her. Spend time with her. Have her live with him. He possessed an unbeatable spell. He could do anything. Be anything he wanted. He could make the sea burn. He could fly. He'd make Nalini proud of him. As long as he had Perotti in his grasp, nothing was impossible. He kept his eyes on the little man who stood behind the thick stem of a palm.

'You wait right there, Perotti,' he heard his own voice whisper. He'd have to shout. Suddenly he felt light on his feet. His muscles flexed. The long, grey years were behind him. The pain was gone. The tiredness, the despair and the indecision had vanished. The waiter shouted something, but Charles just waved at him one more time and started for the road.

# CHAPTER SEVENTY-TWO

━━━■━━━

Before he saw me his face had been pale. There was agony in it as he got up. He was kind of moonstruck. His eyes were glazed. He stood there for a minute and he swayed as though he carried the whole world on his shoulders. He sat down again and he rested. I heard myself sigh with relief. He sat there for a long time. She must have told him something that had unsettled him. Or maybe it had been Sam. Or both. I watched him and then, all of a sudden, I saw him look at me. Recognition flared up in his eyes and I knew he'd seen me. He got up again and he put his raincoat on. I don't know why. It was a hot day. He left a few coins on the table. He waved to the waiter. But all the time his eyes were stuck on me. They seemed demented. I wasn't going to stay, but the mesmerizing scene across the road unfolded like a slow-motion movie. I had all the time in the world.

He waved at the waiter again and turned toward the street. He looked at me. An insane, savage smile lit up his face. The speed of things changed. He came flying towards me like a missile. His limbs had the agility of a tiger. His energy was awesome. The man who came at me from across the road was the old Charlie again. I saw a wild-eyed, young face cutting the air. I saw the movie-star looks of a hero.

'Perotti,' he called. I read his lips repeating my name again and again as he ran. He had his raincoat on, and the material lifted itself into the air. Charlie looked like a vampire with a grey cape. His eyes were fixed on me like a beam. He saw nothing else. I needed to get away and couldn't move, but my mind raced. I couldn't face him. What was I going to say? How was I going to change things? Did I regret having told Nellie where he was?

'Perotti. Perotti,' his lips screamed. It was time to go, but my legs did not obey my brain. I couldn't move. A Harley Davidson came roaring through the traffic. Horns sounded as the shiny machine zigzagged to avoid the cars. I yelled back, 'Watch it, Charlie', but only a whisper came. Charlie was nearly upon me. Just a few yards to go. 'Run, Charlie,' my voice pleaded. A truck stopped to let him cross, and then I heard the howl of the bike as it overtook the truck and crashed at Charlie head-on. There was nothing I could do. There was nothing anyone could do. A police car chasing the bike ran over his fallen body. Tyres screeched and the traffic stopped, but the engines still thundered like in a race. I was stuck in the ground like a tree, and I thought I heard the sickening sound of breaking bones. For a few seconds he lay there still. Then he tried to get up. He looked in my direction one more time and smiled, and then he fell. People ran to him. It was all over.

'You don't just quit on me like that, Charlie,' I said. I said it loud. Maybe I screamed. A guy next to me took a step away. Must have thought I'd gone bananas. 'You can't quit now,' I said again. 'Get up, you bastard. Get up and get over here.'

He could have been anything he wanted to be. He could have started a kingdom. He could have been a king. Instead he died like an alley-cat. But then maybe people like Charlie invite trouble. I mean, people in monkey business should stay in the background like I did. Manipulate from behind the scenes. But Charlie was top billing. He was almost famous. You get into problems when you're famous in our business.

Or maybe it was what they call his karma. I'm not sure what it means, but I think it's the number you draw in the lottery of life. Maybe he was a loser. No. Not a loser. He did not mind not having any dough. What he had missed was excitement, and he sure had that in his eyes just before he died.

I saw that old ballad-singer, dressed in her ancient mauve gown. She came over to him and bowed. A flower fell out of her hat and landed on his back. There were people all around. An old guy with a straw hat hopped over on his crutches to take a look. This fascination with death is crazy. Why do people want a preview?

There was nothing I could do there. The police were sniffing around. I couldn't get involved in any enquiries here. I'm strictly legit now. And if I got involved Nellie would find out about me. About how I hounded him for twenty years. Thirty. How it was me he crossed the road to see. Maybe it wasn't his destiny to die where he fell. Maybe it was my destiny to kill him there.

I walked to the hotel and I went to my room. Nellie's screening was still going on down the road. She was going to be too busy to find out what had happened. If it made the local papers it would be bottom of the back page. Just another crazed tourist run over. An open and shut case. Nobody's fault. A nil change in statistics.

For the first time ever I didn't go out at all. For two days I stayed in my room. The porters were instructed to say I was out of town. No exceptions. They played ball. Nellie called and left messages. In her first message she asked me to call. In the second she said she had to speak to me, and in the third she said she'd be over tonight.

She nearly had her father back, and then he died. I had stolen her from her father twice. I had claimed her for myself. No. It didn't go like that. I chased her father away, then I took her. Then I pushed her back to him and then I killed him. Would she ever forgive me for that? Never. Not even God forgives that. Bullshit. She knows nothing.

I won't take any chances. I'll change it all. Change my name if need be. Disappear from her life completely. I'd only screw things up for her now. Of course, I'll be watching over her. I still know a couple of useful people.

I was never married, but I did have a daughter once.


Charlie is being buried today. Earlier I looked out the window and I saw Sam and Jean walking along the water. Rose was with them. She was dressed in black and looked great. They stopped, and Jean pointed at a stretch of road. She was telling them where Charlie had died. That was the spot. They stood just by my thick palm. His white hair flew with the light afternoon breeze, and his head was down. Rose had dark glasses on and held a handkerchief to her eye. None of them saw me. Then Jean looked at her watch and said something to Sam, and they left. Rose stayed there on her own for a bit, and then she walked away. The Bakers are staying at the Carlton down the road. I reckon they'd have Rose stay there too. Must be going to their room to change. People dress up for funerals. They should go in rags.

I've seen people dress to kill to pay last respects to the guy they've wasted. Most people go because it's expected of them.

Not me. I am going because it's the culmination of our life. I'm going to finish off what he started when he came racing at me. He was coming to say his last goodbye. Charlie said a man must face whoever he is parting from. Face and touch, he said. I won't look him in the eye or pump his hand, but he'll know.

The limousine is down there now. They've just called to say it's ready and waiting. You won't make San Remo on time, Mr Perotti. I said I was coming down.

On the TV they are full of Nellie. She is a cracking success. Her face says she loves every bit of it. I am happy for her, but inside I am in pain. Parting is not like an amputation. It's like dying.

My brain is going funny. I'm all twisted up inside. I mourn the end of my final burst of youth. There's no second chance for us. Charlie's matinee death is the only show in town. Now the show is over, and I have promises to keep.

What for? Who will know?

I will know. And if there is a little bit of Charlie's presence in me, he will know too. If there is a presence? Who am I kidding? He's all over me. All inside my flesh so big he's hammering at my skin.

I am not a religious man, but what if he is in heaven? What if he's changed his mind about killing Paco now he's with the angels all dressed in white? I better wait for a sign.

What if Nellie ends up hating me for leaving her alone? For creeping in and out of her life the way I did? What if she knows? And what if she goes to the funeral? What if Nappaporn is in town? What if Charlie's two women finally meet? And what will Nappaporn tell Nellie if she breaks our secret and talks about me? What if Rose and I . . .?

No more ifs, no more maybes. No hopes, no honour, and no more promises. No revenge.

I'm too old for all this shit. I am retired.

I pack my stuff and walk downstairs. The concierge races towards me and snatches my case.

'Are you staying the night in San Remo, sir?'

'I haven't decided yet. Would you get my bill for me?'

'Right away, Mr Perotti. And . . .'

'What?'

'We did not know the deceased, but our condolences go with you.'

'Thank you.' I should have told them it was me they are burying today.

I pay the bill and get out of there.


Across the road the sun grabs the sea and turns it into a huge silvery screen. Black silhouettes are pasted all over. Trees and cars and boats and people on the sand.

They open the door for me and they salute and wave. My heart is calm and distant.

He'll know I am with him because he's with me wherever I go.

The chauffeur turns back and looks at me. His face is stern.

'To the funeral, sir?'

'No,' I say, and sink into the deep leather. 'To the airport.'